'The Japanese have a saying, "If it stinks, put a lid on it." In *Samurai Boogie*, Peter Tasker takes a firm grip of that lid and wrenches if off with glee. With its abrupt cross-cutting and sudden tight focus on visual detail, *Samurai Boogie* draws heavily on the conventions of Japanese manga comic books; in effect, the novel is a manga in prose. The details of Japanese life are spot-on, from the steamy atmosphere of a noodle stall to the oppressiveness of the summer rainy season . . . For its vigorous pace, the stark authenticity of its setting and its exhilarating immediacy, *Samurai Boogie* is outstanding' *The Times* Metro

'Cyberpunk guru William Gibson has always known that Japan is the coolest place to set a thriller, but no one else has really caught on. Peter Tasker should change all that, by transferring a hard-boiled American private eye mystery to the rain-soaked neon streets of '90s Tokyo. Tasker has created a living, breathing setting with the other-worldliness of an SF novel. Stylish, original and pacier than a shinkansen bullet train. This is manga Elmore Leonard' *Daily Mirror*

'The Japanese setting of Peter Tasker's *Samurai Boogie* is an intriguing cultural contrast . . . There are several touches which make this book fresh and enjoyably different. There's the quirky hero, Mori, his old friends and some unexpected garnishes – and there's a splendid sub-plot involving a sinister computer game tycoon' *Sunday Telegraph*

'A savagely contemporary tale set in sophisticated Japan. So cool it's hot' *The Times*

Peter Tasker is a Tokyo-based writer and commentator. After a career as a top-ranking financial analyst, he is now a founding partner of Arcus Investment, a UK money management firm. He is married with three children.

By the same author

Silent Thunder
Buddha Kiss

Samurai Boogie

Peter Tasker

ORION

An Orion paperback

First published in Great Britain in 1999
by Orion
This paperback edition published in 2001
by Orion Books Ltd,
Orion House, 5 Upper St Martin's Lane,
London WC2H 9EA

A CIP catalogue record for this book is available
from the British Library.

ISBN 0 75283 676 5

Printed and bound in Great Britain by
The Guernsey Press Co. Ltd, Guernsey, C.I.

For Gail

One

A cluster of wooden buildings in the nape of the bay. Red sand, just a patch between the road and the sea. Noise: gulls shrieking, waves pounding, someone twanging a catgut banjo. In the middle of the sand, a square fenced off. And in the middle of the square, something darker, the shape of a coconut.

The nurse comes out of the bath-house, goes trip-trop across the sand, the hem of her kimono in her hand. Through the gate in the fence she goes, then squats on her haunches, long wet hair hanging forward. Knuckles tapping the top of the coconut.

'Hoi! Are you sleeping?'

There is a face on the front, blood-heavy, sweat running down the hard lines of the mouth. It tilts upwards.

'Just thinking with my eyes closed.'

'Thinking about what?' says the woman. 'About me?'

He blinks. Steam rising gently from the sand. Doesn't feel so hot at first, but you end up baking like a crab.

'About a yakuza I knew, used to be a pro wrestler. What they did was mix him into the foundations of the New Kansai airport. There he was, head sticking out of a trench of quick-drying cement, mouth taped up, just watching while they poured in the final load. Some say his ghost is still sitting there, watching the planes come in.'

1

The nurse laughs her disbelief. 'What a horrible story! Why did they do that?'

'Turned out it was a mistake. They're still sending money to his family. Anyway, I'm starting to understand how the guy felt. Can't move your arms and legs, can't even scratch your nose. All you've got left is your head.'

She shifts her position, strong toes pegging into the sand. The kimono slips open over her legs. Golden knees almost touching his cheeks, thigh muscles bending like bows. From pearl-diver stock, maybe.

'You must endure, Mori-*san*. The radioactivity of the sand is already raising your energy levels. That was obvious last night.' Wet hair curtaining her smiling face.

'Glad you noticed.'

'You're more than halfway through the treatment. Another two hours and the men will dig you out. Then this evening I will check your condition again.'

'This evening I've got an appointment, business.'

'Then after your appointment?'

'Time to be checking out. Thanks to your good work, my back pains have gone.'

'Ah. Such a pity.' Sounds like she means it. Acts like it too. Her knees drift open a few inches, showing creamy inner thighs. And she knows he's looking. In his position, there's nowhere else to look.

'I've never had a patient like you, Mori-*san*. Most are so old and ill, aching to their bones. You have power, very deep power. I knew that from the shape of your nose.'

'My nose?'

She's naked under the kimono. He glimpses clear confirmation amongst the shadows. Deep down in the hot sand, his body responds.

'Yes. A strong nose shows a strong spirit.'

'And what about an itchy nose?'

2

She laughs, a full, confident sound you never hear in Tokyo. 'An itchy nose? That means you've been telling too many lies!'

Drawing in even closer, raising herself slightly. Bare knees scrunching the sand, one on each side of his head.

'What are you doing?'

'I have special therapy for an itchy nose.'

The kimono drops over his head, shutting out the bay. Then strong fingers, kneading the back of his neck, pulling him in. The world goes soft hot dark moist.

Seagulls mewling, waves thumping, the woman breathing, slow and serious. Like this, thinks Mori, the pro wrestler would have died a happy man.

Two

In the considered judgement of George the Wolf Nishio, the Mitsubishi StarWagon is the ideal vehicle for the transportation of half a dozen foreign strippers with expired visas. The main point being the high quality of the smoked-glass windows. No one can see in, no matter how bright the street-lights. You stop at a junction, right in front of a police box. No problem. You lean back at the wheel, totally relaxed, an ivory cigarette holder dangling from your lips. The girls carry on with what they're doing – chewing yakitori, darning their stage-gear, gabbling away in Spanish, Tagalog, Cantonese, Vietnamese, whatever.

Another benefit: the in-car karaoke system. Especially useful on long trips like this, when the stress is building. The girls don't like George's singing. They make faces behind his back and think he doesn't see. That just makes him sing all the louder, weepy Japanese ballads that tell of lost sweethearts and long-forsaken home towns. The girls want happy music – funk, Eurobeat, the kind of stuff they bump and grind to on stage. George the Wolf Nishio likes his music tragic, reflecting his philosophy of life.

The StarWagon sweeps up another hill. George glances in his mirror. Two girls are flat out on the bench-seats, resting ahead of the performance. One of the others is playing on a Gameboy. Angel – tallest, sultriest, the biggest breasts –

keeps checking her watch, glancing out the window. Looks like she can't wait to get to work.

According to the club owner in Fukuoka, Angel is supposed to be the star of the show, delivering 'instant brain death' to any male audience. Temperamental, too. The guy showed the scratch marks on his shoulder. Well, tonight she's going to have to pull out all the stops. George spelt it out, no mistake. And afterwards if some balding middle-aged section chief wants to have some fun – or four or five of them for that matter, one after the other or all together – she's going to flash those big white teeth and jump for joy. Because she's dealing with serious people now. The Fukuoka guy told her 'no co-operation, no more passport'. George told her 'no co-operation, no more face'.

George puts down the mike, two hands on the wheel. Can't be late. It's an important conference, this one. Senior syndicate people are hosting construction industry executives and prefectural government officials. Top secret, which is why non-Japanese-speaking girls were requested. The boss could have asked the local outfit to make the arrangements. But they are incompetent, brains like rotten tofu. Instead he entrusts the job to George the Wolf Nishio, sends him all the way from Tokyo. George knows how to get things done. At the age of thirty-five he already has the right credentials, having killed three people – a pachinko parlour operator, a Chinese gangster and an innocent bystander – and spent eighteen months in jail.

Eyes on the road, George flashes that moment – one of disaster, but also great honour. There he was at Narita airport, hauling a ski-bag full of pistols through customs counter No. 4, everything according to plan. Then the customs guy stops him. 'Where you've been, skiing holiday?' 'That's right,' says George. 'What – in Thailand? Open that bag for me, will you?' George looks at the guy, licks his lips. This isn't supposed to happen. 'You know who I am?' he whispers. 'I'm the Wolf!' 'Really? In that case I'm the frilly necked lizard. Now open that bag or I'll open it for you.' It's the wrong guy. George doesn't know it, but the right guy has crashed his car on the way to work. Two airport police drag him away, kicking and cursing.

When his time was up, everyone was waiting for him outside the prison gates, dark suits, all lined up in order of seniority. The boss bowed low, gave him the formal greeting, then a ceremonial envelope containing eighteen months' salary and a special bonus. Honour, loyalty, sincerity – the whole thing. It was hard to hold back the tears.

'Hey, Wolf-*san*! Can't you stop for a couple of minutes?'

It's Angel, bending forward over the driver's seat, wild hair brushing his neck. Tingles like electricity. George registers that Angel speaks quite decent Japanese. How come? Could that be a problem tonight?

'Can't stop. We'll be there in half an hour.'

'No, now! I want to do pee-pee. No pee-pee, I feel bad. I feel bad, no hot dancing. Understand?'

No Japanese girl would talk to him like that. No Japanese man would talk to him like that either. Except people higher up in the syndicate, of course. George swings the wheel, causing her to lurch backwards.

'Hey! Stop the car straight away, or I'm gonna use these stupid boots of yours.'

She's holding one up, must have grabbed it from the bag. The snakeskin boots are the proudest part of George's wardrobe – pointy toes, Cuban heels, a diceboard pattern that gleams venom. Got them from a Yokohama speedhead who'd defaulted on some debt. It had been love at first sight. He'd pulled them off immediately before they'd got too bloodstained.

'Put that down, you dumb whore!'

'I mean it,' she screeches, waving the boot around. She does too. Look at her eyes, pure crazy. Women from these countries are just not civilized.

'Okay, okay. I'll stop at the next place.'

There's a roadside noodle shop signposted, just five hundred metres ahead. George slows, pulls into the little car park. No other vehicles. In fact, the place is deserted, lights off. George gets out, unlocks the side door. Angel's slingbacks hit the gravel She stands there, hands on hips, looking around. With all the frizzy hair, she's taller than he is.

'Come on, then.' He grabs her by the wrist.

'Leave me alone. I don't need you.' She breaks his hold, surprisingly easily. Then she glances at her watch again and George the Wolf Nishio starts to get suspicious. Something funny here. Despite all that fuss, Angel's in no hurry to do her pee-pee. She's waiting for something.

'Get back in the car!' he snarls.

'What's the matter with you?' She backs away, glances back at the road. Now he knows for certain. It's all wrong, just like that time at Narita. He slaps her once, not too hard, doesn't use his chunky wolf-head ring. He tries to wrestle her back through the open door, but somehow she wriggles free. A sharp pain in his ankle: her high-heel shoe. Those big green fingernails raking at his eyes. George wants to hit hard, to hurt. But he can't. The construction industry people wouldn't like the bruises. That will have to come later.

A couple of the other girls are behind him now, yanking at his shirt, scratching his back. That shirt also he loves – black Lurex with white trim around the collar and cuffs. Despite himself, George is starting to get angry.

*

The clock in the empty noodle shop clicks to seven-thirty. They're supposed to be here any time now. Mori sits at the counter, staring at the road, coffee cup in hand. Must be the first cup of coffee made here this decade. Tastes like it too. He waits, roaches rustling through the trash, moonlight on the Formica.

The best plans are the simplest. This one is very simple. The toilets are at the side of the building. Angel goes in the door, then straight out of the window. Mori's waiting in the shadows. Under the cover of the trees, they sprint across the yard, clamber down the rocks. At the bottom, there's an overgrown track leading to a tunnel on the coast road. The whole thing shouldn't take more than a couple of minutes. By the time anyone works out what's happening, they'll be scampering through the tunnel, completely out of sight. On the other side the van is waiting, engine running.

Sounds straightforward, but Angel has to handle the tricky bit first: getting the guy to stop the car in the right place. Mori has spoken to her just once, a rushed phone call, half-drowned in strip music and cheering. She sounds smart enough, tough enough. But according to the doctor she's hot-headed too. The doctor said that's what he loves most about her. Strange, that doctor, at least sixty years old, sadness in the face.

When Mori sees her, he starts to understand. She springs out of the StarWagon, proud, like a guerilla leader stepping out of the jungle. The guy with her is a chimpira, a low-grade yakuza. Mori doesn't know the relationship between them. He only knows she wants out. One look at the guy – violent ugly stupid – explains all that. Time to move. He slips out through the kitchen, gets round behind the toilet and waits.

There is a slow explosion in Angel's head. Accumulated

rage, months and months of humiliation, every part of her body being stared at, pawed, defiled. Men like to do those things, God knows why. But worse still: they don't give you what you've earned with your aching muscles and frozen mind. They cheat and lie with a laugh. Men like the ugly one in front of her, breath stinking of pickled cabbage, grubby hands all over her breasts.

Pepsi and Sondra are out of the car now, hanging on to his back. The ugly one doesn't know how to fight women. He's too close, not covering himself. Angel rakes her heel down his ankle, sinks her teeth into his forearm. He roars something, knocks Sondra away with a flying elbow. But Crystal is there instead, hanging on to his shoulder, fingers clawing for his face. Angel's rage hardens. She twists away, swings in again with a precise head-butt to the nose. The man grunts shock, hands rising to his face. That leaves his groin open. Angel reaches down, gathers it into her hand.

There's not much that Angel doesn't know about the male groin. This thing she first did when she was fourteen, one of her uncles squirming on top of her. Now it's instinct: the other thing in reverse. You grab, twist, squeeze. You don't need to pull. You just keep on squeezing twisting squeezing. Like wringing a flannel.

The ugly one's roar turns into a squeal. Like the pig he is, thinks Angel, smiling with triumph. He ducks down, flails at her, but her grip is iron. Never let go, that's the way. While she's squeezing twisting squeezing, the man has no strength, no power to hurt.

Sondra is behind him now, dancing around, a beer bottle in her hand.

'Hit him, Sondra!'

She hesitates, never done it before.

'Hit where?' she wails.

'Top of the head,' yells Angel. 'Hard!'

9

The bottle smashes. Beer foam flying everywhere, Angel finally lets go.

A burst of noise: the chimpira's angry bellowing; feet scuffling the gravel; women screaming in four different languages. Mori peers around the side of the building, sees the bottle smash on the man's head, sees him crumple to the ground. Angel spits on him, scuffs gravel into his face. The other women stand around, hands on hips, suddenly quiet. One bends down, dabs at the top of his head with a handkerchief. Mori chooses his moment to step out of the shadows.

'Looks like we've got a problem,' he says.

Silence. Six hot gazes on his face.

'Is your name Mori?' says Angel, finally.

'That's right.'

'You don't look like a detective.'

'Thank you.' He gives a little bow.

'What about this pig?' She scuffs at the chimpira again.

Mori glances down – blood bubbles, gurgles, fingers twitching. 'We'd better get going. He could wake up any moment.'

'Best we kill him now, throw him in the sea.'

'Best we don't. Best you stay out of any more trouble. Your friends should get to a phone box and call the police.'

'Are you crazy?' says Angel, fire in her eyes. 'Everyone coming with Angel, of course.'

'Out of the question,' says Mori firmly. 'Much too dangerous.'

She stamps her foot. 'That means Angel stays here. That means we kill him now.'

'My instructions from the doctor . . .' Mori stops in mid-sentence. Instructions mean nothing to Angel. The doctor probably means nothing either. She sits down on the gravel

10

next to the chimpira, slips a flick-knife from her pocket. It has a ladies' blade, light and lethal. She slices the collar off George's shirt, starts feeling for his jugular. He gurgles louder, eyelids flickering.

'Ugly life, ugly death,' announces Angel, teeth flashing like pearls in the moonlight.

Mori opens his mouth, closes it again. She would do it, no question. Just like bleeding a pig for the village festival.

'Okay,' he sighs. 'Everybody get your things and follow me.'

George is woken by two things that blend together: the pain throbbing in his groin; the cicadas skreeking right by his ear. He slowly discovers, with ascending degrees of anger, his face in the gravel, his nose mashed, his shirt bloody and ripped. Then, staggering to his feet, something truly horrible. Where are the girls? They've disappeared, all of them! This is the worst thing that has ever happened to him. His guts ice over when he thinks of the boss's face. No honour, no respect this time.

Cursing, he busts down the door of the deserted noodle place, looks in the kitchen. Nothing but cockroach crap. Clock on the wall says seven-fifty. They have to be somewhere close. George goes to the kitchen door, stares out across the yard: empty dark silent. But just as he turns to go, something sparkles in the moonlight, something half-hidden in a clump of couch grass.

George the Wolf walks over, scoops it up. It's a sequinned tassel, the kind the girls whirl from their nipple-caps. He flashes Angel's breasts, her laughing face, then drops the tassel and grinds it with his heel. His head wound blazes with pain. His injured groin pulses, sick and cold. But now, as he walks to the edge of the cliff, his lips are twisted into a smile.

*

Progress is fast. They scramble over the rocks, down the path to the coast road. No lights, no cars; not now, not later. This is the middle of nowhere, remember. Ahead the tunnel is a circle of black in the cliff. Mori gets there first, waits for the girls just inside. Right behind him is Angel. She runs like an Olympic athlete, head back, long strides. The next four arrive together, slump against the tunnel wall, sucking in air. Mori gestures for silence, stay out of sight.

Way behind is Pepsi, heavy bag across her shoulder, breasts jouncing from side to side. White ankle boots with stiletto heels. Good for stomping out a strip routine, not so good for middle distance running. Mori glances up at the top of the cliff. No sign of any movement. Pepsi gasps the last ten yards, then – just at the entrance to the tunnel – one heel catches a divot in the tarmac. The girl skids, stumbles, legs and upper body moving on definitely different courses. Mori tries to catch her but she's already crashing to the ground.

'Waah,' she wails, and the sound bounces around the tunnel. The bag ruptures, releasing pink negligee, leopard-skin G-string, vibrator, Vaseline, mouthwash. Everyone freezes. Mori raises his hand, peers out of the shadows. Again nothing. But Angel is at his shoulder, pointing at a dark smudge amongst the trees.

'You should have let Angel kill the pig,' she hisses.

Now the smudge has disappeared. Pepsi is on hands and knees, scrabbling her stuff back into the busted bag.

'Forget that,' snaps Mori. 'No time!'

His torch beam dances on the tunnel walls. Patter-patter go the girls' feet. Pepsi's stuff stays on the ground, waiting for the fishermen coming home next morning.

George the Wolf, between two trees, peering down into the gloom, when – 'Waah!', floating on the sea wind, a cry of female panic. The kind of sound he knows well. He shifts his gaze. Over in the tunnel, has to be. He listens again, but nothing now. He turns, runs for the StarWagon, all pain forgotten.

There's still time to get them to the conference, win some respect from the senior syndicate people. He won't say anything rough to the girls, pretend he's taking the whole thing as a joke. Then on the way back, that whore Angel, he'll change her attitude for good. Change her appearance too.

George has the engine revving before the door slams. The StarWagon's tyres eat gravel, spit it out against the fence.

The legend on the side of the Nissan Escargot minivan is the same as the one on Mori's peaked cap and the breast pocket of his overalls – Kaneda Floral Services. There's plenty of room in the back for a good selection of wreaths, potted plants and bonsai, but the thing wasn't designed to carry six healthy, well-proportioned young women. Five get in, and already it's a tangle of limbs and hips and breasts.

'Let me in the passenger seat,' says Angel, who has the longest limbs, curviest hips, heaviest breasts.

'Absolutely not,' snaps Mori. 'You'd be identified immediately.'

'Come on,' she pouts, cocking her head back. 'Angel can pretend she ordinary Japanese office girl. Maybe a sweetheart for you, detective-*san*!'

Mori's patience is wearing thin.

'Shut up, get in the van, and stay there for the next three hours!'

'But there's no space!'

She doesn't know anything about space, that's clear. She should try the Yamanote Line at rush hour. Mori grabs her wrist, twists her arm behind her back, then shoves her face first into the wall of bodies. It gives, as it always does in the end.

'Hey!'

He slams the door on pressed flesh, squeals, cheap perfume. The 650-cc engine whines into life. The peak of his cap low over his eyes, Mori moves up carefully through the gears. He's not going to outspeed anyone in this thing. He has to rely on camouflage.

The StarWagon thunders along the highway, up and down the rolling hills, its speed alarm going beep-beep-beep. George is looking for a right turn to the coast road, getting pretty frustrated to find nothing, mile after mile. After all, there has to be a road somewhere! The yam-heads living in the fishing villages must be provided with some means of reaching the outside world. The dashboard clock winks eight o'clock, the time he's supposed to be at the meeting. George keeps his foot flat on the floor. The speed-needle stays jammed off the gauge.

There! Some sort of farm track leading between two hills. No choice. He jams on the brakes, swings the wheel, gets a whiff of burning rubber.

The track is narrower, more basic than he thought. The StarWagon rocks along the rutted mud, tree branches thumping the roof, bugs splatting the windshield. Squinting through the darkness, George hums a ballad of spring in the snow-country. Now he's relaxed. Japanese engineering he trusts more than the love of a mother or the hatred of a sworn enemy.

Then unbelievably the track ends. George slows just in time. Ahead is a gate, all chained up, behind it a field containing row after row of tea bushes. And beyond that – the sea glinting in the moonlight, the sound of the waves. The coast road he doesn't see, but it can only be a few hundred yards away. The gate is made of wood. The tea bushes are waist-height. George knows what to do. It'll be just like the movies.

Except that this gate isn't balsa-wood. First time the StarWagon bounces off, engine screaming. George curses, backs up a hundred yards, tries again. Second time he takes it at fifty, third gear. Thump! The impact throws him sideways. Noise of metal shearing, wood splintering. One headlight smashed, wing mirrors ripped off, but he's through, ploughing through the tea bushes. These are surprisingly stubborn too, but George is in no mood for compromise. Foot down, he takes them out by the roots. Clumps of plant life sail into the starry sky.

Mori drives slowly, one eye in the mirror. Behind him the girls are gabbling, fighting, laughing. He's starting to enjoy the scenery – the dark hills, the churning sea, the dusty road. Five miles, and just one sign of life – an old man on a bike, a fishing-pole slung over his shoulder. He raises a hand as the Nissan passes. Mori waves back. The world is as empty and still as when the gods first made it.

Until something happens. A hundred yards ahead a vehicle comes crashing through the tangle of vegetation and spins round in the middle of the road, tyres squealing. Mori doesn't recognize the StarWagon at first. One wing is crumpled, the front bumper is dragging sparks off the tarmac, and there's half a tea bush hanging off the radiator grille.

'That shitpig!' yells Angel from somewhere behind. 'I knew he would come.'

'Quiet!' growls Mori. He slows down, sounds the horn: two high-pitched beeps. You have to act the part. In his breast pocket, a pair of wire-rimmed glasses. He puts them on and waits for the StarWagon to move.

*

This time George really can't believe what's happened. He finally makes the coast road, and the engine has cut out on him, won't restart. He turns the key, but all he gets is the spastic cough of the starting-motor. The clock winks ten past eight. He bashes his fists on the steering-wheel, tears of frustration welling. Even Mitsubishi has let him down.

'*Beep, beep.*'

But wait a moment: some good luck at last! There's a guy in a light van, some tofu-brained delivery man waiting to pass. George needs that van. He's going to take it, track down those whores, get them to the conference. Drag them by the hair from the bumper if necessary. He pulls his pistol out of the glove compartment, sticks it into his waistband at the back.

Just what Mori hoped wouldn't happen. The chimpira jumps out of the StarWagon, moves with heavy purpose. Somehow he must have worked it out. Must be smarter than he looks.

Or maybe not. He's got a strange rigid smile on his face. He's making little bowing gestures, pointing at the Star-Wagon. Mori winds the window down a couple of inches.

'What's the matter?' he says, giving his best shot at the local accent.

'Engine problem,' says the chimpira, still grinning grotesquely. 'Wonder if you could give me a hand to fix it.'

'Don't know much about engines.'

'Me neither. I'm just a tourist, down here for the fishing.'

No, he is exactly as stupid as he looks. Standing there, blood all over his chimpira shirt, shark's tooth pendant round his neck, greased-back hair. There's no tourist on earth who ever looked like that. And there's something in his mind. Mori knows that straight away from the way he's standing there, smiling so ugly. Still, Mori can't just ignore the guy. He has to stay in character.

'I'll do what I can,' he says, opening the door of the van.

George the Wolf observes the delivery man getting out of the car. Spectacle frames that went out of fashion a couple of decades ago, the same half-witted drawl as all the other peasants down here. But the man is big, well muscled around the shoulders for someone in the flower business. Used to be a sportsman maybe. To be on the safe side, George moves a step away. Then his hand slips behind his back, feels the handle of the pistol. He needs that van. Respect, loyalty, sincerity: everything demands it!

Angel hears the words, doesn't like them. The ugly is one not the type to talk to a stranger like that. Never friendly, only loudmouth bully or crawling coward. She eases the side door, opens it a crack. Eye to the space, she sees this –

Mori getting out of the car, yawning, stretching out his elbows like he's tired from driving. But he's standing in a funny way, weight on the back foot.

'Let's have a look,' he says. The ugly one is standing sideways-on to Angel. She watches his hand groping under his shirt at the back, closing around the black metal. Mori knows something's wrong. He's moving in closer, but not fast enough. He's waiting too long, wanting to be sure. Angel sees it all in slow motion, understands how it will end. Mori making his move late, the gun barrel swinging towards him. The ugly one blasting him back against the side of the van, bang, bang. Too easy. Angel is going to make it difficult.

'Hey, you!' she shouts through the crack. 'You shit-eating pig, aren't you?'

Like a bee-sting on the balls! The ugly one spins round,

spitting fury. Mori seizes the moment, uses it – front foot lashing fast and high. Wolf takes the impact just under the heart, goes staggering backwards, arms wheeling. The gun goes off, a blast at the moon. Mori follows in, grabs the wrist. Wolf puts two hands to the gun, raises it above his head. Stupid fighting: so keen to keep his weapon he leaves himself open. Angel understands how this will end too. No need to do anything now.

Mori releases the wrist, hits hard to the stomach – once, twice. The ugly one doubles up, retching, still holding the gun. Mori grabs the arm, twists it against his knee, elbow smashing downwards. Wolf shouts in angry pain. The gun goes skidding across the tarmac. Mori skips backwards, then in again: a snap-kick, square in the chest. The ugly one reels back against the sea wall, steadies himself with a hand. He tries to come forward again – bellowed curses, wild punches. Mori in control, switching stance, breathing deep and smooth. Another kick, this time the full weight of the body behind it. The sea wall is just knee-height. Wolf hits it at speed, flailing, rolling, toppling over the edge. Angel, leaning against the side of the van, waits for the splash. Then she starts clapping, loud and slow.

'Bravo, detective-*san*!' she calls out. 'In the sea, just like I said!'

In his dreams George the Wolf Nishio cries tears of joy and gratitude. Gratitude that he has been fitted out in the most georgeous, eye-catching clothes. That the bodies of beautiful women are at his command, craving his touch. That he receives all respect and honour due to the young prince of Japan's most powerful syndicate. But his dreams dissolve in the hard light prising open his eyelids, the cold water slopping over his legs. He weeps again for their passing. Reality is coming. He knows he isn't going to like it.

And he's right. George finds himself alone, lying in a pool of water in some kind of boat. It's a small one, barely big enough to hold him. It bobs on the waves, the water washing from side to side. There's pain in his head, in his arm, in his groin. But wait – there's worse than all that, much worse. Look at his ankles, tied together with a red brassière. And his hands are stuck behind his back, also tied fast. He pokes up his head, sees that the boat is roped to a pine tree at the end of a rocky promontory. Twenty yards of straggly rope is all that's keeping him from the open seas!

How? Why? Suddenly the memories come pouring back: Angel's eyes shining as she reaches down for his groin; the other women squealing away in foreign languages; that delivery man circling around in a karate stance. That was no florist, no way. They were all in it together, had to be. Now other more ominous images: the construction people, waiting impatiently for the girls they'd been promised; his boss's face when he hears what happened. George the Wolf Nishio lies back down in the pool of water, takes a deep breath and opens his mouth wide.

Two schoolkids cycling along the coast road hear a strange noise, out there on the other side of the bay, a long quavering howl, almost like a wild animal in pain. Neither says anything. At this time of year, the wind plays funny tricks.

Mori makes for the prefectural capital, changes his clothes in a pachinko-parlour toilet, rents another vehicle. A StarWagon Lucida, definitely the best for the purpose. He does the switch-over in an empty parking lot, then goes to give back the van.

'How did the shoot go?' says the florist.

'Pretty good,' says Mori, handing over the other half of

the money. 'But it all depends on the art department. If they don't like it, we have to do it all over again.'

The florist nods happily as he counts through the banknotes. All over again means double.

'It would be an excellent thing for the name of a humble business like mine to appear in a magazine. Such a thing has never happened.'

'I'll make sure you get free copies,' says Mori. 'Call me any time.' He smiles cheerfully, slides the phoney business card onto the counter: 'Chizuo Nakamura – Freelance Photographer'.

The florist bows, still a little suspicious about something. Mori is just turning to leave when in walks Angel. The florist's mouth drops open. Suddenly his doorway is full of woman – big hair, big cleavage, denim cut-offs tight as a drum.

'That car no good,' says Angel, hooped earrings shaking indignantly. 'No place for girls to lie down.'

'Shut up and get back in there!' snaps Mori.

Angel wags a finger at him. 'Hey, cool down! Treat me right or I'm going to tell the doctor.'

'Wait a moment,' stammers the florist, eyes glued to Angel's areolae, dark stars under her thin white T-shirt. 'What kind of photos are these? What kind of magazine do you work for anyway?'

'Special collectors' stuff,' says Mori over his shoulder as he moves purposefully towards the door. 'No need to worry about a thing.'

'But – *hoi* – wait!'

'Stop! Let go of me, Mori-*san*!' Angel tries to shake off his grip on her wrist.

Mori doesn't let go. He twists her off balance, bends down, hauls her on to his shoulder in a fireman's lift. Heavier than he thought. She yells, thrashing her feet in his chest as he marches down the street. Turning the corner into the parking lot, Mori sees the florist come rushing out of the shop. He's worried about his shop's reputation. He's going to make a fuss. Mori dumps Angel on the pavement, wheels round to face the music. The florist comes up close.

'Don't forget to send those free copies,' he whispers.

An hour later Mori is gunning the StarWagon up the expressway. Behind him the girls are listening to disco music on a tinny cassette player, shovelling down cup noodles, gossiping, laughing and quarrelling in half a dozen languages. Angel sits in the middle, her chatter the fastest, her laugh the loudest. Some women are pretty scary, thinks Mori. But you must never let them know it.

Three

Rainy season hangover. The sky too low, pressing down on the city like a lid. Slow grey drizzle, east to west, dawn to dusk. Everything soaking, dripping, streaming. The big wet.

Mori stands at the window, gazing out over the rain-blurred streets. Pressure headache. The chipped coffee cup shakes in his hand. Down below: a tide of umbrellas, surging along the pavement, swirling around the subway exit, dividing into streams at the multi-flow crossing. They don't know they're making patterns, but they are. Everything runs in patterns. You just can't see the ones you're in.

Mori swills down the last of the Kilimanjaro, puts a record on the turntable. Ornette Coleman, 'The Shape of Jazz to Come'. Plenty of hiss and crackle, but you can't beat vinyl for true sound.

The coffee finally starts working on his synapses. Last night: a pot of Okinawan rice-liquor, with a decomposing viper curled in the bottom. Drinking companion: an ex-boxer whose sister is the 'Number Two Wife' of a senior man in the immigration bureau. Six new passports delivered, all paid for with the doctor's money. Angel insisted. The doctor just did what he was told.

Mori walks across to the other wall, gazes at the little shrine on the shelf. Laid out for the gods are a shrivelled tangerine, a riceball wrapped in seaweed, a jar of sake bought from the vending-machine across the street. With business at such a low ebb, the gods shouldn't expect any better. He closes his eyes, claps his hands, prays for good things to come – prosperity, health, energy. Used to be he never believed in that stuff. Used to be he didn't need to.

He sits down heavily, drawing a groan from the old sofa. Nothing to do this morning but watch the rain on the window, listen to Ornette blowing through the crackles and hisses, wait for the phone to ring.

The phone rings.

She wants to meet in a Parisian-style coffee-bar in Aoyama, which is the most Parisian-style place in the whole world, Paris included. But the prices are upper-end Tokyo, which means upper-end of the entire known universe. According to the window display, three inches of chocolate-covered goo costs what Mori usually pays for a full bottle of Suntory White whisky.

The clapboard door swings shut with a crash. Mori stands there shaking the moisture off his raincoat, breathing Okinawan liquor fumes over the croissants. A slick-haired waiter rushes towards him, consternation on his face.

'Dear customer! We do not allow wet umbrellas. Please use this!'

He hands over a polythene sheath into which Mori tries to slide his heavy-handled broken-sparred old umbrella. It doesn't fit. Mori's efforts leave the polythene in tatters, a pool of water between his feet. He tosses the umbrella at the waiter, who catches it shoulder-height, copping a faceful of rain.

Mori turns, scans. The young Alain Delon stares back at him from a poster on the wall. Now that's a nice raincoat, nice hat too. From the speakers in the ceiling, Serge Gainsbourg croons filthy-tender. At the tables sit expensively dressed women hiding their curiosity behind screens of cigarette smoke. Which one looks like the mama-*san* of an exclusive Ginza nightclub? Could be any of them except the frowzy housewife type in the corner.

The frowzy housewife type gets to her feet, waves him over. Of course, behind the bifocals, she's not so frowzy. She just isn't trying, which is understandable when you have to keep the charm machine running from eight to two, night after night, week after week, year after year. Kimiko Itoh is tall, with porcelain-pale complexion, no make-up. Age: anywhere between thirty-five and fifty. The only clues to her profession are eyes and voice. Eyes: alert while the rest of her face is smiling. Voice: as sugar-coated as one of the confections in the window.

'Mori-*san*? It's an honour to meet you. As I said on the phone, you were recommended by an ex-employee of mine, Junko Hayashi . . .'

Back in the 1980s, Junko had something going with a cram-school proprietor, a regular customer at the hostess bar where she worked. She was busy manoeuvring him into a divorce when a problem came up. There was a video she had once imprudently starred in, and a sleazy 'talent-scout' who was trying to hawk it to a chain of love hotels. Mori had got a yakuza friend to pose as Junko's cousin. His performance was so persuasive that the talent-scout left for Hokkaido and a new career in the dry-cleaning business.

'Right,' says Mori, lowering himself gingerly on to a fake antique chair. 'And how is she these days?'

'Very fine. We went on a golfing holiday last autumn. The Gold Coast. You know, Australia.'

Mori makes a polite noise. His thoughts: unlike the detective business, cram-schooling is pretty much recession-proof. Parents are always going to want their kids to do better than the others. So that they can get into better high schools than the others, so they can get into better universities, so that they can get into better companies, so they can afford to spend more money than the others on cram-schools for their own kids.

The waiter comes over with a tray of sticky creamy things. Kimiko Itoh spears one with a tiny fork. The waiter puts the tray under Mori's nose. Nauseous, Mori closes his eyes, 'killing with silence' until the thing has been taken away.

'So what are your terms?' she says, flicking at a glacé cherry with a fingernail.

'Depends what kind of problem you've got,' says Mori, crooking a stubby finger into the handle of his coffee cup.

'How about something complicated, like a potential murder?'

Mori smiles, which makes his face ache a little. 'Murders are expensive,' he says.

'Money is for spending, isn't it?' she replies, smiling right back.

Especially other people's, thinks Mori. Junko Hayashi is living nicely off education fees. A Ginza mama-*san* would live off something higher grade than that. Mori soon finds out what that something is – the Japanese government budget.

The dead man, explains Kimiko Itoh, was a senior bureaucrat at the Ministry of Health, a close friend of long standing. Also majority shareholder in a Ginza nightclub, guesses Mori. And in all probability the provider of a luxury apartment in central Tokyo, a condo in Hawaii or somewhere similar, fur coats, golf club memberships, shopping sprees to Milan and other necessities to the lady presently sitting across the table. His death must have been quite a loss.

She continues with her tale.

Masao Miura is one step away from the position of

vice-minister, shogun of the entire health bureaucracy. He is ambitious, dedicated, enjoying his power and influence to the full. From the day he entered Tokyo University Law School he has been groomed as one of the best and the brightest, the wielders of ultimate power in the Japanese system. Now it's within his grasp. And then he dies suddenly. The press reports it as '*karoshi*', death from overwork. The kind of thing that seems to happen on a regular basis in these tough times. Except that a few days before his death Miura had told his high-maintenance lover that someone was following him, that she was to watch out for anything suspicious.

'And did you see anything?' Mori asks.

Kimiko Itoh shakes her elegantly coiffed head.

'So what makes you so sure about the murder?'

'He wasn't suffering from stress. In fact, he was in great shape. We just came back from Bali, a UNESCO conference on ageing. And then there's the autopsy.'

Mori leans forward. The fake antique chair creaks worryingly.

'What about the autopsy?'

'There wasn't one,' says Kimiko Itoh. 'The wife refused it, even though it would probably be necessary to get the full "*karoshi*" pension.'

'Really? You seem pretty knowledgeable about the details.'

'He explained them to me. Actually, he drafted that law in my apartment.'

Mori pauses to take a noisy sip of his coffee.

'So you suspect the wife of an insurance scam?'

The well-plucked crescents above Kimiko Itoh's eyes arch imperceptibly upwards.

'How did you guess?'

'Not difficult,' says Mori.

*

26

'How did you guess?' says Mori, a couple of hours later.

'Not difficult,' says Shima. 'If this Itoh woman was in the wife's place, it's exactly the kind of thing she'd do herself.'

'How can you possibly know that?' protests Mori. 'I mean, you haven't even met her.'

'I don't need to,' smiles Shima. 'I know the psychology of women in the water-trade. The ones that live off men the best are the ones who despise them the most. Two sides of the same coin.'

'Pretty cynical thoughts, Detective Shima.'

Shima nods happily at the compliment. He is the philosopher of Yoyogi police station. Also its only member to view Mori as anything other than a disturber of the delicate network of mutually beneficial relations between police and policed that keeps the district running.

The two men are sitting in a tiny noodle stall perched on a pavement behind Shinjuku station. Rain patters on the plastic tarpaulin that constitutes roof and walls. Steam billows from the cauldron. The proprietor, a grizzled old man wearing a grubby bellyband, shakes more spice on to the writhing noodles. His choice of location has been in violation of city ordinances for the past three decades.

'The wife is certainly the first place to look,' says Mori. 'But maybe it's all a mistake. Maybe all this stuff about being followed was stress-induced too. You know, persecution complex.'

Shima nods. He raises the noodle bowl to his lips, puffs out his sweaty cheeks before he starts slurping. There's almost as much moisture on his face as on Mori's umbrella. The reason is in the bowl: the 'red lake of hell', fieriest noodle broth in the whole of Shinjuku.

'You see the problem,' continues Mori. 'Without anything more, I don't even know if this is a real case or not.'

'Anything more?'

'You know – any suspicious circumstances. The usual stuff.'

'Huh?'

Shima knows exactly what Mori wants. He just likes making him spell it out. The two men have been friends since they met face to face in a karate gym in 1972. Their relative status was a little different in those days. Mori was an arrogant student at an élite university. Shima a shaven-headed tough who had chosen his career path after seeing the riot police in action on the TV news. Mori got knocked out in that first match-up, a 'mistake' as the sneering young cop failed to pull his punch. After their second match-up, Shima had to spend his summer bonus on a set of new front teeth. Now a quarter of a century on, Shima is an inspector, father of two teenage daughters, a man who prefers hunching over a 'shogi' board to practising his karate moves. And Mori? For Mori, the 1970s have never really ended.

'I need your help, Shima-*san*. A high-profile guy like that – somebody must have put in a report.'

Shima takes another good long slurp. Then, scowling slightly, he dabs his mouth with his hand-towel. For a man who has just drained a bowlful of liquid fire, he looks remarkably self-possessed.

'A report?' he says. 'Might be something somewhere, I suppose.'

That's what Mori was waiting for. He finishes his beer, thrusts a thousand-yen note at the old man, who waves it away. The usual ritual: Mori leans over, slides it under the grubby bellyband.

'By the way,' says Shima, buttoning up his raincoat, 'I've got a question for you too. I want to know how you stop your girlfriends from getting jealous?'

'Girlfriends? What girlfriends?'

'Come on, Mori-*san*! I hear you've got five exotic ladies staying over at your apartment. You must be exhausted.'

He chuckles. Mori gives a noncommittal grunt. The women were exhausting, though not the way that Shima thinks.

'Just friends of a friend,' he says. 'Actually, they all left Japan this morning.'

The two men stand up, filling the tiny space. Drops of condensation, shake loose from the steel struts, plunge into the frothing cauldron. The old man hollers his gratitude. Mori pushes through the tarpaulin, walks out into the thin purposeless rain.

He gets back to his office in the early afternoon. Times are still tough in this part of Shinjuku, unless you're a pawnbroker, loan shark or pyramid sales scammer. Many buildings have had 'For Rent' signs up for years now. Mori's building is full because it's got the cheapest rent in the area. It's got the cheapest rent because, first, there's no elevator, second, there's no air-conditioning, third, a sizeable earthquake would reduce the whole place to rubble in ten seconds flat. Nonetheless the tenants keep changing. The ground-floor restaurant went bankrupt last year, replaced by a warren of 'karaoke boxes', cubicle-sized rooms where you can sing, booze, do whatever you want for three hundred yen an hour. For some reason, high-school kids like it a lot.

Up above, the two yakuza have closed their English language school, replaced it with another form of extortion racket, leasing out rubber plants for hotel lobbies and company reception areas. On the next floor the mysterious trading company is still there, its office as silent and dark as ever. As Mori clumps past he scans the ads pasted to the door.

'*The World's Cheapest Water-Purifier – Guaranteed to Eliminate all Microbes and Chemicals!*'

'*The Famous Chinese Slimming Soap – 80% Discount!*'

'*Anti-Odour Tablets, as Featured in Major Weekly Magazines! Smell Thoroughly Clean, Right From the Inside!*'

Mori has heard something about that last one. He stops to inspect the fine print: 'enjoy intimate romantic relations with full physical confidence ... originally developed for medical use ... eliminates all unpleasant odour of bodily wastes and secretions ... replaces with a choice of relaxing scents ...'

A few examples of the relaxing scents are given. Apparently, thanks to the advances of science, you can sweat lavender, piss pine forests, fart lemon and honey. Just the product for this unreal city at this unreal moment in human history. Mori continues up the staircase, shaking his head.

And on the top floor the building's oldest tenant, slowest rent-payer, provider of fragments of reality to anyone willing to pay the price. Written in faded characters just above the letter box: 'Kazuo Mori – Economic and Social Research Services'.

The company's president, finance director, head of sales, chief operative and only employee stops dead in his tracks. The light is on inside, Thelonius Monk tinkling from the stereo. Look closer: the lock has been forced, not difficult with a knife or screwdriver. For a few long moments Mori is as still as a statue. Then soundlessly he eases the door half an inch open ...

'Hey, detective-*san*! Angel been waiting for you all afternoon.'

She is sprawled on his sofa munching an apple. She looks a little different – smart new raincoat, wild hair packed up in a scarf. Mori walks over to the music machine, lifts the needle from the record.

'What's going on?' he says suspiciously. 'Was your flight cancelled or something?'

'Not cancelled. The others all gone to Narita airport. Me – I changed my mind. I want to stay in Japan.'

Mori's anger ignites like a gas-burner in a Korean barbecue. 'You crazy woman! Have you any idea of what that chimpira's going to do if he finds you?'

Angel stands up, all the better to give it to him right back, at point-blank range. 'That guy your fault. Angel say better kill him, and you refuse two times. Why you do like that?'

'Why?' roars Mori. 'Because here in Japan we don't kill people like animals. That's why.'

Angel takes a step forward. Mori takes a step back. It was a mistake to try and compete on volume. Angel's lungs are as healthy as her tonsils, which he now gets to see close up.

'You don't, no! You just take Asian young girls and treat them like animals. ALL JAPANESE MEN ARE PIGS! BIG DIRTY PIGS!'

These words get heavy individual emphasis, loud enough to distract the high-school kids from whatever they're doing down below in the karaoke cubicles.

Mori squeezes his eyes shut, waits for the ringing in his ears to subside. 'Listen to me,' he says finally, wagging his finger like a teacher. 'You have to leave Japan as soon as possible. It's just too dangerous here. People are going to be looking for you, very bad people.'

Angel looks at him, then suddenly slaps him on the shoulder and gives a loud peal of laughter.

'Detective-*san*,' she says. 'I like you! You are very nice man.'

Now Mori is feeling even more uncomfortable. He walks over to the coffee-percolator, pours in a handful of freshly

31

ground Kilimanjaro. Angel sits down on the sofa, legs crossed. She's wearing a pair of brand-new slingbacks.

'Detective-*san*, let me tell you about the city I use to live. In one district there's a rubbish heap as big as Shinjuku station. It stinks so bad you couldn't go near. All the rotten stuff, all the shit – one little sniff would make you fall down on the ground.'

Mori switches on the percolator, turns. She's looking him straight in the eye, not laughing any more.

'Families live and die in that rubbish heap, detective-*san*. Bodies are buried there, not just dogs. Every day the children go to the market to steal food. Sometimes they take too much. After that the market people come with guns. They take the first children they see, shoot them like rats.'

Angel's voice is calm, matter-of-fact, as if she's describing something she saw on TV. Mori listens, thinks, She sold the passport already, bought the raincoat and those shoes. He doesn't blame her. He knows this is no TV documentary.

'You Japanese like to talk about your home town. That rubbish heap is my home town. My little cousins are still there, two of them, stealing food and clothes to stay alive.'

Mori says nothing, gets a couple of mugs from the cupboard. The one with the broken handle he keeps for himself. Angel goes on talking.

'So far I been in Japan almost one year. I get much money from the doctor, send it home. Now my mother and sisters move to nice place. Already everyone getting happy, see.'

'Good time to get out, I'd say,' said Mori.

The coffee's too strong for Angel. She wrinkles her nose like a schoolkid.

'Not yet. My mother needs medicine for her stomach, my little sister wants to go to college. And as for dangerous –

I've seen many dangerous things, many dangerous people. I am pretty dangerous person myself, you know.'

She's smiling again, flashing those big white teeth. And she's pulling something from the pocket of her raincoat.

'Here's the passport,' she says, getting to her feet. 'I give it back to you – that's why I came here.'

'It's yours,' says Mori.

'No, it's yours. If I need it, I'll come and ask again.'

She leans forward, kisses him on the mouth. Mori pulls her in – taut body, hair tingling like electricity – but she breaks away with another laugh.

'That's why I like you,' she says. 'You never put a hand on any of us young girls. You not a pig, detective-*san*.'

'Thanks,' says Mori drily.

Angel disappears through the door. Mori listens to her slingbacks clattering on the metal staircase. He sips his coffee, wonders if she's telling the truth, how old she is, what she looks like naked.

Mori spends most of the afternoon on the phone. He uses a heavy black model which sits in the middle of his desk, a dominating and reassuring presence. A mobile would be more convenient – he recognizes that. And these days they more or less give the things away free. But all the same he refuses to sign up, just as he has refused to buy a laptop computer, a personal organizer or a fax. The reason? Half inertia, half rebellion against the unnecessary. Also he suspects that mobile phones may cause brain cancer. One thing's for sure – if they do, nobody will say anything until it's much, much too late.

The calls he makes are not particularly fruitful. Finding out such basic facts as where and when Miura died turns out to be surprisingly difficult. He calls the ministry, the coroner's office, several hospitals, the research department of a major newspaper. He pretends to be a relative just back from the US, a bank manager, a junior colleague. Finally he pieces together some hazy details. Miura had a heart attack at work. A security man discovered him shortly after midnight. He was rushed to the ministry's own clinic, but too late to do any good.

Run this movie in your mental screening-room –

There's shirtsleeved Miura, alone, toiling late into the night on some complicated legislation vital to the nation's future. Suddenly he feels breathless, staggers out into the corridor when – bang – his overtaxed heart starts to spasm. He tears frantically at his collar, slumps to the ground, draws his last breath right in the centre of the organization to which he has sacrificed his life.

A sad movie. Inspiring even, if you're the kind of person who's easily inspired. Story-wise, it more or less hangs together. Top bureaucrats pride themselves on the long hours they spend at work. At budget time they bring in sleeping bags and clean shirts and don't leave their offices for weeks. A really ambitious man would need to demonstrate fanatical devotion. Otherwise he wouldn't get the peer approval that's the key to success in any big organization.

Except that Kimiko Itoh says it's all wrong. And she was close enough to the man to know. Well, supposing she's right. Supposing Miura's wife had him murdered. The hitman would need to sneak into the ministry in the small hours. Then he would have to employ a method that could be disguised as a heart attack. Why bother? Why not just stage something simple like a car accident?

First thought: Kimiko Itoh may be mistaken, perhaps lying. She's bitter at the loss of her sponsor, keen to stir up trouble for the wife. Second thought: Kimiko Itoh is the client. What the client says goes, especially when she's the only major client on the horizon, your apartment is worth thirty per cent less than what you bought it for six years ago, and the muscles of your lower back keep staging wildcat strikes against the unfair demands you make on them.

Conclusion: shut up and do the job.

Mori starts with the obvious: the nameless security man. He picks up the phone, gets through to the chief of security at the ministry. He uses one of his favourite personae – a grand-toned, long-winded academic from the National Foundation of Cultural Research. If anyone ever cared to check, there are at least five institutions of that name, each containing dozens of men called Tanaka.

'What kind of humble assistance can I offer?' comes the reply, cautiously respectful. The man has been trained to obey, to respond to exactly the sort of bluster that Mori now produces.

'I am an acquaintance of the fine bureaucrat who met such an unhappy end two weeks ago. I wish to express gratitude to the individual on your staff who found him in those distressing circumstances.'

'I see.' Puzzled, but not suspicious.

'A small barrel of sake will be arriving at the ministry in a few days' time. It's a top-quality Niigata band, and it absolutely must be drunk at precisely eight degrees centigrade. Not any warmer, not any colder. Do you understand me?'

'Uh – of course!'

'Now if you could please give me the full name and title of the individual concerned.'

'You mean Kaneda? That's going to be difficult, I'm afraid.'

'Difficult! What does that mean?'

'Well, he's no longer with us here in the ministry. He's been transferred.'

'Transferred where?' Mori snaps.

The chief of security is sounding defensive. Insecure, in fact.

'Uh – well – it hasn't been decided yet. But if you send the sake to me personally, I'll make sure it reaches him. I hope that is acceptable . . .'

'Completely unacceptable!' howls Mori and returns the telephone receiver to its cradle with a satisfying crunch. Something you definitely couldn't do with a mobile.

Mid-afternoon Mori goes for a soak in the tiny bath-house round the corner. For a quarter of an hour he sits there in the steam, legs outstretched, a flannel on his head. As usual, the water is vindictively hot. The only other customer is the manager of the pachinko parlour in the next block. Mori tries to pump him about the new IC-controlled machines they've brought in – how many times a month they get reprogrammed, what parlour they were in before – but the man doesn't want to answer. Instead, he wants to talk about how customer numbers keep declining, how the local syndicate is squeezing him, how anyway there are just too many pachinko parlours for the district to bear. Mori grunts unsympathetically. This guy changes his BMW every year, has a mistress who appears on TV commercials, a skiing lodge up in the Japan Alps and a beach house in Shimoda. All that out of the money that people like Mori pump into his machines in order to see those silver balls go flying. And still he complains! He should swap places with Mori for a few months. He should ride to work on a fifteen-year-old Honda. He should live in eighty square metres of floor space financed with a thirty-year loan. He should spend his evenings trading gossip with brain-dead low-lifes, rummaging through trash-bags, waiting for hours on end outside love hotels, camera at the ready. Then he might have something to complain about.

The pachinko guy gets out of the bath. He looks a little happier for having run into Mori. The feeling is not reciprocated.

Mori lies back in the bath, watches his limbs slowly turning puce. He wonders about Kaneda. For some reason the man is being kept under wraps. It's probably worth finding out why. But how many Kanedas are there in Tokyo? Tens of thousands, just as there are tens of thousands of Itohs and Shimadas and, indeed, Moris. Locating the right one is going to cost money. But, as the lady pointed out, what's money for but spending?

In this city all information is easily available, if you only know who to ask. But who to ask – that itself is information which takes years, maybe decades, to acquire. What you need – the skill of a fly-fisher, the endurance of a Zen monk. You have to coax, tease, ease it out of uncountable late-night drinking sessions, favours that have been traded and retraded, conversations that go round and round like a Möbius strip. The golden rule: you don't search for the information. The information searches for you.

When Mori needs to find out something about some-body, he usually asks Kazuko. Mori and Kazuko have a great relationship – they've never met, never will. He got her name from a man who has never met either of them. And that man's name came from the brother of a lawyer who once did good work for the company owned by a friend of someone who wouldn't be alive any more if it weren't for Mori. That's how Mori got Kazuko's name. At least he thinks so. Truth to tell, it all happened so long ago that he's pretty much forgotten.

Kazuko works for a consumer finance company listed on

the first section of the Tokyo Stock Exchange. She sounds about the same age as Mori himself, and she seems to have worked in every department of the company. She knows more about the business than almost anyone. Probably including the president, a jovial old thug who devotes most of his time and energy to his hobby of speedboat racing. Certainly including the chairman, an ex-bureaucrat who has 'descended from heaven' to a slumberous and lucrative sinecure.

Kazuko knows a lot of things about a lot of people – about one hundred and twenty million people, to be precise. You give her a name, one or two details. She calls back later with date and place of birth, names of relatives, school grades, height, blood type, strength of eyesight, criminal record, salary, average telephone bill, taste in rental videos, and so on. The usual reward for her efforts: fifty thousand yen transferred to a tiny Osaka bank. Account name: Tabuchi Industrial Services. Kazuko's name is not Tabuchi. So who is Tabuchi? That is a question that Mori will never ask.

As soon as he gets back to the office, Mori makes a call to Kazuko. The conversation is brief. He gives her a name, a place of work. She says just one word: 'understood'. Then he sits down on the sofa and waits. He nibbles a steamed bun. He swigs down a stamina drink – containing caffeine, royal jelly and garlic – bought from the vending-machine across the street. He scans the evening paper. The Giants win a double-header, a committee of intellectuals claim that the Nanjing massacre never happened, a senior politician demands a supplementary budget. In other words, business as usual. And as for that sly-eyed, smooth-cheeked politician, enough lacquer on his hair to constitute a fire risk – wasn't he involved in some financial scandal a few years ago? Mori recalls testimony before the Diet, mumbled apologies, protestations of memory loss. Now the man's back, as if nothing had happened. That's the way the system works. Steal fifty thousand yen from a convenience store and you get locked up. Loot a few trillion from a housing-loan company and you get a seat in the cabinet.

Just before six Kazuko telephones from a call box. Mori writes down Kaneda's address and phone number. The other stuff he can do without.

Another piece of bad luck: when he calls, there's no one at home. That means a visit. Location: an unlovely bedtown half the way to Mount Fuji. So take the Honda through the clogged streets? Or strap-hang in a jam-packed train for an hour and a half? Mori's conclusion: individual discomfort is less stressful than the collective kind. He gets his helmet and gloves from the cupboard.

Night-time, the city reduced to water and light. Puddles, windows, beacons, rivulets, reflections etched on wet tarmac. The whole neon empire hazed in drizzle. Ten thousand headlights in the slanting silver rain.

Mori's Honda nudges through the back alleys, thunders along the expressways, glides past the tailbacks like a ghost. It takes longer than he thinks, as getting anywhere in this city always does. Finally, just before eight he arrives.

The Kaneda residence is on the fifteenth floor of the newest high-rise in a cluster of eight. All around are disused rice paddies full of pieces of junk. At the bottom of the building, hundreds of bicycles stacked in neat rows. Mori parks the Honda, scans upwards – every apartment has the same gun-metal grey door, the same tiny balcony. Probably bigger than Mori's place, cheaper too. Still, he would hate to live here. No noise, no human mess, nobody, nothing: an ideal place to go mad.

Mori ascends the damp concrete emptiness, raps on

Kaneda's door. Silence, darkness. A pencil-light through the letter box reveals the place has been cleaned out completely. Mori's thoughts – why do things have to be so difficult? Why doesn't he get any breaks any more?

He gets a break. The elevator hums into life, rises again to the fifteenth floor. There are other human beings alive in the world after all. The evidence appears: a hulking teenage male, in baggy trousers and dyed 'tea-colour' hair. He walks tough, talks tough too when he sees Mori.

'Hey! What you think you're doing?'

Heavy-shouldered, stocky as a judo champ. An earring dangling, a nose-stud, and something shiny in his eyebrow. Looks like the kind that squeezes protection money out of smaller kids, hangs around the fringe of biker gangs, goes 'hunting' drunken salarymen on Friday nights. Nice ordinary boy, really.

'Ah, good evening,' says Mori, turning to face him. 'I'm paying a visit on Kaneda-*san*.'

'Well, he's not here, is he, uncle?'

Uncle! Now that really rankles. Doesn't anyone teach these kids respect any more? Mori thinks about giving him a short introductory course. He would start by removing the facial ornaments, very quickly. But that would be pointless. Mori came all this way for information. So instead he smiles a clenched-jaw smile.

'Then could you please tell me where to find him?'

The hulk enjoys that. It gives him a chance to be unpleasant. He comes closer, pushes his acne-ridden face at Mori. Big pupils, sharp smell of paint thinner.

'Maybe I could, but I'm not going to. I'm not going to tell you anything!'

He laughs, as if he's just said something exceptionally witty. Mori's patience snaps. It's been a hard day, frustration all down the line. He takes a step forward.

'Now listen to me, you pimple-faced idiot...'

A door opens. A face emerges, a middle-aged woman in a faded cotton kimono.

'Supper's waiting for you, Shin-chan. Hurry up, it's your favourite.'

She's smiling and cooing as if he were a cute little eight-year-old. Can't she see what a mini-Godzilla she's spawned?

'Who's that?' says the woman, darting nervous eyes at Mori.

'He's a suspicious guy,' brays Godzilla Junior. 'When I asked him what he was doing, he threatened to beat me up!'

Mori smiles indulgently. 'That's a misunderstanding, I'm afraid. But your son was quite correct to challenge me as he did. In fact, I'd say that our society needs many more public-spirited young men like him. Now let me introduce myself...'

A name card for every occasion. The one Mori takes from his wallet carries a job title calculated to instil maximum awe in the recipient – 'Special Investigator: West Kanto Tax Bureau'. Now there is no Kazuo Mori working at the West Kanto Tax Bureau. In fact, there is no West Kanto Tax Bureau at all. And the phone number given is of a pink cabaret in Ikebukuro where the music is too loud for anyone ever to pick up the phone. These are facts that could easily be checked in a couple of seconds. But the woman is not going to check. If she were the type that would – because she wondered, for example, why a tax investigator would wear a creased leather jacket and jeans that looked as if they could stand up and walk on their own – then Mori would have chosen a different name card.

The conversation is brief, but Mori gets what he wants. Kaneda and his wife moved out about a month ago. In the middle of the night. Without saying anything to anybody. Which was strange, because they had been quite a friendly

41

couple. With a son the same age as Shin-chan, also a keen judo-player. Gone, without even saying goodbye.

Kaneda's next-door neighbour is affronted, puzzled. Mori is not puzzled. He has a good idea why Kaneda didn't even say goodbye: because he didn't know he was going.

Four

George the Wolf Nishio forgets that he is wearing his best white trousers. He gets down on his hands and knees, presses his forehead to the tatami mat. But the syndicate's young prince is unforgiving.

'Tofu-head,' he snarls, placing his foot on the back of George's neck. 'Your stupidity has cost us a major contract!'

Cheek squashed to the floor, George utters whimpering words of apology and shame. He hates the young prince more than ever – the aftershave, the Armani suits, the business-school jargon.

The old boss sits a few yards behind, silent, face like thunder. He's wearing a formal kimono – black silk, deep sleeves. George is grateful for that. It shows respect.

'No more mistakes,' warns the young prince. 'Our business needs trustworthy people, smart people. Not drunken monkeys. Do you understand?'

The young prince's foot is now grinding against his nose. George closes his eyes. How can you have a real yakuza whose hobbies are wine-tasting and racquet-ball? Who analyses the gambling market on a laptop computer? Who socializes with musicians and architects? A true conservative of the heart, George deplores the growing influence of the young prince and the other 'economic yakuza'. But he doesn't want to cross them either – the man's ruthlessness is legendary. So instead he just whimpers.

'Get ready now,' says the old boss. He sounds more tired than angry. George's heart brims over with gratitude. He would do anything for the old boss, anything. A recurrent fantasy: one day the old boss gets fed up with the young prince. He asks George to dispose of him, using any means he likes. In some versions George chooses piano wire, in others a power drill . . .

Thump! The young prince's foot drives into George's lower stomach, knocking him on to his back. Then two of the others grab him by the elbows, haul him towards a low table in the centre of the room. On it are some rolls of white calligraphy paper, the stuff the old boss has hand-made from mulberry leaves by a craftsman in Kamakura. Next to the paper is a short sword, one from his personal collection. The edge looks razor sharp.

The others step back to the side of the room. George unrolls the paper, lays his left hand flat, fingers splayed. Sweat glistens on his brow, trickles down his spine.

'Hurry up,' groans the young prince. 'I can't waste any more time on his nonsense!'

George gazes at his little finger – so naked, so innocent. Thirty-five years it's been with him. Now it's time to part. How will it feel to make a fist with just four fingers? To squeeze a woman's breast, to clutch a steering-wheel?

'What's the matter? Are you scared?' That sneering voice again. George lifts the sword head-height. For some reason the blade is wobbling as if it's got a life of its own.

'Cut it!' roars the young prince.

Eyes squeezed shut, George slams the sword down on the paper. On impact his left hand shoots backwards. The little finger stays in the centre of the paper.

'YAAAAH!' The wolf howls, loud and high.

The pain is sharper than he expects, much sharper. The blood is messier than he expects, much messier. And the rage is stronger than he expects, much stronger. Rage at the young prince, lips now twisted into a supercilious smile. Rage at the whore, Angel. But most of all rage against the phoney delivery man whose scheming has robbed him of all respect and honour!

Typical rainy season, looks like evening all day long. Feels like it too. Mori leans back on his Honda, peers through the wet grey air.

At first he thinks there must have been some mistake. He expected an élite bureaucrat to live in ordinary middle-class style. The stereotype: arrogant maybe, but puritanical, hard-working, dedicated to the service of the nation. Well, scrap the stereotype. Look at the guy's house! Mori had no idea such places even existed in central Tokyo.

He cruises around the block, marvelling. This is what he sees. A huge plot of land – entrances front, back, and side. Through the fence – glimpses of a carp pond, a bamboo grove, a wooden teahouse that looks as if it has more square metres than Mori's entire apartment. The main building is a traditional three-storey structure, with red-tiled roof and long swooping eaves. It faces due east, the ideal for prosperity and health.

The Honda grumbles to a halt. Mori feasts his eyes on the graceful lines, on the ultimate Tokyo luxury – space. Then a red light in the wall starts flashing, and Mori turns away, pretends to be examining a map. The gate swings open to let out a maroon Jaguar with darkened windows. Mori scans the woman through the windscreen wipers. Mid-thirties, short hair, stern mouth. A grieving widow? An accomplished murderess? The Jaguar swishes through a puddle, spraying muddy water over Mori's leg.

Mori rides around a couple of shopping areas, makes enquiries. At the first he's a 'shiatsu' masseur on the

45

lookout for rich customers. At the next he becomes a salesman of cut-price reliquary items: this month the urns are an especially good deal. The locals know all about Miura's death. It's not hard for Mori to get them talking. There's always plenty of interest in other people's misfortunes.

This is what they tell him. Miura bought the place five years ago, had the old building knocked down. Quiet couple, no children. And what kind of woman is the wife? Usual élite type: remote refined traditional. Teaches tea ceremony twice a week. Studies flower arrangement at the Sogetsu Hall every Thursday afternoon. So is there anyone else living in that huge place – housekeeper or relative? There isn't.

Today is Thursday. The time is two o'clock in the afternoon, though you wouldn't know it from the bruised sky. Mori heads back to Miura's house.

This time he's a despatch rider, with a clipboard and an envelope bulging with documents. The street is empty, but all the same he presses the bell, shuffles impatiently from foot to foot. A few minutes' wait, then he strides around the corner to the garden door. It's a catch job, old and rusty. Mori takes a screwdriver from the envelope, slides it through the crack, gives the head a sharp thwack with his flat of his hand. On the other side of the door, the catch goes flying.

A wealthy house, but the security is pathetic. That's because there's no crime on the streets of this city. The serious people are busy with fraud, extortion, blackmail, bribery, money-laundering, bid-rigging, loan-sharking, game-fixing, insider-dealing, trading in weapons, endangered species, spoilt meat, counterfeit software, forged currency, child pornography and immigrant labourers. And these things require a high level of public order to conduct properly.

Mori slips a lock on the kitchen window, climbs in over the sink. The place looks even bigger from the inside. He moves through huge rooms, whole sections of which contain nothing but carpet. What's the point of all this space? For someone who has spent the last quarter of a century living and working in cluttered six-mat rooms, it's enough to provoke agoraphobia.

He noses through a few cupboards – nothing but books, magazines, chintzy tableware. Where would they keep important stuff? A house like this must have a study. In the hallway there's a large staircase, with walnut banisters. Mori goes up, stealthily. The banisters creak. The stairs creak. Even the ceiling creaks.

At the top of the stairs, a long corridor. At the end, a sliding door with panels of translucent paper. Behind it, a hunched silhouette. Human, male.

Mori takes a half-step backwards. A floorboard groans. The silhouette stays motionless. So does Mori. Stillness. The only sound the patter of the rain.

Go forward or back? Mori's instincts decide. He moves down the corridor like a cat, slow motion, rolling his weight over each step forward. At the sliding door, he waits a lifetime. Then his fingernails open a millimetre of light; he lines his eye to the crack.

What he sees – a face the colour of dead blood. A ferociously contorted mouth. A spiked helmet.

Mori tugs the door open another few inches. The samurai gazes at him with bellicose glee, just as it has been gazing on everyone for the past century or so. There are plenty of other antiques in the room too. On the wall, a Noh mask. In the alcove, a wooden statue of the seven gods of good luck, insanely happy with their bags of rice and

47

baskets teeming with fish. Next to the window, a shelf of mud-brown tea bowls. The kind that might cost you two thousand yen each or two hundred thousand or twenty million, depending on how you felt about that configuration of murky whirls and blotches. And under the shelf a traditional wooden chest, made of gleaming cherry wood. Mori has never taken out a life insurance policy, but if he had he would keep it in a fine antique chest like that, with all his other important documents. Probably in the bottom drawer, with its imposing wrought-iron handle.

The drawer is locked, which is encouraging. If he had a chest like that, where would he keep the key? Somewhere not too far away, of course. Somewhere in the room.

Mori looks in the other drawers. He peers behind the Noh mask. He shakes all the tea bowls – gently, of course. Not there either. He stops, thinks, looks around. That samurai figure – the helmet isn't quite straight. Mori eases it off. And there is the key, balanced on the crown of the old guy's polished wooden head.

Actually, there's not much in the drawer, just a stack of folders. Mori dumps them on the desk, scans. The first contains bills, credit-card statements and account books from four different banks. Three of the accounts are small stuff. But the fourth, which is in the name of Age Care Corporation, holds more money than Mori will ever earn in his entire life. The second folder contains miscellaneous stuff – family photos, exam certificates, a plastic file of name cards of doctors, academics and other worthies. The last folder is puzzling: inside are floor plans and photos of two small office buildings in Yokohama.

But no life insurance policy, no signed agreement with a contract killer. Nowhere anything to back the dark suspicions of Kimiko Itoh.

So Mori grabs the folders, is about to stuff them back in

the drawer when one slides from his hand. The contents shower the floor – letters, name cards, photos. Cursing, Mori drops to his haunches, starts shovelling everything back into the folder. Then freezes. One of the name cards is eighty per cent hidden under the rest of the mess. Still the remaining twenty per cent grabs his gaze, won't let go. The reason: that corner of paper belongs to a name card more familiar to Mori than any other in the world. He picks it up, confirms, 'Kazuo Mori: Economic and Social Research Services'.

Suddenly there is a noise outside: tyres on the gravel. Then a car door slams. Voices: male and female, close.

No time to lose. Mori dumps everything in the drawer, locks up, slips the key under the samurai's helmet. The old guy looks a few degrees jauntier than he did before. Mori shuts the sliding door with a thwack, races along the corridor.

Clop-clop, the sound of wooden sandals coming along the path. Mori takes the stairs three at a time, reaching the bottom just as the handle of the front door turns.

A woman's voice. 'Please enter, sensei. It is an honour to invite you to my humble dwelling.'

The front door swings open. Mori glances around desperately. There is a cupboard behind the stairs, the door half-open. He dives inside. Fortunately there is enough room to house a couple of sumo wrestlers.

A man's voice, booming, pompous. 'This is an excellent opportunity, I think. Very few pupils are qualified to appreciate my most advanced work.'

They are inside now, approaching the cupboard. Mori huddles in a corner, buries himself in coats and scarves. The cupboard door is pulled open and for a few seconds light floods in. An umbrella is tossed inside, a couple of raincoats hung up. Then the door slams shut.

49

Woman's voice. 'Shall I help you prepare the equipment?'

Man's voice. 'Not necessary. Please prepare your body instead.'

Woman's voice, timid, dubious. 'Prepare my body? What do you require?'

Man's voice. 'Go and take a hot bath. Your muscles must be soft and supple.'

The woman goes upstairs. The man wanders through the ground floor rooms, chanting a Noh chorus in a low sonorous voice. What Mori should do now is clear – sneak out of the cupboard, through the front door and back to his Honda as soon as possible. But he doesn't. Why? Because he is curious. What kind of person is Miura's wife? Why has she got Mori's name card? And what kind of flower-arrangement lesson needs the pupil to take a hot bath? So Mori waits in the darkness of the cupboard, fake fur tickling his nose, rain dripping on his feet.

A quarter of an hour later she comes back downstairs. Mori waits another five minutes for the flower-arrangement session to get into full swing, then ventures out of the cupboard. He slips across the hallway, listens.

The man's voice issuing instructions. 'Don't move your head. Keep your breathing absolutely steady.'

It sounds as if they are in the tatami room at the back of the house. Mori pads through the empty spaces, testing each floorboard before shifting his weight. One step, freeze. One step, freeze. The seconds drip by. There is the door to the tatami room, half-open, ten yards away. Slowly, silently, Mori closes the gap. He hears the man murmuring a Noh chant. The snick of his clippers as a plant stem is severed. Not a peep from the woman.

'Good,' grunts the man. 'Now all is ready.'

Mori reaches the door, waits, cheek against the cool of

the doorpost. He is just edging his gaze into the room when there's a flash of blinding white light.

'Next I will try from the other side.'

Nothing happens. Mori is stone. He doesn't move an eyelash. Then the Noh chant restarts. The sound of clicking, fiddling. Mori judges the moment, darts a glance into the room.

A detective gets to see a lot of strange things in his work. Sometimes Mori thinks he has lost his capacity for surprise. But now his jaw slackens and his eyes widen. He is surprised.

Here are the reasons, in ascending order of impact. First: the woman is naked. Second: she is inside the room's alcove, the place where you expect to see a ceramic bowl or a painted screen. Third: she is upside down, back against the wall, legs folded over her head. Fourth: there is something between her scissoring thighs, something which the sensei is leaning forward to adjust.

Satisfied, he moves away, giving Mori an open view. What he sees: leaves, twigs, grasses, two tulips bobbing gently on their long stems.

The sensei crouches behind the tripod, fiddles with the focus, then stands up again, hands on hips.

'There's too much movement,' he barks.

'But, sensei . . .' gasps the woman.

'Quiet! You must freeze every muscle in your body!'

The woman takes a deep breath, closes her eyes.

'This is an especially complex work,' the sensei grumbles. 'Every element is the product of intense meditation . . .'

He steps behind the tripod again. The camera flashes three times. Mori ducks out of sight, then pads his way back to the hallway, leaving the flower-arranger and his arrangement alone together. He eases open the front door and makes a silent departure.

Outside the rain has stopped temporarily. Or rather the moisture is no longer forming particles and falling to the ground. Instead it just hangs in the air. Mori mounts the Honda and heads back to Shinjuku, home of non-stop performance art with no tuition, no textbooks and one hundred per cent audience participation.

Evening modulates into night. Mori sits at his desk, sips Suntory White on the rocks, considers what he has learned. A man is dead. A lady who knows him well suspects the wife so employs a detective to check the situation out. But the wife also has the name card of the same detective. Why? Where did she get it from? The one person who might know would be the lady herself, Kimiko Itoh. Mori glances at his watch, a fake Rolex bought third-hand from a local fortune-teller. It's just after seven o'clock. A hard-working mama-*san* should be at her club already. He phones. Kimiko Itoh isn't there. Mori leaves a message.

Next problem: Kaneda. The man who found the body has been hustled out of sight. Not even his neighbours know where he is. So who does? Mori rings the ministry again, pretends to be a cousin of Kaneda who needs to contact him on urgent family business. It doesn't work. They tell him to put his urgent message in a letter and they'll forward it through the internal mail system.

Third phone call: Mori calls Shima to see if he's managed to turn up any police information. He has. In fact, there's a full report on file, detailing the exact circumstances of Miura's death.

Shima's voice brims with pride in the efficiency of the police bureaucracy. Mori can hardly believe his luck.

'So what does it say?' he asks impatiently.

'Just the usual stuff,' says Shima complacently.

'The usual stuff? What is that supposed to mean?'

'Precisely that – the usual stuff for an accidental death. There's nothing suspicious here at all. No case for you, I'm afraid, Mori-*san*!'

First Mori thinks, So that puts an end to the whole frustrating business. Second he thinks, Not yet it doesn't.

'Shima-*san*, could you send over a copy of that report? Just for my notes?'

'Send it over?' says Shima. 'That would be a serious breach of regulations.'

'It certainly would,' says Mori apologetically.

Shima gives a groan of weary exasperation. At that moment Mori knows he has won.

'All right,' says Shima. 'What's your fax number, then?'

Mori doesn't have his own fax machine. Instead he gives the number of the machine owned by the two yakuza who run the shrub-leasing racket downstairs. When he knocks, he finds them in a middle of a mah-jong game with the manager of a nearby love hotel. They all stand up, give him the formal greeting. Conscious of Mori's status as the building's senior tenant, they are more than happy to extend the favour.

'You must have good friends in the police department, Mori-*san*,' says one of the yakuza, gazing at the stretch of 'Internal Use Only' documentation spilling out of the machine.

'Some good friends, also some good enemies,' replies Mori. He rolls up the paper before the yakuza has a chance to inspect it more closely.

The yakuza looks reflective. 'In our business such good contacts could be very useful,' he states. He removes a half-smoked Seven Stars from his cigarette-holder and fits another one. Obviously a health-conscious kind of person.

Mori smiles pleasantly. 'Well, if the guys at Shinjuku

police station want to rent any rubber plants, I'll tell them where to come.'

For a moment the yakuza looks puzzled. Then he stands up and gives a bow.

'That's extremely kind, Mori-*san*. We are humbly grateful for such consideration.'

Now the other yakuza is doing the same. Mori bows right back, gets out quickly. He remembers that a sense of humour is not a traditional yakuza characteristic.

Back in his office, Mori scans the report that Shima faxed. Like the man said, there's nothing unusual: time and place of death; statement from security guard Kaneda; statement from a doctor; excerpts from health records indicating previous heart problems; comments from colleagues indicating heavy workload. Conclusion: the loss of this valuable public servant highly regrettable, but no grounds for further investigation, all procedures having been carried out strictly according to the rules.

He goes through it again. No, there's absolutely nothing there to spur his interest. What a waste of time! He scrunches the fax paper into a ball and hurls it at the bin. It bounces off the rim. Obviously. It's that kind of day. That kind of year. That kind of decade, actually.

Mori needs some calm. He puts on a record – Bill Evans at the Village Vanguard. Then he pours himself another shot of Suntory White, gazes out over the city.

Shinjuku is shimmering, glossy-wet as a whore's mouth. Cars roar the curve on the flyover. Their headlights refract in his whisky glass, dance shadows on the wall behind.

The shadow of a question is dancing somewhere in the back of his brain. What is it? Bill Evans helps him think, so does the Suntory. Mori scoops up the balled paper, straightens it out, runs through it one last time. The question materializes. It is a simple one: who wrote the report? There is no name, no stamp, no indication even of what department the writer of the report belongs to. He rings Shima again. Shima says he will check. Five minutes later he's back with the reply, and this time he doesn't sound so proud about it.

'What?' says Mori. 'You mean your people just took a report by the ministry's own security team and copied it out on official paper?'

'Basically that's right,' says Shima flatly.

Mori's astonishment is mixed with rising excitement. 'And the police declare there are no grounds for suspicion, even though they've done no investigation, no verification at all.'

'Right.'

'So for all you know Miura might have been beaten to death by the Minister of Health himself?'

Mori hears Shima sucking air through his teeth. He pictures the policeman's big square brow furrowed with discomfort.

'Not very likely,' Shima says finally. 'This is the Ministry of Health we are talking about here. These are people who devote themselves to safeguarding the health of the nation . . .'

That comment shows the difference between them, thinks Mori as he puts down the phone. Shima is plenty cynical about women, but when it comes to the élite – the people who live to control other people – he is as credulous as a child. That is why he would never be any good at Mori's job. And why Mori would never be any good at his.

The Taipei Rolex tells him that it's almost eight o'clock. That's more than enough overtime, especially as he doesn't get anything for it at all. Anyway, Mori has plans for what's left of the evening. First of all a nearby Korean barbecue is running a rainy season special – 'All you can eat for two thousand yen'. Do they have any idea what's coming? Mori has been preparing himself all day – light breakfast, just a couple of riceballs for lunch. He'll fill his stomach to bursting point: plate after plate of tenderloin, rib, liver, guts, tongue. Then he'll ride over to Ikebukuro. There's a little art house cinema in a basement under a pink cabaret. Tonight they've got an early Tarkovsky movie, just the single showing. It'll end in time for him to catch the last set in the jazz café round the corner. The singer is an old girlfriend. It's the first time she's come to Tokyo for years, first time they'll have met since her divorce.

Mori pulls on his raincoat, switches off the light. As he closes the door, the phone starts ringing. He gets the feeling that answering it would disrupt his evening. He answers it anyway. His evening is duly disrupted.

The call is from Kimiko Itoh. She has decided not to go to the club tonight. The reason – she's too busy packing. Early tomorrow she's flying to Italy for a shopping holiday. And after that she's going on to Scotland for golf. Of course Mori could ask the questions he wants to on the phone. But that wouldn't be enough. He needs to look into her eyes when she answers. That's why Mori's plans for the evening have to change. Why an hour later he's standing in the foyer of a luxury apartment block in Azabu, brushing the rain out of his hair.

According to the government, ninety per cent of all Japanese people are middle-class, or think they're middle-class, which comes to the same thing. Strange, then, that Mori comes across so few of them in his work. Most of the people he meets have hardly any money at all. And if they do get some from somewhere, it soon disappears again, trickles through their fingers in bills and debts and hard-earned pleasures. Then there are others who have so much they could never even count it. Usually these people don't work for it in the strict sense of the word. They just know where to find the big flow, and how to divert some of it in their own direction. And once they've figured out how to do that, no matter how fast they spend it, the total keeps on growing. The first category includes all of Mori's friends. The second category includes his best clients. There's no doubt in which one Kimiko Itoh fits.

The intercom buzzes.

'Come up, Mori-*san*. Sixth floor.'

The glass security door whirrs open. Mori's boots sound on the black marble floor. His mind limbers up with some mental arithmetic. How about the monthly rent here? More or less than his own annual mortgage payment? How about one of those speckled carp in the atrium pool? More or less than the resale value of his Honda?

Kimiko Itoh is waiting at the door. On her face is a welcome smile of total Ginza professionalism. She is wearing a black dress with a large silver buckle. Mori knows nothing about fashion, is proud of the fact. Still, there's something about the way this dress is cut – something about the tucks and flares and pleats – that suggests that quite a bit of thought went into putting it together. More, for example, than went into the production of his own raincoat, which Kimiko Itoh peels off his back and hooks on to the coatstand, where it hangs down like a soggy sheet.

She puts her palms on her knees and gives a little bow. 'Welcome to my humble home. It's a great pleasure to receive you here.'

Mori winces. This woman is so polite it hurts.

'Please come this way. We were just about to have our evening meal.'

We! Mori has the feeling that he's intruding on something private. 'I'm sorry . . .' he mutters. 'I didn't realize you were entertaining tonight . . .'

Kimiko Itoh gives a well-practised giggle, hand over mouth. 'Please don't misunderstand. There's no one here but Kenji and me. Kenji's not used to strangers at all. He's still so young...'

'Ah.'

She turns her head, coos out, 'Kenji! Here, quick! Come and meet Mori-*san*.'

Mori hears the groan of a chair-leg on parquet. From her tone of voice he pictures a smooth young guy, sullenly arrogant. Maybe her favourite from some Roppongi host club. Mori gets ready to meet him, then stops, shifts into a karate stance. Kenji appears at the end of the corridor, takes one look at Mori, then comes hurtling straight at him, teeth bared.

'Don't worry,' says Kimiko Itoh. 'He's only playing.'

Kenji leaps. Mori grabs him by the collar, manages to twist his head sideways before the full weight of his body crashes into Mori's chest. The back of Mori's head smacks against the wall. They both fall to the ground, roll over. Kenji springs to his feet first, glares downwards at Mori in fierce triumph. Mori slides backwards on the polished wooden floor. Kenji edges after him, yellowy eyes, slavering mouth.

'Not so many strangers here,' says Kimiko Itoh. 'It'll take him a few minutes to get used to you.'

'It'll take me more than a few minutes to get used to him,' says Mori, hauling himself gingerly to his feet.

Kenji is big and ugly and comes from Germany. He ought to be running around the Black Forest, tracking down bears or tearing baby deer to pieces. Instead he's stuck in a sixth-floor apartment in Azabu, Tokyo, Japan. The experience isn't doing him much good, mentally or physically. He's too fat. His coat is blotchy. His eyes are dull and gummy. Mori almost feels sorry for him. Especially when he sees what's dangling from the dog's collar – a metal oblong the size of a cigarette lighter. An anti-barking device. When it senses sound waves, it administers a sharp electric shock to a tender area of the dog's neck. Pavlov's principle works. It doesn't take long for the dog to learn the value of silence.

Kimiko Itoh reads his gaze. 'I had to put that thing on him,' she says. 'It was a condition of moving into this building.'

'It must hurt.'

'Not any more it doesn't. These days he doesn't even try to make any noise.'

Mori nods. 'In other words he's become a true Japanese citizen.'

'Hah?'

So Kimiko Itoh has no sense of humour either. That's no surprise. Whoever started this myth that Ginza hostesses are fountains of sparkling wit? In his time Mori has met hundreds. The most elegant girls from the most exclusive clubs, places where one glass of watery whisky can cost you a month's salary. His assessment: For intelligent conversation you'd be better off with some tattooed punkette from a massage parlour in Kawasaki.

Kimiko Itoh leads him into the sitting room, pours two glasses of white wine. Mori knows nothing about wine. He picks up the glass, peers inside. Aren't you supposed to smell it? He sniffs tentatively. Kenji sits on the sofa, unblinking eyes trained on Mori's groin.

'So how is the investigation going?' she says, lifting a folded fan from the table. 'Have you made any progress?'

'Quite a bit,' lies Mori. 'But I don't want to get into specifics yet. There are just a few points I'd like you to help me clear up.'

'Of course,' says Kimiko Itoh. 'What would you like to know?'

'I'd like to know what kind of contact you've had with Yoko Miura.'

Crack! Kimiko Itoh opens the fan with a flick of her wrist. It's hand-painted, cranes and turtles on a gold background.

'Contact? I'm not in contact with that woman at all. I've never even met her!'

Mori takes in a mouthful of wine, almost retches. It is unbelievably sweet. He glances at the label: 'Liebfraumilch'. Be sure to avoid that one in future.

'So how do you explain the fact that she's got hold of my name card? Who else could have given it to her?'

'Yoko Miura has your name card? That's impossible!'

'Not impossible,' says Mori. 'I've seen it with my own eyes. This afternoon, actually.'

He grabs a handful of salted peanuts, starts feeding them into his mouth. Anything to get rid of the taste of that wine.

'Look, I told you not to contact that woman. Why didn't you obey my instructions?'

This is a new voice – lower, faster, with traces of a tough Osaka accent. Hearing it, Mori feels he knows a lot more about the life of Kimiko Itoh.

'I didn't contact her,' says Mori mildly, 'but you must have. How else could you two ladies be interested in the services of the same detective?'

It's not all that hot in the apartment, but Kimiko Itoh is suddenly fanning herself very fast. 'I think Junko made a mistake about you,' she snaps. 'She said you were totally reliable.'

Mori flips another couple of peanuts in his mouth. 'I do my best, but I can't get anywhere without the right information.'

'You've had more than enough information, Mori-*san*.' She glares.

'What do you mean? You don't like my methods?'

Kimiko Itoh jumps to her feet. Kenji sits up on the sofa, teeth bared, as noiseless as ever.

'It looks to me as if you haven't got any methods. I'm cancelling the contract immediately. There are plenty of other detectives out there who understand how to do what they're told!'

Too true, thinks Mori as he walks out through the marble atrium. Competition is tough. Profit margins are under stress everywhere, so are principles. Maybe he ought to go straight back to the woman's apartment, apologize, tell her he'll do anything to get the job back. He certainly needs it.

He stops in front of the fish-pool, considers. There're still a couple of peanuts in his hand. Absent-mindedly he tosses them into the pool. The biggest fattest fish gets there first, manages to suck both peanuts into its dilated maw. After that it does a strange thing. It does a couple of brisk circuits of the pool, then suddenly leaps out of the water and bellyflops on to the gleaming black floor, where it skids around thrashing its tail. Mori needs several attempts before he manages to grab hold of it and fling it back. Now the fish is rotating feebly in the water, unable to work out which way is up. Mori knows an omen when he sees one, knows when it's time to make his departure.

Mori straddles his two-wheeled time machine, fits on the helmet. The Honda starts first time, as always. Head down, Mori goes slicing through the deliquescent night, on his way to a cramped little jazz club in the back streets of Ikebukuro.

Five

What George the Wolf Nishio likes most about being a yakuza: men are scared of him; women are scared of him; he eats, drinks and screws for free, top quality in every case; and he gets to meet sportsmen, ballad singers and other idols of his youth. They're all scared of him too.

What George dislikes about being a yakuza: boring routine, hanging around doing nothing; having to grovel to the young prince and others like him with no respect for the traditions; dealing with ditch-rat chimpira, yam-head bumpkins and crazed foreign whores.

As a rule, George only volunteers for what he considers to be the most challenging jobs. There have been some good examples this year.

January – the manager of a classy new disco in Roppongi is refusing to pay the standard 'service charge'. George comes up with the solution himself. Friday night, just before twelve, he loads three rice sacks onto the goods elevator, takes them down to the basement. After jemmying a door that faces on to the pounding dance floor, supposedly the biggest in Asia, George slashes the sacks open with his knife. Result: three hundred squealing rats racing through the jungle of legs.

February – a 'progressive' mayor decides to hold a referendum on the construction of a waste-disposal dump. Bad news, since this project would bring great benefits to the public, and particularly to certain close associates of the old boss. George studies the situation. He learns that the mayor's daughter is a student at Yokohama University, that she likes to hang out with a group of reggae musicians. He has a word with one of them, gives him some money and a little bottle of sleeping potion. Result: some high-quality photos, good enough to print on to hand-bills and stick on to every single utility pole in the mayor's electoral district.

March – an up-and-coming bicycle star fails to throw an important race, despite clear instructions. George and another guy break his legs with baseball bats. Result: he retires from the sport, and other up-and-coming racers learn to do what they're told.

April – a major meat-processing company breaks its unwritten agreement with a group of people who have been 'arranging' its shareholders' meetings for the past thirty years. These people also happen to be on good terms with the old boss. First, George tries the indirect approach. He hires a bunch of rightist agitators to circle the company's headquarters in a sound-truck, bellowing out obscenities at an ear-splitting decibel count, nine to six, five days a week. Unfortunately this doesn't work, so George has to take the direct approach. He gets hold of some AIDS-infected blood, syringes it into a few packets of pre-fried skinless sausages, sends them to the company's finance director, parcel delivery. A threatening letter is copied to a few weekly magazines. Result: agreement renewed in a matter of days.

Those are the kind of jobs that give George a sense of fulfilment. It's specialist stuff, requiring intelligence and creativity. Not many people could handle it. In fact, no one could handle it with quite the same panache as George the Wolf Nishio.

Intimidating the owner of a provincial chain of pink cabarets – now that's something different, not specialist work by any means. So when the old boss explains that he has this out-of-town job, standard muscle work, George says nothing. He just stares at his bandaged hand, wondering how long it will take for the twinges from his missing finger to fade away.

'Wolf-*kun*!' says the young prince suddenly. 'This is just the job for you, isn't it?'

The disrespect is fierce, a blowtorch on his cheek. George looks up, eyes narrowing. That fantasy again. If only the old boss would give him the word, tell him to get rid of the young prince once and for all. George would give anything for the chance to carve the character for 'Wolf' in that smooth pretty-boy face.

'What you mean?' says the old boss.

The young prince smiles, gloatingly. 'This is not far from the place where Wolf lost those girls the other week. He should go there again, in order to study the geography of the area!'

The old boss looks at George. His expression is totally serious. George loves him for it. The old boss knows that a man's honour is not a joking matter.

'Well, Wolf-*kun*, what have you got to say?'

It only takes George a split second to make up his mind. He gets down on his hands and knees and bows so low that his well-oiled quiff brushes the floor.

'I beg to undertake this task,' he says hoarsely. 'Please entrust me with the responsibility.'

The young prince stares at him, incredulous. The old boss nods his head. 'That's settled, then. I want you to go up? there as soon as possible. It's important to show respect to the local people who have requested our help in this matter.'

So typical of the old boss – to demand respect for those slow-witted split-tongued bumpkins who run the local rackets. Still, that's why the old boss was the old boss, and why the young prince could never replace him. *Giri* and *ninjo*, duty and magnanimity. They don't teach that in American business schools. And without it you're nothing, just a common criminal.

They file out of the old boss's study. The young prince's eyes are heat-beams on George's neck. No doubt he's wondering why George volunteered for such a routine job, in a place that has such unpleasant associations. George keeps his mouth shut. There are certain matters of high emotional intensity, concerning honour and respect, that the young prince would never understand in a thousand years.

Mori allows himself the morning off. In fact, he doesn't crawl out of his futon until it's nearly over. Lisa sneaked out just after dawn. Mori saw her go. He was pretending to be asleep, face half-buried in the coverlet. Why didn't he get up? Because he could think of absolutely nothing to say.

What Lisa left in his apartment: a cassette of her band doing some Billie Holiday songs; a few lipstick smudges on the pillow; a few scrunched-up tissues on the tatami mat. What she left in his mind: those mocking eyes; that mocking voice; a ghost-kiss from another world, the one called the past.

'You look just the same,' he said in the café, just after she finished her set.

'What, with all this grey hair?'

She shook her frizzy mane. Yes, there was plenty of grey hair. Mori hadn't noticed.

'It kind of suits you.'

'Is that flattery? If so, it's about as clumsy as your saxophone-playing.'

He laughed. She once coaxed him into playing his sax for

her. Must have been the last time he picked the thing up. But he was right. Those strands of grey hair do suit her, so do the strong lines around the mouth. They make her look what she is: unbowed by time.

Mori has plenty of grey hair himself. It doesn't suit him. It makes him look out of focus, a man getting older at the edges. He can still see the young man in the mirror, staring out, wondering what went wrong.

Mori's breakfast – black coffee, toast, a baby octopus. He eats it out on his tiny balcony, amongst his collection of cactuses. He finishes about the time the bullet train is due to pull into Kyoto. He can see her, a couple of hundred kilometres away, walking down the platform in her big round sunglasses, as totally composed as ever.

Some women are like songs. You think you've forgotten the tune and the words, but it's all there in the back of your head.

Mori gets into the office just before three. No need to hurry because there's nothing to do. That's how bad conditions are. Up until now there's always been routine work of one sort or another. Now there's absolutely nothing on the horizon. No missing husbands, no embezzling secretaries, no love-hotel stake-outs. Even his old staple, the pre-marriage background check, has dried up completely. Have people stopped feeling shame at the prospect of acquiring a brother-in-law caught shoplifting twenty years ago, or a mother-in-law who once had a mental health problem? Don't they care any more what kind of family they're marrying into, what impurities might have slipped into its bloodline sometime in the distant past? They do, of course. And always will, as long as Japan is Japan. The problem is more basic: these days they don't have the money.

What happened to the money? Where did it all go?

Nobody knows. Or at least the people who do know aren't saying.

Mori sits down on the sofa, goes through his mail. Nothing important – just bills, coupons, flyers. Great deals are available everywhere – office rentals, take-out sushi, two hours in a love hotel, eternity in an IC-controlled high-rise funeral home. Everything's getting cheaper and cheaper. Everyone feels compelled to undercut everyone else.

Mori's sombre mood takes a turn for the worse when his eyes fall on a rain-smudged flyer which looks as if it's been produced with a child's printing set.

'Problems? Social, Economic and Private Research Carried Out At Lowest Prices Available. Mr Problem-Solver Guarantees Payment by Results Only!'

Mori picks up the phone, dials the number. The voice at the other end is male, young, wearyingly enthusiastic.

'Hello, this is Mr Problem-Solver speaking! All problems solved at guaranteed lowest prices in Japan!'

'I got a problem,' says Mori, adopting a sad quavering voice appropriate to a sad quavering character with a serious private problem.

'Please go on,' says Mr Problem-Solver brightly.

'It's about my wife,' continues Mori. 'Sometimes she goes out in the evenings and doesn't come back until the next morning. She says she's staying with one of her old schoolfriends, but I don't know whether to believe her. Now could you tell me your price to help with something like that?'

'With pleasure!' says Mr Problem-Solver, sounding like he means it. 'What you need is our personal surveillance service. It's highly discreet and it's very cheap.'

'How cheap?'

'Two thousand yen an hour.'

Mori almost chokes. Two thousand yen! That's almost

half what he usually charges. It's less than the rate for a bouncer in a pink cabaret!

Mr Problem-Solver takes Mori's stunned silence the wrong way.

'Is that within your budget?' he enquires anxiously.

Mori decides to push a little further. 'I'm not sure. You say you guarantee the lowest rates. Is that really true? I've heard it's possible to find personal surveillance services at around fifteen hundred yen an hour these days.'

'Fifteen hundred yen! Please tell me where those rates are available. If I can confirm them, we will certainly offer cheaper. That is a promise.'

'There's a guy called Mori, of Mori Research. He's also guaranteeing the lowest rates in the country. You can't both be the cheapest, can you?'

'Let me make some enquiries, honoured customer! If I could just have your name and number...'

Mori slams the phone down. Dissatisfaction, up to the brim.

The phone rings. Mr Problem-Solver already? Mori snatches it, adopts his most uncompromising growl. 'Mori Social and Economic Research. Who's there and what do you want?'

'Ah, Mori-*san*, at last! My plane's due to take off in a few minutes. I've been calling all morning, you know.' It's the voice of Kimiko Itoh, hurried, slightly peeved. In the background loudspeaker announcements, plane noise.

'I was out,' says Mori drily. 'A new case I've been working on.'

'You really ought to switch on your answering-machine.'

'It's broken.'

The kind of phone that Mori has pressed to his ear doesn't come with answering-machine functions. Instead he had a separate unit attached to the phone's Bakelite casing by a couple of stripped copper wires. It often breaks down in the rainy season.

'That's a shame. Anyway, the reason I'm calling is about last night. It was wrong of me to criticize you like that.'

'It certainly was,' says Mori, without thinking what he's saying.

Kimiko Itoh says something else, but the sound of her voice is drowned out by a loudspeaker announcement. 'This is the final call. Will Passenger Itoh please hurry to the gate? This flight for Milan is now closing.'

'I can't hear,' says Mori. 'What did you say?'

'I said you were absolutely right. I want you back on the case as soon as possible.'

'Wait a moment – last night you said—'

'Forget about last night,' jabbers Kimiko Itoh. 'I can't explain now. My plane's leaving...' Her voice fades out, then re-emerges. 'There'll be a special bonus for you, Mori-*san* – an extra thirty per cent of your fee. Come on – please say yes. It would be...'

An extra thirty per cent! What's the matter with the woman? He doesn't have the chance to find out. More noise: another loudspeaker announcement; the shriek of a jet engine.

'Yes,' bellows Mori. 'Can you hear me? YES!'

When the noise clears, the line is dead. Mori imagines the elegant Ginza mama-*san* charging for the plane, Hermes shoulder-bag bouncing from side to side. Anyway, the important thing: Mori is back on the case. He doesn't have nothing any longer. He has something.

Which puts him in a genial and forgiving humour. So when the phone rings and a voice he recognizes as Mr Problem-Solver's starts speaking, he decides to play along.

'Is that Mori-*san* of Mori Research?'

'That's me.' Not sad and quavering this time. Instead, calm, businesslike.

'I have a problem,' says Mr Problem-Solver, as breezy as before. 'I'm looking for some expert help.'

'Really? What kind of problem might that be?'

'Well, I'm worried about my wife. Sometimes she goes out in the evening with her old schoolfriends and she doesn't come back until next morning.'

'Doesn't come back?' says Mori feelingly. 'That's terrible!'

'Yes, it is. Anyway, I'm looking for a good, cheap personal surveillance service. How much will you quote me per hour for following my wife around?'

'Nine hundred yen an hour,' says Mori, no hesitation.

At the other end of the phone there is a kind of gulping noise. Mori presses home his advantage. 'Is that all right? If it's too much for your budget, we might be able to make a special deal.'

Several seconds of silence. When Mr Problem-Solver does finally speak, his voice has lost its bounce. In fact, it's little more than a croak. 'Nine hundred yen! But that's less than the rate for a part-timer in a yakitori restaurant.'

'That's right,' says Mori. 'Before I went into this business, I used to work in a yakitori restaurant myself. They fired me for mixing up the orders.'

'You got fired from a yakitori restaurant?'

'Sure. That's why I decided to become a detective – it doesn't need so much brain-work. Now if nine hundred yen is too much, I'll give you a twenty per cent discount for three days' work. How about that?'

The phone clicks dead. Mori smiles. Mr Problem-Solver now has a few economic problems of his own to solve. Like how to run a business on the kind of income stream that would barely tide a college student over the summer vacation.

Mori lets the receiver slip from his hand. It drops onto its cradle with a *ding*.

Now, back to the Miura case. For some reason, Kimiko Itoh has decided to raise the stakes, making it potentially the most lucrative job he has had for years. But still there's nothing to grab on to and pull, just lots of puzzles, lots of strangeness. A missing security guard. A name card in a drawer. A police report made without a police investigation. Questions that lead to questions, suspicions that hang in the air. The whole thing is as murky as a bowl of newly stirred miso soup.

Mori slumps on to his sofa, ponders. Bureaucrats – an invisible army of occupation. They don't need to leave their concrete fortresses down in the Kasumigaseki district. Their weapons of control – regulations and edicts, constantly shifting administrative guidance, permissions, licences, subsidies. Their tactics – simulation and dissimulation, unpredictability. What you are taught at school – these are the people the public should thank for building modern Japan. What you realize later – these are the people who write the textbooks.

What do ordinary citizens know about the bureaucrats and their work? Not much. What does Mori actually know about the inner workings of the ministry of health, its personnel structure, its methods of enforcing its influence on the wider world? Nothing at all. So how could he find out? If he were an ordinary citizen, he couldn't. It's a closed world. The bureaucrats themselves aren't talking. They go in at the age of twenty-one, work for three decades, then 'descend from heaven' into richly paid sinecures at some private organization with a need for bureaucratic indulgence. And the way the system works, almost every private organization of any substance – company, school, hospital, religious foundation – has just that need, hot pressing and insatiable. The newspapers aren't talking either. Every ministry maintains its own press club on the premises where writers from the big papers go to get spoon-fed with information. So it's the same old story. No one who knows is talking. And the ones who are talking don't know.

Except Taniguchi, that is, Taniguchi knows, and he talks – or rather writes. Taniguchi writes and writes and writes, as if his life depends on it.

Mori picks up the phone, calls Taniguchi. It's time to get some deep background.

This doctor is a funny guy, thinks Angel. What he asks for is so little, something any woman in the world can do. And in return he gives so much. He gives clothes. He gives the use of his house and car. He gives money, more money than Angel has ever earned. This generosity is frightening. It makes Angel think of a world where you can buy anything whenever you want, and still you're sad all the time.

That may be why a man like the doctor needs Angel. When she came back, he cried like a child, put his wet face in between her breasts. He was happy. They were both happy, and in Angel's experience with men that doesn't happen often.

Today she has been doing something else that makes them both happy, wandering through the boutiques of Harajuku, trying on the latest fashions. The doctor likes to go into the cubicles with her, just to watch her dressing and undressing. He doesn't say much, just stands there beaming. The assistants don't like that, but they don't show their feelings. They simper politeness, call out greetings in those silly high-pitched voices that Japanese women use to please men. Angel can imagine what kinds of things they say about her afterwards, their real feelings in their voices. But that doesn't trouble her at all. It makes her smile.

When they've finished shopping, they go to an ice-cream parlour and Angel orders a huge fruit sundae, with cherries and strawberries and chocolate and coffee ice cream. The doctor has a cup of English tea, and sits there watching her eat. He loves watching her eat ice cream. When they're at home, he asks her to eat it in a special way, the same way as he likes her to eat bananas. A simple thing that seems to make him happy. And Angel loves ice cream, no matter what way she has to eat it.

The doctor is like a nice father, very different from her real father, who was angry and drunk all the time. He saved her from the shitpig in the white suit, found a good man like Mori to bring her back. For if the doctor is like a nice father, Mori is like a strict brother. Angel has five brothers, and it's the eldest one who's like Mori. He's a teacher way out in the country, knows nothing about the city any more. But he's calm as a lake, strong as a mountain. Once he decides to do something, he doesn't stop until it's finished. He's a serious man, and Angel likes men to be serious. No easy smiles, no laughing words. In Japan only Mori is a man like that. All the others are playing.

More rain – lukewarm, soft, falling on the city in great gauzy curtains. Mori takes the expressway to Asakusabashi, arrives at Taniguchi's office just after five.

Calling it an office is something of an exaggeration. Taniguchi lives and works in a six-mat room in a building that makes Mori's look like a triumph of modern engineering. Mori reckons that his own place couldn't survive a quake stronger than intensity 5 on the Japanese scale. He reckons that Taniguchi's building wouldn't survive a tanker-lorry taking a wrong turning.

Materials: spongy wooden beams; plasterboard bolstered with corrugated-iron sheeting. The roof is on askew. The front wall is covered with – possibly held together by – some sort of creeper, tough and ugly enough to thrive in the fume-choked air. There are just three floors. On the first is a tiny yakitori joint. No seats, just a single bench, long enough for half a dozen people who know how to eat and drink without moving their elbows. On the second is a nightclub a couple of zeros cheaper than Kimiko Itoh's. The hostesses are young and friendly, mainly trainees from a nearby beauticians' school.

'You're looking well, Mori-*san*. Same as ever.'

'You too.'

Now that isn't strictly true. In fact, Taniguchi looks awful – grey face, puffy bloodshot eyes. He stands there looking at Mori, an unconvincing smile on his face. Mori knows that his own smile is equally unconvincing. There's a subject that cannot be avoided, no matter how much they both might try.

'Would you like a drink of something?'

'Thanks,' says Mori. 'Have you got some green tea?'

Taniguchi looks a little confused. 'Well – no – I meant . . .'

Mori knows what he meant. Taniguchi always was a heavy drinker, even back in the old days when he was a rising star in the social affairs department of the Gendai *Daily News*. After he got eased out – at the request of a senior politician whose finances he had been investigating at the time – his drinking bouts got longer and wilder. Then came the divorce: inevitable, as everyone but Taniguchi himself could see. From the point of view of his wife, the deal no longer made any sense. The man she had married – or rather that her parents had married her to – was supposed to become an élite opinion-former, plugged into the hidden circuitry of influence that controls the pistons and pulleys of the Japanese industrial state. Instead, what

74

happens? Her husband turns into a freelance muckraker whose exposés of political and business scandals appear in low-grade weekly magazines, usually sandwiched between pornographic manga and show-biz gossip. Her father, a top official at the national broadcasting corporation, must give a little shudder every time he passes a newsstand.

Taniguchi gets two cups, pours in some green tea from a Thermos flask. Then he goes to a cupboard and gets out a heavy earthenware bottle. It's shochu, a cheap Kyushu brand distilled from barley.

'This is tea-ceremony, Taniguchi-style.' He grins apologetically and pours half an inch of the barley spirit into his cup. The fumes rise to Mori's nostrils, raw and rank. Taniguchi points the bottle's mouth at Mori's cup. Mori shakes his head.

Taniguchi swills the stuff down, pours himself another cup. This time the quantities are more like fifty-fifty. The greyness slowly fades from his face. Mori eases his way carefully into the conversation. He starts with a couple of gentle digs about the Gendai Giants' poor performance in the double header against the Kansai Tigers. Taniguchi shakes his head, trots out the usual excuses. He may no longer be an employee of the huge Gendai information–entertainment conglomerate, but he's still a fierce Gendai Giants fan. To him, they're not just Japan's number one baseball team, supported by more than seventy per cent of the population. They are gods, and the Gendai Dome is their sacred shrine. Mori, on the other hand, is anti-Giants to the core. Always has been, always will be.

They talk about the Giants' star pitcher. One of the magazines that Taniguchi writes for snapped him coming out of a love hotel with a female newscaster from the Gendai network.

'No wonder he looks so sluggish these days,' says Mori.

'All heroes are men of lust,' smiles Taniguchi, quoting one of his favourite proverbs.

'But not all men of lust are heroes.'

They've had that exchange before, half a dozen years ago. Mori remembers it clearly. Taniguchi? Almost certainly not. He blocks out the past, everything except the baseball statistics.

Taniguchi fixes himself another cup of twenty-per-cent-proof green tea. The conversation edges towards more serious topics. Mori compliments him on his latest project: an in-depth analysis of the shady dealings behind a huge new development on the Tokyo waterfront. As is often the case with Taniguchi's articles, the money trail that he has uncovered is so convoluted – involving city hall, major trading houses and trust banks, religious foundations, political support groups, and special purpose corporations registered overseas – that half a page has to be devoted to a flow chart of eye-straining complexity.

'You did a good job,' says Mori. 'It must have taken a lot of time and effort.'

'A couple of months, on and off,' says Taniguchi, casual.

Mori knows what Taniguchi means by on and off. There are only two things left in the man's life – drinking and working. And how much did he get paid for the piece? For a low-grade magazine like that, one hundred thousand yen would be the maximum. Hardly enough to keep him in alcohol for the duration.

'Well, you certainly nailed them. Anyone reading that is going to feel pretty angry about paying residents' taxes.'

'You're wrong there, Mori-*san*. Nobody's going to get angry. Nobody cares any more.'

'What do you mean?' says Mori, puzzled.

Taniguchi bangs his fist against the table, sending green tea slopping from the cups.

'You know what I mean!' he roars. 'You know exactly what I mean!'

Quite suddenly Taniguchi is incandescent with fury. Red-faced, neck tendons as taut as bow strings, he launches into a breathless rushing tirade about the degradation of modern society.

'Everyone likes to blame politicians and bureaucrats,' he thunders. 'Everybody likes to read these scandalous stories. But it's just pornography, some sort of moral masturbation. In the end we keep on electing the politicians, keep on asking the bureaucrats for special favours. If the politicians and bureaucrats weren't there, we couldn't do anything ourselves! That's how low this country has got. Schoolgirls, priests, university professors, doctors, policemen, engineers – they're all selling themselves. Show me a salaryman who doesn't cheat his expenses. Show me a shopkeeper who pays his taxes properly . . .'

He pauses to wipe his brow, swallow more tea. Then the words come tumbling out again. No logic, no pattern. Mori has never seen his old friend like this before. It's disturbing. Taniguchi was always short-tempered. Now his personality has been soaked in a highly inflammable mixture: alcohol and tragedy.

'It's got to stop, Mori-*san*. If it doesn't stop, this whole country will sink. And if it does sink, it won't matter at all. It's the war – after we lost the war, there's nothing left. All morals, all values have gone. People are so stupid these days. They have such stupid empty faces. What's the point of living amongst such people? What's the point of being alive?'

Taniguchi wails the question like a woman rejected by a lover for the first time. He buries his face in his hands, shoulders heaving. There's a silence which demands to be broken.

77

'Think I'll get us both a coffee,' says Mori, getting to his feet. He goes to the corner of the room that serves as a kitchen and boils up some water. Right next to the little stove is a makeshift bookcase of planks and concrete blocks, the kind of thing a student might have in his rooms. This is where Taniguchi keeps the books of pre-Meiji history that he loves to read. In the middle of the top shelf is a stack of CDs. Mori picks one out – Mahler's Eighth, the Gendai Symphony conducted by Dmitri Rostropovich – and slips it into the CD player. Big music fills the room.

Mori deliberately takes his time with the coffee. When he turns round, a cup in each hand, he's surprised to see Taniguchi looking straight at him, calm as ever.

'Sorry about that,' says Taniguchi, almost cheerful now. 'I suppose I'm overreacting. Things have been difficult since Hiromi died.'

This is the topic that can't be avoided: the suicide of Taniguchi's daughter three years ago. Compared to that, the loss of his job and his wife were nothing, the tears of a sparrow. Mori understands this with his mind. But, never having had wife or child or prestigious job, he can't feel the true weight of it. He knows he's unqualified, and it makes him feel clumsy.

'She was a cute girl. You must miss her badly.'

'Yes, she was cute, too cute to die like that.'

Automatically Taniguchi glances at the row of framed photos on the wall behind his desk. All are of Hiromi, none of his wife. A five-year-old Hiromi standing at a shrine, in her orange kimono. A junior-school Hiromi practising the violin. A high-school Hiromi solemnly clutching a tennis racket. A college-age Hiromi sitting on a park bench, head nestling against a boyfriend's shoulder. Four frozen moments from a life that ended much too soon. Mori can't help but think of the other photos that will never be taken:

at her graduation ceremony; in full wedding regalia; nursing a baby.

The Gendai Symphony shifts up a gear. Taniguchi is smiling a strange kind of smile. Mori thinks back to the last time he saw Hiromi. It was in a Shimbashi sushi restaurant, just a few months before she swallowed those pills. Sure she'd been quiet that evening, but she was always quiet. There was no indication that the pressure of university entrance exams, the stress of the divorce, bullying by her schoolmates, or whatever it was – Taniguchi never said – was pushing her beyond her limit.

The room is drowning in Mahler. Taniguchi suddenly stands up, goes and turns down the volume.

'You came here for a reason,' he says. 'How can I help you?' Brisk, alert – he seems to have recovered completely.

'Ministry of Health,' says Mori. 'One of the top officials died recently. Someone asked me to take a look.'

'Someone?'

'A mama-*san* in the Ginza. She's got some crazy idea that the guy was killed.'

Taniguchi picks up the shochu bottle, tips what's left into his coffee.

'Tell me about it,' he says.

So Mori gives him the story, condensed version, leaving out the missing security guard, the name card and a few other details that Taniguchi doesn't need to know. Taniguchi listens, nods, sips his Kyushu coffee. Then it's his turn. He gives Mori the full inside story of the Ministry of Health, from the late 1950s to the present: the power struggles; the scandals covered up; the links with senior politicians; the shadowy deals with abortion doctors; old-age home developers; pharmaceutical companies; banks 'nominated' to manage the social welfare fund. Intrigue, ruthless greed, betrayal – Taniguchi manages to make top bureaucrats sound like a yakuza gang perpetually on the verge of internecine warfare. Which is why his journalism makes such good reading.

'So what about Miura?' asks Mori. 'Where did he fit into all this?'

'Miura? Right in the middle, of course. You don't get into his position without trading some pretty big favours with some pretty important people. That man knew how to work the system like Rostropovich works an orchestra.'

'So is that where his money came from? I saw his house – it's like a daimyo's castle.'

Taniguchi slurps his coffee, frowns. 'Money was never a problem for Miura. Don't you know who his wife's father is?'

Mori shakes his head. 'Her father? No, I haven't heard anything.'

'Seiji Toriyama.'

That makes Mori sit up straight. He doesn't follow the twists and turns of the political world, but he knows that Toriyama is head of a new political grouping that holds the balance of power in the Diet. Also that the man's star is on the rise.

'The Toriyama family owns half of Kumamoto Prefecture. In fact, Miura was offered one of the Lower House seats there. If everything had gone right for him, in a few years' time he would have made Minister of Health in a Toriyama cabinet. Maybe prime minister himself one day. He was cunning enough to be a good politician, ruthless enough too.'

Now that is interesting. A new landscape of suspicion opens up in Mori's mind.

'Is there anyone who wanted to stop him? A rival in the ministry, perhaps someone outside in the political world?'

Taniguchi gulps down the last of his coffee. 'You mean,

wanted to stop him so much that they'd have him killed? Well, there's no one that comes to mind immediately. Of course I'll make some enquiries if you like.'

'Thanks,' says Mori. 'Of course we don't know that he was killed. It's just one woman's idea. Still, if anything occurs to you, let me know.'

'Understood,' says Taniguchi, nodding along to the music. He's had enough, wants Mori to go. Mori's curiosity is far from sated, but he decides to oblige. It's only when Taniguchi staggers to the door that Mori realizes how drunk he is. A real alcoholic: talks fluently even when he can't stand up straight.

As Mori is pulling on his raincoat a question forms in his mind. 'You said Miura was ruthless, cunning, and so on.'

'Right.'

'It made it sound as if you actually met him.'

'I did,' says Taniguchi quietly.

Mori lets the belt-buckle drop from his hand, gazes blankly at his old friend. This is big news. Why didn't Taniguchi say so before? 'So – what did you think? Was he the kind of guy someone might want to kill or not?'

Taniguchi doesn't need pause for thought. 'No question about that,' he answers.

What does that mean? Mori wants more, but Taniguchi isn't giving. He switches to some trivialities about the next Giants game, hustles Mori out of the door, sends him on his way.

Mori clumps down the shaky wooden staircase, that shochu smell in his nostrils. Only seven o'clock, but already a karaoke is booming in the club downstairs. He thinks a wave of gloomy thoughts. You assume your world is strong, your relationships, your future. All illusion. A man's life is like a racing kite. Strung tight, it soars and swoops and dances in the wind. But break a single spar and the gusts will tear it apart. Look at Taniguchi, once so swift, so agile. Now so broken, earthbound for ever.

Not that Mori himself has anything to worry about on that score. The kite with his own face painted on it crashed to earth a couple of decades ago.

A youthful indiscretion – five hot-headed radicals in helmets and masks break into the university offices, find secret files on students' political activities, set fire to them. Four have influential families, are let off with a warning. The fifth gets identified as the leader. He's expelled a couple of weeks before graduation, meaning that he's blackballed from employment at all major companies and institutions for the rest of his life. The kite called Mori has never been airborne since.

Mori straddles his Honda, points it at Shinjuku. These good old days – what was so good about them anyway? There were no teenage prostitutes then? No dishonest bureaucrats, no weak-brained intellectuals? On the contrary, prostitution was one of the biggest industries in the country, and selling your daughter to pay off debts was standard practice. Bureaucrats and businessmen didn't need to swap envelopes of money. They planned military campaigns in order to enrich themselves and called it patriotism. As for the intellectuals, the whole lot of them swung from Marxism to nationalism to democracy, changing their principles like schoolgirls change their favourite pop singers. Taniguchi should know that. It's all there in his beloved history books.

Mori's conclusion: present-day values are corrupt. The values of the past were just as corrupt. And the values of the future will be corrupt too. Which for a private detective is quite a comforting thought.

The Honda swishes through the rain-slick streets. The crystal towers of Shinjuku get closer.

Six

Mori eats dinner in his office – a broiled eel take-out, with a bottle of Kirin 'First Malt' to wash it down. You see all kinds of fancy beers nowadays. Mexican, Chinese, Belgian, you name it. Nice, if you're the kind of person who likes collecting labels. If not, you may as well stick with Kirin. There's that cold burn when it hits your mouth, a taste you remember from the first sip stolen from your father's glass when his back was turned. Mori's father drank Kirin every night of his life. It was always waiting on the table when he got out of his bath. Now Kirin keeps losing market share. The more market share it loses, the more bottles of 'First Malt' Mori drinks.

Rain runs down the window in neon rivulets. An Eric Dolphy album on the turntable – 'Last Date' – bought a year ago from a collector in Sendai. A few scratches, but nothing to obscure the harsh dignity of the bass clarinet.

Mori glances at the evening paper, half-open on the desk. Front-page photo: Seiji Toriyama delivering a speech at the Keidanren Hall. Slim, oval face, floppy hair. What does Mori know about this man? Suave character, aristocratic background. Big reformer, of course, whatever that means. Mori scans the text. Today Toriyama's calling for: 'a comprehensive political and economic restructuring'; 'a new vision for the new century'; and 'a rebirth of national confidence and pride'. The big business chiefs seated at the table behind him are beaming with satisfaction. They obviously like what they hear. Newspaper columnists and TV people seem to like him too. The polls say that women like him. Even his political rivals treat him with respect. In fact, everyone likes him, except Mori. Mori dislikes Toriyama because he can't work out what the man is all about. A liberal? A reactionary? There's no way of telling. He hides behind fine phrases like a lizard behind a silk screen.

The music dissolves into clicks and hisses. The needle lifts. After that final note faded, Dolphy laid down his horn for the last time. Dead at the age of thirty-six. Why does it have to happen like that? Because a true jazzman is something like a samurai, willing to risk everything, every time, just for one authentic moment. That's why dead men's music sounds so full of life. And, these days, why living men's music sounds so dead.

The phone shuts down Mori's thoughts. At the other end a familiar voice, expert-sugary-polite. It's Kimiko Itoh, wanting to explain the roots of their misunderstanding the other night. Mori flashes Narita airport, the loudspeaker announcements, the Ginza mama rushing for the gate.

'Wait a minute,' says Mori. 'What happened? Did you miss the plane?'

'Thank you for your kind concerns, but they are unnecessary. I was just in time.'

'I thought you were going to Italy.'

Her plane took off four hours ago. Italy is at least ten hours away. It doesn't make sense. Kimiko Itoh reads Mori's puzzlement, gives a little titter of amusement.

'I'm in the plane now, Mori-*san*. You see, there's a phone service available for the use of first-class passengers.'

Mori says nothing. His mind is wrestling with two concepts. First: Kimiko Itoh is calling his office from a point several kilometres above the middle of the Russian steppes – and sounding just as casual as if she were in a phone box in Shinjuku station. Second: she is travelling first class to Europe. First class! Mori rarely flies anywhere. But when he does he sometimes wonders, as he pushes his way to the back of the plane, what goes on behind that curtain, exactly what you get for the incredible sum of money demanded. A two-girl oil massage from the hostesses, sushi made on the spot by a top chef? Now he knows. They have telephones in there. More than a little disappointing.

Kimiko Itoh's explanation is unlikely enough to be credible. She got Mori's name card from Junko Hayashi late last year and wrote down the details in her address book. The name card itself she put in the drawer of her bedside table, forgot about it. After Mori left her place last night she went to check. The name card had gone. Then she remembered something – a conversation with Miura, just a couple of months before he died. He asked her if she'd ever used a private detective. She said no. Kimiko Itoh's conclusion: Mori's name card got into Miura's house because Miura took it himself, without asking.

More than ever, Kimiko Itoh is sure that there is something wrong. She wants Mori to redouble his efforts, to concentrate all his energy on the Miura case, let nothing else get in the way.

'You mean, just drop everything else?' says Mori. 'Hmmm – that would create difficulties for someone in my position.'

Difficulties because there is nothing to drop, and might not be for months. But Kimiko Itoh doesn't know that.

'I understand your position perfectly,' she coos. 'That's why I suggested the special bonus when I called earlier. But perhaps thirty per cent is not enough to compensate you for these difficulties that you mentioned.'

'Not enough?' breathes Mori, the phone suddenly light in his hand.

'Fifty per cent would be more sensible. And if you succeed in solving the case, there'll be another thirty per cent. How about that? Would it help you concentrate, Mori-*san*?'

Mori tells her that it would. And he follows up by telling her to be sure to have a pleasant holiday. Kimiko Itoh says that she certainly will, safe in the knowledge that Mori is devoting himself to cracking the Miura case. Then she describes what she sees from the plane window – winding rivers, mountains tinged orange by the setting sun. Here it's beautiful, she tells him.

Mori glances out of his own window. What he sees – Shinjuku, the night-time version. Neon anarchy, a jungle of messages. Crowds of salarymen trudging through a labyrinth of alleys. Wetness, darkness, fearful density. Here, he tells Kimiko Itoh, it's still raining.

What do you do when the ninja who has been chasing you through the backstreets finally corners you? What do you do when he draws a silver throwing-star from the sleeve of his kimono and cocks his wrist, ready to embed the thing in your throat? You do the only thing you can. You duck.

Richard Mitchell ducks, just in time. The throwing-star goes whirring over his head, slams into the wooden pillar behind him. The points of the star are razor-sharp, glistening with snake venom.

'*Hoh!*' The ninja gives a grunt of surprise, reaches for another star. This time he won't miss. Mitchell edges backwards against a pile of bulging rice sacks. Glimpsed out of the corner of his eye, a silhouette behind a paper window.

'Here is safety! Come quickly.'

There's a geisha, beckoning him inside. Mitchell hesitates. The ninja glides forward, the star glinting in his hand. No choice – dive! The ninja's fingers move in a blur. Mitchell hurls himself at the paper window, goes crashing through the splintering frame. Behind him the throwing star slices into the sack, sending a stream of rice spilling to the ground.

The geisha leads Mitchell to the room with a steaming bath. 'That man may not follow you here. These are the rules of our city.'

A sigh of relief. The rules of the city are incomprehensible, but for the moment he is safe. Mitchell scans the geisha – blackened teeth, shaven eyebrows, an arrangement of jewelled combs and clips holding up her hair. 'What do you require, honoured customer?' she says, bowing low.

Mitchell remembers the phrase he was given. 'I am seeking the sword of Musashi.'

'I can help you find the sword. But first you must enter the bath.'

No choice again. The geisha giggles as Mitchell strips off his dusty clothes. He washes himself, back turned, then lowers himself shyly into the water. The kimono drops from the geisha's porcelain-pale shoulders. She slides into the bath, her breasts in his face, her legs twining around his waist.

Something's not right. Mitchell squirms, tries to raise himself from the water, but the woman's legs lock tight. Suddenly he freezes, pure panic. She's pulling something from her hairpiece, a vicious-looking pin, ten centimetres long.

'No,' breathes Mitchell. 'Please don't!'

The geisha's hand drops below the surface of the water.

'You broke the rules of our city,' she says with a mocking smile.

'It's not my fault! Nobody explained to me what the rules are!'

Too late. The geisha's hand shoots forward. Mitchell squeezes his eyes shut. When he opens them, the water between his thighs is swirling scarlet.

'*Yowww!*' Mitchell tears off the helmet, flings it on to the table in front of him.

'Please be careful with that, Mitchell-*san*. It's an extremely delicate piece of equipment.'

The publicity girl gazes at him with amusement. Her voice has exactly the same lilt as the geisha's.

'S-sorry,' he stammers, heart thumping like a drum. 'But that was amazing ... I mean, it was so REAL.'

'Of course,' says the publicity girl, helping him remove the bulky gloves. 'Our researchers had access to the latest work on neuropsychology and artificial intelligence. This is the first hyper-reality game in the world that incorporates CHI, meaning...'

Meaning Cognitive Holistic Interactivity, a typically wacky acronym. That's why the publicity girl has not only the same kind of voice as the geisha, but the same shape of face as well. Obeying the promptings of CHI, Mitchell's brain somehow constructed the geisha out of the last attractive woman he met before donning the helmet and gloves.

'Have you ever heard the story of the bruises?' says the publicity girl/geisha.

Mitchell nods, his mouth still dry. Apparently one of the research team discovered bruises on his body after a CHI-induced karate bout. When Mitchell heard the story the first time, he dismissed it as a marketing gimmick. Now, after ten minutes in the helmet, he isn't so sure. Sweat is trickling down his back and his pulse is banging as if he has just run a race.

The publicity girl continues. 'In Asian tradition, body and mind are not separate, but different aspects of being. This is the philosophical thinking behind our CHI technology. Very different from the dualism of Western science, I think.'

Where on earth has she got that from? Probably Sonoda, the president of the company. Still, Mitchell isn't about to argue philosophy with her. The new series of games is tremendously impressive, even better than the rumours had suggested. That moment of panic in the bath – he'll be having nightmares about it for months to come.

The demonstration session finishes. In the next room waits a sumptuous buffet – stuffed pigeon breast, Kobe beef, giant lobsters with their antennae still feebly waving. Mitchell avoids his fellow securities analysts. Instead he eats diligently, seriously, grazing up and down the table. In the financial industry these days you never know which free dinner is going to be your last. One false step and you end up like one of those lobsters.

Voice hubbub dies down. There's going to be a panel discussion at the far end of the room. The title, 'Game Culture in the Age of Multi-media'. The panellists: a female game critic; a pet academic; and Yoichi Sonoda, founder and president of SoftJoy Entertainment Systems. A game critic – now there's a thought. You're used to movie critics, book critics, restaurant critics. Nowadays there are people who do the same thing with video games – compare and contrast, explain, recommend. And this young lady is quite a celebrity as a result. Mitchell has seen her on a cosmetic commercial, doing something unforgettable with a stick of lipstick.

The pet academic starts the discussion. He fits the part

89

superbly – lank grey hair, spectacles with big black frames that make him look like a demented owl. He spiels about the future with absolute certainty, as if he has just returned from it in a time machine. In the first five minutes, he gets in mentions of Alvin Toffler, Nietzsche, Yukio Mishima and Marx.

'We are entering a new phase of history, which I have named the second Edo era. The first Edo era was the finest period in Japanese history. We had peace and prosperity and a dynamic cultural flowering, untroubled by foreign influences. Now, thanks to the efforts of far-sighted corporations like SoftJoy, we have a great opportunity to unify and revitalize Japanese culture . . .'

The professor pauses for a sip of water, flicks a strand of hair off his spectacles, then ploughs on with the remorseless power of the truly humourless.

'Remember that before the foreign ships appeared in Tokyo Bay, we had already developed the most advanced popular culture in the world, a culture which united the rich and the poor, the merchants and the warriors. It is my belief that the great artists of the Edo era, the men who created the woodblock prints of the floating world, would be producing game software if they were alive today.'

Applause ripples around the room, led by SoftJoy staffers in their distinctive orange tunics, then Yoichi Sonoda holds up his hand and starts to speak. The financial analysts start scribbling. This is the part of the evening that they have been waiting for.

'You will be happy to know that the new version of the Joystation is meeting its monthly sales targets. As a result, market share had held steady at thirty per cent, just five points below our competitor Mega Enterprises. My target is to raise our share to sixty per cent by the end of the year.'

This is a remarkably ambitious number. Most of the analysts are smiling as they write.

'Ultimately our customer base will extend to all ages, all types of people – from junior-school children to grand-mothers, from salarymen to priests. The prototypes we have been demonstrating here today should give you some idea of what is to come. Truly, as the sensei has forecast, Japan is on the verge of a digital version of the Edo period. Let us all learn to play as our ancestors did. Let us learn to play seriously.'

The staffers lead another round of applause. Mitchell joins in. Sonoda is definitely impressive. It must take ferocious determination to be a successful entrepeneur in Japan, a country where disturbing the established economic order is treated as an almost criminal act. To achieve dominance of an area into which the big conglomerates have been pouring resources for the last decade – that must takes balls of silicon.

Next is the turn of the female game critic. But here comes a major surprise. She starts off with a discussion of the US software industry and the history of intellectual property rights. In other words, Reiko Tanaka turns out to be a highly intelligent woman, articulate and sharp-witted. Mitchell feels cheated, fascinated, confused. All that giggling on banal quiz shows – it was an act? Or is this the act now? Or maybe neither. Maybe this is a woman who just happens to have the looks of a movie star, an excellent brain and a simple, fun-loving personality. What a phenomenon that would be! It only takes Mitchell a split second to decide that he wants to marry Reiko Tanaka.

He edges closer, watches, listens, devours. When the discussion is over, Sonoda and the two other panellists are hustled away by athletic-looking SoftJoy staffers. Mitchell intrudes himself, mumbles pleasantries, forces them to exchange name cards with him. Many people who look fine on TV look pretty strange in real life. Not Reiko Tanaka. She looks sleek, symmetrical, as light as air. She turns her gaze on Mitchell. Sex-rays blast him from close range, strong enough to raise the hairs on the back of his neck. He smiles, mumbles some more. Gratifyingly Reiko seems impressed by his command of Japanese respect-language. He adores her for it, tries to send a marriage proposal through his eyes. It doesn't work. her deflector shield is up. A quick TV smile, then Sonoda is guiding her through the door. Love at first sight, no question.

Two members of Yoichi Sonoda's private think-tank lead him into the elevator. Professor Suzuki is behind him, still jabbering about his digital nirvana. Reiko Tanaka is sulky-silent, as well she might be after what happened last night. But all good things come to an end, even the most successful formats have to be upgraded. The difference between the salaryman and the visionary is as follows. The salaryman acts when necessity demands. The visionary acts when action is unnecessary. There was still much pleasure and warmth between himself and Reiko, much still to be explored. Which is why she is bitter now, why she probably hates him. But if she didn't hate him, it would mean that he was too late, that he had acted like a salaryman. In business and in private matters, Yoichi Sonoda has never acted like a salaryman.

The elevator hums up to the thirtieth floor. It is globular, glass-fronted, goes up and down the side of the building like a bubble in a thermometer. Sonoda gazes down at the jumble of smallness, now quickly getting smaller. The Seikyu Hotel is the only skyscraper for miles around. The brothers who control it also own, amongst other things, the railway system that sprawls over the western suburbs of

Tokyo and the chains of department stores, supermarkets and convenience stores that dominate the shopping streets. As for this hotel, elder brother must have spent much money getting a special exemption to the building code. The rumour – five hundred million yen secreted in sacks of rice and delivered at the dead of night to the house of the desiccated old racoon-dog who was governor at the time.

SoftJoy staffers are waiting to greet them on the thirtieth floor – orange tunics with a black lightning flash down the breast. Average age of employees: twenty-seven. Oldest employee: the thirty-nine-year-old president himself.

Sonoda leads them into his suite. They sit around the sofa, nibbling sushi and sipping white wine. The professor keeps up his monologue, as if he were sitting opposite one of his brighter students rather than his paymaster. Reiko stares out of the window, glum, switched off after her performance on the panel. Sonoda gazes at the bank of TVs on the wall, all running SoftJoy video games downloaded from the new digital satellite channel.

A knock at the door. It is Ochi, head of product development. Sonoda reads his eyes: trouble. They go through into the room that serves as an office, sit down at the table. Ochi sounds worried.

'Our friend has sent disturbing reports about Mega's new format. Apparently he has come across secret plans for a surprise launch in the summer.'

Sonoda nods. Two years ago he managed to develop an 'information source' at Mega – a finance department section leader who happened to be married to the sister of a lawyer who was in the computer club with Sonoda at university. The section leader's wife walked out when she found out about her husband's huge gambling debts and the petty fraud that was paying the interest. She told her lawyer brother, who, over drinks in the Ginza, told Sonoda, who told Ochi to move in at once. It was the kind of chance that comes once a decade.

'That was to be expected. Is there anything else?'

It is clear from Ochi's frown that there is something else.

'Yes. Some of the game ideas are very close to our own prototypes.'

'What? How close?'

'Too close for coincidence. Our source is not a technical man, so his descriptions are not totally clear. Still, from his descriptions I would say that Mega must have had access to our developers.'

'Really! Which ones?'

'There are only a few possibilities.'

Sonoda sprang to his feet.

'I want you to identify the developers responsible as soon as possible. Focus on this exclusively next week. Move the heavens to find these people!'

'And if I do find them, what then?'

Sonoda smiles, hands on hips. 'Then what do you think?'

'I think we should make an example of them. This disloyalty is disgusting. Let us invoke the penalty clauses, bankrupt them!'

Spoken like a true salaryman! Sonoda shakes his head. 'I have a different idea. What you must do is offer them new contracts, at double the money.'

Ochi looks stunned. 'New contracts!' he says. 'You know what that means? They will just carry on feeding our best ideas to Mega!'

Sonoda grunts, turns away. Over the years Ochi has become adept at interpreting the various tones and timbres of his boss's grunts. From this one he understands that Sonoda, first, has registered the proposition, second, finds it logically sound, but, third, nonetheless valueless as an algorithm. Also that Sonoda's previous instructions should be obeyed immediately, with no further questioning. Also that the meeting is now over, and that Ochi should exit the suite by the bedroom door and occupy himself with the remaining guests downstairs. Also that no one else should know about this conversation.

That's how Ochi's brain processes that particular grunt. He clicks the door open, disappears into the corridor. Sonoda stands motionless at the window, gazing down at the labyrinth of neon.

Unfortunate coincidence. Mitchell is heading for the station, a polythene umbrella keeping off the worst of the rain, when Scott Hamada pulls up at the kerb in a chauffeur-driven Mercedes. Hamada is a Japanese-American who works for Silverman Brothers, the largest securities firm in the world. He is objectionable, and knows it.

A window whirrs down. 'Get in,' Hamada calls out. Mitchell hesitates, but he's getting wet, especially around the ankles. Pride has its price.

'Have a cigar,' says Hamada, when Mitchell climbs in. This time Mitchell does refuse. What follows is predictable. After all what's the point of being highly paid and successful unless you can find someone else who isn't to make the contrast? And from Scott Hamada's point of view, who could provide a better contrast than Richard Mitchell?

'Have you heard about new head office?' says Hamada. 'The Silverman Brothers Centre?'

Mitchell has heard of it – a glass tower next to Grand Central Station, with a museum on the ground floor dedicated to 'Silvermans' People and Principles'. Items that will not be exhibited: photos of a junior partner being led out of the dealing room in handcuffs; documents from the SEC investigation into the bid-rigging of a treasury bond auction; busted junk bonds and overpriced IPOs.

Hamada talks the triumphant language of financial capitalism – straddles, strangles, knock-out options, derivative instruments so complicated that even the people who created them have forgotten what they were originally for. He drops hints of mind-boggling bonuses and the difficulty he has in finding new ways to spend them. He makes jokes about the annual Silvermans' junket to the Bahamas, where top-performing staff were entertained by Stevie Wonder and a couple of dozen Hollywood starlets. Hamada fills the car with filthy cigar smoke. Hamada succeeds in his aim – making Mitchell feel profoundly unhappy.

If Hamada is living large, Mitchell is living lean. The past few years have been one long downward slide. Beginning with the three months at Henry Lazarus's hedge-fund operation. Continuing with a six-month stint at a US discount broker, a year with a Dutch pension-fund manager, another six months with a French insurance company, then on to a Japanese securities house wallowing in scandal and bad loans. Final resting-place – a British merchant bank which was almost immediately swallowed up by a German bank.

Buy-side analyst, sell-side analyst, fund manager, trader, salesman, corporate financier – Mitchell tried them all, none with much success. These days the strategies of financial companies are as unstable as the markets they attempt to navigate. These days no one is safe from the tsunami of restructuring, downbuilding, delayering, rightsizing, purging, axing, shafting, sacking, canning. Still, even by these standards, Mitchell's curriculum vitae is not a pretty picture. His current job, he recognizes, is likely to be his last.

'You've just renewed your Buy rating on SoftJoy,' says Hamada, suddenly changing the subject. It's not a question.

He knows for sure, probably got the report from one of his clients.

'That's right,' says Mitchell cautiously. 'What about you?'

Hamada blows fumes out of the side of his mouth, Edgar G. Robinson-style.

'My rating remains a strong "Sell",' he says. 'The new machine is impressive, but Sonoda is strategically vulnerable. All his best games are created by outside developers. What happens if they get lured away, hey?'

Mitchell has heard that argument many times before. He gives his standard answer. 'That's not going to happen. For a start, the developers are all kept under wraps, totally unknown to the competition. Secondly, they'd be nothing without SoftJoy anyway. Sonoda works on each game himself, adding the really slick touches. That's why SoftJoy games sell so well.'

Hamada shakes his head, as if he can't believe how anyone could be so stubborn.

'I respect your tenacity, man, but Mega's gonna certainly roast his ass.'

'Is that so?'

'That's the truth, Ruth. Don't forget Mega has the resources of the entire Mitsutomo group backing them up. If Mitsutomo were a country, it'd be in the OECD, that's how rich it is. Big league stuff, Mitch. You know what I mean?'

Mitchell knows just what he means: two things. First, Hamada means that Sonoda is out of his depth, a little guy going head to head with a huge industrial combine. Second, he means that Richard Mitchell is out of his depth too, a little guy taking a contradictory stance to the top analyst in the sector, who also happens to be backed by the vast technical, financial and political resources of Silverman Brothers.

Mitchell says nothing. Hamada puffs smugness. The SoftJoy stock price has been slumping since the start of the year, a cause for serious dissatisfaction to any investors who put their money where Mitchell's mouth was. The Mega stock price, meanwhile, has been soaring to new highs, thanks to consistently heavy buying by Silverman Brothers. So Hamada can gloat with every waggle of his cigar, and Mitchell has got no comeback at all, nothing.

Mitchell has a minor coughing fit. The cigar fumes are unendurable, Hamada's attitude also. Fortunately, they don't have to be endured any longer.

'I'm getting out here,' he says. 'Thanks for the ride.'

Hamada zips the window down a few inches, peers out. 'This where you live, Mitch?' he says dubiously. Mitchell views the scenery through Hamada's eyes – row after higgledy-piggledy row of squat concrete buildings, festooned with aerials and satellite dishes, strung with a cat's cradle of telephone wires and power cables. A far cry from the luxury apartment complex – with restaurants, health club and in-house tennis professional – that he inhabits himself.

'This is a real people area,' says Mitchell, getting out of the car. 'It's a lot of fun, actually.'

Frogs are croaking in the patch of waste ground next to his building. An old lady pushing a squeaky bicycle comes out of the alley. She stares at Mitchell with unmistakable hostility, then mutters something curse-like beneath her breath.

'That's my landlady,' explains Mitchell lamely. 'She's a real character.'

Hamada flicks ash off his cigar. 'Sounds like you put her into SoftJoy at ten thousand yen,' he grins.

'SoftJoy is a far better investment than Mega,' snaps Mitchell. 'You wait and see.'

Hamada chuckles, pleased that his provocations have hit home. Mitchell stumps toward the door of his building. Rain patters on his shoulders. His landlady mouths another incomprehensible curse. The frogs jeer.

Yoichi Sonoda is a small man with a large head. You need to walk around him once to get a true idea of its size and weight. Then you appreciate the great job his shoulders and neck are doing in holding it upright.

At the moment Sonoda is alone, sitting in the bedroom on the thirtieth floor of the hotel. The sound of the professor's voice comes through the wall. He continues to lecture Reiko Tanaka about cultural theory, but Sonoda doesn't hear him. Sonoda has the ability to switch off sights and sounds that no longer interest him any time that he wants. Now he has switched off the professor's droning voice, Reiko's occasional replies, the hotel room, the raindrops speckling the window, the massive formlessness of Tokyo spreading out to the horizon like a dark swamp.

In his mind Sonoda is playing his favourite game, a multi-dimensional interactive game that has no beginning or end, no rules, no definable goal at all. The purpose is just to keep on playing. Sometimes you are the pursuer, sometimes the pursued – more often both simultaneously. There are hidden passages, sudden betrayals, an infinite supply of ever-stronger enemies. It is a fascinating, all-consuming game, the most real game ever.

Recently a new enemy has appeared, an entity called Mega. It is aggressive, ruthless, with many powerful weapons and allies. But like a dinosaur, its brain is small and slow. Sonoda can predict exactly how it will react to the various lures and false trails that he is laying in its path. Before too long he will construct a trap skilful enough to overcome its suspicious instincts, a trap from which it will never be able to escape.

Timing is all.

Lay the bait. Wait.

Then jerk the joystick.

Seven

Five-thirty in the morning. Mitchell is woken by the rain. Not the sound of it, the feel – wet and cold on his cheek. He opens his eyes. This is what he sees: a dark patch in the ceiling, the shape of Australia. He turns his head. There, on the tatami mat next to his pillow, a pool of dirt-speckled water.

This is a bad start to the day. It means protracted negotiations with Granny Abe, the landlady. Instinctively she will blame him for the leak, just as she blames him for the repeated blown fuses and blockings of the toilet. It'll be there in her rheumy gaze, in her muttered imprecations.

'The foreigner has allowed rainwater to soil the sacred tatami mats! This is the one who damages our earth-less two-pin Japanese wiring system, overloading it with computers and printers and other nonsense. The one whose enormous turds keep blocking up our slender Japanese pipes. Never again will I rent my apartment to such a foreigner!'

That's how Mitchell interprets it, for even in his imagination Granny Abe's mutterings are impossible to understand.

He gets to his feet, rolls up the futon and stuffs it in a cupboard. Water-beads are still forming somewhere in the middle of New South Wales. He gets a rice bowl, sets it to catch the drips. Coffee, toast, TV news. The mayor of some town in Tohoku has been arrested for bribery. Mitsutomo

Bank is writing off a couple of hundred billion yen in bad loans. The birth rate is declining. The stock market is declining. The number of abalone caught by the nation's abalone fishermen is also declining. Nothing good is happening, nothing at all.

The mention of Mitsutomo Bank sets Mitchell thinking about Mega, SoftJoy and his own shaky position as junior analyst at West Bavaria Securities. Maybe Scott Hamada is right. Maybe Mega's next-generation machine is going to be a real winner. If so, SoftJoy is finished. Whereas Mega is a gigantic empire of electronics products – with the top brand name, a movie studio in Hollywood and interests in satellite TV, broadcasting and media all over the world – SoftJoy generates all of its profits from video games. Lose its position there, and the company could well go out of business. Meaning total domination of the market for Mega. And a bonus the size of the GNP of a small African country for Scott Hamada. And the termination of Mitchell's job at WBS.

There's no escaping that conclusion. The SoftJoy stock has plunged thirty per cent since Mitchell recommended it as his 'top pick of the year'. The investors that bought the stock are already disgusted by the situation. If Hamada is only half right in his opinion of what happens next, in a matter of weeks they'll be baying for blood.

What to do? Mitchell could downgrade the stock to 'Weak Hold', citing 'unforeseen adverse developments in the operating environment' or some such tripe. He would be hated for it, of course, mocked and reviled as a lily-livered piker. But he would still have a job.

Or he could stick to his guns, renew his recommendation as a 'Strong Long-Term Buy'. In which case he could be a hero. Or an unemployed villain.

The choice is stark and existential. Believe Scott Hamada,

with his Harvard MBA and number-one ranking from *Institutional Investor* magazine. Or believe your own instincts, as honed by long hours spent playing the games of both SoftJoy and Mega.

Mitchell swills coffee round his mouth. The water goes plip-plip-plip into the rice bowl. Outside the frogs have started croaking again.

Mori gets to the office early, newly energized by the generous bonus that Kimiko Itoh has dangled in front of him. Breakfast at his desk – two prawn dumplings, a banana, coffee. He claps his hands in front of the little shrine on the wall, implores the gods for a little luck, then gets down to work.

First call of the morning – Kazuko, at the consumer finance company. Mori needs to locate Kaneda, the missing security guard. Wherever the guy's been moved to, at some point he will make a bank withdrawal, visit a clinic, rent a video, or do something else that will create a tiny vibration somewhere on Kazuko's invisible spider-web of data. When that happens, she promises to pass the information on to Mori immediately. And Kazuko always keeps her promises. Putting down the phone, Mori wonders – not for the first time – what kind of person she is. If her voice is anything to go by, brisk, no-nonsense, hard to impress. And from the nature of the service she provides, a complex woman, dangerous to cross.

Second call – Inspector Shima, doyen of the Shinjuku police. What Mori needs to know – why would Miura be interested in the services of a private detective? There's a chance – admittedly slim – that Shima might have the answer.

'I could get in serious trouble for talking to you again,' grumbles Shima, as he always does.

'Sure,' soothes Mori. 'But it's nothing big this time. Just some routine stuff.'

'Go on,' says Shima suspiciously.

'I've got a feeling Miura was involved in some kind of trouble.'

'What kind of trouble?'

'I don't know – blackmail, threats of violence maybe. Anyway, something might have been reported.'

Shima gives a well-practised groan of irritated incredulity. 'You mean you want me to check our records on the off chance that some undefined incident might have occurred at some undefined location at some undefined time.'

'Exactly,' says Mori. 'By the way, have you been following the kick-boxing tournament? There've been one or two major upsets already.'

'Is that right?' says Shima, immediately interested. These days his fondness for the martial arts is entirely passive, though nonetheless intense for that. Judo, karate, sumo, kendo, boxing – he follows them all closely.

'The favourite got his jaw broken in the first round. And last year's champion was beaten by a total unknown, a trainee cook from Iwate Prefecture.'

That's sure to set Shima's pulse racing. His father's family were rice farmers in Iwate for as far back as records exist. Therefore anyone hailing from the prefecture – sportsman, political boss, up-and-coming starlet baring her bush in a weekly magazine – is automatically worthy of enthusiastic encouragement.

'Somebody gave me a couple of tickets,' continues Mori casually. 'Tonight's the last stage – from quarter-finals onwards. Still, I don't suppose a busy man like you would be able to find the time . . .'

In fact, it seems that Shima is able to find the time with

little trouble. He informs Mori that he will be waiting outside the hall at seven-thirty sharp.

'And, Mori-*san*, be punctual for a change. We don't want to miss the start.'

The sharpness in his voice comes from experience.

'You know me,' says Mori. 'Never late unless there's an excellent reason.'

Like his Taipei Rolex suddenly adopting a different pace to the rest of the universe. Or the Honda getting temperamental. Or Mori just plain forgetting.

Fine – that's done. Now to lay hands on some tickets. The tournament is sold out, of course. Meaning that some enterprising yakuza group probably bought up half the entire issue of tickets before they even went on sale. The man who knows about these things is a pawnbroker who operates out of a small shop a couple of blocks away. He calls himself Kubota International Services, although his real name is not Kubota and the services he offers are of a totally domestic nature. He will buy things from you for a lot less than they are worth. He will sell them on to someone else for more. And he will never ever ask any questions.

A five-minute walk and Mori's standing at the entrance, slapping the rain off the folds of his raincoat. He wanders through the shop, past stacks of out-of-date electronic equipment, shelves of bric-à-brac, dead men's clothes, discoloured bronze Buddhas. The man who has decided to call himself Kubota is sitting at the counter, wiping over a glass case which contains a stuffed mongoose attacking a stuffed cobra. It's an impressive item of home decor. The mongoose's teeth are vicious. The cobra is coiled to strike.

'What do you think, Mori-*san*?' he says, looking up. 'Which one of these would you put your money on?'

'The snake's got first shot,' says Mori. 'But it's his only shot. Miss and he gets his throat ripped out.'

'So you'd choose the mongoose?'

Mori peers through the grimy glass. 'No, I'd probably choose the snake. He looks cool enough under pressure. Probably done it a few times before.'

They chat lightly about the weather, the new Porpoises pitcher, an especially good tempura restaurant which has just gone out of business. Mori mentions the kick-boxing tournament. As expected, the man who has decided to call himself Kubota knows where to find some tickets, front row. There's a woman working in a pink cabaret around the corner whose sister is married to a junior yakuza who specializes in sporting events. A word in the right place and the tickets will be ready by mid-afternoon.

Mori glances at the pile of dog-leaved books beside the counter. Dostoevsky, Camus, Thomas Mann: an unusual selection for this part of town. Mori picks out a handful, buys them for the price of a bottle of Suntory White. The man who has decided to call himself Kubota looks mildly grateful, rolls up the banknote and slides it into the back of an ancient valve radio on a shelf in front of him. Then he spits on his rag and goes back to wiping down the glass case. Inside, the mongoose and the cobra carry on glaring at each other.

On the way out Mori picks up a flyer that he notices lying on a broken-backed chair by the door. The print job is better quality than the one he saw before, but the wording is almost the same. 'Mr Problem-Solver will take care of all social and economic problems. Guaranteed – the cheapest rates available!' Mr Problem-Solver clearly hasn't got the message. How can the guy hope to solve other people's economic problems when he's got no understanding of his own? It looks like a face-to-face meeting is going to be necessary.

If there's one thing that makes George the Wolf Nishio nervous – apart, that is, from the old boss when his ulcer's playing up – it's flying. Planes are scary because you have no control. Threats don't work, or bribes or appeals to duty and obligation. You just have to sit back and hope for the best. The only real solution: ample quantities of alcohol.

So George makes sure to have a couple of beers with his breakfast. Then, in the departure lounge at Haneda airport, he takes his time guzzling a half-bottle of bourbon and some low-grade sake bought from a vending machine. When he swaggers aboard, having kept everyone waiting for ten minutes, he finds that the plane has to stay on the tarmac until another slot clears. Half an hour later it finally goes bucking and jerking through the cloud cover. By now George has emptied his hip-flask of Korean brandy and he's starting to feel pretty queasy. There may also have been a problem with the snacks he ingested in the small hours of the night before – pickled gherkins, mashed crab-brains, slivers of raw horsemeat spiced with ginger. Anyway, whatever the reason, George's stomach starts to churn and beads of sweat roll down from under his mirror shades. And that's the point at which the captain tells everyone to fasten their seat belts because the plane is heading for heavy turbulence.

George is dressed to impress. The yam-heads in the countryside won't have seen anything like his jacket – mauve suede, with black lapels and side panels. Or his shirt, which has the luminous image of a horned demon on the back. Or his leather trousers, held up by a belt with a silver buckle the size of a fried egg. These clothes can't be bought in any regional superstore. In fact, they can't be bought anywhere. He had to use his initiative to acquire them. The belt, for example, came from an off-duty GI and cost George a split knuckle and a broken toe.

In the next seat is a salaryman with a briefcase open on his lap. He has been trying to ignore George for the whole flight, the usual thing. Now he's absorbed in reading a thick report packed with charts and tables. George suddenly feels lousy, cold and hot at the same time. He stares in consternation at his gleaming leather trousers, his suede jacket which he brushed so carefully before putting on. This could be a disaster.

Aware that George is leaning across the seat, the salaryman tries to turn away. But it's too late. George grabs that briefcase in both hands, yanks it onto his own lap.

'What do you think you're doing?' squawks the salaryman.

'Shut your mouth,' George hisses, knuckling the man's cheek for emphasis. He bends over and his stomach heaves – once, twice, three times. When he's finished, the briefcase is swimming with a *mélange* of the morning's booze and the night before's snacks. Taking care nothing slops out, George snatches a couple of pages of typescript from the man's hand and wipes his face with them. Then he drops them in the briefcase and clicks down the lid.

A quick check. Jacket, shirt, trousers – all spotless. George heaves a sigh of relief, hands the briefcase back. He will not lose face with the yam-heads after all.

'Is everything all right, honoured customer?' A prissy-looking stewardess is standing in the aisle, peering down at them.

'Go away and die, elder sister,' growls George. The salaryman gulps, says nothing. With his stomach voided, George starts to feel much better. For the rest of the flight he sleeps, legs stretched out into the aisle.

There are two local guys waiting for him at the airport. Iba, the tall gangly one, has got such a split-tongued accent that George has to ask him to repeat almost everything. Not that he makes much sense anyway. The other one, who is called Sakamoto, looks and acts as if he's mentally deficient.

The car they've brought is just what you'd expect – a twenty-year-old Lincoln Continental with plenty of dents and a top speed of fifty kilometres an hour. For some reason the interior smells strongly of stale catpiss. Sakamoto drives like an old lady with senile dementia, accelerating into the curves then braking sharply halfway through. Both men are wearing clothes that went out of fashion at around the same time as their car was made. George glances at his watch. With a bit of luck, this won't take long.

But it does. First of all there are formalities to be observed. They have orders to take him to the gang headquarters which, the way they tell it, is in the centre of the local entertainment district. Well, the local entertainment district consists of two narrow streets of cinder-block buildings with hand-painted plywood façades. There are a couple of pink cabarets, a pachinko parlour, a strip theatre with a sign advertising a 'corn-on-the-cob' show. No evidence of any customers at all.

The gang's office is above a dingy noodle shop which Iba rates as serving 'the best fried rice omelette in the whole prefecture'. Lying across the doorway is a black and white cat with half of one ear missing. George wonders if it sleeps inside the Lincoln.

Sakamoto leads him upstairs. George waits for the local chief in a cramped anteroom filled with boxes of ten-year-old porno videos.

The local chief, Sada, is no ordinary yam-head. He is a friend of the old boss from way back and deserves to be treated with respect. The two of them set up a black market in rice just after the war. The old boss used his profits to build up a power base in Tokyo. Sada spent his share on women and gambling. According to one story, he once got so deeply into debt that he was forced to challenge a champion fighting dog to a fight to the death. The dog lost in round one.

So it's a something of a shock when Sada comes into the room in a wheelchair with his head tilted to one side. His eyes are watery, the flesh is hanging off his face in leathery folds. In short, the man is at least half-dead. George bends a leg and makes the formal greeting, word-for-word perfect, just as the old boss would want. Then he listens as Sada croaks gratitude and explains what has to be done. What with the accent and the fact that his voice-box is all clogged up, it's pretty hard to understand what Sada's saying. Still, to ask a lot of troublesome questions would show a lack of respect. So George waits until they are out on the street again to get a clearer idea from Iba and Sakamoto. They give it to him in stereo – the braying bumpkin on one side, the stuttering moron on the other.

This is what George learns. The owner of a chain of pink salons is refusing to pay the increase in the operating licence that Sada's people are demanding. Worse still, he has been seen associating with officers of the 'United Prosperity Coalition', an Osaka-based syndicate that has been expanding aggressively into neighbouring prefectures. So this isn't just about money. It isn't just about face. It is about long-held territorial rights. That's why they needed someone from Tokyo. All they want George to do is stand there and look tough. The other side will get the signal, 'Go any further and you risk a nationwide gang war.'

They get into the purulent Lincoln, drive through the empty streets. The yam-heads tell him more. It turns out that the pink salon guy has got pretty extensive interests. He started out with massage parlours, love hotels and soaplands and built up quite a little empire. More recently he has diversified into meal provision for schools, garbage disposal for hospitals and other stuff. George starts to feel a twinge of unease. He didn't bring his gun.

Forty minutes in the car. Drizzle modulates into fog. Daylight slinks off to a far corner of the sky.

The pink salon the guys have chosen is a prefab building not far from the expressway. Apart from the pachinko parlour next to it, there are no other signs of life for miles around. Discreet, and nicely sited for the long-distance hauliers who go thundering down the coast all hours of the day and night. Right now there are a dozen giant trucks in the parking lot. The pink salon guy evidently has a sharper business sense than Sada's people, with their depopulated 'entertainment area'.

George gets out of the Lincoln, stands there chewing on a toothpick. The pink salon is huge, one of the biggest he's ever seen. Disco music is pounding away inside. There are a couple of bouncers at the door eyeing them.

What's the matter, Wolf?' says Sakamoto. 'Is there some problem?'

'The only problem is your brain,' snaps George. 'When you were born, the doctor must have dropped you on your head.' Sakamoto glances at Iba, a stupid little grin on his face. The grin says, 'The tough guy from Tokyo is getting nervous.' Well, that's true. George is getting nervous. Not because he's scared, but because the situation is all wrong. The information is bad. The preparation is bad. The people he's working with are monkeys.

George walks up to the entrance, grins at the bouncers, flashes twenty thousand yen.

'What do I get for this?' he says.

One of the bouncers grins back. Depends how much time you've got, he says. Two girls for two hours, three girls for one hour or – special deal – four girls for half an hour.

The bouncer sounds calm, not at all fazed by the sight of the yakuza from Tokyo. George nods, walks inside with Iba and Sakamoto following behind like turd trailing from a goldfish.

The interior is dark. The disco beat is a sledgehammer. A mama-*san* appears, guides them to a booth at the back of the cavernous room. George judges there are at least thirty such booths altogether, half of which are occupied. That means probably twenty girls working, good revenue flow. Needing more than two bouncers to protect it. George the Wolf Nishio takes a deep breath. He's starting to like this less and less.

They order drinks, girls. Three appear. Young, surprisingly attractive. They take off their T-shirts and dance on the table. Micro miniskirts, fluorescent G-strings thrust in the men's faces. Sakamoto is grinning like a split coconut. Glancing under a grinding crotch, George notes that two big guys have appeared from a back room, are taking seats right by the door. He picks up a cocktail fork, slips it in his pocket.

Sakamoto is starting to drool. He puts five thousand yen on the table, has the girls peel off their G-strings. Iba pulls the whisky bottle to his mouth and starts glug-glugging. The men sitting near the door are staring at them, impassive. George bends over to Iba, hisses in his ear, 'Maybe this isn't such a good idea.'

'Leave it to us,' sneers Iba. 'We can handle this without your help.'

He takes another swig of whisky. One of the girls starts fiddling with Sakamoto's zipper. The men by the entrance are muttering to the two bouncers. It won't be long before they make their move. George suddenly stands up.

'I'm going to take a piss,' he says.

George weaves his way between the booths to the back of the salon. Last glimpse of Sakamoto – trousers down below his knees, girl bent across him. Iba is having a car-wash – a naked girl on each side, pushing breasts into his face. The booths around them are being vacated, girls leading their customers over to the far side of the room.

George knows the layout of this kind of place. He has been in enough of them in his time. He walks past the toilet, slips behind a curtain and down a short corridor to the emergency exit at the side of the building. Outside the air is warm and wet. George pauses to listen. He can hear nothing but the sledgehammer thump of the music. He goes round the back of the pachinko parlour, then doubles back to the car park, taking up an observation point between a couple of trucks.

What happens next is predictable. The two bouncers are suddenly called inside. A couple of minutes later they emerge, hauling Iba's limp body by the arms and legs. His shirt is in shreds and blood is pouring down his face in streaks. The bouncers dump him at the side of the building and give him a two-minute stomping. Next comes Sakamoto – no trousers, squashed nose, burbling incomprehensible insults. Or maybe they're comprehensible to the bouncers because one of them suddenly grabs him by the back of the neck and slams his face into the concrete wall. Apparently unsatisfied, the bouncer takes a few steps backwards and repeats it. Sakamoto stops burbling.

These people, decides George, are reasonably serious. While the two bouncers are stuffing Sakamoto head-first into a garbage-can, he tries the door on the truck nearest him. It's not locked. Stealthily, he climbs inside, crouches down behind the driver's seat. Which turns out to be a smart move. The four big guys come out with baseball bats and start scanning around the car park, peering under the trucks. No sign of George, which obviously makes them feel somehow unfulfilled. One of them gazes at the Lincoln Continental, calls to the others. George winces. The car is stupid, old-fashioned, bad in every respect. But he can imagine what it means to old man Sada. If the old man could see – or hear – what happens next, he would weep tears of fury.

Glass shatters. Metal squeals as it buckles. The baseball bats keep on smashing, clanging, crunching, drowning out the disco beat. They must be Unified Prosperity people. No one else would dare. George seethes.

Eventually the noise stops. Footsteps head back to the pink cabaret. George lifts his head above the seat, gazes at what remains of the Lincoln. It's a pitiful sight. There's a deep crater in the roof, the hood has been twisted off, the doors battered into all shapes. This disgrace must be avenged, properly. The old boss would demand it.

George bides his time. Fifteen minutes later, more footsteps. The truck driver opens the door, hauls himself up into the driver's seat. He smells of whisky, hums a ballad as he starts the ignition. Behind him George stays silent, small. It's not until the truck has been rolling for a couple of kilometres that George gets off the floor, jams the cocktail fork in the side of the guy's neck and tells him to pull into the next farm track on the left.

'You're going to get in trouble for this,' says the trucker, suddenly sober.

'So are you,' growls George. 'Drunk driving – that's a serious offence.'

He moves smoothly, just like the hero of one of those yakuza movies he loved as a kid. He uses an oily rag as a blindfold, ties the guy's hands behind his back with his own headband. When he's satisfied that it's good and tight, George hauls the guy out of the truck and shoves him into a paddy-field, where he stumbles around for a few seconds then splats face first into the mud.

George finds what he needs in the back of the truck: a tyre-iron, a monkey-wrench, a plastic tube, an empty gasoline can, a sports newspaper. He uses the tube to syphon gasoline out of the tank, stuffs the mouth of the can with paper. Then gets down on his hands and knees and fiddles around with the truck's accelerator pedal.

It only takes a few minutes to do what he wants to do. The driver is sitting on his knees in the middle of the paddy-field, waiting for him to go. George obliges, taking the truck with him. He heads back the way they came, headlights dimmed. The road is deserted. The rain has more or less stopped.

Back at the pink salon it's business as usual. The two bouncers are outside, smoking cigarettes and chatting. They don't see anything strange about the big truck idling to a halt at the entrance to the car park. By the time they realize that something is wrong, it's too late.

George has to move fast. He uses his cigarette lighter to light the paper sprouting from the gasoline can, then slides out of the door. One of the bouncers recognizes him, comes forward. Inside the cab the gasoline can erupts. The bouncer stops dead, hands on hips. George reaches inside, uses the tyre iron to lever the accelerator down to the floor, jams it into place under the brake. The truck surges forward, gears screaming like a herd of crazed elephants. The passenger seat is a ball of flame. The bouncers scatter, yelling scared. The truck picks up speed and George goes flying, shoulder smashing into the tarmac. He rolls over, looks up to see the full force of the Mitsubishi Guts, Japan's top-of-the-line commercial freight vehicle, go thundering towards the entrance of the pink salon.

What happens next is beautiful, worth one hundred times the pain shooting through his arm. It's Japanese engineering versus Japanese construction. And engineering wins, hands down.

A mighty crunching ripping sound. The truck smashes clean through the front wall, engine roar rising to a whine. Panic screams inside. Orange flames billow from the cabin window, reach out to catch wood and plastic. Support beams shear into two. The roof of the building tips a couple of feet at the front. The truck twists sideways, wheels squealing on lino-board. Curtains and cushions ignite. Half-naked women go running out the emergency exit. Pandemonium, of the most gratifying sort. Sada's Lincoln Continental has been well and truly avenged.

George would like to stay and watch some more, but decides against it. Police and fire people will be on the scene before long. Anyway, he has things to do. He slips away down the road, nursing his injured arm. After he has been walking for around ten minutes he sees a schoolgirl on a moped coming the other way. Unbelievable, it must be one of those rare days in life when everything goes right.

George waits crouched in the shadows, then runs out and knocks her off the moped, which goes careering into a tree. Fortunately the machine is undamaged. Not so the girl. She sprawls on the tarmac, concussed. George grabs her by the arms, hauls her over to the side of the road and shoves her into the ditch. That, he figures, is his good deed for the day.

Shima watches the kick-boxing with rapt attention. Occasionally he gets really excited and starts making little punches in the air. Mori leans back, thinks of other things while his eyes follow the choreography of fists and feet.

His own favourite sport is professional wrestling, the reason being that you know it's phoney from the start. With most other sports you can never be sure. Take sumo wrestling for example. A good proportion of bouts are fixed in order to preserve the hierarchy of wrestlers. They don't want some unknown guy coming along and disturbing the dignity of a grand champion. It wouldn't be right. Baseball? The boyfriend of the sister of one of Mori's ex-girlfriends was involved in fixing a Japan Series in the late 1980s. Boxing? The yakuza go directly to the umpires. Athletics? A festival of pharmaceuticals. No, sport is something you can only take seriously when there's nothing at stake.

The cook from Iwate fights with diligent violence. In his first match he knocks out the defeated finalist from two years ago. In the next, urged on by Shima's yells, he gets off the floor to outpoint the all-Kanto champion. After that there's a thirty-minute break before the final. Mori and Shima go and sit on the steps outside. They drink beer from the can, watch fashionably dressed office ladies hurrying through the rain.

'By the way,' says Shima casually, 'there was something you asked me about, wasn't there? What was that exactly again?'

To someone who knows Shima as well as Mori does, this is a promising start.

'It was just a bit of fact-checking,' says Mori. 'You know, about that bureaucrat Miura.'

'Ah, yes. Miura.'

A pair of shapely legs go flashing past on the other side of the street. Shima's gaze follows.

'I don't suppose you had a chance to look at the records yet?' says Mori.

Shima rolls some beer around his mouth, apparently bored by the whole topic. This is even more encouraging.

'As a matter of fact I did,' he says.

'And nothing interesting came up?'

Shima shrugs. 'Certainly nothing that would interest the police.'

Mori turns to look at him. Shima stares straight ahead, pretending not to notice.

'How about something that might interest me?'

'That's for you to judge, Mori-*san*.'

Shima reaches in his jacket and pulls out a plain brown envelope. Mori pockets it, offers gruff gratitude. They finish their beers and go back inside to watch the final.

It features the Iwate boy against a guest fighter from Thailand. Shima is soon on his feet, roaring out advice, cursing the referee, groaning with anguish whenever the Iwate boy takes a blow. Mori stays seated. From the clashes of energy, the balance of trade in kicks and punches, there is only one way this can end. The Iwate boy goes rushing in like a mongoose. The guy from Thailand stays coiled like a snake. And when he strikes, the accuracy is devastating.

The Iwate boy goes down twice, both heavy blows. And both times he gets up too soon. Shima shouts louder. He admires the fortitude, the contempt for the truth of the situation. Mori admires it too, but he wouldn't recommend it. The Iwate boy's next rush is slower, wilder. And the Thai's strike is harder, much harder. This time the Iwate boy doesn't get up. In fact, he doesn't move at all. Shima sits down heavily, a rueful look on his face.

'Maybe next year,' says Mori.

'Definitely next year,' says Shima. 'He's got everything it takes.'

Except guile and wisdom, and they come from fear. The mongoose doesn't fear the snake, which is why it keeps on rushing in. The snake fears the mongoose. That's why it has to make sure, first time.

Sada sits slumped in his wheelchair, head on one side, listening while George the Wolf Nishio explains how he single-handedly faced down half a dozen Unified Prosperity guys, avenged the vandalism of the Lincoln and reminded the pink salon owner of the value of sincerity and obligation. When George has finished, Sada says nothing, doesn't even look up. For a moment, George thinks the old man might have died already. Then the one side of his mouth twists open to reveal broken yellow teeth, grey gums.

The croaks and wheezes are interpreted by another of Sada's men, a moon-faced thug with a bull-neck and a gleaming pate.

'The boss is sorry that you have been put to such trouble. Tomorrow he will write a letter to your boss in Tokyo thanking him for your excellent work.'

George smirks in delight. Respect and honour are returning to him. He can feel it almost physically.

Old man Sada croaks some more. Dumpling-face bends down to listen, rolls of fat glistening on the back of his neck.

'The boss offers you our full hospitality for the rest of your stay here. Anything you want, any service you need – just tell him and it's done.'

George bows sincerity, head ducking deep, arms rigid at his side. There is indeed a small service that he is about to request. One that should lead to the full restoration of honour and respect.

Eight

In the rainy season Yasuo Takeda doesn't open his florist shop until eleven. From experience he knows that not many people come by in the mornings. Anyway, most of his business is commercial these days – funerals of local dignitaries, openings of pachinko parlours and restaurants, various political events. The orders usually come through in the afternoon, via fax or phone. So by eleven-thirty all he has accomplished is to set up the cactus display, cover it with polythene and drag it outside. After that he sits behind the counter sipping barley tea and leafing through the wodge of manga magazines that he has been subscribing to ever since leaving middle-school. That was eighteen years ago. The manga haven't changed much since then, neither has Yasuo Takeda.

The door flies open. Four men peer in. Takeda jumps to his feet, sings out an enthusiastic welcome. But these are not ordinary flower fanciers. That is obvious at first glance. In fact, they look as if they've stepped straight out of a low-grade manga. The first through the door is fat and as bald as an egg. Then comes a tall one with a bandaged head, followed by another wearing a plastic nose-splint. Most disturbing of all is the last man – mirror shades, circus clothes, face of vicious thinness.

'Are you Takeda?' says the one with the nose-splint.

'That's right,' says Takeda, his voice quite a bit higher

and faster than usual. 'If there's anything you require in the way of flowers or horticultural items, I'd be honoured to provide it.'

Mirror shades scans the shelves.

'Would you now?' he says. 'Well, let me see. Have you got any top-class non-organic fertilizer?'

Takeda brightens. Maybe these men are members of some kind of gardening club. He shows them the bags of fertilizer, explains the different suitabilities for different kinds of plant.

Mirror shades nods approval. 'How about some tools?'

Takeda points out a display rack hung with trowels, clippers and hand-forks. Mirror shades picks up a hand-fork, weighs it thoughtfully in his palm, then suddenly turns and stabs it into a bag of fertilizer. Then he pulls it out and slams it in again and again, as if into the guts of a dying man. Fertilizer showers out of the ripped bag, forms a little black hill on the floor. Takeda stares at it, horror-struck. These are not gardening people after all.

The one with the bandaged head grabs his arm, twists him to the ground.

'You recommend that stuff,' says mirror shades. 'Now you can show us how good it is.'

'What do you mean?' gasps Takeda.

'Eat it!'

Takeda has read enough manga to know better than to refuse. Eyes squeezed shut, he pushes his face into the mound of fertilizer.

'Take a mouthful!' says mirror shades. Takeda takes a mouthful.

'Chew!' says mirror shades. Takeda chews.

'Swallow!' says the mirror shades. Takeda swallows.

'Good,' says mirror shades. 'Now for some weedkiller to wash it down.'

Takeda chokes. Fertilizer shoots from his mouth. The four men peer down at him.

'Are you ready to co-operate?' says the fat man with the naked head.

'Yes, I am,' says Takeda, more sincerely than he has said anything in his life before.

What they want – the guy who borrowed Takeda's van for a couple of days just before the start of the rainy season. In fact, the way they glance around the shop, it looks as if they expect him to come through the door any moment. Takeda explains he hasn't seen the guy since then, has no idea of his current location. That causes the one with the nose-splint to scoop up a handful of fertilizer and hurl it in his face.

'So he's not a friend of yours?' says the one with the mirror shades. Takeda shakes his head vigorously.

'Explain who he is, then.'

Fortunately Takeda remembers quite a lot. Squatting on the floor in front of the mound of fertilizer, Takeda states what he knows. That the guy said he did advertising spreads for glossy magazines. That he was really in the porno business. That he was using a South-East-Asian woman, a crazy luscious one. Here Takeda's hands signify a large and well-shaped pair of breasts. And here the weird one picks up the hand-fork and slams it into the fertilizer sack one more time.

'What was his name?' growls the one with bandaged head.

Takeda has that too. 'Nakamura,' he chirps. 'I've got his name card in my desk drawer.'

'Get it!'

Takeda gets it, hands it to the one with the mirror shades. He scans it, then points at the phone.

'Call him now,' he says. 'Ask him when the photos are going to be ready.'

In fact, Takeda had been wondering whether to do that for the past few days. After all, he is entitled to a complimentary edition of the finished product. He dials the number. It rings a dozen times without reply.

'No one there,' he says lamely.

'Give it to me,' roars mirror shades. He snatches the phone, dials. After half a minute his face suddenly clenches like a fist.

'What did you say?' he roars into the phone. 'Go away and die!'

With that, he tears the receiver free of its cable and hurls it against the wall. The casing shatters. The others gaze at him in amazement. Mirror shades ignores them, turns to Takeda.

'You idiot,' he snarls. 'That was the number of a phone booth in Ueno Park!'

The one with the nose-splint is still puzzled. 'You mean this Nakamura guy gave a fake phone number,' he says.

'His name isn't Nakamura, you brain-rotted monkey! If he fakes his phone number, he fakes his name as well. That's obvious, isn't it?'

Mirror shades is bellowing like a crazed man. Takeda doesn't move. He just squats there in front of the mound of fertilizer wondering how much of it he'll be forced to eat. Of course the name card was fake. He should have realized that. After all, wasn't the guy using some other name too? What was it the girl called him as they were leaving the shop? Takeda thinks back frantically, replays the scene frame by frame.

There's the woman, standing in the doorway – big hair, big earrings, dark areolae tight under her T-shirt . . .

123

Mirror shades sucks deep breath through his teeth. He gazes down at Takeda, ugly hate in his face.

'You lied to me,' he hisses.

Then the guy walks up to the woman, bends down, lifts her off her feet ...

'What shall we do with him?' says the one with the nose-splint, prodding Takeda with his toe.

'Shall I get the weedkiller?' says the one with the bandaged head.

Big eyes flash anger. Slingbacks slice the air. Tropical lips spitting hot words ...

'No weedkiller,' says mirror shades. 'You two hold him. You get me that hedge-cutter over there ...'

The bald one lifts the hedge-cutter off the shelf, scissors the gleaming blades in front of Takeda's face.

Hot words? What words? Takeda closes his eyes, tries to focus one last time before the scene slips away. But already rough hands are reaching under his armpits, hauling him upwards. A wail rises from the depths of Takeda's being.

'Let go of me, Mori-*san!*'

Mirror shades jabs a forefinger into his adam's apple. 'Mori-*san?* What are you talking about, tofu-head?'

'Mori,' squawks Takeda. 'The man's name is Mori!'

Even mirror shades takes pause at that. Takeda's manner is unmistakably that of a man who is telling the truth.

Mori eats lunch at a conveyor-belt sushi place on the southside of Shinjuku station. The quality's not great, but with all dishes two hundred and fifty yen a pop what can you expect? What Mori likes is the attitude of the cook, who is silent and efficient and treats every customer the same. This is because he's a robot, a couple of metallic hands that grasp, slice, and squeeze all day long. So he doesn't have magazine articles about himself stuck on the wall and make you listen to his anecdotes. He doesn't make up the bill according to his mood. He doesn't display a temperament to match movie director Kurosawa's. He gives you peace and quiet.

Mori chews peace and quiet, two thousand yen's worth, a little rubbery. After that he spends half an hour in a dingy jazz coffee-bar – unlimited refills for three hundred yen, Miles, Mingus, Stan Getz. Then he goes into a pachinko parlour where he knows the machines well, buys two trays of silver balls. His concentration is off today. The balls have almost all gone when he gets one right into the central tulip. It springs open then, remarkably, stays open long enough for him to slot another half-dozen balls straight between the gaping petals. His own accuracy astonishes him. The machine flashes, chimes, starts puking silver balls. Enough of them to buy conveyor-belt sushi every day till the end of the month. Mori leaves the place triumphant, filled with new faith. Faith in himself. Faith in the pachinko industry. Faith in the universe. There's always a special spot hidden somewhere. You've just got to locate it and all the barriers open up, all the silver balls flow straight to their destination.

Back at the office, Mori goes to the cabinet, pulls out the Miura file that he made this morning. The Miura case deserves its own file because it's a real case now. The contents of the envelope that Shima gave him last night make that clear. If Mori plays this one right – as sweetly as he played that pachinko machine – there's a good chance of pocketing that special bonus that Kimiko Itoh dangled in front of him.

The file is pretty slim so far: just a few pages of his own scribbled notes; Shima's envelope; the original police report of Miura's death. Mori picks out the envelope, goes through the contents again.

Two pages of typescript – photocopies from police

records. The first page describes a complaint made by Miura's wife: telephone harassment by persons unknown. The date of the complaint: early Febrary, just about the time Kimiko Itoh noticed that Miura was acting edgy. According to the note on the next page, the police immediately requested the phone company to monitor the line. Apparently there was only one more call after that. Finally there's a copy of a letter from Miura's wife saying that she's deeply grateful for the fine work of the police, she's satisfied that the harassment is now over, and she doesn't want any more valuable resources to be wasted on such a trivial matter. The date on the letter: four days before Miura's death.

So it looks as if half of Kimiko's suspicions are right. Miura did have reason to be scared. But the other half are probably wrong. Miura's wife wouldn't be involved in the harassment. On the other hand she must know more of the circumstances of her husband's death than what appeared in the official report. The next step, then, should be to look a little closer at this whole incident. Is there any way to find out more about the anonymous phone calls? Yes, there is a way.

The way's name is Takeshi Shinohara and he's a mid-ranking executive at Nippon Telephone and Telegraph. Five years ago there was a problem with his daughter. Emi Shinohara got sucked into one of the religious cults that are springing up like bamboo shoots. In double quick time they drained her mind and her bank account. Then they got her going on the accounts of the design studio where she was working. Bringing in the police would probably have ended Shinohara's career and his daughter's marriage prospects. So he went to Mori instead.

Mori calls Shinohara, asks some hypothetical questions

about nuisance calls. Shinohara explains how the monitoring system works. Mori asks if the calls are recorded. Shinohara says yes. Mori asks how long the tapes are kept. Shinohara says they don't use tapes any more. Everything is digital these days. Everything's in a computer somewhere. Mori asks if what goes into the computer can be got out without too much trouble. Of course, laughs Shinohara. That's the whole point, isn't it? Mori stops the hypothetical. He tells Shinohara exactly what he wants.

Head down, Mitchell marches through the drizzle. He is trying to do the impossible: to walk faster than the rest of the crowd that is surging across the multi-flow complex of zebra crossings. He bangs into wet shopping bags, takes umbrella jabs in the side of the neck, squeezes between shoulders and elbows – all because he is late for an important meeting. At three-thirty Mitchell is due to give a TV interview to World Business Network. The subject: the Japanese video-game industry. His fellow interviewee: slick Scott Hamada of Silverman Brothers.

Television interviews are an important part of a financial analyst's job these days – they help build 'profile'. World Business Network has good coverage, syndicating to media companies all over the world. An interview like this will probably be shown in airports and hotels all over South-East Asia, on cable in the US, on satellite in Europe, on in-flight video on planes criss-crossing the globe, on stock price terminals in every major financial centre. So it's an ideal forum for Mitchell, a chance for him to transmit his bullishness on SoftJoy to all corners of the world. The only problem: he has never appeared on TV before.

He gets to the studio late, wet, sticky in body and mind. A cute girl asks him if he wants to be made up. No, he says. Then yes. Then no again. The set is unbelievably small and tacky, just a plywood desk with a few chairs behind it. Mitchell sits down, faces the bank of TV cameras. On one side of him sits the interviewer, short hair, sexy in an elfin sort of way. On the other sits Hamada, his face covered with a patina of orange powder. He's wearing silver collar studs (collar studs!) and a tie that oozes hand-knit designer expensiveness. He gives Mitchell a friendly wink. Friendly – who does he think he's kidding? This is war.

A mike is fitted to Mitchell's lapel. He is told not to touch it, not to stare at the camera, not to rock his chair up and down. The director counts down the opening. Mitchell scratches his nose, wonders what to do with his hands. He runs through his opening sentences, all of which sound clumsy, profoundly dull-witted . . .

'Action!'

This is live. People in Hong Kong and Singapore and Australia are actually looking at him right now. Can they tell how much sweat is rolling down his back? How much his nose itches? For one mad moment lurid obscenities flood his mind – sexual perversions, racist slurs. He could say what he liked! No one would be able to stop him in time. He swallows drily, sneaks a sidelong glance at Hamada. The man looks as calm as Buddha.

'Hello, everybody. Welcome to Global Market Trends . . .'

The interviewer chirrups brightly, reciting her words from a teleprompter above one of the cameras. The lights are hot on Mitchell's forehead. His whole face feels as if it is made out of cardboard.

'Today I have with me two experts on the video-game industry – Scott Hamada of Silverman Brothers and Richard Mitchell of West Bavaria Securities. Many people believe that competition will increase dramatically his year and weaker formats will be forced out of the market. What would you say to that, Mr Mitchell?'

Mitchell wants to say that the premise is wrong, that SoftJoy is excellently positioned to recover its previous dominance. But somehow every one of his carefully prepared sentences flies out the back of his head. His mouth opens, but what emerges is a long croaking sound, strange even to his own ears.

'Uggerrr . . . gerrrrrr . . .'

'I'm sorry, Mr Mitchell.'

'Uggerrrr . . .'

The interviewer's smile becomes a rictus. Mitchell's head is throbbing strangely. Maybe he's sick. He grabs at a glass of water on the table, gulps, wipes his mouth with the back of his hand. Which lets Scott Hamada slip into the gap. He holds up a well-manicured forefinger.

'If I could just say something here . . .'

'Certainly, Mr Hamada.'

Her relief is palpable. So is Hamada's glee.

'I think there are three clearly distinct issues that we need to examine here. Point one – the structural problems resulting from . . .'

Mitchell watches in despair. The guy exudes confidence. How does he do it? Maybe it's innate. Maybe American securities analysts are born TV operators, like Scandinavians are born skiers. More likely, Silvermans sends its staff on a media skills programme, with someone like Harrison Ford giving the lessons.

Mitchell tries to butt in, but once Hamada has got going he's impossible to stop. The words keep coming, well cadenced and plausible. And what the words say is that Mega Enterprises is the company to watch. Mega Enterprises is powerful, innovative, is going to develop all sorts of synergies with its Hollywood movie company and its

European satellite broadcasting company. Anyone getting in the way of Mega Enterprises is going to be blasted off the map.

With just a few minutes left to run Mitchell spies an opening. He seizes it, no time for subtleties. The words rush from his mouth.

'Mega's a formidable competitor, no question ... but I think Scott's enthusiasm may have been coloured by the large bond issue that his own company is leading in the Euro markets ...'

See how he likes that – the equivalent of an unprovoked knee to the groin. Mitchell is as good as accusing him of professional dishonesty.

But Hamada isn't ruffled. He gives a little smirk, comes straight back.

'Our relationship with Mega goes back a long, long way. We understand the company very well, and investors who have followed our advice have profited handsomely. On the other hand investors who have chosen to back Mega's competitors have lost out big-time.'

'The trend's already changing,' said Mitchell, cheeks burning. 'Take a look at the shipments projection for the summer ...'

'Forget projections,' cuts in Hamada. 'Let's stick to the facts here, shall we?'

He folds his arms across his chest and pantomimes a sad shake of the head.

'No, the shipments tell the story,' Mitchell blusters on. 'They show quite clearly that ...'

Show what? He pauses, desperately scans his memory. Nothing there! He's clean forgotten. And another gap has opened up for Hamada.

'Here are the realities, folks,' says Hamada crisply. 'Mega's stock price has been one of the best performers in the market this year, reflecting the company's superb fundamentals. Meanwhile, what has happened to the stock price of SoftJoy?'

It sounds like a rhetorical question, but Hamada is gazing straight at Mitchell. The interviewer turns to him expectantly. The camera swivels, its huge black eye staring into his soul. He has to say something, anything.

'Well – uh – you see, I'd say stock is in a consolidation phase. This is a temporary phenomenon – uh – quite healthy actually.'

Now he's open for the knock-out punch. And Hamada delivers it with brutal efficiency.

'But not so healthy for people who bought at over twelve thousand, right? Mega is soaring, SoftJoy is collapsing. That is the market's judgement. And the market ain't wrong. The market is never wrong!'

Mitchell has plenty to say to that. For example, that the market could well be wrong this time, since it has been dominated by the heavy buying of Silverman Brothers itself – for tame mutual funds, for its proprietary book, for the huge pension accounts it has under management. But before he has time to organize his thoughts the elfin interviewer breaks in, thanking them for their valuable insights. One of the staff is standing behind the cameras, holding up a card that says, 'Ten Seconds!'

Mitchell interrupts her savagely. 'Hold on a minute, will you? I've got one last point. Sure, the stock price has entered a consolidation phase, but if you look back over the past two years . . .'

'No time for that now, I'm afraid, Mr Mitchell.'

Another card is being held up now. It says, 'Close Now!'

'The relative performance shows quite clearly that . . .'

Behind the camera people are gesturing frantically for

Mitchell to shut up. He ignores them, ploughs on for a few last incoherent seconds.

'. . . bottoming out . . . great chance to buy more . . .'

'Okay!' yells the director, and the lights go on. It's over, but it's not okay. Mitchell sits there, mouth half-open. Suddenly he knows exactly what to say. He wants to tell people in Hong Kong and Australia and hotels in the Middle East and airports across South-East Asia that SoftJoy's games are the best in the world, that the company is certain to succeed in the end. But there's no chance now. The cameras are dead. The studio is just a dusty room, with Mitchell sitting alone at the plywood table in the middle.

In the past few days the effects of the hot sand therapy have started to wear off. The muscles of Mori's lower back are twisting and hardening again, which makes him walk with a slightly stooping gait, which makes him feel ten years older, which makes him tense and irritable, which makes the muscles in his lower back harden and twist some more. He has plenty of time to kill before meeting Shinohara, so he goes to the bath-house round the corner, spends half an hour soaking muscles, thoughts.

On the way out, he finds a pile of fliers from Mr Problem-Solver lying on the table next to the door. Same message, much better print job this time. Mori turns to the old lady who hands out the towels.

'Where did these come from?' he demands.

She looks up from the hand-held TV that she watches all day long.

'A young man brought them this morning,' she says. 'Very polite and pleasant he was.'

'Really?' says Mori sourly. 'And what did this pleasant young man look like?'

The old lady's mottled brow furrows. 'Well, he looked a little bit like you, Mori-*san*.'

'Like me?'

'Not now, of course. Like you used to look when you first came here.'

Mori nods his thanks. When you're old, you remember what happened twenty-five years ago as if it happened last year. And what happened last year you don't remember at all. There's something enviable about that. Except that when Mori gets to be her age, twenty-five years back will be what is happening now. And there's nothing memorable about what's happening now at all.

Shinjuku is subdued under the low skies, the soft grey rain. Mori tramps up the metal staircase to his office. No high-school kids hanging around the karaoke boxes. The plant-leasing yakuza haven't come back from lunch. On the third floor the premises of the little trading company are as dark and empty as ever, but there's a new sign pasted to the window:

MENTAL REVOLUTION!
LEARN HOW TO CONTROL YOUR LIFE
ACCORDING TO THE STRATEGIC
WISDOM OF GREAT MILITARY LEADERS.
LEARN WILLPOWER! LEARN CREATIVITY!
SPECIAL INTRODUCTORY OFFER OF
15 EASY-TO-FOLLOW VIDEO-TAPES.

Smart idea, thinks Mori. Because people don't really want to control their lives. They want stability and security, and for that they need someone to tell them what to do. Willpower, creativity? Just follow the lessons. Democracy, a liberalized economy? Here's the manual, do what you're told. That's what the system relies on. Works well too, most of the time. Anyway, does anybody really control his own life? Not those great military leaders, that's for sure. They were just whirled along, improvising frantically through all the chaos and slaughter. The winners look back at what happened and call it strategy. As for the losers: whatever they did and thought, nobody cares.

The patterns are invisible, ever-shifting.

Control is illusion.

Battle is improvisation.

Back in his office Mori sits down at his desk, traces Mr Problem-Solver's address on the map. It's not far away, just ten minutes on the Honda. He picks up the phone, gives him a call.

'Are you well today, Mr Problem-Solver? I hope so, because I'm coming round to see you right away.'

'Please feel free to visit at any time,' says the voice at the other end. 'The best prices and services in the country are guaranteed.'

'Liar,' says Mori.

'What's that?' squawks Mr Problem-Solver. 'Who are you anyway, and what is the nature of your problem?'

'I'm Mori,' says Mori. 'And my problem is you.'

Mr Problem-Solver's office is above a noodle shop in a tiny 'pencil building' with a tiled façade of nose-bleed red. The building is more modern than Mori's, but also more cramped and somehow more temporary-looking. The elevator is not large enough to open an umbrella in. The little window on the third floor looks out on the blank concrete of the flyover ramp, close enough to reach out and touch. Presumably you get used to the vibrations and the fumes after a while.

'Mr Problem-Solver – Economic and Social Research' reads the sign on the door. And underneath, 'Knock Before Entering'. Mori knows a sign very similar to that, the one attached to the door of his own office.

134

Originality is clearly not one of Mr Problem-Solver's strengths.

He knocks and enters at the same time. Mr Problem-Solver looks up from his desk.

'Come in,' he says.

'I am in,' says Mori.

What Mori was expecting – a bullish young tough, probably a college judo champ or something like that. What he sees – a slightly effeminate guy with a shy smile and hair flopping down over his eyes. What could the old lady in the bath-house have been thinking of? Mori could never have looked like that, no matter how far back you went.

'Good to see you,' says Mr Problem-Solver, getting to his feet. 'My name is Uno.'

He's actually quite tall, and well muscled around the shoulders. Mori turns away, glances around the room. In the bookcase: row after row of manga comic books, lurid science-fiction stuff. On top of it: a CD player and a stack of CDs, all trendy rock bands with nonsensical names.

'Listen – how old are you?' says Mori.

'Twenty-one,' says Uno, without hesitation. It sounds as if he was expecting the question.

'Twenty-one!' explodes Mori. 'That's much too young!'

'So how old were you when you started out?'

Mori ignores that piece of impudence.

'You should be at college,' he says.

'I quit at the beginning of last year,' says Uno, flicking the hair out of his eyes.

'What were you studying?'

'European literature.'

Mori purses his lips. 'That's good stuff. You shouldn't have quit. You'll never get the chance again.'

'The teachers were useless. I wasn't learning anything.'

'You'd have learned more from them than you'll ever learn in this place.' Mori waves his hand around the room.

'Not so,' says Uno, frowning slightly. 'I think I can learn a lot here.'

'A lot about what?'

Uno looks embarrassed. 'A lot about life,' he says.

Mori sits down heavily on the sofa. He slaps his hand on his thigh, and guffaws with laughter.

'Why is that so funny?' asks Uno, genuinely puzzled.

'It's not really,' says Mori, and starts laughing all over again.

They drink coffee, talk about European literature. Uno's an intelligent guy, surprisingly well read. His favourite writers are Italian post-modernists that Mori has never come across. Mori tries to explain what he gets out of his own favourites, Camus, Kafka, Thomas Mann.

The walls vibrate as trucks roar along the flyover. Down on the ground floor the waitress yells out the noodle orders, one of which prompts Mori to look at his watch. Unbelievably he's been here half an hour already. He gets to his feet, picks up his helmet. Doing so, he notices something in the cupboard next to the coffee-jar. A silver trophy. It makes him think of the one he keeps at home, University Karate Champion, 1972.

'You win that?' he asks Uno.

'That's right. The year before last.'

Mori nods approvingly.

'Nice work. And you're still carrying on now?'

'I had to give up,' says Uno with a sigh. 'I did something to my elbow. It more or less ruined my backhand.'

Mori stares at him blankly for a moment, then makes for the door. No resemblance there, none whatsoever.

It takes Mori forty five minutes to get down to the Ginza. Shinohara is already waiting for him at the specified place, the menswear section of Mitsushima Department Store. In fact, when Mori arrives Shinohara is in the process of trying on a dapper fawn raincoat. Mori glances at the price ticket. Six hundred thousand yen, the price of a brand-new Honda.

'You're not thinking of buying that, are you?' he asks, horrified.

'Maybe,' says Shinohara. 'Somebody passed some gift coupons on to me. I've got to spend it somehow.'

Got to spend it somehow, words that Mori has never been able to utter in his life. The mighty river of yen continues to pass him by. As for Shinohara: since they met last, he has been going up in the world. He is now head of a division responsible for equipment procurement and installation.

They chat briefly, then Shinohara hands him an envelope. Mori squints inside – a couple of sheets of type script.

'That's good,' he says with a smile. 'After what you told me, I was expecting a memory disc or something like that.'

'You can have one if you want,' says Shinohara, buckling the belt of the raincoat. 'What kind of sound system have you got on your computer?'

'I haven't got a computer.'

Shinohara adjusts the lapels of the raincoat, draws himself up to full height.

'Then you're better off with the text,' he says. 'It's totally reliable, produced by our own voice recognition software. Still, if you need the actual recording, I can get it for you.'

'Don't bother,' says Mori. 'I've got what I need here.'

He leaves Shinohara preening himself in front of the mirror. The envelope he wraps up and puts in his jacket pocket. What does the typescript say? Mori kills the thought, doesn't even touch the envelope until he gets back to the office. Some kind of detective superstition – look too hastily, not giving full attention, and the only real clue in the case might just dissolve into nothing.

Nine

It doesn't dissolve into nothing. It leaps out from the page and grabs him by the throat. Mori sits at his desk, guzzles a glass of Suntory White, relives a three-month-old conversation between a dead man and his tormentor.

MIURA: Hello! Is anybody there?

CALLER: It's almost time now, Deputy Vice-Minister

MIURA: You again! What do you want?

CALLER: We know all about you, everything you've done.

MIURA: I don't know what you're talking about.

CALLER: Did you think you were going to get away with it? Did you think you were too important to fall?

MIURA: Listen, I don't know who you are, but maybe we should meet soon. You've obviously got some mistaken impression of me.

CALLER: Meet? Do you think I'm stupid?

MIURA: I just want to clear things up.

CALLER: Well, I'll let you into a secret. We have met, many times already.

MIURA: What do you mean?

CALLER: We met last night for example. You didn't notice me, of course.

MIURA: Really?

CALLER: Yes, really. I was sitting opposite you in the train. It was the ten-thirty from Kasumigaseki station.

At the other end, you took a taxi to your house, as you usually do. Before getting the taxi you dropped into a convenience store and bought a weekly magazine and a packet of cigarettes. The cigarettes were Seven Stars, your favourite brand.

MIURA: You must be crazy.

CALLER: But not crazy enough to carry on talking to you for any longer. I expect the police are going to be here any minute.

MIURA: Who are you? Tell me.

CALLER: You can call me Black Blade. Revenge is my game. Goodbye, Deputy Vice-Minister. It's almost time.

MIURA: What? Wait a moment!

CALL OVER.
CALL ORIGINATED: PUBLIC PHONE-BOX IN
TOKYO STATION.
TIME: 9.30 a.m. SATURDAY 5 MARCH

Mori swills down the Suntory, pours himself another. This is disturbing stuff. Firstly, because the caller is no ordinary nuisance-maker. He's investing plenty of time and trouble in his programme of harassment. Secondly, because just two days after this call Miura sent his letter to the police asking for the monitoring to be ended. Why would he do that? From the look of the conversation he seemed worried enough at the time. With good reason, too. Black Blade? Revenge is my game? It sounds childish, but also pretty scary.

Mori opens the filing cabinet, dumps the transcript in the Miura file, together with a record of his expenses and some scribbled notes. The notes are mainly questions. And so far the answer to every question has thrown up more questions, more concealment. But it's a real case, no doubt about that. From now on it deserves his undivided attention.

The phone rings: Shima.

'There's a problem,' he says. 'We've got a foreign woman down here who keeps asking for you.'

'Asking for me? What for?'

'She claims you've got her passport.'

'Ah – that woman!'

'What's this all about, Mori? Are you running a side business or something?'

'I can explain,' says Mori. 'I'll be there right away.'

When Angel walks into a bar, the place gets noisier, livelier. When she laughs, other people laugh too. When she gets angry, the others go small.

Always remember your friends – that's what her father told her. Remember your enemies too – that's what her mother told her. Her father was killed in a street-fight when she was nine years old, beaten to death like an animal. Her mother has seventeen grandchildren.

Tonight Angel is with her friends. The doctor's gone to Los Angeles for a medical conference, leaving Angel enough pocket-money for the next two weeks. Except that Angel's not going to keep the money for the next two weeks. Most of it she intends to blow over the next two days – on meals with her friends, presents, movies, lots of fun. If she needs some more, she knows how to get it, quite fast and safe.

They are in a little restaurant in Ogikubo, six of them, all good friends. There's plenty of spicy food, a karaoke machine with songs in eight different languages. Angel is happy to see their faces as they gossip, joke, croon gleeful imitations of singers unknown in Japan. The other girls need a night like this. They are going through tough times,

141

no one like the doctor to take care of them. Instead they have to deal with stupid chimpira, dirty nightclubs in the middle of nowhere, cheap-charlie customers, up to a dozen a night. Angel looks at the woman holding the microphone now. Estelle has been in this city for three years, illegal the whole time. She's just a couple of years older than Angel, but tonight she looks middle-aged. Three months ago she said she'd found a good guy, the manager of a pink salon in Nagoya. It turns out the guy threw her out soon after, didn't even pay her wages. Now she looks so pale, used up somewhere deep inside.

The bar is crowded, noisy. Someone walks in, takes a seat behind her, but Angel is having too good a time to pay any attention.

'Hey, isn't this a famous sexy girl?' A voice in English, just a couple of feet behind her. Angel knows it. She turns round to face her enemy.

'I hear many people looking for you, Angel. When they find you, maybe you don't look so sexy no more.'

Chen-li: tall girl from Shanghai. Beside her a Chinese guy, thin face, hard eyes. Chen-li knows everybody, everything. Chen-li makes introductions, takes commissions. Chen-li supplies stuff that keeps you going, night after night. It's free when you don't want it. When you do want it, she makes you pay big.

'Where's my money?' says Angel, banging her hand on the table. She feels a hot bubble of anger swelling within her.

Chen-li purses her lips: born actress. 'What money?' she says.

'You know what I mean,' says Angel. 'Those two perverts.'

She doesn't want to think about it. They tied her up, hurt her. The cigarette burns took weeks to heal.

142

'I reckoned those guys were just right for you,' says Chen-li, dipping her chopsticks into the noodle bowl.

'What do you mean by that?' says Angel, getting to her feet. The hot bubble is about to burst. She can feel it.

'You enjoy too much,' says Chen-li, grinning. 'You enjoy try anything, right?'

Angel's rule: when you're ready, don't say anything. Move before anyone realizes what's happening. The Chinese guy doesn't realize what's happening. He looks up curiously as Angel puts her hand under the tablecloth, lifts it with a jerk. Bowls, knives, chopsticks go flying.

'*Yayee!*' shouts Chen-li as the hot soup pours into her lap. Angel gives her no time, dives across the table, hands closing around her neck. The chair topples. The two women roll on to the floor. Somewhere behind, Angel's friends are yelling encouragement. She hardly hears them. Chen-li does girl-fighting, kicking and biting. Angel punches her in the face, hard. Chen-li grunts in pain. Now the Chinese guy is wrapping an arm around Angel's neck, pulling her upwards. Angel twists free. She grabs a noodle bowl off the table and smashes it across the side of his head. Flying through the air – noodle broth, blood, fragments of porcelain. The Chinese guy's head thumps the floor. She thinks about hitting him again, decides against it. He's not getting up for a while.

'Knife! She's got a knife.'

Chen-li crouches a couple of yards away, something gleaming in her hand. A stream of bright blood is running from her nose.

'Come on, sexy girl,' she snarls.

Angel waits for the moment, one hand resting on a stool. Chen-li takes a deep breath, comes rushing, knife slashing. Angel picks up the stool, hurls it in her face. Chen-li goes down. Angel dances around her, stamps on her knife hand.

The knife goes skidding. Angel bends down, knees in her back, winds a hank of hair around her hand. Now – time to make sure. Angel hauls the woman upright, leads her across the room. Chen-li squeals, scared, pleading. Angel pulls her down, smashes her head on the wooden table, once, twice –

'That's enough.'

The cook has come out of the kitchen. He stands in the doorway, a meat-cleaver in his hand. Angel knows him. In fact, she did some things he wanted, a long time ago when there wasn't enough money for good food.

'Hey, sorry,' says Angel.

'Get out of here straight away. All of you.'

No one is going to argue. The Chinese guy gets unsteadily to his feet, puts a hand-towel to his bleeding scalp. Chen-li is lying across the table, half-conscious, hair soaked in beer and noodle broth. Angel reaches into her pocket, pulls out her wallet. Forty thousand yen, just what she was promised for the session with the two guys. The wallet has another pocket, inside it one hundred thousand yen wrapped tight in polythene.

'How about a loan, Chen-li?' she coos into her ear. Chen-li snuffles blood and noodles. Angel takes the money, stuffs it into the back pocket of her jeans: half for Estelle; half for the cook.

Take care of your friends.

Take care of your enemies too.

The problem comes later. The salaryman customers got out of there as soon as the fight started. One of them must have called the police because the street outside is full of sirens and flashing lights. Cops grab the girls, yell questions. The girls yell back in Thai, Vietnamese, Portugese. The cops make them go back into the restaurant. The place is a mess, but Chen-li and her boyfriend have disappeared. The cook says he was in the kitchen, didn't see what happened. The cops are angry. They were expecting shootings, stabbings, gang warfare. What they got: jabbering women; broken plates on the floor. They need to save face. They need to have something official. So they grab Angel, demand her passport, place of residence, place of work. When the answers don't come, they take her back to the police station, lead her inside like a prize hostage. Their smiles say it all: you don't get one like this every night.

Mori gets down to the police station at nine o'clock. Shima's not there, but Mori knows he'll have put in some words. The rest is ritual. And ritual always has to be observed correctly.

They put him in a room, make him wait ten minutes. The two patrolmen that brought in Angel appear, say they are thinking of charging her.

'What's the offence?' says Mori.

'We haven't decided yet,' says one of the patrolmen.

He explains. According to the anonymous caller, there was violence and intimidation. But the anonymous caller has disappeared. The victims of the violence have disappeared. There are no witnesses who make any sense.

The other patrolman scratches his head.

'Many problems with foreigners these days,' he says. 'That puts a lot of pressure on us, you know. People want results.'

The man's drift is clear. 'People' means bureaucrats in the police agency. 'Results' means a good healthy uptrend in arrests, with underperforming police stations likely to suffer the consequences in next year's budget.

Mori nods in sympathy. 'These are difficult times,' he says.

'This woman wasn't carrying her passport,' the cop continues. 'That's illegal for a foreigner, you know.'

145

Mori flashes the passport, comes up with a story about Angel being an honours student who has come to Japan to further her deep interest in the economy and culture. The police don't believe it, of course, but that doesn't matter. What's important to them is that an acquaintance of Shima is prepared to come down and spin such a story on Angel's behalf.

They lead him into the interrogation room. Angel is sitting in a wooden chair, elbows on the table, sulky-bored.

'You've caused everyone a lot of trouble,' says Mori sternly. 'I want you to make a full apology.'

Her eyes flash rebelliously. 'Hey, I've done nothing bad! Who says Angel has done something bad? There's no proof at all!'

Mori winces, glances at the two expressionless cops. 'You don't understand, do you? It's not a question of proof. These are the police.'

'But I don't admit any bad thing!'

Mori bends down, mutters in her ear. Remember this: in Japan apologizing and admitting are two complete different things.

'Now apologize,' he says, taking a pace back. 'Do it right, will you?'

Angel does it right. She undoes a couple of buttons, stands up and gives a nice big bow, letting her shirt hang loose to show plenty of cleavage. It's just a gesture, but the cops appreciate it.

'All right, Mori,' says one of them. 'We're going to let her off this time.'

'We just need someone to guarantee that she behaves all right. You'll do that, won't you?'

Angel look at him, smiles her big smile.

'Of course,' says Mori, and leads her out of there before she does something to change their minds.

146

What can you guarantee about a woman like Angel? Nothing, except that she's always going to be trouble for someone. Mori intends to make sure that next time it isn't going to be him.

Outside on the street he hands her the passport, tells her to take the next plane home. She nods – big grin, raindrops glinting in her frizzy hair.

'Thanks for helping me,' she says. 'You good guy, Mori-*san*.'

'Not a pig, right?'

'Not a pig at all. You better than the doctor, even.'

Suddenly she puts her hands around his neck, gives him a hug. Lithe muscles stretch against him, a body temperature higher than his own. Mori closes his eyes, breathes in heavy female warmth. Already his resolution is melting.

But Angel pulls away.

'I have to go now,' she says. 'My friends are waiting for me. Maybe next time, okay?'

'Maybe,' says Mori.

Angel crosses the road, heels clicking across the wet tarmac. When she's gone, the night seems quieter, slower, smaller.

Mori rides home on the Honda. His back muscles are in worse shape now, locking into a hard aching mass that sends twinges up into his left shoulder. There's a blind masseur who operates from a room above a pachinko parlour, quite close to the station. Mori decides to drop in. As usual the conversation is disconcerting.

Mori sits cross-legged on the floor. The masseur stands behind him, thumbs digging into his clavicles.

'You need to drink more water, Mori-*san*,' he mutters. 'Your ears are starting to stick out.'

'My ears?' says Mori, frowning.

'That's right,' says the masseur. 'It's a sign of ageing. A

newborn baby's body is mostly water. An old man's body is dry.'

'You're saying I'm turning into an old man?'

The masseur grunts assent. 'The process actually happens in the kidneys, but it shows up first in the ears. They dry out and start curling up like dead leaves.'

Mori sits pondering that while fingers like steel pegs knead his back muscles into submission.

'You are worrying much,' continues the masseur. 'That is why your body twists into these painful shapes. What is it that worries you?'

Mori shakes his head. 'I don't know – money problems, I suppose.'

'You should stop worrying about money. Old men think about money more than sex. Young men think about sex more than money.'

'Really?' says Mori uneasily. 'Is it thinking about money that makes you get old? Or is it getting old that makes you think about money?'

The masseur is using his elbow now, grinding small circles into the small of Mori's back.

'Both, of course,' he said. 'Body affects mind, mind affects body.'

'So what should I do?'

'Think about money less. And drink more water, Mori-san. If you don't, your genitals will dry up like dead leaves too!'

At this the masseur cackles with laughter. He has a strange sense of humour.

When the session is over, Mori goes home, cooks himself a swordfish steak. Watching it sizzle, he thinks about what the masseur said. Money – sure, it's looming larger. In the old days Mori never wanted it, never did anything to get it. But he never wanted to have no money either. He just assumed that some – not a great amount, just a sufficiency – would always be there somehow. He doesn't assume that any more, not since the price of the apartment he bought in 1992 went into continuous freefall. His life savings are in this apartment, a thirty-year loan too. How can you stop thinking about money problems when you're destined to sleep inside an enormous one for the rest of your life?

The swordfish is chewy, salty, plenty of juice. Mori thinks about women, one in particular. Tonight he doesn't drink whisky. He drinks half a litre of water instead.

Besides Angel there are five other girls in the big circular bed. They are laughing chatting munching spicy crackers watching a Jackie Chan video on the high-definition TV set. In the living room another half-dozen girls are dancing to the latest Michael Jackson album. Feet pound the floor. Sometimes there comes a sound of furniture toppling or plates smashing, but that doesn't matter. Everything will be cleared up, as good as new by the time the doctor gets back. Good luck is for sharing, Angel believes. Good luck is for having fun.

Angel likes men. But spending a lot of time alone with one man, no matter how smart he looks or how nice he talks – that gets boring quickly. Men are so moody and proud, obsessed with sex. Women understand how to enjoy themselves properly. Look at Estelle there. Listen to her laugh as she tries on that jacket, the one the doctor bought for Angel in Singapore. Her face lights up, and she prances around like a fourteen-year-old girl. Everyone else laughs too. Despite everything that's happened to her, Estelle knows how to have a good time.

'Hey, Angel!' calls one of the girls from the lounge. 'Maybe you should marry this guy and settle down. Then we could have a party here every night!'

'Right!' says Estelle. 'That would be great, wouldn't it?'

Angel nods, takes a swig of beer from the bottle. But maybe it wouldn't be so great, she thinks. What makes it great now is that it can't be done all the time? Because this isn't her place, isn't her city, isn't her country. One day she'll go back to her own place in her own city, and she'll make sure that her children never need to come here, never need to have someone like the doctor taking care of them. They won't have fun like this, won't need to.

'Estelle!' she shouts. 'There's a velvet jacket in one of those drawers. Why don't you try it on?'

Ten

Tokyo station: the biggest, busiest, ugliest in the country, maybe in the whole world. Every morning a million somnambulist salarymen traipse through its catacombs. They don't need to open their eyes. They have microwave receivers implanted in their skulls, digital mapping on the insides of their eyelids. But if you don't have access to the data, you could get lost in this maze of corridors, tunnels and staircases. You could end up walking for the rest of your life.

Today being Saturday, the crowds are a little slower, a little less dense. Still, rush hour is rush hour, and Mori struggles against the flow, moving inwards and sideways when everyone else is moving out. There are hundreds of public phones in this station – on platforms, at noodle-stands, next to the banks of ticket-machines. Mori has no idea from which one Miura's nuisance call was made. The only way to find out is to check them all.

It takes him an hour to find it – at the back of a newspaper kiosk on the central concourse. There are three phones together, old models that take coins, not cards. The people using them now have their backs turned to the human river behind them, their hands cupped to their ears to ward off the blaring din of loudspeaker announcements. They are oblivious to all around them, and the surging

151

crowds are oblivious to them. Nobody would recall anything about this scene at all.

This is the place from which the man who identified himself as Black Blade made his last intimidating call to Miura's house. Black Blade? That's a strange name, the sort of thing you might find in a manga comic book. 'Revenge is my game,' he'd said. Again that's a childish sort of threat, hardly something you could take seriously. If it weren't for the fact that Miura is dead, it would be laughable.

The office girl who has been using the phone slams the receiver down on the cradle and turns round, hoisting her bag on her shoulder.

'Excuse me,' says Mori.

She raises her eyes and looks through Mori as if he weren't there. It's the look that everyone gives everyone else in a place like this. For if you really looked into all the faces that confronted you, if you tried to read every expression, the effort would make you sea-sick.

On the spur of the moment Mori picks up the phone, dials the number of Miura's house. Five rings, then she answers. Mori says nothing, puts the phone down. Then he picks it up and does it again.

'Who's there?' says Mrs Miura. Mori glances to either side. The people using the other phones are paying absolutely no attention.

'My name is Black Blade,' he says, trying to make it sound as sinister as possible.

'You again!' She doesn't sound as surprised as he was expecting.

'That's right,' says Mori. 'I haven't gone away, you know.'

'Your voice is different.'

Mori puts his hand over the receiver. 'Revenge is my game,' he intones.

'What about our offer? Isn't it enough money for you?'

152

Offer? What offer? Mori pauses for a moment.

'I need to think about it more,' he says finally.

'Why don't we meet? I can explain everything.'

'Meet?' says Mori, surprised.

'You choose the place and time.'

She sounds suspiciously confident. Someone has been coaching her, thinks Mori.

'Shinjuku station,' he says. 'Seven o'clock tonight – in front of the pedestrian tunnel on the west side.'

'Wait – how will I know you?'

Mori thinks fast. 'I'll be carrying a red travel bag, with the JAL logo on the side.'

Then he puts down the phone before she has time to ask any more questions. On either side of him office girls natter away in worlds of their own.

Mori goes back to his office, lets some coffee work on his synapses, mulls over what he knows. Miura told the police that the problem with nuisance calls was over, no need to continue the monitoring. But it wasn't over. There had been other contacts, quite recent too, from the sound of things. Mrs Miura had offered the caller money, was expecting him to accept it. Why would she offer money to a man who might have killed her husband? Only one possible answer to that: to keep him quiet. The caller had dangerous information of some sort, information that could still do damage. 'Revenge is my game,' he'd said. Revenge for what? More questions leading to other questions. More murk.

Mrs Miura would be waiting for him at the station this evening. Probably with a couple of dozen detectives lurking in the shadows. Mori thinks, This is a good way to get arrested for murder and extortion. He also thinks, It's maybe the only way to find out what's really going on. He needs to be there tonight. He needs to have back-up, someone reliable who knows nothing about the case at all.

On the spur of the moment, he picks up the phone and calls Mr Problem-Solver. Is Uno the kind of guy to be sitting in his office on a Saturday morning in the vain hope that someone is going to call through with some business? He is. And today he's right. For once someone is going to give him some business on a Saturday morning. Mori smiles as he puts the phone down. Long ago he too used to come in to work every Saturday morning, just like millions of other employees of small- and medium-scale companies all over the country. In those days, Mori thought that the more time you put in, the more diligent you were, the better the results. He hadn't realized then that it's not a question of hours and effort. Because, in the end, being a detective is not really a job at all. It's a life.

Mori gets over to Uno's place just before twelve. They talk a bit about baseball, European movies, favourite noodle shops. Like Mori, Uno is strongly anti-Giants. Like Mori, he prefers Buñuel to Bergman. Unlike Mori, he can't take his noodles too spicy.

Then Mori gets to the point.

'You say you offer the lowest rates in the country, right?'

'Right,' says Uno cautiously.

'So what if a client asked you for two hours' work this evening, a simple observation job.'

'Simple observation? Hmmm ... fifteen hundred yen an hour.'

'And what if someone else – me, for example – were quoting twelve hundred?'

'Then I'd do it for eleven-fifty.'

'You wouldn't turn it down?'

Uno shook his head vigorously. 'I don't turn anything down. I've got to build up a reputation in this business somehow.'

Mori smiles at that one. What kind of reputation is there

in staking out love-hotel car parks or scouring the backgrounds of happily engaged couples in the hope of finding a bankruptcy or a rare blood disease?

'Eleven-fifty,' he muses. 'That sounds very reasonable. You've got a deal.'

'Fine,' says Uno, nodding enthusiastically. 'Who is this client, by the way?'

'Me,' says Mori, moving towards the door. 'Come on – some preparations are going to be necessary.'

There's a man called Jiro – nobody is sure of his family name, maybe he isn't sure of it himself any more – who's been living around the west exit of Shinjuku station for the past twelve years. Jiro lives in a pre-fabricated structure that he has designed himself. It is highly functional, the use of space being classically parsimonious. The basic materials he has employed – two enormous cardboard boxes, a blue plastic tarpaulin, some hessian matting. From a polythene bag he has created windows. From some string and a square of plywood, he has created a little door that opens and closes. Inside there are piles of books, blankets, a radio, a gas lamp. It is easily the biggest cardboard house in the whole cardboard city that is forever shifting and spreading around the precincts of Shinjuku station. This is unsurprising since Jiro is one of the most senior residents. It is Jiro whom the newcomers consult when they want to know what they may and may not do. It is Jiro whom the charity people warn when city hall is about to start one of its periodic campaigns against the homeless.

Mori knows Jiro. Whenever he passes the cardboard city, they exchange a few words. Jiro's a man of strongly conservative opinions, which he delivers whether anyone is there to listen to them or not. He believes that Japan should re-arm as soon as possible. He thinks that women should walk a few paces behind their men. The state of the world, as revealed in the used newspapers and magazines that he reads all day long, fills him with dismay. Sometimes Mori thinks that it's all an act. Jiro can be pretty alert when he wants to be. A couple of years ago Mori needed some help. Late one night a trading-house executive was beaten up at the taxi-stand, his briefcase stolen. The briefcase contained records of financial transactions between the executive and the female proprietor of a Ginza boutique. The police didn't find any witnesses, but Jiro did. A friend of his living in a nearby doorway not only saw what happened but could even identify the two chimpira responsible. All Mori had to do was to pay them a visit and convince them to give the briefcase back.

Today Mori has another favour to ask Jiro, nothing as complicated as last time. All he wants is for Jiro to rent out his cardboard home for a couple of hours. Jiro is happy to oblige. He gives a short rant on the flaws of the education system, then wanders off clutching the six-pack of beer and yakitori lunchbox that Mori has provided.

Uno gazes in consternation at the cardboard house.

'You're expecting me to get in there? What's the point of that?'

Mori raises a querulous eyebrow. 'Remember – I'm the client. You do what I say.'

'But it's so dirty,' whinges Uno. 'I mean, there are probably fleas!'

'Fleas! That's if you're lucky. What about the poisonous spiders?'

Uno folds his arms, shakes his head. 'This is no joke. I'm not spending two hours in there.'

Mori pokes a finger in Uno's face.

'*Hoi*, are you trying to back out of a job you've accepted? That's no way to build a reputation, is it? Once you've agreed to take something on, you've got to follow it through to the end.'

Uno takes a step back, surprised by the anger in Mori's voice.

'I'm not trying to back out,' he says. 'I was just wondering if there wasn't a different way.'

'There's no different way,' says Mori gruffly. 'This is the way I've decided. Now shut up and go and get changed.'

He hands Uno a bag containing a torn undershirt, a paint-flecked windcheater and some shapeless polyester trousers. These are Mori's own clothes, at least twenty years old. He keeps a heap of them in the office cupboard, uses them for intensive trash-sack rooting and other heavy work. Uno puts them on in the toilets. They fit well enough, which is no surprise since Uno is almost exactly the same height and build as Mori.

'Not bad,' says Mori, 'but we need to get you looking a little more realistic.'

They go to an alley around the back of the station. Mori finds a can of coffee, pours it over the windcheater and trousers. Uno winces. Mori slaps him on the shoulder.

'That's just the start,' he says.

There's a heap of trash in a corner of the alley. It contains all that Mori needs. Facial grime is supplied by the tyre of a derelict bicycle. Skin blotches for hands and neck are supplied by grease from the chain.

'Now what about your hair?' muses Mori. 'It looks as if it's just been washed.'

'It has just been washed,' says Uno ruefully. 'I wash it every morning.'

Every morning! That's what the young men of this city are like these days. Super-fastidious, obsessed with germs and smells. It's not surprising the birth rate is plunging.

The last item Mori needs is lying amongst the detritus of

an old lunchbox – a plastic bottle of soy sauce, still half full. He picks it up, squeezes a little lake of sauce into Uno's hair and rubs it in like a barber rubbing in a handful of conditioner.

'Not bad,' he says, stepping back to admire his work. 'Maybe I should be one of those people who work on movie sets. What do you call them?'

'You mean make-up artists,' says Uno, his face streaked with dirt, his hair matted and spiked.

Mori nods. No make-up artist could have done better, given the circumstances. Now it's time for the cameras to roll.

At ten to seven Mori is leaning against a food-counter located a couple of hundred metres from the tunnel entrance. His position offers an excellent view of the suburbs of cardboard city. Jiro's place is directly opposite, though Jiro himself is not at home. Instead, a visitor is making himself comfortable, curling up in the little doorway and scanning the passing crowds with a baleful eye. Mori gobbles octopus dumplings, browses a sports newspaper, occasionally glances over at the tunnel entrance. On the floor beside him is a shopping bag overflowing with Uno's clothes. Underneath Uno's clothes is a red JAL travel bag.

As far as Mori can see, everything looks perfectly normal. The crowds of shoppers stream through the tunnel. The denizens of cardboard city sit beached, remote from the relentless flow of activity going on all around them. Occasionally people stop at the entrance of the tunnel, but it is always to light a cigarette or to peer at a map or to turn and hurry back the way they came. No sign of Mrs Miura, no sign of any police presence anywhere.

Uno stands up and stretches, hands above his head. That is the signal to say the coast is clear. A few seconds later, he sits down again, curls up in the doorway. Uno looks the part. But that's no surprise. Most people would look the part just as well. Because these days the gap between most people and the denizens of cardboard city is no thicker than a sheet of paper. A few pieces of bad luck – a job loss, a family break-up, a few missed loan repayments – and that's where you end up. Time was these homeless were crippled veterans, crazy people, hopeless alcoholics. Not any more. You can see it in their faces – ordinary faces, imprinted with shock and shame at what's happening to them.

Mori waits, sips coffee. A group of street musicians appears from the other end of the tunnel. They form a circle, start clapping hands and jangling guitars. One of them leans a placard against the wall: 'CHRISTIAN ALLIANCE FOR HOMELESS SUPPORT.' They use the English word 'homeless', written in phonetic script. Using foreign words makes things sound different, less personal somehow. One of the musicians has put a hat on the ground for people to throw money into. Nobody throws in any money. People walk by, pretending not to see. Because seeing, really seeing, would be too scary.

Uno gets up, stretches again: all clear. Then Mori sees her, coming from the direction of the big department store on the corner. Mrs Miura is wearing an olive-coloured raincoat and brown suede ankle boots. She passes in front of Mori, no more than ten yards away, walking quickly towards the entrance of the tunnel. The last time Mori saw this woman she was upside down in the alcove of her reception room, playing the part of a human vase. Now she looks brisk, determined. A formidable woman, thinks Mori as he swills down the last of his coffee.

Mrs Miura takes up a position halfway between Uno and the entrance to the tunnel. She stands with her back to the wall, apparently lost in thought. For someone who is on the point of confronting a dangerous killer, she looks remarkably calm. The place that she has chosen to stand is a little surprising – not at the entrance to the tunnel, where she would be easiest to find, but in a sort of recess. Uno gets up, stretches, this time puts his hands above his head twice. That signal says that he is sure that it's okay, that Mori should come over immediately.

Mori surveys the scene, tries to find a pattern in it. There is a pattern hidden somewhere, waiting to emerge. He can sense it from Mrs Miura's tense figure. She doesn't glance around to try and identify the person she is supposed to meet. She doesn't move at all, in fact. Why is that? Answer: because she's been told exactly where to stand. Mori turns, scans behind him, then to either side. No sign of anyone suspicious – just the constant flow of faces, voices, feet, all moving at the same pace, all disappearing into the tunnel. He orders another tray of octopus dumplings, waits another five minutes, munches, watches. Still nothing. Mrs Miura stands stock-still. Uno squats in front of his new home, ready to observe the contact.

It's time. Mori picks up the shopping bag, pulls out the red travel bag. A young salaryman comes rushing towards the counter. Mori hastily covers up the travel bag again. The young salaryman buys a pack of caffeine-flavoured chewing gum.

'Excuse me,' says Mori. 'I wonder if I could ask for a favour. It's a silly thing, really.'

The salaryman turns to Mori, smooth eager face, definitely not a cop.

'What kind of favour? I'm in a hurry, you know.'

'It'll only take a couple of seconds,' says Mori. 'You see that woman over there in the olive-coloured raincoat? She's my wife. I want to give her a surprise for her birthday. If you could just go over and give her this bag...'

'What's inside?' says the salaryman, slipping a stick of chewing gum into his mouth.

Mori scratches his head. 'Well – uh – it's hard for me to say . . .'

'Hard to say!' frowns the salaryman. 'Well, I'm not going to carry a bag for you without knowing the contents. For all I know it could be a bomb!'

He turns to go. Mori puts a hand on his shoulder.

'All right, I'll tell you. Actually, it's underwear. Not the sort you get in an ordinary department store, if you understand what I mean.'

Mori gives a sheepish grin. The salaryman grins right back. 'I understand exactly. All right, I'll do it. But make sure you give her a proper birthday party!'

Mori hands him the red bag. The salaryman hangs it over his shoulder, slips into the crowd. Mori watches the red bag moving towards the tunnel entrance. Is the salaryman going to fulfil his task properly or is he just going to march off with the bag himself? No problem – for better or for worse, salarymen always do as they're told. The red bag passes in front of Uno, the street musicians, then approaches the recess where Mrs Miura is waiting. Mori moves away from the food-stand, cuts through the crowd to a staircase that leads up to ground level. There he takes a few steps, turns and watches.

The salaryman is within twenty metres of Mrs Miura now. He takes the red bag off his shoulder, prepares to hand it over. She doesn't acknowledge him. In fact, she turns away from him, starts walking in the opposite direction, along the wall to where the street musicians are playing.

Except that the four street musicians have stopped playing now. They have put down their guitars and placards and are walking rapidly towards the salaryman. The salaryman stops, shouts something at Mrs Miura. He throws down the red bag, turns toward the tunnel entrance. The street musicians break into a run, shoving shoppers out of their way. The salaryman sees them coming, starts pushing through the crowd himself. But the musicians move faster, scattering people ahead of them. They catch the salaryman at the tunnel entrance, wrestle him to the ground. As if by a single instinct, the crowd clears a space. People turn their heads, gaze down at the tangle of limbs. But they can't stop and watch. The pressure of the moving bodies all around them is too great.

The salaryman is back on his feet now. He seems to be shouting something, gesticulating towards the food-stand. It's a good time to be elsewhere. Mori submerges himself in the human tide pouring up the staircase to the department store.

Half an hour later Mori is back in his office waiting for Uno to call. But Uno doesn't call. Probably gone home to wash, thinks Mori. And then off to some unisex beauty salon to have his pores scrubbed clean and his hair tricked and teased back to shape. For a young guy like Uno that would be a more urgent matter than making a report to his client.

Mori flicks through the evening paper, browses the report of last night's Giants match, then puts a disc on the turntable. Roland Kirk: dead from a stroke at the age of forty-two. The man could play three instruments at the same time – saxophone, clarinet, nose-flute. Mori tried that once when he was a student. It sounded like a mess. The record playing now, Kirk made after his first stroke, when one side of his face was more or less crippled. Somehow he worked out a different embouchure, just kept going till the end. Maybe that's what brought on the second stroke.

Maybe the man was killed by his own music. If so, Mori envies him deeply.

Two hours pass: time enough for Uno to get himself shampooed, manicured, waxed and plucked. When the call finally comes through, Mori's Taipei Rolex points to six o'clock. Uno's words come out in a rush.

'Mori-*san*! Are you there? That was really something, wasn't it? I mean, those guys pretending to be musicians – they fooled everyone, didn't they?'

'They certainly fooled you,' says Mori, sourer than he intends. 'Where've you been anyway?'

'I've been continuing the investigation!'

Uno's voice brims with enthusiasm. Mori's heart sinks.

'You've been doing what? You had no instructions to do anything except observe and report to me. Isn't that what we agreed?'

'Well, that's just what I did,' says Uno. 'I observed and now I'm reporting the results. They could be pretty important too.'

Now he sounds hurt. Mori sighs exasperation.

'What do you mean, important? We saw the same thing, didn't we?'

'We saw the same thing in front of the tunnel. I'm talking about what those guys did next. Where they went.'

'Where they went? You followed them back to the police station.'

'Not a police station,' says Uno archly. 'They weren't cops. Of course, if you're not interested ...'

'I am interested,' snaps Mori. 'Get over to my office as soon as possible.'

Twenty minutes later Mori hears footsteps ringing on the metal stairs. Uno knocks on the door, walks inside. He is still grimy-faced and sticky-haired, still wearing the same stain-spattered clothes. He looks around, nods approval.

'This is a great place,' he says.

Mori follows his gaze – battered sofa, filing cabinet, shelves of books and old jazz albums.

'What's good about it?'

'The atmosphere. It suits you just right, Mori-*san*.'

That's a dubious compliment. Mori has started to hate this office. Every year he decides to find somewhere better: a place with air-conditioning; a Western flush-toilet; sound-proofing good enough to mute the growl of the city. Every year he fails.

He throws Uno a change of clothing, fixes two glasses of Suntory White on the rocks, gets ready to listen. Uno washes, changes, talks.

This is what happened.

The musicians grabbed the salaryman, hauled him towards where the woman was standing. Uno decided to get closer. He stumbled towards them, waving his arms around and singing the national anthem under his breath. Everyone ignored him, the four musicians included. The salaryman was jabbering that he didn't know what they were talking about, that he had been given the travel bag by a guy waiting over at the food-stand. One of the musicians sprinted off to the food-stand to check. He soon came back shaking his head. At that the other musicians shoved the salaryman against the wall and started crowding in on him. It looked like they were trying to intimidate him into confessing. Uno didn't see exactly what happened next, but the salaryman suddenly went limp. In a matter of seconds, a couple of medics appeared with a stretcher and rushed him up the spiral staircase to street level. Uno followed, improvising a rant on the dangers of immigration. He got to the top just in time to see the salaryman being slid into the back of a white station wagon, an oxygen mask clamped to his face.

'Interesting,' says Mori. 'I wonder how they got the ambulance people to co-operate like that.'

'They weren't ambulance people,' says Uno smugly. 'I knew that as soon as I saw them.'

'You did? How?'

'From the hands. The knuckles were all mashed up, just like yours. Now it's possible that one ambulance man might be a karate player. But two at the same time? That's just too much of a coincidence, isn't it?'

Mori nods, impressed. 'Go on,' he says.

'So then the musicians ran past me and got into the ambulance. I asked myself what Mori-*san* would do in these circumstances. Would he just go back to his office and write a report? Probably not, I thought. Mori-*san* would want to know more. Was that the right answer?'

'It was right,' allows Mori.

'So I got into a taxi. The driver took one look at me and told me to get out. I said it was a matter of life and death. I said I was a relative of the sick guy and please follow the ambulance all the way to the hospital. Except that it didn't go to any hospital.'

Uno smiles triumphantly. Mori gives him the question he's waiting for.

'All right, so where did it go?'

'It went right into the centre of the business district, no hospitals anywhere around. Then suddenly it turned into one of those big underground car parks.'

'And then what?'

Uno frowns. 'And then I'm not sure.'

'You're not sure?' explodes Mori. 'You mean, you didn't look any further?'

'Of course I looked further,' protests Uno. 'That's what took me all this time. That car park has got six levels, and I checked every single square metre.'

'But you couldn't find the ambulance?'

Uno gives a shrug. 'That's right,' he says sheepishly. 'I must have missed it somehow.'

Mori swills down the last of the Suntory, leans back in his chair and stares at the ceiling.

'Hey, there's no need to get angry,' says Uno. 'I did my best, didn't I?'

'I'm not getting angry,' says Mori, his gaze fixed on a spot in the middle of the ceiling. 'Where did you say this car park is again?'

'In the business district, right where the head offices of the big trading houses are.'

Mori sucks in air through the side of his mouth. If his suspicions are correct, the Miura case has suddenly taken on a much darker complexion.

Uno turns to the bookcase. 'Look – I can show you on a map if you like.'

'No need for that,' says Mori, getting to his feet. 'Come on, let's go out and eat. What kind of food do you like?'

Uno explains that his preference is for Mediterranean cuisine, nothing too oily, with a carafe of Chardonnay to wash it down. Mori leads him through a urinous alleyway to a tattered awning lit by a couple of paper lanterns. The legend reads 'Dragon's Whisker', and beneath, in faded letters, 'Paradise of Famous Dumplings'.

'Welcome, company president,' shouts the man behind the counter as Mori ducks through the awning. 'What's this? Have you brought your handsome son with you tonight?'

He beams at Mori, his face as round and fat and well steamed as one of the famous dumplings. Mori shakes his head. 'This guy? He's not my son. He's a competitor, keeps undercutting my prices.'

The cook laughs. 'Another company president, then.'

'That's right,' says Uno. 'And one day I'll be competing on quality, just like you.'

They eat dumplings, then more dumplings, then more again. Dumplings fried and steamed. Dumplings containing chicken, shrimp, minced beef, sweet bean jam. Dumplings round, crescent-shaped, pyramidical. Dumplings covered in sesame seeds. Dumplings reeking of garlic. Then they lighten up with egg soup and chopped melon, all the better to be ready for the next plate of dumplings. Alcoholic refreshment: Chinese rice spirit, poured piping hot onto crystals of brown sugar. The bill: non-existent. A few years back Mori helped the owner trace his sixteen-year-old daughter, who disappeared one night after a family quarrel. It took Mori three weeks to find her – living with a chimpira who was using her to pay down his gambling debts. Eri said she would come back only if Mori promised to keep quiet about what had happened. Mori promised. Then she made her father promise to let Mori eat for free. He promised too. In Mori's opinion, Eri would make a good trade negotiator.

After that Mori took Uno to one of the few beer gardens that opens in the rainy season. It's on the roof of a twenty-storey office building not far from Shinjuku Park. There's a stage in the middle of the roof, and in the hot summer evenings they put on mud-wrestling or topless female sumo or striptease games. In the rainy season they rig up a canopy of blue plastic for the benefit of beer drinkers who like to sit and watch the water falling from the sky.

Uno says he doesn't drink beer usually. He says he can't, there just isn't enough space in his stomach. Mori tells him that since they're almost the same build there can't be a real physical reason. Instead, the problem must be psychological, and psychological problems must be challenged straight

167

on. They drink beer. After the first three flagons, Uno reports that it's getting easier.

'We'll have another two,' says Mori. 'After that we can go to a club I know. They've got really nice girls there, junior college students. They'll be all over a trendy young guy like you.'

'No thanks,' says Uno, wiping his forehead with a hot towel. 'I'm not interested in that kind of thing.'

Mori should have guessed before — there's something too neat, too fussy about the guy. He glances from side to side, then leans across the table.

'You mean you're gay,' he whispers.

Uno smiles. 'Does that bother you?'

'Not at all. Some of my best clients have been gay. In fact, it could be a good niche for you to develop. 'The cheapest gay detective in Shinjuku — write that on those fliers of yours and you'll probably get three times as much business.'

Uno takes a deep draught of beer, leaving a moustache of froth on his upper lip. 'Well, I'm sorry to disappoint you, but I'm not gay. The problem is I've got a steady girlfriend.'

Now Mori is really confused. 'Steady girlfriend? So what?'

'So I'm not interested in going to this club you mentioned. This is a serious relationship.'

Mori stares at Uno: bright serious eyes, beer moustache.

'Are you sure you made the right choice of career?' he says.

'I think so,' says Uno. 'We had a thorough, very adult-type discussion on the subject. At first she was opposed, but then she came round to my point of view. And now most of her friends are telling her it's pretty cool to be engaged to a private detective. She's even starting to think like that herself!'

'Engaged!' Mori leans back in his chair, blows out his

cheeks. The idea takes time to sink in. 'Well, at least you've got one benefit there,' he says finally.

Uno looks puzzled. 'What's that?'

'You'll be able to get the pre-wedding investigation done for nothing!'

Mori chuckles at his own joke. Uno doesn't give even a flicker of a smile. He buries his face in the flagon of beer. Mori takes that as a sign that the topic is closed. He orders a plate of split peas, chomps them in silence, shooting them straight from the pod into his mouth. What kind of woman has friends who think it's cool to be engaged to a private detective? Answer: the kind of woman that no private detective should be associated with. Imagine meeting these friends. Imagine their faces, the questions they'd ask.

Uno changes the subject, wants to know more about the incident in front of the tunnel. How did Mori know there was a trap? Instinct, says Mori. It comes with experience. Uno wants to know more. Who was the woman anyway? Why was she so suspicious? Mori explains the principle of client confidentiality. Uno says he understands it well enough, but thinks it shouldn't apply any more.

'After all, I'm working on the case too now,' he says.

'Wait a moment,' says Mori. 'I gave you a specific assignment which is now complete. That's different from working on the case itself.'

Uno belches beer. He's starting to slur his words.

'Give me another assignment, Mori-*san*. I can help you. A complicated murder case like this needs two men, not just one.'

Mori raps his knuckles on the table. '*Ho!* What makes you suppose this case has got anything to do with murder?'

'I don't suppose,' says Uno. 'I know for sure. I have the information.'

'What information?' snaps Mori.

'That's confidential,' says Uno, draining his beer with a smack of the lips.

Mori sighs, raises his gaze to the dark rain falling from the dark sky. 'All right, then,' he says after a pause. 'In that case maybe I will give you another assignment.'

Uno grins in triumph. 'All right, then. In that case maybe I'll tell you what you want to know. It happened when the musician guys had hold of that salaryman.'

Mori leans forward. 'What happened exactly?'

'As I told you, they shoved him up against the wall and started crowding in on him. They were talking in low voices, not loud enough for anyone to hear, but then the salaryman panicked. He yelled out that he hadn't killed anyone, that he had never heard of Miura or Nakanishi. That's when they did whatever they did that knocked him out like that.'

Electricity shoots up Mori's spine, lights a bulb in the back of his skull.

'Say that again,' he breathes.

Uno says it again, twice.

'Now I've fulfilled my part of the deal,' he says, arms folded across his chest. 'So what's this new assignment you're going to give me?'

Mori had been going to send him to observe Mrs Miura's house for a couple of hours, not that anything useful would result. Now, though, he has a better idea.

'Nakanishi. I want you to go through the newspapers, public records, anything else that comes to mind. Look for an unsolved murder with a victim called Nakanishi.'

Uno looks unimpressed. 'Go through newspapers? That's work for a librarian, I'd say!'

'You mean, your fiancée's friends wouldn't think it's cool,' snorts Mori. 'Well, maybe not, but checking and assembling information is what this business is all about. The sooner you realize that the better.'

And the sooner you realize what this business is really like – what kind of things you have to do, what kind of person you have to become – the better for all concerned.

'Another beer?'

'I've had enough,' says Uno, staggering to his feet.

Mori smiles. 'Okay – let's move on to that nightclub I was telling you about.'

George the Wolf Nishio sits in a Roppongi bar watching a country-and-western group on the stage in the corner. Lonesome Luke Segawa and the Prairie Boys, one of George's favourites. They make music of a keening purity, as tragic as any he has ever heard. The bar is a small one, just a cramped corner on the twentieth floor of a building that the old boss acquired a couple of years back. George doesn't know the full story – something to do with a trust bank, a political faction leader and a real-estate company whose only assets are uncompleted golf courses and unsaleable resort condos – but the old boss was eager to replace the existing tenants as soon as possible. He asked George to encourage turnover. The existing tenants soon left. George found new ones such as the Happy Trails Bar and the Wet Banana Theatre Club.

It is part of George's duties to keep an eye on these establishments, making sure there are no problems with the rowdy elements sometimes found in Roppongi these days. Generally his mere presence – sprawling on a chair near the door in his white suit and mirror shades – is enough to do the trick. In fact, George is so effective that many people take one look inside then go back the way they came. Tonight, for example, the only other occupied table is the one behind him, where a group of long-haired students are quickly getting drunk. The other customers swallowed their drinks and left shortly after George's arrival. But that's no problem, all the better for enjoying the music.

Lonesome Luke is in good voice, high and quavering. George pops a Benzedrine tablet, washes it down with a mouthful of Wild Turkey. There are many things on his mind. Thanks to his performance in the countryside, he is back in the old boss's favour. That brings its own problems, as George fully understands. Specifically, the young prince's people will be watching harder than ever. Then there is the question of the man Mori, said by that rot-brained florist to be in the porno business. Well, George knows most of the big names in the porno business, and preliminary enquiries have drawn a complete blank. Still, George intends to keep trying, because that's the kind of man he is – the kind of man who lives for honour and respect. That is why he walked into Abebashi Prison with a smile on his lips. That is why he will not rest until the man Mori has been made to pay.

Lonesome Luke takes off his stetson, ducks his balding head to acknowledge the applause. He doesn't smile. In fact, his dark care-lined face looks more miserable than when he was singing. George approves. Lonesome Luke is no drunken monkey of a pop singer. He is a man of sincerity.

One of the Prairie Boys changes his banjo for a Dobro guitar. He lifts it carefully, strums out a few ringing chords. Lonesome Luke takes a harmonica from the pocket of his denim shirt, raises it gravely to his lips. George sits forward, anticipating those first mournful bars. What's it going to be – Hank Williams or Slim Whitman?

Problem: a sudden clamour from behind. George turns. The students are shouting in loud stupid voices. At first George can't make out what they are saying. When he does, he is aghast.

'Yah – heavy metal!'

'Hey, uncle! Let's hear some heavy metal!'

They have girls with them. The girls are laughing, mouths wide open. George glances at the stage. Lonesome Luke stands frozen, his face as expressionless as a weather-beaten old gravestone.

George gets up, walks over to their table, glares into a drunken red face.

'Too much noise!' he hisses. 'Behave with proper manners in a place like this!'

'We want heavy metal,' squeals one of the girls.

'Shut your mouth, you rot-brained whore.'

'What did you say?' says the biggest of the students, getting to his feet. 'Who do you think you are, anyway?'

Unbelievably, he puts a dirty paw on the shoulder of George's newly pressed jacket. George knocks it away with a snarl of outrage. There's a silver cocktail fork handily placed on a nearby plate. It wouldn't take a second to snatch it up and bury it in the guy's windpipe. But that would be unprofessional. The manager doesn't want police trouble, not over stupid stuff like this. On the other hand George can't just walk away either. If he did, he wouldn't be George the Wolf Nishio.

Everyone's watching – the manager, the waiters, Lonesome Luke himself. George pulls his briefcase from under his chair and clicks it open in front of the student's nose. The way he does it nobody else can see inside.

'Hey, ditch-rat,' he says, putting his hand inside the case. 'You know what this is?'

The student nods his head. Suddenly he's sober.

'You want to hear some really heavy metal?'

'No.'

The other students say nothing. They're looking up at the big guy, catching his fear.

'You want to apologize for this rudeness, right?'

The student nods again, eyes wide. George grins.

'That's good. Now get down on your hands and knees and crawl over to the stage.'

The student hesitates for a second, then does what George says. Lonesome Luke stares sombrely into space, doesn't even acknowledge the guy's existence. That's good too. Lonesome Luke know how to hold his dignity.

George gets behind the student and rams a sharply pointed toe-cap up between his thighs. The student squeals like a woman.

'Silence!' roars George. 'Get your face down, and stay there until the music's over!'

Eyes shut, the student presses his forehead against the wooden boards. The girls are silent now, no more drunken giggles. George goes back to the table, fills his whisky glass and gulps it down in one. With the police becoming less understanding these days, he rarely carries a gun in Roppongi. Tonight is a fortunate exception. Fortunate for everyone because no gun would have meant fists and knives and broken glasses. Which would have meant screaming, blood everywhere, no chance to hear Lonesome Luke's next song.

George turns to the women, grinning ugly-polite. They're in a state of shock. He raises a buttock and eases out a fart, slow and sardonic.

Then the Dobro chimes again. Lonesome Luke puts the harmonica to his mouth and blows a couple of chords. George recognizes the melody at once. It's Hank Williams.

Eleven

The hangover Mori wakes up to is a classic: pressure headache; blurred vision; a whole rainy season happening inside his head. Memories of what happened after the beer-garden take some time to demist. It was a good evening, that much he knows. He closes his eyes again, sees the laughing faces, smells the perfume. The girls in the nightclub were alive with energy and fun. Uno drank well, danced well too. And as Mori expected, the girls wouldn't let him go. Mori left him there, the last customer in the place, with his shirt off and his hair falling over his eyes.

Careful breakfast – a rice-ball, a couple of tangerines, no coffee. After that Mori switches on the TV for the tail-end of the weekly current affairs programme. The subject is political reform, the absolute necessity for it, as everyone agrees. Leaders from all the major factions are present – a row of dark suits and earnest reassuring faces. The interviewer asks whether the governing coalition, which includes all the major parties, is going to survive until the end of the year.

The acting head of the Kaneshita faction explains how he is 'exerting all his efforts to establish a framework that will facilitate the necessary consensus'.

His bitterest rival, a man whose burning ambition shattered the unity of the old party, smiles and nods. He believes that 'it would be wrong to rule out the possibility of somewhat severe winds blowing towards the end of the year'.

A third states that 'flexibility could be said to be the number one priority for working towards national renewal'.

Familiar words, familiar face. It is Seiji Toriyama, looking older and wearier than he appeared in the newspaper photo. Since Mori found out that Toriyama is Mrs Miura's father, he has been paying more attention to the political scene. He squats in front of the TV, watches the interviewer attempt to probe further.

'Toriyama-*san*, it is believed that you are the key man in the political landscape this year. If your support is withdrawn, the cabinet must fall. And in that case there would be a strong possibility of a Toriyama cabinet being established . . .'

He pauses, probably expecting the same thing as Mori: modest chuckles, followed by the usual stream of verbiage about 'reform' and 'national renewal'. Instead, though, Toriyama goes on to the defensive.

'Well – uh, let me say first – bearing in mind the different opinions that can be held on this matter – that it would be better to continue to discuss the situation thoroughly until it becomes appropriate to take more steps forward . . .'

Toriyama stumbles to a halt. He looks ill at ease, distracted. His left eyelid, Mori notices, has developed a twitch.

The interviewer tries again. 'So are you saying that you will continue supporting the cabinet, whatever the other parties may decide?'

Toriyama squirms in his chair. 'What I'm saying is that there are voices calling for stability and it is not necessarily wrong to take that into account. In the words of the proverb, the bridge should be crossed cautiously, tapping it to make sure it is strong . . .'

The interviewer turns his attention to the acting head of the Kaneshita faction, a past master of verbal obfuscation. The discussion gets even more convoluted. Mori's hangover gets worse. Politicians – why can't they talk like ordinary people? Do they talk like that to their wives and mistresses too? Still, Toriyama is usually much smoother, more commanding than the old faction leaders sitting on either side of him. Today he looks and sounds terrible, as if he's got a two-day hangover to rank with Mori's.

Outside the rain is slowing. Mori switches off the TV, guzzles down a stamina drink, gets ready for his standard hangover cure: half an hour of karate practice in the grounds of the local shrine. Fight pain with pain.

The shrine is deserted, just an old one-eyed cat watching quizzically as Mori goes through his routine. His legs don't kick as high as they once did, his fists don't move so fast, but it doesn't take long for the adrenalin to start flowing. Mori pirouettes on the slippery stone surface, grunts from deep in the stomach, fills his lungs to bursting point with the damp air. The hangover is soon defeated, though the one-eyed cat doesn't look impressed.

As Mori's body works, his mind works too. He thinks over the events of yesterday. That unfortunate salaryman: attacked in the street, drugged, hauled off to a mysterious destination. It shouldn't take long for the 'musicians' to figure out that he had nothing to do with Miura's death. Salarymen are straightforward types. They don't go around committing serious crimes, at least not unless their company gives them instructions. If it had been Mori who had been hauled away, the situation might have been a little more tricky.

The ploy with the bag was a good one – it reaped dramatic new information about the Miura case. Black Blade is certainly no ordinary stalker. He is suspected of involvement in two murders, Miura's and the man called Nakanishi's. Even more important is the identity of those who are doing the suspecting, people who disguise themselves as musicians and medics and operate from the heart of the business district. Mori has his own ideas about those people, but he needs elucidation. And, once more, the man to give it to him is Shima.

Mori gets home, just after midday, dripping with a mixture of rain and sweat. He rings Shima, asks him if he's got time to meet. Shima says fine, no problem, he has to come to Shibuya this afternoon anyway. That surprised Mori. He can't imagine Shima choosing to spend his precious free time in one of Tokyo's busiest shopping areas.

'I need to buy a violin,' explains Shima. 'It's a congratulations present for Mari-*chan*.'

'Congratulations? For what?'

'For passing her driving test,' says Shima proudly.

The picture that comes into Mori's mind: a shy-faced girl in junior-school uniform trying to peer over the top of a steering-wheel. When was it that Mori last saw Shima's elder daughter? Eight, ten years ago? It seems like just the other week. Time is definitely moving faster these days. The future arrives way before you're ready.

Shibuya bustles with young people, seethes with their spending. Pubs, clubs, snack-bars, boutiques, daytime discos, love hotels, karaoke boxes, game centres – a whole lush ecosystem nourished by the disposable incomes of sixteen- to twenty-five-year-olds. These kids live at home as long as they can, coax pocket money out of their parents and grandparents. They don't want to grow up, and who can blame them? When they do, their disposable incomes will get disposed of fast enough.

Mori forces his way through the sea of bodies, trying to

keep his bemusement under control. 'Ambient trip-hop garage trance' – what does that mean? How is anyone supposed to know? These kids are a strange tribe. They like to communicate not face to face but with pocket pagers and handyphones. The language they use is a mish-mash of slang and catchphrases from comic books and TV programmes. The girls look like aliens, with their light brown hair and fake tans. The boys get their arms and legs waxed smooth, change the shape of their faces with plastic surgery. When Mori was twenty years old, he wanted to change Japanese society from top to bottom. These kids are only interesting in changing the way they look.

Shima is waiting in a fast-food joint, a large parcel on the chair beside him.

'Cost me a couple of months' salary,' he grumbles. 'Still, it should be worth it. She's going on tour with the youth orchestra soon.'

'Youth orchestra!' says Mori, eyebrows raised. 'Sometimes I wonder if Mari-*chan* really is your daughter.'

'*Hoi!* What's that supposed to mean?'

Mori shrugs, goes to the counter and gets himself a yakitori riceburger. Shima's sense of humour isn't what it was. Perhaps his own isn't either.

Mori sits down, takes a munch out of the riceburger.

'So what's the problem this time,' says Shima testily. Mori gets right to the point.

'What can you tell me about this new intelligence agency, that was set up a few years ago. You know, the thing the papers call the Japanese CIA.'

Shima frowns. 'That's highly delicate, Mori. I wouldn't get involved if I were you.'

'I am already involved,' says Mori. 'Their people almost snatched me off the streets yesterday. By the way, the headquarters is in the business district, isn't it?'

Shima sucks noisily at his tofu shake. 'Yes, I'm told that they do have some facilities there. Frankly I don't know much more than that.'

'If they were planning some kind of operation in Shinjuku – let's say they were hunting for someone dangerous – wouldn't they notify you in advance?'

Shima gives a hollow laugh. 'We'd be the last to know,' he says. 'These people do what they like, when they like. It's all top-secret stuff.'

'So who controls them?'

'That's top secret too,' says Shima. 'Anyway, why would they want to snatch someone like you? I thought you quit your subversive ways twenty-five years ago.'

Shima may have given up karate, but he still knows how to jab. And his political views haven't moderated since the two men first met. As far as Shima is concerned, healthy political scepticism is on a par with terrorism.

Mori swallows the last of the riceburger. 'It's got something to do with that Miura case I told you about. It looks like Kimiko Itoh was right about the murder angle.'

'That doesn't explain anything,' says Shima with a shake of his head. 'They shouldn't be interested in an ordinary murder case. They're supposed to be concerned with serious threats to national security.'

'And what constitutes a serious threat to national security?'

Shima wags a finger in Mori's face. 'You should know better than ask. That's top secret, of course.'

Sunday evening Mitchell spends alone in his apartment, waiting for the phone call. The rain drums on the roof, runs down the window pane in fat streaks. On the tatami mat there are three rice bowls now, each positioned to catch a different leak. Mitchell sips green tea, frowns into the screen of his computer. He's just reached a new phase of the simulation game he's been playing. At last he's through world five, home of angels and demons, and into world six, home of the gods.

These days Mitchell rarely goes out in the evenings. Being short of money in Tokyo is like being short of water in the Gobi desert. You can't move, can't do anything. So Mitchell stays at home instead, feasts off instant noodles and plays computer games. What he has found: SoftJoy games are consistently the most exciting and innovative. That is why he has been so bullish on the stock price. The company deserves to succeed. Mega, producer of unimaginative trash, deserves to fail.

The drumbeats get stronger. The leaks drip faster. From outside comes a faint wailing, a creature in bad pain somewhere. Mitchell goes to the window, peers out nervously into the dark. It takes him several seconds to identify the sound as the product of a human voice. The old woman who lives in the ground floor is listening to a traditional folk song on the radio. No words, no melody that he can trace – just a long rhythmic caterwaul. Mitchell sits down again, but the sound won't leave his mind.

The phone rings. It is the call he has been dreading. He lets it ring four times – enough to show nonchalance, but not slackness. On little things like that his career might depend.

'Hello, Richard. How are you doing?' she says.

'Fine,' lies Mitchell. 'Where are you calling from, Sasha?'

'I'm on my way to Charles de Gaulle. There's a meeting in Frankfurt this evening.'

'Really? So how's the weather in Paris?'

Sasha de Glazier, head of global research at WB Securities, gives a loud groan.

'Don't talk to me about the fucking weather. I don't do weather talk. You should know that, Richard.'

Sasha talks as she lives, fast and impatient. You can't get much more global than Sasha. She's half Lebanese and half Argentinian, a fluent speaker of French, Spanish and Italian. She lives in planes and hotels, has close friends in every city that has a serious financial market. She gets bored if she stays in the same country for more than two weeks, or works for the same company for more than two years. Unfortunately for Mitchell, she's only been with WB Securities for eight months.

'So what do you want to hear first,' raps Sasha, 'the good news or the bad news?'

'Whatever you like, Sasha.'

'Hey – if I was doing what I liked, I wouldn't be wasting time talking to you. Come on – good news or bad news?'

'Good news,' says Mitchell promptly.

'Right. The good news is you're not going to be fired just yet.'

A wave of relief hits Mitchell, starting in his heart and coursing straight to his brain.

'In my view, you ought to be terminated straight away – with minimum severance terms. However, the Bavarians have just put a temporary freeze on firings. They've taken it into their heads that there has been too much staff turnover since I arrived. Can you believe that?'

Mitchell can believe it without difficulty, though he doesn't say so. Since Sasha joined the firm, hardly a week has gone by without some analyst or economist walking out the door or being propelled through it.

'So now for the bad news. From here on, your salary is going to be strictly performance-linked. As your recent performance has been dogshit, that means a cut of thirty per cent. You also go on to my personal watch list. Unless you can demonstrate clear and substantial improvement, you'll be the first to walk the plank when I get the Bavarians to change their minds. Do you hear me?'

Mitchell hears it so well that his ears are on fire.

'Don't disappoint me, Richard. I hate to be disappointed.'

The phone clicks dead, but Sasha de Glazier remains in Mitchell's mind. She is a big woman, looks more Latin than she sounds on the phone. Late thirties, at a guess, with a wide brow and long hair brushed back tight. The last time Mitchell met her was in Hong Kong. She didn't pay much attention to him at the time, being busy firing half the South-East Asian research department. Now she has turned the fury of her ambition right on him.

Mitchell leans back in his chair, tries to analyse the situation objectively. Sasha is a Maoist manager: she revels in tumult, hates stability. The consensus-loving Germans are trying to slow her down, but they need someone like Sasha if they are going to get anywhere in the modern financial world. Trying to stop her from firing people is a doomed effort, King Canute with the waves lapping around his ankles.

So how long will it take? Mitchell's judgement – two months, maximum. First she coaxes the big new budget out of them: 'Hey – do you want to be serious global players, or are you just going to sit on your butts and carry on lending money to stinky little companies in the Black Forest?' Then she waits a bit before delivering the ultimatum: 'You gave me the budget. Now either give me the freedom to manage it or fire me.'

Sasha doesn't bluff. Her newly won freedom to manage the budget will be manifested in the instant dismissal of Mitchell. She won't care what she pays for the replacement. In fact, the more of the Bavarians' money she spends the happier she will be. And the Bavarians will be happy too, convinced that they are one step further on the way to becoming serious global players. Everyone's going to be happy, except one Richard Mitchell.

Outside the rain spatters. The unearthly voice drifts up from below, wailing centuries of pain and loss and resignation. Mitchell closes his eyes. Under his breath he starts to join in.

Yoichi Sonoda sleeps four hours a night. Anything more he considers a waste of time. Ever since his high-school days, Sonoda has been obsessed with not wasting time. He doesn't drink alcohol. He doesn't hang around in night-clubs or discos or fancy restaurants. Most evenings Sonoda spends working, either with his inner group of advisors or on his own. Tonight he is alone, reviewing the business plan for the second half of the year. If his eyes get tired, he will put on a mask and sleep on the couch. If his eyes don't get tired, he will keep on working till dawn.

As he reads, he jots notes into the palmtop computer which he always keeps within reach, even when he's sleeping. Occasionally he turns to the game console on the table beside him and tests a manoeuvre with the joystick. On the giant screen that covers the far wall five-headed dragons rear and snarl, muscled superheroes race through mazes of flame, oceans part and volcanoes erupt. Sonoda's hand moves in sharp, measured jerks. His eyes are unblinking, serious.

What he sees does not impress him. These are the latest games that Mega has put out. As usual, the visuals are strong and fast. But there is no narrative power, no emotional engagement with the images that flash by on the screen. You could never get lost in one of these Mega games. You would never think about it all day long, rush to get home to play another instalment because it has become more real than your everyday life.

Sometimes Sonoda thinks that he is the only person alive who understands what that really means. It means something as big as TV, but interactive, participatory. Something not just for kids, but for adults, whole families, old people living alone. You don't just sit there and stare at it. You enter. You assume an identity. You act, feel, choose.

Sonoda picks up his phone, touches his memory key.

'Yes, hello . . .' The voice at the other end mumbles drowsily.

'Wake up, Ochi! I have urgent business to discuss.'

'President Sonoda! What time is it now?'

'The time is irrelevant. I want you to update me immediately on the Mega problem. The scrambler is on so you can talk freely.'

'Mega?' It takes Ochi a few seconds to gather his thoughts. He's the kind of man who prefers being asleep to being awake.

'Yes, Mega. Have you succeeded in identifying the developers who leaked our new game ideas?'

'The investigation has been narrowed down to four suspects, President. I will interrogate them personally tomorrow.'

'Excellent. When you find the one responsible, let me know immediately. There's no time to lose.'

'Understood!' barks Ochi. But he doesn't understand. A man like Ochi isn't capable of understanding how the game must be played.

Twelve

Monday morning Mori gets to his office early. Suddenly the bonus that Kimiko Itoh offered him is looking more attainable. Mori needs that money. He needs a new turntable, a new sofa, new cylinders for the Honda. He also needs to pay down more of the housing loan, clear his arrears on the office rent. According to the blind masseur, money troubles can accelerate the ageing process and twist the body into strange shapes. If that's true, then a successful conclusion to the Miura case could cut down his medical expenses as well. No more acupuncture, moxibustion, hot sand baths. No more blind masseur either.

Uno calls soon after ten.

'Thanks for taking me out on Saturday evening,' he says. 'I learned a lot.'

'No problem,' says Mori. He can't resist the obvious question. 'By the way, how long did you stay in that last place?'

'Stay? Actually I left soon after you did.'

A few supplementary questions pass through Mori's mind, but he leaves them unasked.

'A detective needs to spend time in places like that,' he says. 'It's important for cultivating information sources, all part of the job. I hope your fiancée understands that.'

'Me too,' mutters Uno.

Mori pauses to take a mouthful of coffee. 'If not, why

don't you let me talk to her? I can explain all the different aspects of a private detective's job . . .'

'That won't be necessary,' says Uno hurriedly. 'Now, about Nakanishi. The news isn't so good, unfortunately . . .'

It isn't good at all. Uno went to his old university yesterday. He managed to talk the janitor into opening up the library and spent all afternoon going through newspapers. Nowhere did he find any mention of a murder involving a victim called Nakanishi. Then first thing this morning he called up the Home Ministry pretending to be an academic doing research on crime statistics. Again, there was nothing.

'Strange,' muses Mori. 'Maybe it was made to look like an accident somehow.'

'You want me to look at all the accidental deaths too?'

'No, that would be a waste of time. There are far too many.'

Uno sounds disappointed. 'So what else do you want me to do? I'm as involved in this case as you are now!'

'Wait a moment,' growls Mori. 'I can't carry on paying you one thousand five hundred yen an hour to come up with nothing!'

'No problem,' says Uno, quick as a flash. 'Why not pay me by results instead? No results, no cost to you. If I come up with something, you can pay me two thousand yen an hour.'

Mori almost chokes on his coffee. He takes the receiver from his ear, stares at the grease spots on the ceiling. What Uno has just suggested breaks every rule in the unwritten commercial code of the private detective industry.

'Are you still there, Mori-*san*?'

'I'm here.'

'So what do you think of my offer? This is a great opportunity for me, you know. Working on a real murder case with someone as famous as Mori-*san* – that's the kind of thing only happens once in a lifetime.'

Uno is definitely learning. Knowing how to identify people's weaknesses – that's one of the keys to success in this business. And flattery Mori considers to be one of his own greatest weaknesses. The other one is women. Put the two together and the combination can be devastating.

Mori sighs. 'All right, you win.'

Uno gabbles his gratitude. 'Please let me receive your acceptance of my heartfelt thanks. I would like to express deep appreciation of—'

'Enough of that,' snaps Mori. 'Here's what I want you to do. You told me you read a lot of science fiction and fantasy and that sort of thing, right?'

'Yes.'

'Well, I'm looking for information on a character called Black Blade. Could be in a movie, a TV show, a manga comic book, anything.'

'Black Blade?'

'That's right. Have you heard the name?'

Uno pauses. 'Hmm ... maybe – uh – well, I'm not certain, to say the truth...'

'Then make certain,' says Mori. 'This is important stuff, could be the key to the whole case.'

'Sounds like more librarian-type work.'

'Consider it a missing person search. Except that the person we need to find is a fictional character of some sort.'

'Understood,' says Uno crisply. 'You won't regret this, Mori-*san*. I really would like to express heartfelt appreciation of your—'

Ding! Mori drops the receiver onto its cradle. 'Won't regret this' – he certainly hopes not. When this case is over, he really does need to meet Uno's fiancée. He needs to explain that her boyfriend's choice of career could do with another one of those thorough, very adult-type discussions.

Mori gets himself another cup of coffee, then calls up his own contact in the Home Ministry. Not that he doubts Uno's diligence, but it's always possible that they didn't believe his assumed identity or just decided to hold something back. After all they are bureaucrats, and for bureaucrats information is something to be hoarded, not handed out to strangers like packets of tissue paper. But Mori's contact has nothing to add. Mori tries again – missing persons, serious woundings, attempted arsons. Still no trace of a Nakanishi anywhere. Conclusion: accident or cover-up. After all, Miura's death wouldn't have registered in this kind of search either.

The morning dribbles by. Lunch is light – prawn pilaff and iced tea in a nearby coffee-bar. The owner likes to proclaim proudly that he opened for business on the very month of the Tokyo Olympics, and there are pictures of Japan's twenty-five gold-medal winners on the walls. Mori once told him that by the look of the carpets and upholstery the decor hadn't changed since. This place could qualify as a Designated Cultural Monument, he said. That's possible, said the owner. And at the same time maybe you'll qualify as a Living National Treasure. Mori laughed at the time. After all, Living National Treasures are usually wrinkled old men, masters of fossilized art forms like classical puppet theatre and ancient court music. Nothing could be more remote from his own experience. Or so he thought. How long ago was that conversation? Fifteen years? The world has changed a lot since then, Mori too. The time of wrinkles and failing eyesight doesn't seem so far away. Nor does the time when his own working methods will seem like a quaint anachronism. If he's still going in another fifteen years, stumbling around after two-timing wives and swindling secretaries, he'll certainly deserve an award of some sort.

Mori snaps the head off a prawn, chases away his gloom by concentrating on the Miura case. Nakanishi: it's quite a common name. There must be hundreds, maybe thousands of people called Nakanishi who die every year. So what is distinctive about this particular Nakanishi? Nothing, except for the fact that his death excited the attention of the intelligence bureau. But that could be the significant point. It suggests that Nakanishi must be an important figure in the eyes of the guardians of 'national security'. Just like Miura. So could Nakanishi be another bureaucrat, perhaps even a colleague at the Ministry of Health? It's certainly worth checking. And the best way to check is to consult someone with detailed knowledge of all the major ministries. One man comes to mind, a man who has devoted his life to peering through the 'black mist', that miasma of scandal, financial finagling and behind-the-scenes intrigue that has cloaked the Japanese establishment for as long as anyone can remember. Mori decides to pay another visit to Taniguchi.

It's two o'clock when Mori's Honda pulls up outside Taniguchi's place. The tiny yakitori restaurant on the ground floor is just closing for the afternoon. A young man wearing a rolled headband is squatting on his haunches in the doorway. He has a bicycle race tip-sheet in his hand, a toothpick jutting from his mouth.

'You're looking for Taniguchi-*san*,' he says as Mori passes on his way to the stairs.

'That's right. How do you know?'

'He said you were coming. He said to tell you to wait until he gets back.'

Mori frowns. He just called Taniguchi fifteen minutes

ago. Still, he shouldn't be surprised. Punctuality is one more attribute of the élite journalist that has been dissolved in alcohol and grief.

'He's gone out? How long for?'

'He didn't say, but it's probably not long. At this time of day he often goes to the supermarket to get some drinks. Anyway, you can come inside, if you like.'

Mori nods his thanks, steps into the darkened restaurant and takes a seat at the counter. The master is standing at the sink, elbow deep in dishwater. He turns, yells at the young man to go and get Mori some fruit.

'Young people lack common sense these days,' he grumbles beneath his breath.

'Sorry to cause bother,' says Mori.

'It's no bother. Anyway, I hear that you're an old friend of Taniguchi-*san*'s. That's good because I've got a few things to ask ...'

He dries his hands in his apron, comes round to the other side of the counter. Mori has an idea what the few things may be. He's not wrong.

'It's a sad thing to see, a man like that. What I was wondering – being that you're an old friend – is whether you think he needs medical attention?'

'Medical attention? What do you mean exactly?'

The master looks embarrassed, then he taps the side of his head with his finger.

'The poor guy's going funny,' he says. 'Wandering around in a daze, talking to himself all the time – sometimes he doesn't even know where he is!'

The young man brings Mori a slice of watermelon and a glass of iced tea. Mori nibbles, sips, thinks back to Taniguchi's outburst during his last visit. Yes, his old friend seems to be having difficulty in keeping control. No surprise there, really.

191

'Taniguchi-*san*'s had bad problems,' he says. 'You know about his daughter, don't you?'

The master leans forward, close enough for Mori to smell the pickles on his breath.

'That's who he talks to!' he whispers. 'His daughter. We hear him all the time . . .'

Mori doesn't know what to say. He knew that Taniguchi was suffering, but he had no idea how deeply. After all, three years have passed since the death of Hiromi.

'Living on his own is not good,' says the master. 'He should go out more, instead of staying in that tiny room all the time . . .'

'But doesn't he go out to research his magazine articles?'

The master shakes his heavy face. 'Not any more. He says that he prefers to employ young people to do all the legwork. What he means is that in his state he wouldn't be able to interview anyone properly or anything like that . . .'

The master breaks off and lifts his gaze. Mori turns to the door. Taniguchi is standing there, hair plastered to his forehead by the rain. He looks confused, lost. The master makes a jovial comment about the recent Giants game, and Taniguchi's face immediately lights up into his old smile.

'Great teamwork,' he says, picking up an umbrella from the stand at the door. 'That's what the Giants are all about – not star players, but teamwork!'

The master stands up, throws him a phantom pitch. Taniguchi swats with his umbrella, cups his eyes to watch the phantom ball sailing into the phantom bleachers.

'There it goes,' he whoops. 'A sayonara home run to win the Japanese Series!'

Craning his neck, Taniguchi suddenly loses his balance. He reels sideways. An arm thrusts out and an empty beer glass goes flying to the ground. Taniguchi stares at the broken glass as if he can't believe it's there.

'What's going on?' he roars. 'What shit-for-brains put that glass in my way?'

The master glances at Mori, shrugs, kneels to pick up the fragments.

Taniguchi stomps up the stairs to the six-mat room that serves him as both office and apartment. In his hand is a shopping bag clinking with jars and bottles. He trails water, the sweet smell of sake. Mori follows a couple of paces behind.

Taniguchi slumps down on a cushion, pours out a couple of glasses of shochu, uses the remote controller to switch on the stereo. The room swims with Mahler. Taniguchi's shochu disappears in one gulp. He immediately pours another with a shaky hand. Mori glances over at the alcove. The black-rimmed photo of Hiromi stares out at him, twenty years old for ever.

Mori mixes his shochu with lemonade – thirty parts to seventy – then nudges into the conversation.

'You remember Miura – the Ministry of Health guy married to the daughter of Seiji Toriyama.'

Taniguchi guzzles, nose wrinkled. 'Miura? Yes, how are you getting on? Any leads there yet?'

'One or two,' says Mori. 'Nothing decisive, though. Actually, there seems to be another murder tied in somehow, a guy called Nakanishi. That's what I came to ask you about.'

'What do you want to know?' says Taniguchi, turning down the music.

'Well, I'm trying to trace this Nakanishi. I thought he might be another bureaucrat or maybe related to the bureaucracy somehow. Have you come across anyone called Nakanishi who's died recently?'

'Hmmm ... what kind of area did he work in?'

Mori sips tentatively at his shochu. 'No idea.'

'So how do you know he's a bureaucrat?'

'I don't – it's just an instinct.'

Taniguchi shakes his head, grins. 'That's the difference between a detective and a journalist. You base your research on instinct. I base mine on logic.'

Mori looks at his old friend keenly. Here's his lead-in to the most delicate part of what he has to say. 'Talking of research, I understand you don't do much yourself any more.'

Taniguchi's brow darkens. 'Really? Who told you that?'

'A friend of a friend. He says you've got some young guys doing all the research for you. He reckons you're not in good enough shape to do it yourself any more.'

A calculated approach: sting his pride. Taniguchi still considers himself to be an ace investigative journalist, despite everything that has happened. Devotion to his work is the one source of value left in his life. Mori is expecting a stormy response. He gets it.

Taniguchi drains his glass, bangs it down on the low table in front of him. 'That's nonsense, complete lies! I do all the serious work myself. Nobody else could do what I do, nobody else knows what I know.'

'So why have someone else do all the legwork, then?'

Taniguchi is agitated. His hands flutter in front of his face like wounded birds. 'Because . . . because I want to pass on my knowledge, my experience of what this world is really like. Otherwise when I'm gone, there'll be nobody, nothing left at all.'

Now Taniguchi is staring at the photo of Hiromi, a blank expression on his face. Mori feels clumsy. He leans over, pats Taniguchi on the shoulder.

'You ought to see a specialist,' he says. 'Get yourself fit again, then you'll be able to handle all the research yourself. This world needs you, Taniguchi-*san*. It really does.'

Taniguchi hauls himself to his feet. 'You asked about Nakamoto?' he says.

'Nakanishi,' says Mori. The delicate part of the conversation is clearly over, but Mori intends to return to it on his next visit. Because what he said he meant. The world does need Taniguchi, especially now that the black mist is swirling so strong and thick that the whole landscape looks like being enveloped.

Taniguchi goes to the old wooden dresser that he uses as a filing cabinet and spends fifteen minutes leafing through newspaper clippings, interview reports and old personnel lists. Mahler swells and ebbs and swells again. Mori sits at the low table, sipping at his shochu and browsing through a book that Taniguchi wrote a few years ago about the Kobe earthquake. It is a depressing tale of bungling, cover-ups and infighting over the division of reconstruction funds, spelt out with Taniguchi's usual precision and clarity.

Finally Taniguchi comes up with three candidates. Yoshio Nakanishi, deputy chairman of the Urban Renaissance Research Council: died three years ago. Kenji Nakanishi, official in the patent bureau: died last year. Tsutomu Nakanishi, diplomat: died in March this year. Mori writes the details into his pocket book, finishes his shochu, gets up to leave.

'Take care of yourself,' he says. 'There are plenty more books like that waiting to be written.'

He points at the Kobe earthquake book.

'Too many to count,' says Taniguchi. 'Anyway, don't worry about me. I'm just a journalist. You're the guy with the dangerous job.'

Mori thinks about that as he tramps down the narrow staircase. For sure a private detective makes enemies, many of whom are ruthless and violent people. But Taniguchi's enemies are on a different scale, powerful organizations and individuals who would pay vastly more for his silence than anyone ever would for Mori's. From that point of view, Taniguchi's job might be the more dangerous.

Mori gets back to his office just after four. He spends the next hour on the phone following up the leads that Taniguchi provided. The first call is to the Foreign Ministry. Mori becomes an old schoolfriend of Tsutomu Nakanishi keen to get in touch after so many years. What he finds out: the unfortunate diplomat died on his first overseas posting, drowned off the coast of Spain. Calling the Patent Office, Mori becomes a section chief in the R&D institute of a medium-size electronics company. What happened to Kenji Nakanishi, a man who provided so much assistance in the past? Sad story: knocked over by a car on his way home late one night. Yoshio Nakanishi turns out to be the most difficult to trace. Mori becomes a lawyer representing someone claiming to be his illegitimate son. He discovers that the Urban Renaissance Association is a subdivision of the Real Estate Research Council, which is itself a consultative body attached to the Ministry of Construction. The problem is that the Urban Renaissance Association only meets six times a year, and the Real Estate Research Council itself keeps no records of its own staff.

'But this is an urgent matter,' Mori presses. 'The young man that I am representing is anxious to clear up the uncertainty as soon as possible...'

The woman at the other end of the phone sounds dubious. 'A young man, you say? What age would he be?'

'Twenty-one,' says Mori promptly.

The woman laughs. 'Well, in that case I don't think you've got the right person. The average age of people at the Urban Renaissance Association is well over seventy! Of course, some of them are still pretty active...'

Mori gets it ... these organizations exist to provide

sinecures for retired bureaucrats! He decides to call the Ministry of Construction directly.

'My name is Nakamura,' he says. 'I am chief of the president's office at Mitsukawa Corporation. This is a strange request, I know, but our president's elder brother recently discovered that one of his old army comrades passed away three years ago . . .'

Mori gets bounced from extension to extension, from bored office lady to haughty junior functionary, but he keeps his patience. If you bluster convincingly enough, if you sound like you're used to getting your way, the information comes through in the end. The golden rule: nobody ever checks.

Finally Mori is given the number of a separate organization, one responsible for administering the activities of all the 'special corporations' under the ministry's control. The woman who picks up the phone is surprisingly co-operative, answering all his questions without demur. Mori guesses that she's pleased to have something to do for a change.

Yoshio Nakanishi, it turns out, retired from the Construction Ministry thirty-three years ago. After a spell as advisor to a major real-estate developer, he joined the Urban Renaissance Association. That was the same year that Mori Economic and Social Research Services was established. Mori thinks back. Since then he has clumped up the metal staircase to his office roughly six thousand times. To do the equivalent, Yoshio Nakamura would have had to work one thousand years.

More to the point – three years ago Yoshio Nakanishi died at the age of eighty-two, after a long convalescence.

So where does that leave the investigation? Which is the real Nakanishi – the drowned diplomat, the old man dying of a fatal disease or the patent official hit by a car? Black

197

Blade would be unlikely to travel to Spain, or to bother with someone so close to death. That leaves Kenji Nakanishi as the most likely candidate. A junior official in the patent office? Somehow it doesn't feel right. And hunting down the details of a traffic accident three years ago is going to be a tiresome and time-consuming business. Taniguchi hires people to do all the tiresome and time-consuming things for him. Maybe Mori should do the same. Maybe he should formalize the relationship with Uno, give him a permanent role as performer of everything tiresome and time-consuming. At no more than twelve hundred yen an hour, of course. Not a bad idea, thinks Mori, and reaches for the phone. Just at that moment, it starts to ring. Uno! Mori knows it from the vibrations. He can hear the man's voice buzzing in his head even before he picks up the receiver.

'Hello, hello! Hello, hello!'

Right first time. Mori holds the phone a couple of inches away from his ear.

'Mori here, of Mori Social and Economic Research.'

'No results, no pay,' babbles Uno. 'That's what we agreed, right?'

'Right.'

'Well, I've got results. Just half a day, and I've found the missing person!'

'Missing person? What are you talking about?'

Uno's voice brims with pride. 'Those were your own words. Consider it a missing person search, only the person is fictional. Well, I've found him. I've found Black Blade!'

Mori feels his own excitement rising. He forgets why he was planning to call Uno.

'That's great,' he breathes. 'Now, don't move – I'm coming round straight away!'

Fifteen minutes later Mori is in the tiny elevator humming up to Uno's office. He finds Uno sitting in the middle of the floor surrounded by piles of science fiction paperbacks, manga comic books and movie magazines. He grins confidently, raises a fist in the air like an American tennis player.

'So what have you got for me?' says Mori, squatting down beside him.

'I've got this!' Uno picks up one of the magazines and thrusts it under Mori's nose. Mori stares at the open page. Written in lurid wavy script: 'Black Blade – Revenge is My Game!' Underneath: the figure of a crouching ninja, with black mask and black cloak.

'Tell me about it,' says Mori.

'There's nothing much to tell. This is an advertisement for a video game, one of the biggest hits at the moment.'

'A video game!' Mori wasn't expecting that.

'That's right. Do you ever play video games, Mori-*san*? They're getting a lot more sophisticated these days. You might like them.'

'You're joking,' growls Mori.

'Well, anyway. That's what Black Blade is – the hero of a hit video game.'

Mori takes another look at the picture. Black Blade is a formidable-looking character, heavily muscled around the shoulders, with a throwing star in one hand and a short sword in the other.

'So what's the idea exactly?'

Uno shrugs. 'I'm not sure exactly. As I understand it, the players take on the role of Black Blade. They go around hunting down greedy merchants, corrupt officials and so on. There are more and more traps, the game gets more and more difficult . . .'

Mori purses his lips. 'Corrupt officials? Where did you get that from?'

'I read a review of the game in one of the other magazines. Made it sound pretty interesting, actually.'

'Show me,' says Mori tersely.

Uno digs out the magazine. Mori sits down at Uno's desk and studies it closely. Surprisingly, Uno is right – it does sound quite interesting. According to the review, a lot of serious thought went into the game's development. High-resolution computer graphics were used to recreate the interiors of actual Edo-era buildings, and the street scenes were devised under the guidance of recognized experts. The music is authentic, so is the language used by the characters. Even the hero has a basis in history, or at least myth – a ninja whose master was assassinated by a group of rich townsmen. After that he spent his time secretly punishing the unjust and helping the poor.

'See,' says Uno. 'The concept is more sophisticated than you expected, isn't it?'

'I suppose so,' says Mori.

'That's the sales point of the company that produced it. SoftJoy games have always got something special about them.'

Mori gazes at Uno's bright enthusiastic features. 'You spend a lot of time playing these things, do you?'

'Not a lot of time, really. No more than five or six hours a week. Of course, when I was still a student it was many times that.'

'So you've got one of these console things at home?'

'I've got three actually – all different formats.'

Mori shakes his head. There's not much difference between twelve-year-olds and twenty-two-year-olds these days. The twenty-two-year-olds are just bigger.

'Let's go and do some research,' he says, heading for the door. 'The kind you're really going to enjoy.'

On the ground floor of a pencil-building close to Mori's

office there's a shop which specializes in cut-price computer equipment. Years ago it used to sell top-of-the-range audio stuff. Mori hasn't been inside since then. It has never occurred to him to buy a computer, a disk-drive, a memory-board, a high-speed modem. Nonetheless he has noticed one thing – the place seems to be cheap. The bargain sale boasted on the stickers in the window has been going on for years, the discounts getting ever deeper, the inducements to buy that bellow from the loudspeaker getting ever more frantic. Mori and Uno step inside, and Mori feels as if he's stepped into a different world, one where he understands nothing at all.

'Welcome, honourable customer! Everything here is blisteringly cheap, special discounts even on the special discounts!'

The speaker is a skinny youth with a straggly Vandyke beard.

'Video games,' says Mori brusquely. 'Where do you have them?'

The skinny youth points at a doorway. 'All software in there,' he says. 'What are you looking for anyway – CD-ROM, cartridge or mini-disk?'

Mori glances helplessly at Uno.

'Cartridge,' says Uno. 'The format is the Joystation.'

The youth leads them through the doorway, shows them a wall-rack of garishly coloured game cartridges.

'Are you looking for any one in particular?' he says.

Mori nods. 'Have you got one called Black Blade?' he says.

'Of course. That's the best-selling title in East Japan at the moment. It just went straight to the top of the list.'

He turns and points to a leaflet pinned to the wall. It's some sort of list of best-selling video game titles. As he said, Black Blade is right at the top – number one position.

There's something about this place – the colours, the lights, the strangely named products – that makes Mori's head hurt.

'I'll buy one,' he says, and slaps a five thousand yen note onto the counter. The game costs him six thousand five hundred.

They go back to Mori's office, find a spare helmet for Uno, then head for Uno's apartment. Uno is not an experienced motorbike passenger. His hands clamp tight under Mori's arm every time the Honda banks into a turn. Rain patters on their shoulders, speckles their visors. By the time they arrive the grey light is thickening, neon streaking the tarmac.

Uno's apartment is in Hachijoji, an area swarming with students in Mori's day. The students are still there, except they don't look like students any more. They're well-dressed, docile, contented. Mori was ferociously discontented back then, and he's still discontented now, albeit with different things. He hopes to stay discontented, one way or another. It's discontent that keeps him going.

The apartment is pretty standard: two rooms in a mock-brick building of six storeys. The area is semi-commercial, semi-residential. On one side of the building – a liquor shop, huge sake barrels on the pavement. On the other – a small clinic for cosmetic surgery. Uno lives on the third floor, just above street level. He pushes the door open, ushers Mori inside. It's much tidier than Mori was expecting. Nice bushy plants by the window, no plates or piles of books on the floor. Uno sits down on a stool, unwraps the cartridge and slots it into a plastic console about half the size of a lunchbox.

'That's a Joystation?' asks Mori, surprised.

'That's it,' says Uno. 'You thought it was going to be bigger, didn't you?'

Mori nods. He had assumed that it would be about five times the size.

'No need,' says Uno. 'It's linked up to the personal computer in the bedroom. That's where all the processing gets done.'

So Uno has a personal computer in his bedroom. He probably lies there late at night, absorbed in on-line communication with people he will never meet in his life. When his girlfriend comes round, does the computer ever get jealous?

Uno goes to a cupboard, pulls out a shiny black helmet with a thick visor.

'I thought you never rode a motorbike,' says Mori.

Uno shakes his head, enjoying every minute. 'This isn't for a bike. It's the audio-visual response system.'

'What is that supposed to mean?'

'It means circular sound, high-resolution liquid crystal displays, a Chi-interface.'

'A what?'

Uno taps the top of the helmet with his fingers. 'In here – a kind of field of oscillations and pulses. It works directly on the brain. That's what makes these games so exciting.'

'Really.'

'Yes, really. You want to try?'

Mori smiles, shakes his head. Uno slides down the visor, kneels in front of the plastic console. In a matter of seconds he is totally absorbed in the game, right hand clicking the buttons on the console, left hand jerking the joystick. Mori watches him gradually become more animated, bobbing his head, making little grunting sounds. Mori gets up, goes into the kitchen – again remarkably neat – and searches for coffee. There is only Nescafe, so he settles for a cup of green tea made with a tea bag. Back in the main room, Uno is breathing deeply, shoulders rolling.

'How long does it go on for?' calls out Mori. But Uno doesn't respond. The tinny echoes of shouts and music can be heard from inside the helmet. Mori taps him on the shoulder. Still nothing, so Mori bends down and pulls the jackplug out of the console. The tinny sounds stop.

'What's happening?' says Uno, sliding up the visor. His cheeks are flushed, eyes shining.

'You're not supposed to be having fun,' says Mori. 'You're supposed to be doing some research. Now explain – what's going on in there?'

Uno explains – kabuki, teahouses, evil money-lenders, lecherous tax collectors, mysterious questions pinned to walls, messages hidden in sake bottles, ambushes, poison, treachery.

He takes off the helmet, hands it to Mori. 'You'll never understand unless you try yourself. It's like being there, right in the middle of everything.'

Gingerly Mori puts it on. With the visor down, the world goes dark, a cinema just before the projector starts running.

The projector starts running. Images all around, bright, fast, rushing past his eyes. Noise – footsteps, the cry of street-hawkers, lute music from an upper window. Mori's pulse quickens. Someone is behind him, someone whispering a question in his ear. He turns to face a geisha – white face, tiny mouth, hair heaped with jewelled combs. A bath? She's asking him to come inside, a bath has been prepared. Been prepared? How did they know he was coming? Mori refuses, turns away. Swarming faces, shouts – a lacquered palanquin being carried through the street by jog-trotting men in indigo kimonos. A beggar in a cart looks up at Mori, face twisted into a gap-toothed grin.

'Do you know who that is?'

Mori shakes his head.

'He's the one. He made the stuff that killed your friend's wife.'

Mori remembers now. A dealer in Chinese medicines, dispensing poison to the enemies of the shogun. The palanquin rushes past.

'He's going to the teahouse over the river,' says the beggar. 'If you sneak in the back door, you can catch him unawares.'

Mori nods, but he doesn't trust the beggar. His hands are too clean. Mori moves cautiously through the crowd, pushing his way towards the bridge. The sky is pure blue, sun glinting on the river. Glancing to the left, Mori sees the snow-capped outline of Mount Fuji rising above the curved roof of the kabuki theatre. Down below men in straw hats are poling skiffs along the glinting surface of the river. The whole scene is as vivid as a picture.

Then Mori stops dead, shocked to his core. This whole scene actually *is* a picture! The curve of the bridge, the disposition of the skiffs on the river, even the colour of the sky – he recognizes it all from a woodblock print by Hiroshige. And the bulk of Mount Fuji, looming much too close to be real – that's straight out of one of Hokusai's works. Mori watches the palanquin disappear into the crowd on the other side of the bridge. The people jostling by – look closely at their faces. Blurred, empty, they're walking illustrations. Mori feels a surge of panic. He's lost in a world of lies and traps and secrets, a world constructed and controlled by others. He puts his hands to his head, grabs at the helmet.

'Take this thing off me,' he roars.

Two men are moving towards him, samurai with their hands on their swords.

'Didn't you hear me? I said take this thing off!'

One of the samurai smiles. 'To cross this bridge you must fight,' he hisses.

'Get out of my way,' bellows Mori, heart thumping.

The first samurai draws his sword, edges closer. Mori jerks the joystick. One move – he slices off the man's hand. Blood spouts, deep gouts shooting on to the dusty ground. The blurred face twists into a caricature of pain. Mori grits his teeth, strikes again – this time a side-swing. The man's head separates from his body, goes flying over the side of the bridge.

'*Hoh!*' shouts Mori, exhilarated. He jabs at the other samurai, who dances backwards. Other samurai have appeared from somewhere, making a circle around Mori, edging closer. They're nervous, he can feel it. Mori wheels, thrusts. The samurai yell in confusion, back away again. This is getting enjoyable. Mori singles out the biggest of them – thick top-knot, carbuncle in the middle of the forehead. This man will be the next to die. After that, the others will scatter, run back jabbering in fear to whoever paid them. How does he know that? Instinct, solid and sure.

'*Hoh!*' he yells again. Then, 'What?'

The world has gone black. The bridge, the river, Mount Fuji – all have disappeared into nothing. Mori closes his eyes, takes a deep breath. The noises have gone too; no more street cries, no more lute music.

Slowly he lifts the helmet off his head, gazes into Uno's grinning face.

'What did you think?' says Uno. 'Pretty realistic, isn't it?'

Mori glances at the clock on the wall. Amazingly he spent fifteen minutes playing the game. The time flashed by in an instant.

'Realistic?' he says, wiping the sweat off his brow. 'That's not exactly the word I'd use . . .'

This room is realistic, a small concrete box, hardly

distinguishable from any of the other concrete boxes you have to live your life in. Reality – dull, colourless, totally lacking in any meaning other than what you bring to it yourself. In contrast, the world inside the helmet is heavy with meaning, too much meaning, shaped and layered by clever persons unknown. Mori finds the whole thing stiflingly oppressive.

Uno pulls out a low table. They sit down, drink green tea with dried squid snacks. Uno explains the intricacies of video games to Mori: the different formats; the different generations; the different segments of the market. There are gambling games, science-fiction games, games in which Japan won the Pacific War, games in which you can recreate the evolution of the human race, adding your own mutations. There are also many detective games though – as Uno says with an apologetic smile – they're not very popular these days. In fact, nothing stays popular for more than a few months.

Mori chews squid, ideas. The man he's looking for must be an obsessive player. In fact, playing Black Blade might have been what tipped over an already disturbed mind, provoking him to re-enact the scenes inside the helmet. It's certainly possible. After just fifteen minutes, Mori's head is still buzzing with images and voices. That field of oscillations and pulses, what Uno called the Chi interface – it clearly has some effect.

Black Blade is supposed to revenge himself on high officials. Miura was a top-ranking bureaucrat. It makes a certain kind of sense. Mori sips tea, ponders.

'How many units does a game need to sell to become a hit?' he asks.

Uno sucks air through his teeth. 'Let me see – around five hundred thousand, I suppose . . .'

Mori grunts in dismay. The person he's looking for could

be any one of those five hundred thousand. That's far too many to give any kind of practical help to the investigation.

Mori glances at the clock again. It's time to be going. He gets up, mutters thanks, steps out into the corridor. Down on the street below: high-school students pulling beers from a vending machine; a taxi-driver urinating against a wall; grannies lugging shopping bags; the traffic lights bleeping 'Greensleeves'. How would Hokusai have handled that? He'd probably have fitted in Mount Fuji somehow. He usually did.

At the head of the staircase Mori suddenly stops. A strange thought has occurred to him. Maybe nothing, maybe something. Anyway, certainly worth checking. He goes back to Uno's apartment, pushes the doorbell. When Uno opens the door, he stands there in the rain, points a finger.

'You were talking about the video-game market. You said nothing stays popular for long, right?'

Mori talks fast. Uno looks startled, but he can see that Mori needs an answer.

'Sure. That's why the big companies like SoftJoy and Mega have to keep on bringing out new games all the time – twenty or thirty a month, usually.'

'And the guy in that store told us that Black Blade has just gone straight to number one in the bestsellers' list. Those were his exact words, weren't they – just gone straight to number one?'

'Yes, I think so. Why are you asking?'

'Because I want to know something. I want to know when this game was first released.'

'First released? I think it says somewhere on the plastic case. Why is that important?'

'Don't ask questions,' snaps Mori. 'Just get me that case.'

Uno disappears into the apartment, comes back with the case in his hand.

'Here's the release date,' he says, pointing to a line of figures on the side. 'Almost a month ago now.'

'A month ago! Are you sure?'

Mori stares, eyes popping. There's no mistake. The game was put on the market almost six weeks after Miura died!

'What's this all about?' says Uno. 'Is it important?'

Mori tells him it is, but not the reason. He needs to get back to the office, make some phone calls.

Uno looks impatient. 'So we're making progress, right? What's the next thing you want me to do?'

Mori turns for the stairs. 'No time now,' he says over his shoulder. 'I'll give you the details tomorrow.'

'Hey, tell me more,' yells Uno. 'Wait – I'm coming with you! Just let me get my shoes.'

But Mori doesn't wait. He jogs down the stairs, crossing the path of a young woman in a red raincoat at the entrance to the building. She hurries past, barely registering his presence. Glimpsed face – sharp, serious, efficiently pretty. Outside on the street Mori straddles the Honda, glances up to the corridor on the third floor. The red raincoat has stopped outside Uno's apartment. The door is open. Uno's voice floats down, pleading, defensive. Mori revs the Honda, lets out the clutch. A strong bet: Uno won't be going anywhere this evening.

In the opinion of George the Wolf Nishio, the end of the Cold War has been a distinctly mixed blessing. There are benefits, no question. George himself has dealt in teenage prostitutes from Vietnam, cheap handguns from Poland, speed from Vladivostok. But in his day-to-day work, the disadvantages are more obvious. In particular, the unpleasant necessity of co-existing with the Snakehead.

When mainland Chinese mafia groups first started operating in Japan in the early 1980s, they were deferential, willing to show respect to their betters. In business terms, they were mere sub-contractors. But with the arrival of the Snakehead, all that changed. The Snakehead held a virtual monopoly on a lucrative new market: the smuggling of Chinese peasants to work in sweatshops and construction sites. Demand was explosive, supply limitless. Snakehead groups grew more and more powerful, began to diversify into drugs and gambling.

The kind of Chinese George has to deal with changed too. They used to be rough and simple types, awed by everything around them, keen to learn as much as they could. No more. The new breed are ex-People's Army, cold-eyed, well funded. The real problem: they are not scared. George does not like dealing with people who are not scared of him. He finds them scary.

So when a man called Wang calls George up, says he has something interesting to tell him, George feels pretty ambivalent. Wang is a sinister individual, said to have killed a chimpira who double-crossed him, chopped up the body and fed it to pigs. Still, the two men have co-operated before, profitably. This is how it worked.

Stage One. Wang went to Shanghai, equipped with ninety travel packs, which he sold for ten thousand US dollars a piece. Each travel pack comprised a blue Terylene suit, a white shirt, a bogus name card and a free berth in the hold of a Japanese trawler leased by the old boss.

Stage Two. George and Wang got hold of a container truck, drove it down the Japan Sea coast. Four-thirty a.m., the call comes through on Wang's mobile phone. It's from his deputy on the fishing boat, now hoving into local waters. Wang goes out in a little motor boat, ferries them through the freezing mist, twelve at a time.

Stage Three. The next day ninety salarymen are delivered in container trucks to work sites all over central Japan. They don't speak any Japanese, but are willing to work for one third of the going rate, uninsured, untaxed. But they do bear some hefty deductions. Twenty per cent of earnings is payable to Wang's people, another twenty per cent to the old boss.

That was nearly three years ago now. These days Wang does everything himself, has heavy presence in drugs and gambling and the 'ejaculation industry'. He's growing fast, much too fast for George's liking.

They meet in the back room of a restaurant in Yokohama's Chinatown. Decor – gold embroidered silk screens, marble floors, glittering chandeliers. Wang sits at a low table, surrounded by young Chinese men with eyes like the black stones on a go board.

'Good to see you,' says Wang, not bothering to get up. George isn't going to bow, not to one of these guys. Instead he nods, mutters some bland words of greeting. George always feels uncomfortable when status relations are unclear. Is Wang a status inferior? In the traditional sense, yes: after all, he is Chinese, and at least five years younger than George. But in another sense, no: he is rich, powerful, has dozens of underlings who would kill for him at a moment's notice. And now he is offering George a favour, as if he were a high-ranking syndicate member helping out a junior. George doesn't like that, but the favour being offered is one that he needs.

Wang beckons George to sit down. 'You are looking for a man called Mori,' he says.

'That's right,' says George, startled. 'How did you know?'

Wang smiles, thin, cold. 'Some of the people you asked do business with us too.'

That's bad news. It meant that Wang is pushing directly into the old boss's franchise.

'You know this Mori?' asks George.

Wang flicks his fingers. One of the young men leaves the room, comes back leading a tall Chinese girl with a bandage wrapped around her forehead.

'This woman is Chen-li. She will tell you what you want to know.'

Chen-li nods, kneels down demurely at the table. This is what she says. The whore Angel is her enemy. After they fought in a restuarant Chen-li has been trying to trace her. She discovered that Angel has been bought by a middle-aged doctor, name unknown, is living with him somewhere in Yokohama. She also discovered that Angel was brought back to Tokyo by a private detective called Mori.

George lights up inside. 'Private detective? Are you sure?'

Chen-li is sure. She even knows where he's based – somewhere in Shinjuku.

George stammers his gratitude, says he will work hard to return the favour. Don't worry about it, says Wang with an easy wave of the hand. It's always a pleasure to help an old comrade. And – who knows – there may be a special favour we'll need some time in the future.

Two young men lead George back to the Mazda Roadstar – walnut dashboard, calfskin seats – that he has just borrowed from a real-estate broker who owes some favours to the old boss. The real-estate guy doesn't know he's lent it yet, but when he finds out he won't object.

The Mazda is parked more or less diagonally, back wheels up on the pavement. George pulls a string of keys out of his pocket with a flourish.

'Cute little car,' says one Chinese guy, blank face.

'Just like my younger sister's,' says the other, his pronunciation so lousy it makes you wince.

The lack of respect would normally send George into a paroxysm. Tonight, though, his spirits are ebullient. The man Mori is finally within his grasp! Only when he is tearing along the expressway, thirty kilometres per hour over the limit, does he start to wonder about the special favour that Wang has in mind.

Shinjuku, nine o'clock – neon puddles, tramping feet, ghostly karaoke echoing down empty corridors. Mori sits at his desk nursing a glass of Suntory whisky. The revelation about the release date of Black Blade has turned the whole Miura case upside down. He isn't casting around in the dark any more, searching for dead men called Nakanishi or missing security guards. He has a definite focus of enquiry: the company called SoftJoy, supplier of electronic hallucinations to mindless juveniles of all ages.

Somewhere in the SoftJoy organization is someone who calls himself Black Blade, a disturbed character probably responsible for two murders. How to get closer? Uno is not the person for a job like that. An inexperienced private detective who competes on price is hardly going to coax incriminating information out of a secretive outfit like SoftJoy. Even Mori himself would have difficulty without cover of some sort, an excuse to get in and ask questions. Who would have that kind of excuse? Who could just walk into a major software company and question the top people about their product development process? Mori cracks an ice cube between his teeth. An idea has come to mind – a weird one but, then, all good ideas look weird at first. And so do many bad ones too, of course.

Mori rattles the ice cube between his teeth, picks up the phone.

Thirteen

Mitchell has been told by many people – ranging from taxi drivers to immigration officials, from bankers to 'body-conscious' Roppongi girls – that Japan has only four seasons. They say it proudly, implying that no other place on earth is in the same happy condition. They rarely mention the fifth season, the rainy season. With good cause.

The rainy season brings unpleasantness. It brings the slob face to face with the consequences of his own slobbishness. It makes things grow: fungus on plates in the sink; slime in the bath; a clump of tiny mushrooms where the window was left open and the rain soaked the tatami. It makes dirty socks stink. Of course, dirty socks are supposed to stink. But not like this. Nothing has ever stunk like this before. This is a biochemical hazard.

The rainy season brings out the cockroaches. They scurry around after dark, rustle through the trash, compete to excrete in the most daring places – in the washbasin, on the computer keyboard, on the rim of the cooker.

The rainy season washes the world grey. Buildings, clothes, trees, salarymen's faces – all different shades of grey.

Mitchell craves the end of the rainy season, but it's only halfway through. Wet days stretch out ahead, as far as the eye can see.

A typical evening at home. Mitchell is squatting in the

middle of his unmade futon, playing a newly acquired video game. Raindrops plip into the half-dozen rice bowls on the floor. Sounds outside the window – frogs croaking, helicopters droning. Granny Abe's radio wailing the rainy season blues.

A new sound, the phone ringing. Mitchell glances at his watch, and his stomach lurches. It's too late for Yoko, Keiko, Sachiko or Rika. But it's not too late for Sasha de Glazier. This could be it: instant execution. Mitchell clears his throat, picks up the phone. He's determined to face the axe with the aplomb of Sir Walter Raleigh.

But there's no axe, not yet anyway. The voice at the other end is utterly non-global. Mitchell recalls the face that comes with it, the deep-set eyes, the lines around the mouth. Mori – they haven't met for almost a year! Now, why would a private detective be calling him so late in the evening? And why would he be making a feeble attempt to flatter, complimenting Mitchell on his excellent Japanese and his deep knowledge of Japanese companies? You don't have to be a trained analyst to get suspicious at this point.

And when the man suggests meeting for a drink in an hour's time in order to discuss old times, those suspicions are bound to deepen. But you go all the same. Because you've been feeling pretty bored lately, and whatever Mori has got to say, whatever convoluted problem he wants to tangle you up in, the experience is unlikely to be boring.

Mori puts down the phone, pours himself another glass of Suntory White. Unorthodox problems call for unorthodox solutions. The foreigner may be clumsy, but he's trust-worthy enough for someone who works in the big money game. That was proven in the circumstances in which they first met, escaping from a group of religious maniacs. Since then they've got together a couple of times, drunk sake, toured a few nightclubs. Still, they don't really have a lot in common. Mitchell likes Roppongi discos and Hollywood movies. Being a foreigner he has trouble making the necessary distinctions – between jokes and insults, between good cheap sushi and lousy cheap sushi, between women who are truly dumb and those who are just pretending. The guy speaks decent Japanese; Mori can understand almost everything that he says. And because he understands what Mitchell is saying, he sees that foreignness isn't a question of language at all. Mitchell talks about Japan and Japanese all the time – comparing, summarizing, judging. And the Japan that he talks about is a place that Mori has never been to in his entire life.

The last time the two of them met was in a Latino bar near the big Yotsuya crossing. Fragments of the conversation stick in Mori's mind. They were drinking sour Brazilian liquor. On the dance floor office girls were wiggling and jiggling, thirty minutes of carnival before the last train to the suburbs.

Mitchell mentioned that he was working for the Germans, didn't seem too excited by the idea. Mori asked what exactly he was doing. Mitchell answered that he was supposed to be in charge of growth technology. Is that interesting? asked Mori, doubtful. Could be worse, said Mitchell. Gives me the chance to study companies like Mega Enterprises and SoftJoy.

That's where the fragment breaks off. Mitchell hit the dance floor. Mori slipped off into the night. Now it's time, almost a year later, for the conversation to be resumed.

Mitchell sits waiting for Mori in a Korean barbecue on the south side of Shinjuku station. He sips beer, stares out of the window, watches people hurrying through the fizzling rain. Mori pulls up to the kerb on his motorbike, immediately recognizable even in his helmet. How old is this guy? It's hard to judge. Looking from a distance at the calm oval face and the thatch of hair, you'd say anything between thirty and forty. Closer up, when you see the lines and the flecks of grey, you'd say anything between forty and fifty. From the way he talks, you'd say centuries.

Mori walks into the restaurant, raises a hand in greeting. Mitchell gets up and bows – surely the Japanese thing to do – but Mori waves him back impatiently, as if he'd said something foolish. Mitchell remembers – this is a tense and difficult character. No smiles, no etiquette, no hesitant, delicately weighted enquiries. Usually when Mitchell stands close to Japanese men three or four inches shorter than himself, it makes him feel large, forceful. With Mori, though, he feels as light as paper. It's as if the man is made out of some super-dense material, several times heavier per cubic inch than ordinary flesh and bone.

The last time they met – vague memories, an evening fogged in Brazilian liquor and pounding drums. Some tipsy girls from an advertising agency were dancing. Mitchell went to join them, swapped name cards, scored with one of them later that weekend. Anyway, he was throwing his limbs around to the music, making good eye contact, when he suddenly realized that Mori's chair was empty. This is a man who doesn't samba.

Mori sits down, orders chilled beer and rice and beef soup.

'Make that two,' says Mitchell.

'How spicy do you want it?' asks the waiter.

'Strong as you've got,' says Mori.

'Same for me,' says Mitchell, trying to copy Mori's characteristic half-grunt half-growl. It doesn't come out right, and the waiter gives him a strange look. Nobody else talks like that, at least no other Japanese that Mitchell has ever met.

'There's a favour I need to ask,' says Mori. 'It's about a company called SoftJoy. Remember, you said you were following it pretty closely.'

'That's right,' says Mitchell uneasily. 'It's my number-one recommendation. What's the problem, exactly?'

Mori sketches the outlines of the problem in frustratingly vague terms. Someone at SoftJoy was involved in a certain incident. The person concerned appears to have been obsessed with a hit video game well before it was released on to the market. So Mori wants to know how games are actually developed, how many people are involved in the process, how easy it is to get hold of their names.

'Their names?' says Mitchell, trying to hide his amazement. 'That sort of information is highly secret.'

Mori narrows his gaze, frowns. 'Well, getting hold of secret information is your job, isn't it? I mean, if you've only got the same information as everyone else, what's the point?'

Mitchell sighs, thinks about explaining the concept of efficient markets, free and fair disclosure, the perils of insider trading. Then he gives up. He has tried the principles of finance on Mori before. It was hopeless, no more effective – to use a phrase he'd learned from Mori himself – than pissing on a frog's head.

The chilled beers arrive – huge frosted mugs, shards of ice bobbing inside. Mitchell takes a draught, pauses to think. He certainly needs to know more. 'Incident' – that's a suspicious sort of word. In Japan short wars are sometimes described as 'incidents'.

'So what kind of incident was this exactly? A crime of some sort, I suppose?'

'You could say that.'

'A serious crime?'

Mori peers at a spot on the wall some distance above Mitchell's head. 'Well, it was certainly serious enough for the guy who got killed.'

Mitchell's beer-mug bangs down on the Formica. 'What? You're telling me that some SoftJoy staffer has been involved in a murder? And it's related to one of their products?'

'Two murders, actually,' says Mori.

Mitchell gazes across the table, mouth open. Images jumble in his brain: the police raiding SoftJoy's offices; the stock price falling like a stone; Scott Hamada grinning; Sasha de Glazier's long fingernails closing around her mobile phone. Mitchell leans back in his chair, groans in humilation.

'What's the matter?' asks Mori. 'You don't want to get involved?'

'I'm involved already – up to my neck! If you want any help from me, you're going to have to give me the whole story, right from the beginning.'

Mori looks dubious. 'That's difficult. The background is confidential.'

'No good,' says Mitchell shaking his head. 'Any information I've got is confidential too!'

Mori's eyes bore into him, but Mitchell doesn't flinch. He can't afford to, not with his career hanging in the balance.

'All right,' Mori says finally. 'But first of all we eat.'

The waiter brings two bowls of rice and beef soup. The liquid inside is orange-streaked, shimmering.

'Too strong for you?' asks Mori.

'Not at all,' says Mitchell.

'Well, drink it like this.' Mori raises the bowl in both

hands and takes a long noisy slurp, after which he wipes his mouth with a hand-towel.

Mitchell picks up his bowl, peers inside. Close up the stuff looks even stranger, possibly radioactive. Only too aware of Mori's expectant gaze, he tilts the bowl towards his mouth, closes his eyes, guzzles. The shock is immediate, electric. Mitchell just manages to control the impulse to jerk his head backwards. His lips burn, his tongue sizzles, his tonsils ignite. Still Mitchell carries on drinking until finally pain is overlaid with numbness. Then he slaps the bowl back down on the table.

'Good?' asks Mori solicitously.

Sweat on his brow, tears in his eyes, Mitchell nods. For the next quarter of an hour, Mori does all the talking.

Mori leaves Mitchell outside Shinjuku station, points the Honda in the direction of the fifteen-million-yen net liability that he calls home. The meeting went well. Mitchell seemed to understand the problem, promised to help. All Mori wants is the names of the people who would have been familiar with the contents of the Black Blade video game three months before its release. Surely that shouldn't be too difficult for someone with Mitchell's credentials? Mori remembers when they first met, on that island controlled by the religious cult. He remembers Mitchell explaining his work. 'I'm a kind of financial detective,' he said, the salient differences being that Mitchell gets paid every month just for showing up to his office, no one tries to kill him when he uncovers inconvenient facts, and he can spend his whole career working on the same small number of cases. Well, the job of any detective, financial or otherwise, is to get hold of information that people don't want to give. As for the information that people actually do want to give out – you have to be very cautious with that indeed.

The Honda roars up the ramp to the expressway. Mori peers through the rain. If he hurries, there may just be time for a massage on the way home.

The train suddenly jerks into life. Mitchell grabs the handrail, manages to prevent himself from collapsing into a cluster of office ladies. Despite the thousands of train journeys he has taken in this city, he has yet to master the art of holding his balance when his legs are swaying in one direction and his shoulders in another. The train is jam-packed, or at least seems to be. In fact, at every station more and more people shove their way on board, manage to find space amongst the press of bodies. No words are spoken, no glances exchanged. Some people are sleeping on their feet, or maybe pretending. Others are scanning the fliers of weekly magazines, watching the day's news scroll past on a digital tickertape. Breath mingles, sweat mingles, flesh presses flesh.

The lesson of Japanese trains: strangers don't really exist. If you're squashed up against someone you know, your skin tingles with the message: Eros or embarrassment. If you're squashed up against a stranger, there's no message at all. You might as well be pressing up against a door or a wall. And to the stranger you're no more than a door or a wall too. You don't really exist. Nothing really exists.

Zen commuting – one art that Mitchell has managed to master in his daily journeys through the bowels of the giant city. Right now his right elbow may be pinned between the shoulders of two salarymen, his hips twisted at ninety degrees to his feet. There may be a wet umbrella dripping down his trouser-leg, a briefcase jammed into his buttocks, a salaryman's breath hot on the side of his neck. His mind, though, is elsewhere, floating high above the clouds.

Mitchell's thoughts concern Mori, SoftJoy, Sasha de Glazier. He needs to get to the bottom of this business, fast. Imagine what Mega Enterprise's publicity machine, backed by the full might of the Mitsukawa empire, could do with a story like this. Non-stop media investigations, consumer boycotts, demands for product recalls – it could be enough to scupper the launch of SoftJoy's next generation machine. Everything would turn out according to Scott Hamada's dire predictions.

So what to do? First of all, it's vital to pre-empt the police. That means helping Mori find out who was involved in putting together this Black Blade game. Easier said than done, of course. Like all SoftJoy games, it will have been developed by an outside contractor. Sonoda is unapproachable, notorious for his paranoid attitude to secrecy. Mitchell is going to need some assistance. Is there anyone he knows who could smooth the way?

Suddenly the train jerks to a halt. Mitchell staggers, twists, grabs. Diagonal glances, silent faces – he was the only one who wasn't prepared, the only one who didn't pay attention to the announcement. The train hums, awaiting the electronic event that will allow it to continue its progress under the city.

Mitchell's mind hums too. Yes, there is someone who could help him, someone close enough to Sonoda to know the details of the development process. But would she agree to help him? Uncertain, but trying to persuade her could be an intriguing challenge.

Fourteen

Angel is woken by the sound of the phone. It's the doctor, calling from Los Angeles.

'What's going on there?' he says. 'Have you got a man with you?'

'Nobody's here,' says Angel sleepily. She glances at the clock on the bedside table. It's nine-thirty, well before the time she usually gets up.

'So how many men have you been with while I've been away?'

Angel does a little calculation on her fingers. 'Twelve,' she says finally.

'Twelve! That's more than one a night, isn't it?'

'One night there were three – all at the same time.'

The doctor's voice goes husky. 'Really? How old were they?'

'They were students that I met in a disco, all young and very healthy.'

'Tell me about it,' breathes the doctor. 'Tell me everything you did.'

'Sure,' says Angel, stifling a yawn. 'When you get back, I'll tell you every detail.'

'I would like to watch that. Will you let me watch next time, Angel?'

Angel giggles. 'Watch? That's naughty of you, Doctor.'

Actually it's about as naughty as he gets. He touches her

breasts occasionally, never anything more. He's a strange guy, this doctor. He doesn't want sex. He wants to want it. When he looks at her sometimes, there's a strange kind of need in his eyes, as strong as a baby's need for warmth. Angel's never asked him this, but she thinks that maybe he's dying.

'Will you let me watch?' repeats the doctor petulantly.

'I'll think about it,' says Angel. 'Anyway, there's a small problem at the moment.'

'What problem?'

'The bank account's empty.'

'Empty already? What have you been doing?'

Angel wrinkles her nose reflectively. 'Well, I've been spending money,' she says. 'To meet these nice boys, I need to look like a nice girl – with nice clothes and perfume and so on.'

'How much money do you want?'

'Just a couple of hundred thousand,' says Angel in her softest, sultriest voice. 'Enough to look nice for all the nice boys. And for you too when you're watching . . .'

The doctor says it's time to go into the conference hall now, but he promises to transfer the money as soon as possible. That's good. Angel needs the money straight away. Not to look nice for any students, because there aren't any students, nor has she been with any other men since the doctor left for America. If it's a holiday for him, it's going to be a holiday for her too. No, the reason that the account is empty is Estelle.

Two hours later, the doctor's brand-new Porsche pulls up outside a grubby concrete block in the back streets of Koenji. Not having a driving licence, Angel parks carefully, smiling at a curious delivery boy bicycling past with his noodle tray high on his shoulder. The bike wobbles, and for a moment it looks as if he's going to crash. Not every day does he see a woman as voluptuous as Angel in her skin-tight designer jeans and halter top of crimson satin. Angel gives him a friendly wave, then disappears into the building.

A man called Kris opens the door of the apartment. He works in the fish market, a good guy but not too bright.

'How's she doing?' asks Angel.

'Better. The doctor says it's all on the surface, nothing serious.'

But for a woman like Estelle the surface is serious too. It's all she's got.

'You should have called me before.'

'She didn't want you to know.'

'Why not?'

Kris shrugs. Angel sweeps past him into the tiny bedroom. Estelle is sitting up against the pillow. Angel flashes her smile, but the first glimpse comes as a shock. Estelle is almost unrecognizable, her face a mass of bruises and welts, one eye swollen up like an overripe fruit.

'What happened?' says Angel.

Estelle mumbles through split lips, so softly that Angel has to bend down to hear what she's saying. What happened is this. Last week a guy came into the pink salon, told her someone outside wanted to see her. Estelle went out on her own. Chen-li was waiting with five Chinese girlfriends. They pulled her into an alley, beat her to the ground with socks filled with coins. Then Chen-li doused petrol on her dress, said she'd roast like a chicken unless she told them what they wanted to know. And what they wanted to know was about Angel.

'What did you tell them?'

'I said you were with a doctor in Yokohama somewhere. I said he paid that detective Mori to get you away from the crazy gangster. I'm sorry, Angel. I was scared.'

'No need to be sorry,' says Angel. 'It's my fault. The fight in the restaurant – that's what started it.'

She squeezes Estelle's hand, kisses her lightly on the forehead. On the way out she hands Kris a thick envelope of money. It's time for Estelle to be going home.

Mori sits at his desk, jotting notes on a piece of paper. The felt-tip pen moves fast, joining characters where they shouldn't be joined, missing out strokes and turning standard patterns into flowing squiggles. At school they teach you to write in simple boxy characters, then get you to think the same way. Mori's teachers certainly did their best, but it wasn't enough.

He makes three columns: one for facts; one for suspicions; one for questions. That's just for convenience, of course. The distance from facts to suspicions is rarely as large as it seems.

FACTS	THEORIES	SUSPICIONS
Miura is dead	It was a murder, covered up	Why necessary to cover it up?
He was stalked by someone calling himself 'Black Blade'	The killer is obsessed with vengeance	What is he avenging?
'Black Blade' is the name of a video game released after Miura's death	The killer works for SoftJoy, the company that markets the game	How many people would be aware of the contents of the game?
A man called Nakanishi is also dead	Nakanishi is also a bureaucrat or an influential person of some sort	What is the relationship, if any, between Miura and Nakanishi?

Mori nibbles the top of the pen, ponders. Kimiko Itoh will be back in another ten days. Progress has been made, but hardly enough to qualify for the bonus-earning break-through. Maybe Mitchell will be able to come up with something in time, maybe not. Anyway, every angle needs to be explored. Mori picks up the phone, calls Uno. The voice at the other end is as enthusiastic as ever.

'This is getting exciting, isn't it? Even Kei-chan was impressed.'

'Kei-chan?'

'I mean, Keiko. That's my fiancée.'

Mori can't hide his irritation. 'What – you told your fiancée about this case?'

'We discussed it,' chirps Uno. 'You see, we discuss everything. That's one of the rules of our relationship. Anyway, what birth sign are you, Mori-*san*?'

At first Mori doubts that he has heard right. 'Birth sign? What do you want to know that for?'

'Keiko was looking at my horoscope in one of the magazines she reads. It says a very important event will happen this week, big enough to change the direction of my entire life. Apparently it's all related to a Sagittarius with an AB blood type. Are you a Sagittarius, Mori-*san*?'

'I don't believe that stupid nonsense.'

'But are you a Sagittarius?'

'No, I'm a Scorpio. And my blood type is ZZ minus.'

Uno, thinks Mori for the hundredth time, is simply not cut out to be a private detective. A man who follows horoscopes in women's magazines will believe absolutely anything. And as for discussing the details of a case with his fiancée – the lack of professionalism makes Mori cringe.

'So let's get into action,' says Uno breezily. 'I've done everything you asked me so far. What's the next step?'

'The next step is to check out a guy called Kenji Nakanishi, died in a car crash last spring. The death could be suspicious. I want you to find out everything you can about the circumstances.'

'Understood!' replies Uno smartly.

Mori put the phone down. This kind of lead has to be followed up, but Mori's instincts are telling him that it's going to be waste of energy. And if there is someone with plenty of energy to spare, it's Uno.

Next call: Shinohara, his contact at the phone company. Mori thanks him for the transcript of the monitored conversation, tells him that he'd like to listen to the recording itself.

'No problem,' says Shinohara. 'What delivery medium would suit you? If your computer's got audio capability, I can arrange for the whole thing to be transmitted to you on-line.'

'Thanks for the offer,' says Mori. 'But if you don't mind, I'd prefer a cassette tape, parcel delivery.'

Lunchtime – Mori hears the cry of a baked-yam seller on the street outside. He runs down the stairs, stops the guy's van and buys one. He eats it in the grounds of a dank cramped little shrine overshadowed by a new capsule hotel. The sky weighs down on his shoulders. The rain hangs in the air, paused. Mori swills down canned coffee, then goes to the pachinko parlour to blow the money he has just saved on food and drink. You've got to be strict about these things.

As soon as he's back in the office a call comes through

from Shinohara. From his embarrassed tone of voice, Mori can guess what's coming.

'It's the first time something like this has happened,' says Shinohara. 'It looks like the domain protection system must have been wrongly deployed.'

'Domain protection system? What are you talking about?'

'That's the program that seals off all high-priority data, makes sure that it can't be deleted or shifted around by unauthorized personnel.'

'So what happened?'

'Well, the data got deleted.'

Mori sucks air through his teeth. 'When did this happen?'

'We can't tell,' mutters Shinohara. 'Somehow or other that information got deleted too.'

'Strange, isn't it? I mean, you gave me the transcript just a few days ago.'

'No, that's different. Let me explain how our domain archiving system works...'

Mori doesn't care how it works, but he listens while Shinohara meanders on about filter-hierarchies and ultra-secure command strings.

'So you think this was an accident?' he says when Shinohara has finished.

'What do you mean?' says Shinohara, puzzled by the questions.

'I mean you don't think someone managed to break in and steal the data.'

Shinohara is shocked by the idea. 'Someone from outside? That would be impossible.'

'You mean, just like the deletion of data that can't be deleted.' That comment was a mistake. It puts Shinohara on the defensive, obliges him to affirm the honour and glory of the company where he has spent the whole of his working life. He embarks on a long explanation of the sophistication of the security system, the unsurpassable excellence of the software engineers who created it. This time Mori doesn't listen at all. Instead he is wondering about the intentions of a certain group of people working out of an obscure building in the heart of the business district.

Mid-afternoon, Mori goes for a soak in the bath-house across the street. The old man is there again, heating up his sluggish blood, singing war songs in a low quavering voice. It's amazing how he remembers the words as he doesn't remember much else – not Mori's name, not the day of the week, not even the name of his own dead wife. Maybe when you get to a certain age the past seems closer. The day you were born must seem like yesterday when you think about where you're going.

'Are you feeling well, grandad?' calls Mori through the steam. The old man raises his hand, keeps on singing.

Back at the office Mori fixes coffee, puts a record on the turntable – 'The Blues and the Abstract Truth', by Oliver Nelson. This copy he bought twenty-five years ago in a little shop in Yoyogi. Sounds like it too, all clicks and bumps from the moment the needle comes down. Mori has to put a five-yen coin on top of the pick-up to stop it from jumping.

The sound of the phone cuts through Mori's reverie. It's a sibilant, nuanced sort of ring – not Uno this time. Mori picks up the receiver, recognizes at once the studiedly neutral tones of Kazuko. As always, she goes straight to the point, no pleasantries.

'The person under enquiry has been located. The address is Matsuda City five twenty-seven, Green Palace Heights eight zero four. Do you understand?'

'Understood.'

The line clicks dead. 'Thank you, Kazuko-*san*,' says Mori

into the purring receiver. Finally the inevitable has happened. Kaneda the missing security guard has opened a bank account, or rented a video, or used his health insurance card, or done something else that has left a trace on Kazuko's super-sensitive financial radar. It's time to pay him a visit.

Richard Mitchell is sitting in a cafeteria located on the top floor of a skyscraper known in the financial world as the 'Tower of Bubble'. In the late 1980s Mitsukawa Real Estate bought the land from Mitsukawa Life, Japan's biggest insurance company, on credit supplied by Mitsukawa Bank. Work on the project was started by Mitsukawa Construction in 1990 and completed a few years later, at the trough of the real-estate slump. Miraculously, despite charging the highest rents in the world, the building has been one hundred per cent full ever since. Or maybe not so miraculous, since the tenants include Mitsukawa Electric, the world's largest manufacturer of memory chips, Mitsukawa Construction, Mitsukawa Life itself and Mitsukawa Bank, which moved in after selling its old head office to the government-controlled Urban Renaissance Corporation.

Mitchell sips cinnamon tea from a small metallic mug. These mugs are part of the cafeteria experience. They are heavy, misshapen, and such good conductors of heat that they can't be held at the base or the rim. If you ask, you can buy one for twenty thousand yen, roughly the same price as a dinner in the Belle Epoque restaurant next door. The famous artist who designed the cafeteria has other works on sale too. There are ashtrays (Yen 35,000) that look like chunks of volcanic lava, stools (Yen 120,000) made from whitewashed automobile tyres, and postcards (Yen 1,500) featuring his latest installation, a heap of smashed-up office equipment that was set on fire simultaneously in Tokyo,

Berlin and Manhattan. But there is no one to buy, for Mitchell is the only customer. The five waiters stand motionless, staring out of the window in an appropriately post-modern manner.

Mitchell glances at his watch. Will she bother to show up? On the phone, she was reluctant until he explained that he had crucial information that might affect the future of the company. Even then she seemed hesitant, unsure whether to believe him or not.

The door swings open. 'Welcome!' call out the waiters in unison. The woman who walks in looks like a librarian on holiday: steel-rimmed spectacles; check shirt hanging over her shapeless corduroy trousers. Mitchell has difficulty in matching her with the fizzy 'talent' who appears on the quiz shows or the stunningly attractive woman who sat next to Sonoda at the panel discussion. When she comes up to his table and smiles a greeting, the resemblance gets a little stronger. Those lips are unforgettable.

'Good afternoon,' says Reiko. Next surprise: she speaks fluent Californian English.

'Thanks for coming,' says Mitchell. 'I was worried you weren't going to make it.'

Reiko sits down opposite him. 'No problem, but there isn't much time, I'm afraid. I'm supposed to be filming a commercial in two hours' time.'

'Commercial for what?'

'For SoftJoy. President Sonoda has asked me to appear in the summer campaign.'

When she pronounces Sonoda's name, her eyes drop and there's a hint of reverence in her voice. Mitchell's jealousy knots and throbs. How do you get a woman like this to think about you like that? Probably by not thinking about her at all.

Mitchell keeps the subject going. 'As an analyst, I'd really like to understand how these games get developed. I mean, how the process is actually managed.'

Reiko raises an eyebrow. 'Uh-huh.'

'I suppose the basic idea has to be approved, then some kind of contract is signed with the developers.'

'That's right.'

'So how many SoftJoy people would get to see the product when it's under development?'

Reiko looks at him keenly. 'SoftJoy people? None, of course.'

'None?' says Mitchell, taken aback.

'None, except for President Sonoda. He handles the contacts with the developers himself.'

'And these developers of Black Blade – how could an analyst like me get in touch with them?'

'You can't. Their identity is totally secret, even now. That's a key part of SoftJoy's strategy.'

'But someone like you could find out, couldn't you?'

Reiko frowns. 'I could, but I won't. That kind of information is the lifeblood of a company like SoftJoy.'

'Look, if you care about the future of SoftJoy, you will help me. One of these developers may have been involved in a serious crime. The whole thing could be extremely damaging.'

Reiko is looking at him as if he were a suspicious stain on a love hotel coverlet.

'What on earth are you talking about?'

'I can't say any more until you give me the names of these developers. Believe me, if we can clear this thing up, President Sonoda will be eternally grateful.'

Reiko stares at him across the table and for a moment Mitchell thinks he has won. But then she pushes her chair back and jumps to her feet.

'Liar,' she shouts at him. 'Why should I tell you anything?'

'Wait, Reiko!'

She bats away his hand and turns for the door. Mitchell slumps in his seat, resists the temptation to hurl the twenty-thousand-yen tea cup to the floor. The five post-modern waiters continue to stare into space, as if nothing at all is happening.

Matsuda City is a long train ride away. Mori gets there just after five o'clock, stops at a police box to get directions. The district where Kaneda lives is a few kilometres from the centre of town. The rain is thinning out, so Mori decides to walk.

Machida is a place with a history. Great battles were fought here in the era of warring states. In the sixteenth century, the castle in the centre of town was besieged by warrior monks, who finally swarmed over the ramparts and slaughtered the forces of the local daimyo. Soon after, they in turn were put to the sword by the army of a rival warlord. Just a hundred and forty years ago, loyalists of the last shogun made a despairing stand on the coastal plain, charging the riflemen with swords drawn. And just a few years before Mori was born, kamikaze pilots took off from an airfield on the far side of the river. Over the centuries Matsuda City has seen the destruction of hundreds of thousands of ferociously sincere men. But you wouldn't know it from looking at the place now. Today Matsuda City is the same as everywhere else: the same railway station; the same grid of streets; the same convenience stores; the same family restaurants; the same clean bright emptiness that you get in all the giant suburbs of the giant city that has spread to fill every corner of the Kanto plain.

Half an hour on foot brings Mori to the high-rise

complex that is Kaneda's new home. It's hardly an improvement on the man's last address – not so vast and impersonal, but not so modern either. There's no rack to park the bicycles, no elevator. Mori has to stump up six flights of damp concrete stairs to reach Kaneda's apartment. He bends down, peers through the letter box. No sound, lights off. Mori takes a flat cap from his inside pocket, slips it on his head and raps on the door of the next apartment along.

Footsteps on the other side of the door. Mori gives a broad smile, just the right height for the peep-hole.

'Who are you?' calls out a woman's voice.

'Kanto Electric Power,' chirps Mori. 'Many thanks for your continued patronage.'

The door edges open a couple of centimetres, still on the chain. One eye peers into Mori's face. 'What do you want?' says the woman.

'An electrical fault has been located in the next-door residence. I've been ordered to deal with it quickly, but unfortunately there's nobody at home.'

'Really? Well, you'll just have to wait till she gets back.'

'When will that be?'

'I don't know,' says the woman, irritated. 'Whenever she finishes her shift at the department store.'

Mori leans in closer to the crack in the door. 'Please give me the name of that department store. I must contact her as soon as possible.'

Behind the door the woman shakes her head vigorously. 'I'm not going to tell you that. I never get mixed up in other people's business. That's my rule.'

Mori glances at his watch. 'You may get mixed up whether you want to or not. If this fault isn't corrected by tomorrow, there could be a major fire. Your own apartment could be at risk.'

The one eye widens. 'My apartment?'

'That's right.'

The strip of face disappears. 'Wait a moment – let me write down the details for you.'

A few minutes later the woman returns, pushes a sheet of notepaper through the crack in the door.

'Thank you,' beams Mori. 'And heartfelt gratitude for your continuing custom.'

Half an hour later Mori walks through the entrance of the Seikyu department store. Like every other Seikyu store, it's a huge aircraft-carrier of a building, occupying a prime site just in front of the railway station. Mori goes straight to the food department, ignoring the shouts of welcome and the baskets of samples that are thrust in front of him. In his student days, he sometimes lived off those samples, spending his lunch-breaks touring the department stores of Shinjuku and Ikebukuro.

Kaneda's wife works in the fresh fruit department. Like all the other staff members, she is wearing a little badge with her name on it. Mori stops in front of the counter, watches her arranging a cluster of bulbous 'cannonball' grapes in a basket of melons, papaya and star-fruit. Her fingers move busily, briskly. She's a strong-faced woman – no make-up, grey-streaked hair pulled back in a bun. Looks like the type who jumps eagerly into middle age, glad to be rid of all the nonsense that comes before.

'Excuse me,' says Mori. 'I hope you don't mind me interrupting your work.'

'That's all right. You're not interrupting.'

True enough, because even as she looks at him her fingers are still tucking, folding, primping.

'Actually, I'm looking for your husband. I need to contact him as soon as possible.'

Sometimes Mori gets tired of the stories he has to spin in

the course of his work. He's got too good at it. Nobody questions him any more, nobody even thinks of questioning. Dull, weary lies, not worth the effort of disbelieving.

Now Mori is an ex-colleague of Kaneda's, a veteran employee in the security department of the ministry. The reason for his visit: he needs to trace some documents that have been sent for storage, just to complete the annual records. His boss told him to go and ask Kaneda in person, as Kaneda's signature was on a document requesting permission to change the storage location of the other documents ... As Mori speaks, he reads boredom in the woman's eyes: boredom with his words; boredom with her husband's colleagues and job; boredom with her husband. Which is exactly the response he wants.

'You say you're in a hurry?' she says. 'Well, in that case, you'd better go directly to the bowling centre on the other side of the station. That's where he'll be right now. Afterwards he'll probably go and get drunk with his new colleagues.'

She says that completely factually, without a trace of humour or disapproval. Mori thanks her, hurries out of the store.

The bowling centre isn't hard to find. It's a four-storey concrete building with a giant red bowling pin sticking up from the roof like a monstrous phallus. There are ten lanes in the bowling hall, four of them occupied. Mori stands at the back, watches the action. One of the lanes is occupied by a group of chimpira in Hawaiian shirts and sunglasses. They bowl badly, feet and arms everywhere, and make plenty of noise, roaring and dancing and chasing after the balls. In the next lane are some serious bowlers, middle-aged men who go through breathing exercises before they start their run-ups. Next to that is group of young salarymen and office ladies. The men swagger back after every strike, slap hands and hunch their shoulders. The women compete at failure, squealing joyously every time a ball goes spinning into the gutter. Their reward: a male colleague bending behind them, demonstrating how to hold the ball right.

The last lane looks the most promising – middle-aged men again, but not so serious this time. Cans of beer are being drunk, cigarettes smoked, octopus dumplings guzzled. A few of them look as if they might be security people: judo-player hips, crewcuts, no necks. What happens next confirms Mori's inference. There is a long rack of bowling balls behind the lanes. Obviously unhappy with his performance, one of the crewcuts decides to replace the ball he has been using. He dumps it in the rack, starts testing the feel of some alternatives. Just at that moment, a third chimpira appears, strides up to the rack. The crewcut seizes on the white ball at the far end, the heaviest on offer. He weighs it, jams his stubby fingers into the holes, grunts in satisfaction. The chimpira stands staring at him, arms crossed.

'Hey, uncle,' he growls. 'What do you think you're doing?'

The crewcut ignores him, bends down, goes through a stiff-kneed bowling action.

The chimpira smacks the back of his left hand into the palm of his right. 'Listen to me when I'm talking! That's my ball you've got there.'

This chimpira looks like a bike-gang graduate – drainpipe trousers, long greasy quiff, a couple of chunky rings on his fingers. He's a big guy, and he's rolled his T-shirt sleeves on to his shoulders to show off his meat.

The crewcut leans back against the rack. He looks slightly puzzled. 'Your ball? I'm sorry, I thought it belonged to the bowling alley here.'

'You don't understand me, uncle,' says the chimpira, grabbing at the crewcut's collar. 'This is the ball that I always use!'

'Let go,' says the crewcut tightly. 'This is my best shirt!'

The chimpira finds that comment highly amusing. He turns to his two friends, who are also approaching the rack.

'Hear what he says!' he chortles. 'Best shirt! It looks as if it should be used as a toilet rag!'

There is the sound of ripping cloth as he yanks his hand backwards. The two other chimpira howl with laughter as he tosses the severed collar high into the air. The office girls stop giggling, the salarymen stop slapping hands. On the other side of the hall the crewcut's comrades are no longer chomping drinking smoking. They stand and watch in silence.

'Now give me the ball or I'll do the same thing to your ears!'

The crewcut shakes his head. 'I'm not giving you this ball. Get another one.'

The chimpira looks as he can't believe what he's just heard. He looks at his friends, shakes his head sadly, then suddenly swivels on his heel and crashes a fist into the centre of the crewcut's square face. The crewcut staggers a few paces backwards, hands clutching at his nose. Then he shakes his head, takes a long noisy sniff and spits a jet of blood onto the floor. His expression is as blank as a slab of concrete.

'Come on, uncle,' yells the chimpira. 'Give me that ball before you get damaged some more!' But there's a ragged edge to his voice. His two friends have stopped a dozen yards away, smiles frozen. The crewcut doesn't reply. Instead, he replaces the ball carefully in the rack, then comes gliding forward in a solid-looking judo stance. The chimpira manages to land one other blow – glancing, on

239

the side of the head – before the crewcut sweeps him off his feet and the back of his head thumps against the ground. The chimpira looks up dazed to see the crewcut hoisting the white bowling ball out of the rack again.

'You wanted this ball,' rasps the crewcut. 'Well, here it is.'

He drops it from shoulder height, straight into the chimpira's groin. The chimpira pukes in shock, loud and long. The crewcut steps over his spasming body, moves towards the other two chimpira with the same purposeful stride. They turn, run for the exit. Applause sounds from the lane at the far end of the hall.

'Bravo, Kaneda! Nice form!'

Kaneda nods acknowledgement, still totally expressionless, then walks off towards the men's toilet. Mori gives him two minutes before following.

Inside Kaneda is bending over a basin, shirtless, washing the blood from his face and hands.

'Broken nose?' asks Mori.

Kaneda glances into the mirror. 'Feels like it,' he says. 'Anyway, this nose has been broken many times before. Maybe this time it's been knocked back into shape.'

'That was done like a true professional,' continues Mori. 'It's a pity you couldn't stay with the ministry in Tokyo. Men like you are not so easy to find.'

Kaneda turns round slowly, dabbing at his face with a towel. He's got a chest like a twenty-litre sake barrel.

'What are you talking about?' he says, eyes narrowed.

Mori smiles confidently. 'We're following up the Miura incident. It's our job to see that there isn't any recurrence.'

Kaneda purses his lips, suspicious. 'So you're with the police?'

Mori feigns shock. 'Are you joking? This is much too important to be left to the police.'

'So who are you, then?'

'Information Bureau,' says Mori, dropping his voice to a murmur. 'I'm sorry I can't tell you any more. We've been closely involved in this whole thing since the beginning.'

Kaneda pauses, stares at him. What Mori guesses he's thinking: does this guy really look like an Information Bureau agent? But since Kaneda's probably got no idea what Information Bureau agents look like, Mori feels on reasonably strong ground.

'I've heard of you people,' Kaneda says finally. 'Anyway, how did you find out where I was?'

'That can't be revealed, I'm afraid.'

'Why have you been brought in?'

Mori waves a forefinger. 'I can't say anything about that either. All our operations are top secret. You understand the situation, don't you?'

Kaneda gives a puzzled nod. Mori claps him on his bare shoulder. 'We're fully aware of your co-operation, Kaneda-*san*. You've done a good job. Now, I just wanted to confirm a few details of what happened the night you found Miura's body.'

'Well, that's difficult,' mutters Kaneda. 'Section Chief Kurata told me not to breathe a word of what happened to anyone.'

'Section Chief Kurata was absolutely right,' says Mori crisply. 'He also has done an excellent job of minimizing information leakage. But this is a national security question now. It is being dealt with from a much larger perspective. Do you understand me?'

Kaneda's brows knit in perplexity. He's having trouble reconciling two opposing demands on his loyalty. Mori's guess: in the end Kaneda will choose to obey the higher authority. That's the basic instinct of all people who work in complex organizations.

At that moment one of the other crewcuts comes

through the door. He glances at Mori, senses the tension in the air.

'What's happening, Kaneda?' he says. 'No more problems, are there?'

Kaneda opens his mouth and closes it. He looks like a schoolboy caught shoplifting.

'No problem at all,' says Mori smoothly. 'I just happened to recognize Kaneda-*san* here. We belonged to the same judo club in our high-school years.'

The crewcut's gaze relaxes. 'Really? Kaneda-*san* must have been a pretty strong player.'

'Much stronger than me,' says Mori with a smile. 'Anyway, we were just going over to the noodle stand to have a chat about the old days.'

He tosses Kaneda the collarless shirt and pushes through the door. Will Kaneda follow? Seconds later he does, and Mori leads the way over to the noodle stand in the corner of the hall. Mori buys a couple of cans of beer and they sit at a plastic table.

'Why do you need the details?' asks Kaneda nervously.

Mori pulls his notebook out of the inside pocket of his jacket. 'I'm afraid I can't tell you that,' says Mori. 'The line our investigation is currently taking is something that can only be revealed to authorized individuals.'

'Authorized individuals? Who are they?'

'I can't tell you that either,' snaps Mori. 'You're not authorized to know.'

Kaneda looks confused again. Confusion has always been one of Mori's favourite weapons.

'Don't worry,' he says, handing Kaneda a beer. 'Just run through what happened that night. I know exactly what to look for. So far your co-operation has been first class, Kaneda-*san*. I'll make sure there's another special mention in the files.'

That seems to satisfy Kaneda. He leans back, talks. Mori listens, writes.

Fifteen minutes later Mori closes his notebook, fits it back into his pocket.

'Did you find what you wanted?' asks Kaneda deferentially.

'Some details may have been of a certain amount of value,' says Mori. 'I shouldn't say any more than that.'

'Of course not,' says Kaneda.

In fact, Kaneda's explanation was of immense value. Finally Mori has discovered exactly how Miura died. He pushes his chair away from the table, gets to his feet. Kaneda jumps to his feet, bows low.

'If you need anything else, please call me any time. And if it's not too rude of me to ask...'

'Ask what?' says Mori.

Kaneda looks embarrassed. 'You see, this is not a good place for me here. The people are second rate, unprofessional. If there's any chance for me to get another good position, like the one I had at the ministry...'

'I'll do what I can,' mutters Mori. This is tough. Kaneda is a good guy, trying to do a good job. When he finds he's been fooled, he will hate himself. And Mori too. Still, being hated is an intrinsic part of the job.

'Here's my name card,' says Kaneda, fumbling in a pocket.

'I can't give you mine, you know,' says Mori sternly.

'Ah – of course.'

Mori takes the card, nods acknowledgement, then stares at it again, his pulse thumping.

'Is anything the matter?' says Kaneda.

'Nothing at all,' says Mori. He puts the name card in his pocket and makes briskly for the exit. What was written there stays etched in his brain: Bunzo Kaneda, Deputy Chief of Security Section, Nakanishi Pharmaceutical'.

George the Wolf Nishio may cultivate the image of wild spontaneity, but in fact he is a believer in meticulous planning. Having been informed of the existence of a private detective called Mori, he takes the trouble of making some discreet enquiries. He talks to a salary loan enforcer, a soapland manager, an ex-cop who helps run a book on sumo tournaments. They give him useful information. Mori, learns George, seems to have no affiliations at all, not even unofficial backing from any of the syndicates. That comes as welcome news, dispelling one nagging fear – that Mori might somehow be on good terms with the old boss or, still worse, the young prince.

The ex-cop is particularly helpful, even directing George towards someone who once knew Mori well. Fifteen years ago Sakura was the senior girl in a massage parlour located two floors under Mori's office. Now she's a forty-year-old speedhead who works the porno cinemas, the only places dark enough and where the men are desperate enough for her to make a living. George finds her where the ex-cop said – taking a break in a fast-food joint opposite the cinema complex. And just like the ex-cop suggested, George has brought her a present: a little ball of silver paper. She opens it up, squints inside at the five grams of white powder, gives a big broken-toothed smile. George grins back at her. She wouldn't look so happy if she knew what it really was – one fifth speed, two fifths starch, two fifths crushed penicillin tablets left over from George's last clap cure.

They sit down.

'This Mori,' says George. 'Tell me what you know about him.'

'What's the reason?' says Sakura, slipping the silver

packet into her handbag. She's a terrible sight – bony arms, greasy hair, skin like old paper. George can hardly bear to look at her.

'I'm thinking of giving him a job. First of all I need to check his credentials, see if he's the right kind of guy.'

'He's the right kind of guy,' says Sakura confidently. 'Don't worry about that.'

'I need to know more. Like, does he work on his own, does he carry a gun, does he have any influential friends or associates? You know the kind of thing.'

George grins pleasantly, but it doesn't seem to be working. Bloodshot eyes gaze suspiciously over the top of the coffee cup. Sakura nods at a payphone on the other side of the street.

'Listen, I'll go and give Mori a call. If he says you're okay, I'll tell you anything you want to know.'

Behind his mirror shades, George winces. Why is this woman so difficult? Why can't she just do as she's told?

'No need for that,' he says hastily. 'Let's go somewhere a little more private, where I can explain the whole problem to you in detail. To tell you the truth, I'm in the mood for some stress relief too.'

He takes a ten-thousand-yen note out of his pocket, waves it in front of her stubby nose. Sakura stares at it, as if hypnotized.

'All right,' she says. 'Let's go to the underground car park across the street. There's a storeroom at the back we can use.'

George heaves a sigh of relief, grabs her by the arm, leads her out of the fast-food joint. Interesting psychological point: everyone has professional pride, even whores. Especially whores, maybe.

They walk down the ramp into the car park under the cinema complex. The guy in the ticket-booth nods at them, casual, maybe thinking of the good meal that the unofficial rent of the storeroom is going to buy him. Sakura waves back, bouncy as a schoolgirl on the way to school. She won't be waving on the way out, thinks George. Probably not moving at all, in fact. He pats the pocket of his jacket, makes sure that his brass knuckles are still there.

Fifteen

Five a.m.: Mori opens his eyes. Something woke him, a noise too close. There it is again, a scrabbling just outside the window, sounds like someone moving across the tiny balcony.

Mori rolls quietly out of his futon, pads towards the curtain, stands and listens. A minute of silence, then the noise is repeated, louder this time, metal scratching metal. Mori takes a slow deep breath, then suddenly jerks open the curtain. What he finds: one of the largest crows he has ever seen, beak like a steel spike, knobbly claws gripping the rail of the balcony.

Mori raps a knuckle against the glass. The crow stares at him, imperious. Mori picks up the baseball bat he keeps in the corner, slides open the window. The crow takes off, long leisurely flaps of its giant wings carrying it to a nearby telegraph pole where it perches, glaring defiance.

These creatures are more like mini-pterodactyls than birds. There are stories of them carrying off cats in their claws, deliberately knocking noodle boys off their bikes, pecking out the eyes of sleeping drunks. And thanks to the high-protein diet available in the trash-bags of the giant city, each generation is bigger, stronger, less afraid of human beings than the last. According to an article Mori read recently, they have the intelligence of Stone-Age men. That makes sense. For independent logical thought, Mori would choose a sophisticated modern-minded crow over more than a few yakuza he's met.

He slams the window shut, goes back to the futon. Almost immediately he hears the 'whump' of the crow's wings as it swoops back to its favoured position on the balcony. Smart bird – it knows he can't be bothered to go through the same rigmarole over and over again.

Five o'clock: too early to do anything useful, too late to go back to sleep. Mori has coffee and riceballs, then jogs up to the shrine on the hill and runs through some karate moves. Afterwards he feels clear, refreshed, ready to confront the two startling pieces of information he acquired yesterday.

First revelation: Miura's death. He was found outside the entrance of the ministry's main building, not in the corridor next to his office. And he wasn't rushed to a private clinic dying of a heart attack. He was already dead, garrotted with a black cotton belt.

Second revelation: the ministry had Kaneda transferred to Nakanishi Pharmaceutical. It's a name that Mori has heard before, a company that has been in the news quite recently. Could a member of the founding family have been Black Blade's other victim? And if so, what would the connection be with Miura?

Kimiko Itoh's bonus is almost within Mori's grasp. What he needs – a little more patience, luck, imaginative energy. And then it will be his to claim.

Mori doesn't go straight to the office. Instead he stops by at the national library, spends the morning going through microfilm copies of old magazine and newspaper articles. It isn't hard to find material about Nakanishi Pharmaceutical. The company's been in and out of the news for at least the past ten years.

This is what he discovers. Nakanishi is actually a

pharmaceutical firm with a small speciality chemicals division attached. It was founded in the mid-1950s by Junichiro Nakanishi, a brilliant research scientist who had earned his doctorate in Germany before the war. Gradually Nakanishi built the firm up into one of the most innovative drug producers in Japan, one more success story of the high-growth years.

So far, so good. But then in the late 1970s came controversy. A citizens' group claimed to have documents proving Nakanishi's personal involvement in war crimes. The charge: he carried out medical experiments on prisoners of war in occupied China, including vivisection without anaesthetic and injection with the bubonic plague virus. According to the documents, Nakanishi was arrested at the end of the war, but managed to get off the hook by passing the results of his research to American intelligence.

When the charges were published in a small-circulation radical magazine, Nakanishi sued for libel. Then the documents disappeared, destroyed in a fire at the home of a left-wing lawyer. Accusations and counter-accusations were traded until it was found that the leaders of the citizens' group had links with a terrorist faction who had hijacked a JAL plane. The group was immediately disbanded and the leaders jailed for subversion.

The 1980s were a good time for Nakanishi Pharmaceutical. Demand was booming for its mainstay products, nutritional supplements and vitamin injections. They became part of Japan's lavish disbursement of aid to developing countries, and in the domestic market they were approved for use in school health programmes and old-age homes. Nakanishi products were included in the box of medicines that every worker receives on joining any major Japanese company. The Nakanishi stock became a darling of the financial market, quintupling on speculation about the potency of an anti-cancer drug the company was supposedly developing.

In 1988 Junichiro Nakanishi died at the age of eighty-three. His funeral was attended by four ex-prime ministers, a Nobel Prize-winning biochemist, and his favourite female ballad-singer. He was succeeded by his son Kenichi, who died at the age of fifty-four just last year. Yes, Kenichi Nakanishi, just one year ago. And, try as he may, Mori can find nothing about the cause or the circumstances.

One last thing that nags and itches – an article published two years ago in one of the less reputable magazines. The subject is Nakanishi Pharmaceutical's ties with the bureaucracy – how cunning old Junichiro coaxed a succession of top-level officials to 'descend from heaven' and join the board of his company. Apparently at one stage there were three former bureau chiefs pulling the strings for him. The article, which is unsigned, is obviously the product of thorough background research. It is also superbly written compared with the semi-pornographic rubbish in the rest of the magazine. In fact, Mori recognizes one or two poetical references. There can be only one journalist in the whole of Japan who would include an allusion to classical Chinese poetry in a paragraph about the funding of non-mainstream political factions.

So here's a question for Mori to puzzle about all the way to Shinjuku. When he asked Taniguchi about the name Nakanishi, why didn't his old friend say anything about Nakanishi Pharmaceutical? After all, just a couple of years ago he had himself written an exposé of the company's connections with the bureau. Two answers come to mind, one of which is improbable, the other extremely disturbing. The improbable one: Taniguchi said nothing because he didn't remember. The disturbing one: Taniguchi said nothing because he did remember.

Mori hears the phone as he stamps up the staircase to his office. He doesn't hurry, counts the rings. There are twenty-five of them, shrill and urgent. Only one person he knows is that persistent. He picks up the phone and his guess is confirmed.

'Mori-*san*!' yelps Uno. 'Where've you been? I've been trying to get in touch all morning.'

'I was at the National Library,' says Mori.

'The National Library!' Uno sounds astonished.

'That's right. When I talked about library work, I meant exactly what I said. Now – what have you got for me?'

Uno's voice quavers with excitement. 'I checked into Nakanishi's automobile accident. That's great news!'

'Automobile accident?' For a moment Mori is puzzled. Then he remembers the unfortunate junior bureaucrat in the Patent Office – run over late one night when he was probably staggering home drunk.

'Actually, not an accident,' gabbles Uno. 'I called the Ministry of Justice. At first they didn't want to give me the information, but I managed to persuade them. There was a woman, quite kind – actually, I arranged to meet her for a drink tomorrow – and what she said was . . . Can you guess what she told me, Mori-*san*?'

Mori's fingers tap irritation on the desk-top. 'No idea,' he says. 'But listen – here's something more important. Remember I said—'

Uno rushes on heedlessly. 'She said it was a hit-and-run incident, never been solved! And what's more, there were only two witnesses and I've got both names. I'm planning to interview them this afternoon. You can come too if you like Mori-*san*, see if we can get anything new about this mysterious white car that—'

'Forget that nonsense,' snaps Mori.

Uno blurt's, injured pride, 'Nonsense? What are you

talking about, Mori-*san*? This is the breakthrough you were waiting for, isn't it? If we can find that white car, we'll have the murderer!'

'Wrong!' says Mori. 'If we find that white car, we'll probably have some miserable salaryman committing suicide. This is a different Nakanishi! The one we're looking for has got nothing to do with the Patent Office.'

Finally silence. Mori fancies he can hear the ticking of Uno's mental clockwork.

'Say that again,' says Uno, slow and quiet.

Mori says it again, then tells him about Kenichi Nakanishi.

'What makes you so certain this is the right guy?' asks Uno, newly tentative.

'The fact that somebody wanted me to think he isn't,' says Mori.

'Hah?'

'Lies lead to truth,' says Mori. 'That's the kind of thinking you need to develop if you want to succeed in this business.'

Uno still sounds confused. 'I see,' he says slowly. 'Anyway, I suppose you want me to check the details of this man's death too.'

'Exactly,' says Mori. 'Get working on it straight away. This is the most crucial stage of the whole case.'

'That's what you always say,' moans Uno.

True. It's what Mori always says, and what he always means. Every phase is the most crucial until you come to the next, just as every shock you meet is the most jarring, every betrayal the most bitter, every frustration the most frustrating.

Mori puts down the phone, walks over to the little shrine-shelf on the wall above the turntable. The offerings need to be replaced soon – the vending-machine sake has almost evaporated, and the tangerine has shrivelled to the size and texture of a golf ball. Mori hopes the gods will understand. He closes his eyes, claps his hands, prays for success and prosperity and other elusive things. If they weren't so elusive, Mori wouldn't need the gods and the gods wouldn't need him.

Mitchell arrives at the office from a company visit, all damp shoes and sweaty shoulders. His mind is full of earnings estimates and asset turnover ratios until he glances through into the branch manager's office. Then he stops dead, heart pounding.

This is what he sees. Standing in the middle of the room is Klaus Hauptman, chief of the branch. Hauptman is a tall heavy-set man with a crescent-shaped scar on his left cheek. It looks like a duelling scar might be expected to look, though the real cause is said to be a car crash on the autobahn. Hauptman is smiling at someone, an unusual event in itself. For some reason he is speaking French, slow and heavily accented but, as far as Mitchell can judge, correct.

'Si c'est possible, je voudrais attendre encore deux ou trois mois.'

Another figure hoves into view, one that Mitchell recognizes, even from the back. From the floor up – gleaming spike-heel shoes, black stocking seams disappearing into grey worsted skirt, long black hair cascading over padded shoulders. Mitchell's heart sinks. There's no mistaking that toss of the head, that icy contralto.

'Le moment d'attendre est passé. Il y a seulement une solution – une déculottage immédiate.'

Sasha de Glazier gets in close, lays her hand lightly on Hauptman's forearm. Mitchell has seen her do that before. Stroking, cheek-kissing and generalized flirting with stodgy but powerful middle-aged men – they probably run a course on it at INSEAD.

Hauptman gives a cheesy grin, wags a finger in her face. He's trying to flirt back, which is a gruesome sight. Mitchell hurries back to the research department, hunts around in vain for a French dictionary.

At two o'clock, Mitchell clicks on his Bloomberg terminal, glances at the day's action. He soon wishes he hadn't. Despite a 'dead-cat bounce' in the Nikkei index, the SoftJoy stock has fallen another five per cent. A swift calculation: the market capitalization of the company has shrunk by four hundred billion yen since Mitchell's 'Buy' recommendation was issued last autumn. What could you do with four hundred billion yen? You could buy six thousand Rolls-Royces, build three hundred fully equipped hospitals in the Third World, send a space probe halfway to Jupiter. Now all that wealth has disappeared, been sucked through the Bloomberg screen into an alternate universe.

Mitchell taps the keyboard, accesses the chart of SoftJoy's stock price. He examines the daily point and figure pattern, the moving average trends, the momentum indicators. What they tell him: the stock price is collapsing. He tries a different, more Japanese approach. How would Yazawa, his old boss, have viewed the chart formation? That zigzag at the peak last November – surely that's a 'temple of three Buddhas'. And the steep drop two months ago that started this latest sell-off – isn't that a 'geisha's suicide leap'? If so, the decline in the SoftJoy stock price should now be in its final phase. Unfortunately the only person who understands the Yazawa method of chart analysis is Yazawa himself. And Mitchell's old boss is still keeping a low profile, shifting his base of activities around 'emerging markets' in countries that lack extradition treaties.

The phone rings. The voice at the other end is female, Californian-accented.

'Thank you for inviting me out yesterday, Mitchell-*san*. I'm sorry I ran out on you like that.'

'Don't worry – I'm used to it,' says Mitchell.

Reiko Tanaka laughs. 'Really? Surely a handsome and successful guy like you has girls chasing around all the time.'

'Not really,' says Mitchell with a half-hearted chuckle. Successful? He's on the point of being fired for the fifth time in six years. Handsome? She doesn't know about the hanks of hair that come out in his brush every morning or the relentless, genetically determined expansion of his waistband.

Reiko continues. 'I mentioned what you said to a certain important person. He is interested in discussing this matter with you directly.'

'Important person?' says Mitchell, puzzled.

'President Sonoda. He invites you to come to his apartment, eleven o'clock tomorrow night.'

'Fine,' says Mitchell. He puts the phone down, gazes abstractedly at the computer screen. Sonoda is famous for shunning publicity, refusing to speak to journalists or financial analysts. The fact that he wants to meet Mitchell in person is a major coup, a highlight in Mitchell's career. But Mitchell feels little excitement at the prospect. The presence of Sasha de Glazier in Hauptman's office suggests that his career in the financial markets doesn't have much longer to run. As if to remind him of the fact, the screen gives a long bleep – the indication of an important trade – and the SoftJoy stock shifts down another half per cent.

Sasha is still in Hauptman's office, both of them standing close to the window. Mitchell approaches, pretending to scrutinize the display board on the opposite wall. He can just catch their voices above the hubbub of the dealing room. Mitchell's schoolboy French has trouble coping with Sasha's rush of words, but Hauptman is reasonably easy to understand.

Hauptman: *Mais cet homme coûte tres cher, n'est ce pas?*

Sasha: *Non. C'est un type comme Mitchell qui nous coûte le plus cher. Il est complétement foutu!*

Hauptman: *Compris. Et le rendezvous est quand?*

Sasha: *A six heures ce soir. Au restaurant Yamato de Ginza.*

'*Complètement foutu*' – something else to look up in the French dictionary. But from the way Sasha spat it out, the meaning is pretty clear. She has in mind the implosion of wealth signalled by the SoftJoy stock price, the thousands of Rolls-Royces that will never be bought, the space probe of Jupiter that will never be launched.

After that the voices move away from the window. Out of the corner of his eye Mitchell sees Sasha pick up her handbag from the sofa.

'*Ciao*,' she coos. Hauptman gives a stiff bow, then puts his hand to his mouth and blows her a kiss. It's an ugly sight. Mitchell winces, moves hurriedly through the dealing room.

At three o'clock, Mori leans the Honda against the side wall of the ramshackle ivy-covered building that contains Taniguchi's office. He didn't call in advance, judging that surprise might be a useful tactic. Inside the little yakitori restaurant the lights are off. The sliding door is a few centimetres open, ballad music floating out from the kitchen. The master appears, mop in hand, catches sight of Mori pulling off his helmet.

'Bad timing,' he calls out. 'Your friend's just gone out again, said he might be gone for quite a while.'

'Really?' says Mori. 'Can I come inside for a while?'

'Of course.' The master disappears into the kitchen, comes out with a glass of barley tea and a plate of strawberries.

Mori thanks him. He doesn't care for strawberries – too sweet – but for the sake of politeness he pops a largish one into his mouth.

'Did you manage to have that talk with Taniguchi-*san* last time?' asks the master, lighting up a Mild Seven. 'You know, about medical treatment for his problem.'

Mori shakes his head. 'He didn't show much interest in the idea.'

'That's what I guessed. He doesn't show much interest in anything these days. Except for the Giants games, of course.'

Mori takes a toothpick, starts prising a strawberry seed out of a cavity. Suspicions form in his mind, manifest themselves as questions. 'You said Taniguchi would be gone for quite a while. Does that happen often? I mean, I thought he stayed inside his apartment pretty much all the time.'

The master puffs contemplatively on the Mild Seven. 'Sometimes he spends an afternoon out somewhere – doing research for his articles, he says.'

'But I thought he had assistants do all the research these days.'

The master shrugs. 'One day he says one thing, the next day he says the opposite. That's all part of his problem, isn't it?'

He taps his finger against the side of his head.

'Does Taniguchi-*san* ever stay out late in the evening?' asks Mori. 'I mean really late – around midnight.'

The strawberry seed is proving surprisingly stubborn. The end of the toothpick snaps off, and Mori has to reach for another.

'That late?' says the master reflectively. 'Not very often, I think.'

'Not very often? You mean that he has done once or twice this year.'

The master looks doubtful. 'Once or twice maybe.'

'What about on March the fifteenth, Friday night?'

The master shakes his head. 'I've no idea,' he says. 'I don't keep records of things like that. Anyway, I thought you were an old friend of his.'

'That's true – I am an old friend.'

'Who just happens to be a private detective.'

The master gazes at him keenly. Mori considers dissimulation. In his wallet he has a collection of name cards, each carrying a different profession. In the end he decides against it.

'Is it so obvious?' he says.

'Completely,' says the master.

'All right, here's the situation. First time I came was to get Taniguchi-*san*'s advice about a case I'm working on. Now I'm starting to think he's mixed up in it somehow.'

The master gives a grunt, as if he had suspected as much all along. 'And if he is, what are you going to do?'

'I don't know,' says Mori. 'What would you do?'

The master tilts his head back, sends a smoke ring floating towards the air-vent.

'That depends,' he says. 'Everything always depends, doesn't it?'

Mori nods. Not a fancy answer, but the only answer that makes sense. Loyalty, friendship, justice, truth – all are provisional. He finishes the barley tea, tells the master that he's going to wait for Taniguchi upstairs. The master nods, turns away without another word.

The building is old and crumbling. Cheap materials have been patched up with cheaper, putting the places that have

258

been repaired in a worse state than those that have not. Like many things in this city, it wasn't built to last but somehow it has. Mori doesn't have much difficulty getting into Taniguchi's room. A steel comb through the jamb, a jiggle of the handle, and the door springs open. Mori stands in the middle of the room, scans. The same mess as before: piles of photocopied documents; magazine articles; scattered manuscript pages written in Taniguchi's elegant hand. Mori picks a couple, glances through them. What he expects: Taniguchi's usual painstaking analysis of dirty dealings amongst the 'iron triangle' of business leaders, élite bureaucrats and political bosses. What he sees: thoughts jotted down at random, no logic, no witty classical allusions.

It would have been better for this country never to have grown so rich. Poor hard-working peasants have nobility and humanity, but rich peasants are arrogant and despicable. Certainly the tidal wave of money is drowning all human goodness. Nobody can be trusted in this age, not the rich and the powerful, but not the ordinary people either. They know about all the corruption, the exploitation of the weak, the spiritual poisoning. Just as long as some grains of rice fall their way, it doesn't bother them at all. So what can be done? I remember the young officers who hunted down the corrupt ones sixty years ago. They were executed as traitors at the time, but soon they were treated as pure-hearted heroes. In today's world also, perhaps only shocking deeds can break through out complacency.

Mori puts the pages back in place on the floor. He thinks back to that strange rant of Taniguchi's a couple of weeks ago. His old friend is in even worse shape than he thought, probably capable of anything. Once upon a time, Taniguchi used to be a pacifist, strongly opposed to Japan having any military capability at all. Now he's a reactionary, nostalgic for a militaristic era that ended years before he was born. What could cause something like that – not just a change of political opinion, but a complete personality shift? Alcohol, the break-up of his marriage, the loss of his daughter – those are the obvious answers, but they don't explain what's been happening inside the man's mind.

And as for those young officers – well, they may have been pure-hearted, but their actions helped send the whole country plunging to self-destruction. Being pure-hearted means being simple. But the world isn't simple, not now, not then. As the master of the yakitori restaurant said, everything always depends.

Mori checks out the filing cabinet by the window. There is a file labelled 'Health', but nothing in it about Miura, nothing about Nakanishi either. That's strange, since Taniguchi must have researched the company in order to write the magazine article. Guess: Taniguchi has another store of documents somewhere. Mori makes a methodical search – behind the books in the bookcase, in the cupboard containing the jars of shochu, under the mattress of Taniguchi's unmade bed. Finally, in the bottom drawer of the bedside chest, hidden under a pile of towels, he finds an old leather briefcase, creased and discoloured. Mori picks it up. Light, almost empty. Mori uses a pair of scissors to spring the lock, takes out a single unlabelled file. Then he sits down on the bed, leafs through the half-dozen sheets of paper inside.

All are in Taniguchi's handwriting. First is the manu-script of the anonymous article about Nakanishi Pharma-ceutical, followed by some pages of notes. One part contains an interview with Miura himself, presumably transcribed from a tape-recording. It begins with some bland requests for information on the procedures used in the clinical trials of new drugs. Then the subject moves to the ministry's policy towards drug-pricing. Finally the questions get more focussed.

QUESTION: So a new drug only gets awarded a higher price than an existing drug if there is proof of 'substantially better performance'?

MIURA: That's right. We are endeavouring to ensure that tax-payers' money is used with maximum efficiency.

QUESTION: But what about the new Nakanishi nutritional supplement? It's been given a price more than double that of similar foreign drugs, even though the American FDA says there is no difference in performance.

MIURA: We do not have to take notice of the FDA. Japan is not under American occupation any longer.

QUESTION: It is also said that members of the drug-approval committee have received generous research donations from the Nakanishi Foundation. Doesn't that break the guidelines that the ministry issued fifteen years ago?

MIURA: Fifteen years ago? Our guidelines have changed many times since then. We don't have to issue them publicly, you know.

QUESTION: Are there any guidelines about the ministry's own people receiving uncollateralized loans from the same source?

MIURA: What are you saying? This interview is supposed to be about health policy in the twenty-first century. Let me say that you are certainly infringing the human rights of the individuals concerned!

QUESTION: Is your wife the ultimate owner of a Hong Kong registered company called Asia Healthy Services?

MIURA: This is outrageous! I will not answer any more questions. If you pursue this any further, I will ensure that you are arrested.

Mori can't help smiling as he reads. He can almost hear Taniguchi's feline tone, see the bureaucrat's angry face. But maybe it's not so amusing after all. The outcome was murder.

The final page consists of a few scrawled notes, not easy to decipher. The content, though, is intriguing.

January 19: Kinjo Restaurant, Akasaka.

7.15: Miura on foot.

7.30: Nakanishi in Toyota Crown.

7.35: Toriyama in Mercedes.

The first time the three have met in the same room for four years. The structure of evil is complete.

9.30: Miura on foot.

9.45: Nakanishi in Toyota Crown with geisha.

10.05: Toriyama in Mercedes. Calls Miura in ministry, thanks him for arranging meeting. Confident about coming election.

That last part is surprising. Mori would never have suspected that Taniguchi was the kind of guy to eavesdrop on a mobile phone conversation. Maybe he'd better stop underestimating his old friend.

Mori puts the papers back in the briefcase, replaces it in the drawer. He closes the door behind him, using the steel comb to ease the lock back into place, then stamps down the stairs, his footsteps loud enough to shake the building to its fragile foundations, his mind racing through the implications of what he saw in the hidden file.

Nakanishi, Miura, Toriyama – 'the structure of evil', linked together in a web of devious transactions. Nakanishi's third-grade drugs get first-grade prices. Toriyama gets funding for his platform of 'political reform'. Miura gets the cash to fund a lavish lifestyle, Ginza mistress included. Mori recalls the contents of the antique chest in Miura's house: the account books; the debentures; the photos of office buildings in Yokohama. No question, Miura was more than just Toriyama's son-in-law. He was his banker too. Miura, together with his wife, were controlling the flow of illegal contributions to Toriyama, probably through overseas companies such as Asia Healthy Services. As a hypothesis it sounds plausible, unsurprising even. The only surprise is that Taniguchi, a man who has been breathing black mist for the past quarter of a century, should consider it sufficient reason for murder.

On the way out, Mori pokes his head into the yakitori restaurant. The master is sitting at the counter in the dark watching a baseball game on a pocket TV.

'Thanks for your help,' says Mori.

'That's fine,' says the master, looking up from the TV. 'Would you like me to say anything to Taniguchi-*san*, give him some sort of message?'

'No message, please.'

'That's what I thought. Anyway, did you find what you were looking for?'

Mori nods. 'More or less. Listen, if it's all right with you. I've got another of those detective-type questions.'

The master takes a long drag at his Mild Seven. 'You're going to ask me if I remember something that happened one night three months ago and I'm going to tell you no.

People who aren't detectives don't remember things like that, and when they do it's usually wrong.'

'It's a simpler question than that. Did Taniguchi-*san* ever talk about video games, playing them or anything like that?'

The master expels a cloud of blue smoke. 'Video games?' he chortles. 'Are you joking? The only entertainment that interests Taniguchi-*san* is baseball.'

Mori thanks him, ducks out through the awning. He is on the verge of wrapping up the entire case, but the connection between Black Blade and Miura is still frustratingly vague. The drizzle is thickening now, rain like lines of steel wire. Mori wheels the Honda away from the wall, wipes down the saddle with the flap of his raincoat. Just as he's fitting on his helmet, there's a tap on his shoulder. He looks round to meet the gaze of the young man who brought the water melon last time Mori came to the yakitori shop.

'I heard you talking to my father,' he says. 'Is it true that you're a real detective?'

'That's what it says on my name card,' says Mori. 'So it must be true, right?'

'Great! You must have seen and done lots of amazing things.'

'Not as many as you think,' says Mori. The conversation has been short, but already it's boring him.

'Anyway, I heard that question you asked. It made me think you must be a pretty good detective.'

Mori stares at him blankly. Obviously this boy is easily impressed.

'I mean, he's never talked to me about video games, only about baseball.'

'And so?' says Mori, irritation rising.

'So you must be a good detective. Because Taniguchi-*san*

really is interested in video games. Just a couple of weeks ago I saw a video-game package lying on his table.'

Mori slides off the helmet, stares into the young man's pudgy face. 'Say that again,' he breathes.

'It was when I was delivering a plate of chicken gizzard to his room. There was a video-game box in the middle of the table. Actually, I asked him about it, but he got angry, refused to talk. He gets angry a lot these days, silly things mostly.'

Mori nods sympathetically. 'I know that,' he says. 'Now, if you want to be a big help, just think back and try to remember what game it was you saw there.'

'Not so difficult,' says the young man. 'That game happens to be one of my favourites.'

'You mean Black Blade.'

The young man laughs with surprise. 'Absolutely right! How did you guess that?'

Mori shrugs modestly. 'Experience,' he says. 'After all, I am a detective.'

On entering the Yamato Restaurant, you are greeted by a row of svelte, doe-eyed young ladies in russet-brown kimonos. They trill enthusiastic greetings.

'Welcome, honoured guest!'

'Please be so good as to enter!'

One of them leads you along a bamboo-lined pathway that bridges a rippling stream, then into a private tatami-mat room tastefully decorated with flower arrangements and charcoal-brush screens.

Behind: a mossy garden, with a waterwheel gently rotating, a large stone lantern, speckled carp gobbling in a shallow pond.

All round: birdsong, the chiming of wind-bells, the soothing sounds of a well-appointed country inn.

There are no windows, so there's nothing to remind you that the restaurant it located on the fifteenth floor of a skyscraper that also contains one of Tokyo's busiest department stores and the head offices of Mitsukawa Insurance and Mitsukawa Cement.

Tonight is Mitchell's first visit to the Yamato. He squats cross-legged at the low table, sipping sake from a thimble-sized cup, picking with his chopsticks at the strange collection of hors d'oeuvres on the crescent-shaped dish in front of him. Everything is tiny, superbly arranged, delicately hued, tasteless. Everything has been made to look like something else. There is a piece of fish-meal cut into the shape of a leaf, a clump of salmon eggs that looks like a flower, a ball of bean-curd moulded to look like a plover's egg. Nothing in this city can be what it is, not even the food.

After five minutes: a voice on the other side of the sliding door, loud and foreign.

'Okay, here we are. If you need to plug in your laptop, go right ahead. They've got modem facilities in all the rooms.'

The unmistakable tones of Sasha de Glazier. Fortunately tonight she's decided to speak English, not German or French or Spanish.

'Great choice, Sasha. You certainly know your restaurants.'

That voice, slick and ingratiating, immediately sets Mitchell's teeth on edge. It's Scott Hamada, tireless booster of Mega Enterprises' stock price, Silverman Brothers' global capability and his own boundless brilliance.

'It's part of the job, Scott. When you have to hire as many people as I do, you get to know an awful lot of restaurants in an awful lot of cities.'

The voices fade down the path. Mitchell stares glumly at a slice of yam disguised as lotus-root. The Bavarians have already lifted the hiring freeze. And as she promised,

Mitchell will be the first to walk the plank. Bad enough in itself, but to be replaced by cigar-smoking Scott Hamada! The thought of it makes him shudder with anguish.

The sukiyaki arrives: first a cauldron of water, then thin slices of raw beef, plates of vegetables, noodles, bean-curd. The waitress lights a burner under the bowl, mixes in soy sauce, then uses long lacquered chopsticks to shovel the materials into the simmering water.

'How long before it's ready?' asks Mitchell.

The waitress smiles again. No doubt she would smile exactly the same smile if Mitchell informed her that he wished to urinate in the carp-pond.

'You speak fine Japanese, foreigner-*san.*'

Mitchell frowns. He knows that foreigners who actually do speak good Japanese never get told so.

'How long? I said. Come on – answer the question!' This time he uses the kind of back-of-the-throat rasp that he's heard from Mori. The waitress's smile ices over.

'It can be ready whenever the honoured customer wishes.' She takes a remote-controller out of her pocket and shows him how to adjust the size of the flame.

'Fine,' says Mitchell, still doing his Mori imitation. 'I'm slipping out for a few minutes, okay?'

He leaves the waitress tending the cauldron of sukiyaki, wanders down the path in the direction taken by Sasha and Hamada. The sound-proofing of the private rooms is pretty good, so he has to lean in close to the sliding doors to catch anything being said. A few waitresses pass him on the path, pretending not to notice what he's doing. Finally he finds the right room, next to a grove of thick bamboo. From the tone of the voices inside, the foreplay is already over.

'It would be a great privilege to work with you, Sasha. Everyone says you're a real professional.'

'I certainly don't tolerate losers. They're like tumours.

You have to cut them out before they infect the whole operation.'

Mitchell nibbles his lower lip. The thought of Sasha with a scalpel in her hand is a disturbing one.

'I'm a winner,' says Hamada. 'That means I'm looking for a winner's package, appropriate to my franchise value.'

Sasha takes that in her stride. 'I hear where you're coming from, Scott. We can put together a pretty imaginative structure – commission bonus, shadow options, points participation in any deals you generate. What nationality is your wife, by the way?'

'Canadian.'

'Okay – if you don't mind transferring her nationality to the Dutch Antilles, we've got this neat tax-minimization programme . . .'

Mitchell's ears burn. He feels as if he's eavesdropping on something pornographic. Needless to say, no elements of this 'imaginative structure' have ever been offered to him. He moves closer, gets his ear right up against the panel. The voices are much clearer now, Hamada's even more syrupy-smooth than usual.

'Interesting,' he says. 'But what kind of numbers are we talking about here?'

'Highly appropriate numbers, Scott. Actually, I've already mapped out a contract for you. Look it over, see if it floats your boat.'

Mitchell squeezes his eyes shut. This is worse than he thought, much worse. At this very moment Hamada is holding a written promise of Mitchell's job. He might even sign it straight away, in which case Mitchell needn't bother showing up for work tomorrow.

Paper rustles. Hamada sounds excited by what he sees, almost to the point of sexual arousal. 'Mmmm . . . uh-huh . . . yeah . . . mmmm . . .'

'Take your time, Scott. I'll leave you alone for a while.'

A moment of pure panic. Mitchell springs away from the door, goes thumping into a kimono-clad waitress carrying a wooden tray one-handed above her head. The tray tips. The waitress squeaks in shock, grabs Mitchell's shoulder for balance. The two of them stagger sideways, collapse to the ground. Sashimi rice noodles go flying, the tray clatters, porcelain shatters . . .

'Whatta fock is going on?'

The contralto is deeper, the Latino accent stronger. Mitchell twists onto his side, confronts spikes-heel shoes, black stocking seams disappearing into a grey worsted skirt. Sasha de Glazier is standing over him, Scott Hamada at her shoulder.

'Mitchell, you goddam klutz,' says Hamada, shaking his head and grinning. 'What are you doing here, for chrissake?'

Mitchell gets to his feet. His jacket and shirt are dripping with soy sauce and sake. 'Never mind that,' he says tightly. 'What are you doing here?'

Hamada's grin stretches to the very edges of his face. 'Oh – discussing various opportunities.'

Sasha says nothing. She gazes at Mitchell with ferocious suspicion. Mitchell has to say something, so he says exactly what he's thinking.

'If you're thinking of hiring this guy, you're making a big mistake, Sasha. He's only got one idea in his head – Mega Enterprises. When that thing implodes, he's finished, nothing left to offer.'

'Oh, really?' says Hamada sarcastically. 'And when do you see that happening? When SoftJoy gets back to the price you made your recommendation, I suppose.'

'Sooner than you think. My sources are telling me Mega's in deep trouble.'

269

'And what sources are these, Mitch? Taxi-drivers, hook-ers?'

Mitchell flushes with anger. 'Highly placed industry people. I'm with some of them right now, working on a deal.'

'Really?' says Sasha. 'In that case, maybe I should come in and hear what they've got to say.'

Disaster looms, a trap of Mitchell's own making! Sasha's laser eyes are singeing his cheeks. Hamada's sneer is eating into his soul.

'Not appropriate at this stage,' he stammers. 'They've demanded total confidentiality. This could be a big one, Sasha. Just give me until the end of the month to bring it in.'

'Big one!' snorts Hamada. 'If you believe that, you'll believe anything.'

Sasha ignores him. Mitchell forces himself to meet her gaze. It's not easy. Doesn't this woman ever blink? Does she glue her eyelids into place every morning?

'Okay,' she says finally. 'Another couple of weeks won't make much difference, I guess.'

'Wait a moment,' protests Hamada. 'This makes no sense at all!'

If Hamada had known Sasha better, he wouldn't have said that. She turns, fixes him with the twin death-rays. 'I make the decisions here,' she says, in a voice some degrees below freezing point. 'Now go back and check that document I gave you. We'll discuss it later.'

Hamada's mouth opens and closes like a dying carp's. That gives Mitchell his chance to make an exit.

Safely back in the little room, Mitchell slides the latch shut, slumps down prone on the tatami floor. The sukiyaki cauldron bubbles and froths, soothing music for a wounded mind. Propping himself up on an elbow, Mitchell levers in more beef, bean-curd, noodles, cabbage, mushrooms. Stress always stimulates his appetite, and sukiyaki is one of his favourite foods. Why? First, because it tastes good, second, there is no correct way to cook or eat it and, third, it looks like what it is – a patternless structureless mess. Like his own life.

Tonight in the city –
ten trillion raindrops will fall from the sky
one hundred billion yen's worth of goods and services will
   be bought and sold
one million commuters will ride the subway home
one hundred thousand neon signs will flicker and wink
ten thousand orgasms will take place in love hotel
   bedrooms
one thousand tiny earth tremors will quiver through the
   alluvial subsoil
one hundred babies will be born
ten people will die in traffic accidents
and one private detective will be gunned down by an
   unknown assailant

George is wearing his favourite jacket – black with maroon panels, large and loose enough to accommodate a pistol in the inside pocket. His mirror-shades he has left in the glove compartment of the Mazda, which is safely stowed in the car park of a children's clinic a few blocks away. Now it is time to make use of the information he pounded out of the old whore last night.

First of all George goes round to the back of the building, looks for an old Honda with Saitama plates. It's there all right, leaning against the wall between two vending machines. George thinks about slashing the tyres, pouring a jar of 'one-cup' sake into the petrol tank. Then he smiles at the futility of the idea. After all, Mori is never going to ride this motorbike again.

Luckily there aren't many people around, just an old man coming out of the bath-house down the street, a couple of high-school kids hanging around the karaoke boxes. George waits until they've gone before making his way up the staircase at the side of the building. Rain drums softly on the metal stairs. George moves carefully, checking each floor before moving up to the next. On the third there is a some sort of trading company, lights off inside. George crouches down at the door, takes the ski-mask out of his pocket and pulls it over his head. It fouls up his slick new hairstyle, tickles his nose. George grits his teeth. He doesn't plan to be wearing the thing for more than a few minutes.

Mori's office is supposed to be on the sixth floor. Confirmation comes from the grubby little sticker on the door: 'Kazuo Mori – Economic and Social Research', printed in faded characters. George can hear music inside, some squalling saxophone stuff that sets his nerves jangling. He takes out his gun, checks it. His mouth is dry, heart pumping surprisingly fast, maybe too many Benzedrine tablets. There's nothing to worry about, nothing at all. Mori's got no gun, no warning of what's going to happen. After what George did to Sakura, she won't be saying anything to anyone for weeks.

George takes a deep breath, puts his finger on the buzzer.

Back in his office, Mori browses the political section of the evening paper with more attention than usual. 'Vision, Leadership and the Spirit of Renewal' – that's the headline over a photo of Seiji Toriyama giving a speech to the American Chamber of Commerce. Apparently the Americans love Toriyama just as much as everyone else. The ambassador has called him the 'grand champion of Japan's reform movement', and Henry Kissinger has agreed to write the introduction to his latest book. The photo itself, though, is a strange one – Toriyama grimacing like the demon-guardian of a temple. Maybe, thinks Mori, the camera caught him reflecting on the fates of his old friends, Miura and Nakanishi.

Uno rings at eight o'clock, says he's spent all day researching Nakanishi's death. The cause is given as a heart attack, but the details are frustratingly vague. According to some reports Nakanishi died in the sauna of a luxury golf club. Others say that it happened at the apartment of an unnamed close friend. In the scandal magazines there were even rumours that he'd committed suicide, driven to it by huge undisclosed losses in the currency markets.

'What do you think?' says Mori.

'Too young for a heart attack,' says Uno decisively. 'He wasn't much older than you, Mori-*san*.'

'It can happen to anyone.'

'But he was in good shape too. This man was a sportsman, ex-champion skier, handicap of five at golf.'

'Really,' says Mori drily. 'And what about the suicide theory?'

'That doesn't ring true either. He'd just taken over as president of the company a few years before. Whatever problems there were he could blame on his father.'

A thought ripples through Mori's mind. Has he been underestimating Uno's potential? That analysis is quite smart. What follows is even better.

'I decided to do some background research, just following my instincts. I found something very interesting, Mori-*san*. Nakanishi used to live in Shirogane-dai, a traditional wooden house. Anyway, eighteen months ago, there was a mysterious fire, burned the whole place down. Fortunately the whole family were away at the time.'

'Are you sure about this?'

'Of course! I've got the names of the neighbours, the people who were working at the fire department at the time. Actually, I've written a report already. Would you like me to print out a copy and bring it round?'

'Sure,' says Mori. 'And listen – you've done good work. There's hope for you yet.'

At the other end of the phone Uno breathes out sharply. 'Thank you, Mori-*san*. I've been waiting a long time for you to say that.'

Mori puts down the phone, sits pondering at his desk. Maybe Uno has got what it takes as a detective after all. Because what it takes now is not the same as it used to be. The world is changing, faster than anyone can possibly keep up. So why not a tennis-playing manga-reading detective who cooks Italian food and treats his fiancée like Mori treats his wealthiest clients? What really matters is the way you think, what you choose to believe and what you choose not to believe.

Mori pours himself a glass of Suntory, puts a record on the turntable – Dexter Gordon, 'Our Man in Stockholm'. There's a bad scratch on the first three tracks, but Mori's used to it by now. He doesn't really hear it. The saxophone's bass notes shake the window in its frame. Mori scans the baseball reports, refills his whisky glass. Track four starts, a slow lush ballad that fills the room. Fills it so well, in fact, that at first Mori doesn't hear the sound of the door buzzer. He glances at the Taipei Rolex. Strange – Uno must have come in double quick time.

'All right,' he calls. He lifts the needle off the record, then turns to the door.

George's finger is poised on the buzzer, a gun gripped tight in his sweaty hand. This is how it's going to work. Mori will open the door a few inches. George will start shooting straight away, chest and stomach. Mori will stagger backwards, collapse on the floor. With luck, he'll still be conscious. If so, George will bend down, stick the gun in his mouth, see the knowledge in his eyes. That is the moment to savour, the moment of moments. Maybe Mori will plead for his life, weeping in fear. George hopes so. Because then George will have the opportunity to say something cool and contemptuous, just like in the movies. What should he say? What are the right words to express the fierce joy of honour restored? George takes his finger off the buzzer, silently tries out a few phrases on his lips.

All of a sudden there is a noise down below, footsteps ringing on the metal staircase. With his face buried in the itchy ski-mask, George daren't turn to look. Instead, he moves away from the door, loses himself in the shadows. The footsteps are getting louder. Whoever it is might be coming all the way up to Mori's office. That would be a problem. He would see George, challenge him. George couldn't risk that. He would have to shoot.

The footsteps have risen to the fourth floor now. George hunches down in a corner of the little landing at the top of the staircase. Dark rain spatters, large drops on the back of his leather jacket. But visibility is poor tonight. It shouldn't be possible to make out George's figure from below. The footsteps stop on the fifth floor, half a dozen metres under where George is crouching. George hears someone whistling softly under his breath, a bunch of keys clinking, then nothing. George waits a couple of minutes, then gets to his feet. He peers over the rail, checks the door on the fifth floor. Nobody there. Whoever it was must have gone inside, very quietly.

George goes back to Mori's door, gets his mind ready again. Inside the room a saxophone is playing, loud and slow. Enjoy the music, Mori – it's the last you'll ever hear. George takes a deep breath, stabs the buzzer a couple of times with his finger. The gun he holds ready, chest-height.

Suddenly there's a noise behind him, too close for comfort. George wheels round, pulse thumping like a drum. Under the mask his mouth gapes in amazement. Two metres away a young guy is straddling the rail of the staircase. He must have climbed up from the floor below. George lifts the gun.

'Don't move,' he says through the clenched teeth.

The young guy drops lightly to the ground. George reads his gaze, hot determination. He doesn't like it. Inside Mori's office the saxophone music has stopped in mid-bar.

'Don't move, I said!' George hisses savagely. The guy glances in turn at the gun, the door, George's face, then the gun again. Then he jumps.

Mori is halfway to the door when he hears the gunshot – so loud, so close – then the sound of footsteps clattering down the staircase. Mori jerks open the door, sees Uno sitting on the ground, back against the railings. He stares up at Mori, earnest.

'Go after him, Mori-*san*!' he mutters. 'Don't worry – I'm all right.'

But Uno is not all right. A patch of blood is spreading across the centre of his shirt, and his face is the colour of tofu. The clattering footsteps are far below now. Mori leans over the rails, glimpses a figure in white trousers dashing out into the street.

'I tried to hold him,' says Uno weakly. 'I did my best, but he got away. That shouldn't have happened.'

Mori squats down beside him. A pool of blood is spreading slowly across the metal floor, dimpled by the rain.

'You did a great job,' says Mori. 'Nobody could have done better.'

Uno nods, eyelids fluttering shut. 'Something strange,' he whispers. 'My feet are so cold, my hands too.'

Mori races back into his office, dives for the phone.

Sixteen

George goes tearing through the maze of alleys, barging his way through clusters of umbrellas. People turn and stare. George snarls in frustration at them, swings wild fists. Why are they staring at him? How can they know what he has done? Then he understands the problem. The ski-mask is still on his face! He ducks into the entrance of a peep club, bounds up the stairs. Halfway up he yanks off the mask, leans against the wall, sucking in air.

That young guy – he deserved it. He ruined everything, all the preparations. But George isn't going to let one failure discourage him. He knows everything he needs to about Mori. He will lie low for a few weeks, then make another strike. And if that doesn't work out, he will wait a few more weeks and try again. He will keep on trying until the business is finished. Because this is not a matter of choice. It is a matter of necessity, driven by the unshakable logic of honour and respect. For the spirit of George the Wolf Nishio to be whole again, Mori must die.

George feels calmer now, but nervous energy is still coursing through his system, screaming for release. A peep club is not what he needs at all. He waits another five minutes, then steps out into the drizzle. A few blocks away is a rent-a-body salon specializing in 'costume play'. The owner is a retired bicycle racer long beholden to the old boss.

'Good evening, Wolf-*san*,' he says when George comes butting through the curtain of plastic beads.

'What have you got for me?'

'Whatever you like.'

He flips open a photo-album of girls dressed as air hostesses, nuns, nurses, schoolgirls, shrine maidens. George chooses the air hostess because she's got a typical whore face – little eyes, big mouth. Just what he needs to vent his energy, quick and nasty.

He sits waiting on the bed in the little cubicle. The woman comes in, smiles and bows low. She asks what sort of thing he wants. Her accent – clumsy, split-tongued – is something George wasn't expecting. It grates like sandpaper, has to be stopped.

Without really thinking what he's doing, George jumps up and thwacks her across the face with the back of his hand. The woman goes flying backwards against the wall, stands there staring at him in dumb shock. She looks so funny that George decides to do it again, twice as hard. This time the whore's head bounces off the wall like a soccer ball. She slides to the ground, glassy-eyed, blood and saliva trailing from her mouth.

George jerks her upright by the wrists, dumps her face down on the bed. All the tensions of the evening are surging within him. He rolls her skirt up over her waist, rips the lacy panties off her buttocks with his bare hands.

For some reason – maybe the little moaning noises she's making, maybe the way the hill of flesh is tilted towards him – George suddenly finds himself in an enormous hurry. He scrabbles trousers and briefs to his knees, dives on top, fingers digging into the woman's neck. No time to be fussy or fancy: he rams blindly through a ring of rubbery muscle. Three savage thrusts, then he convulses with a roar of triumph that rises from the depths of his belly. The whore lies there, whimpering in pain.

Breathing hard and ragged, George slides off, zips up. He has an intense desire never to look at this woman again. On the way out he slides a roll of banknotes into the mama-*san*'s pocket. Usually he doesn't pay anything in this place, but special service deserves special consideration.

Outside the tarmac is running with neon rivulets. George moves briskly through the crowded streets, the raindrops like cool acupuncture on his face. Now he feels easier, lighter, gradually getting reconciled to the extra weeks of waiting before his spirit will be whole again. What he needs to help the process along: a bottle and a half of Wild Turkey, accompanied by the keening voice of Lonesome Luke Segawa.

Uno's fiancée arrives at the hospital at ten o'clock. Mori is sitting outside the operating theatre, trying to read the eyes of the doctors hurrying in and out. They don't give much away. Keiko is wearing the same red raincoat as she was the night before. She notices Mori, glares at him in suspicion.

'Who are you?'

'I'm Mori. We were working on a case together.'

'Oh, the famous Mori-*san*! He talked about you as if you were a god.' There's bitterness in her voice. Her face is pale, pinched with tension.

'He talked about you a lot too,' says Mori quietly.

'Saying what?'

'Well, he said you were the most important thing in his life.'

Keiko stamps her foot on the ground. 'That's not true! The most important thing was this stupid idea of being a detective. We had terrible rows about it almost every week, but he wouldn't listen. Now look what's happened!'

Mori shrugs, nonplussed. Uno had said that Keiko supported his choice of career, thought it was trendy. The way he'd said it had been so natural, so naïvely proud.

Keiko sits down heavily on the bench – arms folded, legs crossed – stares at the wall in front of her. She's different from what Mori expected, harder, more controlled. She's got the ability to channel grief and fear into another emotion, anger. And the focus of that anger is Mori.

'So what happened?' she says, not shifting her gaze from the wall.

Mori gives a brief account: the gunshots; the man running into the night; the ambulance ride to the hospital. What he doesn't mention: the hole in Uno's chest; the pool of blood spreading across the wet metal; the colour of his face under the oxygen mask.

'You mean that you've got no idea who did it or why?'

'Not yet,' admits Mori.

'Surely the god of detectives can do better than that! After all, this hitman was aiming for you, wasn't he?'

'Quite probably.'

She glances at him, pale-lipped. 'It should have been you, Mori-*san*. It should be you in there now, fighting for your life.'

There's no possible answer to that, so Mori doesn't attempt one. Keiko sits there in silence, foot ticking up and down like a metronome. Mori watches groups of nurses walking past, joking and chatting. Periodically messages crackle through the loudspeaker system, telling of cars parked illegally and entrances that are about to be locked for the night. Hospital routine is so reassuringly normal, makes you think of government offices, not death and suffering and loss. On the other side of that door a man is lying flat on an operating table, grim-faced doctors up to their wrists in the bloody mess of his chest. At any moment

281

his heart might twitch for the last time, his spirit might sail away like a paper boat on the river. And what Keiko said was absolutely right. It should have been Mori.

The doors of the operating theatre swing open. A doctor comes out, green tunic, mask hanging around his neck. He stares at Mori and Keiko, then points to Keiko and calls her over. That's a good sign. Mori stays sitting. He watches them talk, watches the smile light up Keiko's face. Then she slumps down on a chair, big sobs rising from deep inside. Mori waits a couple of minutes, then goes over and sits down beside her.

'Your fiancé's a tough guy,' he says.

'He's a stupid guy,' says Keiko, blinking tears. 'I want you to tell him that, Mori-*san*. I want you to explain.'

'Explain what?'

Keiko takes a tissue from her pocket, blows her nose with surprising ferocity. 'About this whole detective business. He never listens to me. He'll listen to you, nobody else.'

'You want me to persuade him to quit?'

Keiko nods vigorously. 'If he doesn't quit, there'll be no marriage. I told him that two nights ago, loud and clear.'

That was the night that she passed him on the street outside Uno's apartment. Mori remembers her face, taut with determination. And he remembers Uno the next day, as bright and enthusiastic as ever. Mori's respect for Uno rises a few more notches. The man's talent for deception is far greater than he appreciated. Maybe Uno was on the right career path after all.

Keiko dabs at her mascara, lips compressed again. The moment of weakness has gone. 'What I'm saying is common sense,' she says. 'You understand what I mean, don't you?'

Mori understands exactly what she means. It's in the way

she looks at him, in her tone of voice – she doesn't want to marry someone who's going to end up like Mori.

'Common sense is common sense,' says Mori.

'Right!' says Keiko briskly. 'He shouldn't be so selfish. He should think about the future. That's what I want you to tell him, Mori-*san*.'

'I'll explain the situation,' says Mori, getting to his feet.

What that means: he'll explain to Uno that he has to make a choice. There's no middle way. Being married to a woman like Keiko and working with someone like Mori are mutually exclusive. 'Think about the future': he'll say that too, but he doesn't expect Uno to take much notice. A few people gave the same sort of advice to Mori when he was starting out. He ignored them. When you're young, the future's too far away to worry about. Then one day you look in the mirror and the future's already over. All that's left is the present – more of it, every day, slipping by faster and faster.

Mori walks down the hospital corridor, passes visitors carrying baskets of fruit, doctors talking golf, nurses chatting about movies and pop singers. The air carries the smell of laundry, old food, disinfectant. Mori hardly notices. He's thinking of paper boats lit with little candles, a procession of them sailing out into the great black ocean. One at least has been washed back to the shore.

Ten o'clock next morning, Mori hears the office phone ringing as soon as he puts his foot on the bottom step of the staircase. He knows that it's his own phone because it has a distinctive sound – a little louder than the others in the building, a little harsher. Mori doesn't hurry – if you hurry, it usually stops ringing the moment your hand touches the receiver – but ambles up the stairs at a steady pace. He opens the door softly, hangs up his raincoat. Then he turns to his desk and snatches the receiver off its cradle in mid-ring.

'Good morning, Mori-*san*,' says Kimiko Itoh. 'Aren't you rather late getting to work today?'

'I had a busy night,' says Mori, trying to hide his irritation. 'A friend of mine almost got himself murdered.'

'What a shame,' says Kimiko Itoh. 'You weren't hurt, I hope.'

'I was supposed to be the target,' says Mori flatly.

'Really? What an exciting life you have, Mori-*san*! Anyway, you're supposed to be working exclusively for me. I hope you are giving proper concentration to the job.'

Mori grunts acknowledgement, reminds himself of the bonus. The private detective business is part of the service sector, meaning that clients expect to be treated like gods. As a successful entrepreneur in another part of the service industry, Kimiko Itoh is well aware of the position. She probably pays out similar bonuses to her hostesses, received them herself in her younger days. She understands how an appropriate incentive can aid 'proper concentration' in difficult circumstances, for example, when straddling some wizened old faction leader with a dodgy heart and a prostate like a satsuma orange.

Why Kimiko Itoh has rung: to get an update on the Miura case. Mori tells her that the murder theory is confirmed, that he has a pretty clear idea of the circumstances, that he has already interviewed a suspect.

Kimiko Itoh sounds impressed. 'So you know who the murderer is?'

'I said a suspect,' says Mori. 'There's no real proof yet, and I haven't worked out the motivation.'

'Ah, motivation! So you don't think that the wife was involved?'

'Unlikely. My thinking is that the whole business is related to a political scandal.'

'Political scandal?' Kimiko Itoh makes it sound as if the concept is one she has never come across before.

'Something to do with the wife's father. Did Miura-*san* ever say anything to you about him?'

'About Toriyama sensei? No, I don't think he did.'

'What about a company called Nakanishi Pharmaceutical? Did he ever mention that?'

Kimiko Itoh trills in amusement. 'You don't understand, Mori-*san*. He would never discuss serious matters with a poor weak-brained woman like me!'

Mori gives a sardonic smile. Kimiko Itoh came from nowhere. Now she lives in a luxury apartment in the most expensive area of the city, flies around the world first-class, goes golfing in Hawaii. That's how weak-brained she is.

'No problem,' says Mori. 'Anyway, the suspect is the key to the whole case. There's a good chance he's going to confess.'

'Really? What makes you think that?'

'Instinct,' says Mori. He doesn't explain that the instinct is based on fifteen years of friendship.

'Excellent work,' says Kimiko Itoh. 'By the way, I'm in Madrid today. There's a museum here called El Prado. Have you heard of it, Mori-*san*?'

'Yes, I have. It's got the biggest Goya collection in the world.'

Mori wonders who she's travelling with. Maybe she's moved with the times, gone for the boss of a digital TV consortium or a biotech company. More likely it's another élite bureaucrat or an up-and-coming politician. That kind of wealth is less visible, but a lot more permanent.

'Goya?' coos Kimiko Itoh. 'Isn't he the one who cut off his ear?'

'That's Van Gogh.'

'So what does Goya do, plants or people?'

'People mostly.'

'You know everything, Mori-*san*. You're a really smart guy.'

Kimiko Itoh puts down the phone. Mori has a strong suspicion that she knows more about painting than he ever will.

He makes himself a cup of coffee, sits down and confronts the dilemma he has been avoiding. What to do about Taniguchi?

In professional terms, the answer is clear enough. Kimiko Itoh is too valuable a client to be fobbed off. Mori should get his hands on as much evidence as possible, then hand the case over to the police. Direct result: a sensational murder trial, splashed all over those same scandal magazines that carry Taniguchi's own articles. Indirect result: shame and misery, mental collapse.

In personal terms, the answer is equally clear. Mori should confront Taniguchi, tell him everything he knows, then make him promise to get medical help. Direct result: a chance for his old friend to rebuild his life. Indirect result: no bonus, no loan repayment.

There are other complications. What about the people from the Information Bureau? They may well get to Taniguchi in the end, regardless of what Mori does. And would Taniguchi accept his offer anyway? And if he does, can he be trusted? After all, at least two men have been killed already.

Mori leans back in his chair, hands folded behind his head, eyes fixed on the blotches in the ceiling. On the desk in front of him the mug of coffee steams untouched.

Then suddenly Mori's thoughts snap. There's a noise at the door, a scratching of metal on metal. Someone is trying to fit a key to the lock. Whoever it is must have come up the staircase as quietly as a cat. Mori creeps towards the door, neck tingling, the noise of last night's gunshot echoing in his mind. On the other side he hears keys clinking, a big bunch by the sound of it. Another one slides into the lock, and this time it turns. Mori waits half a dozen heartbeats, then bulldozes the door open, hurls himself at the figure outside.

'Hey! What you doing, detective-*san*?'

Angel twists away from him, shock in her eyes. Mori drops his hand from her neck, takes a step back.

'What am I doing?' he explodes. 'What do you think you're doing breaking into my office!'

Angel jingles a fat bunch of keys in front of his nose. 'I borrowed these from a friend of mine,' she says. 'I wanted to give you a surprise.'

Mori slumps against the wall, breathing relief. 'Well, you certainly succeeded,' he says.

Angel points to the floor. There's a long thin package lying there.

'That's my surprise,' she says. 'It's a sayonara present. Saturday, I'm leaving, going back to my own city.'

She picks up the package, hands it to him. The wrapping paper is from Mitsukawa department store, one of the most expensive places to shop in the whole of Japan.

Angel gives a little bow. 'Thank you for the things you've done, and thank you for the things you haven't done.'

'Haven't done? What does that mean?'

'You're different from other men. You look at a woman in a different way.'

'Maybe not as different as you think.'

Angel cuffs him on the shoulder. 'All men are pigs a little bit. My father was too.'

They go inside, sit down on the sofa. Mori apologizes for

being so jumpy, explains about the shooting of Uno. Angel looks worried.

'You have big enemies somewhere?'

'Not any new ones,' says Mori. 'That's why it's strange.'

Angel nods thoughtfully. 'There are many crazy people in this city. You take care of yourself, detective-*san*.'

'You too.'

'Just another couple of days, that's all.' Then the clouds pass from her face. 'Hey – let me show you something.'

She takes her wallet from her bag, slides out a photo. It shows a young girl, dark face smiling at the camera. Mori looks closer, recognizes the straight brow, the big eyes. Even as a young girl, Angel had tough beauty, no cuteness at all.

'You've grown up a bit since then,' he says.

White teeth flash. 'You think that's me,' says Angel, gleeful.

'It's not you? Who is it, then?'

'My daughter, Maria. It's her twelfth birthday next week.'

Mori's jaw drops open. For several moments he can't think of anything to say. A line of questions forms in his mind. Such as who is the father, was she ever married, how old is Angel anyway? He suppresses them all, hands back the photo.

'She's going to be a strong woman,' he says. 'Just like her mother.'

Angel shakes her head. 'Not like her mother. Much stronger than that.'

It's time for her to go, they both know that. A kiss on the cheek – tingling hair – then big smiles, big thanks. Angel runs down the stairs soundlessly, like a cat. Cars slow to let her cross the street. There's a red BMW pulled up on to the kerb. Before opening the door, Angel turns and waves, shouts something that gets lost in the roar of the city. Mori waves back, long and slow. Angel climbs into the BMW.

Mori watches it pull out into the stream of traffic, a single particle of colour shooting through the damp monochrome morning.

He goes inside, picks up the package.

Angel wonders what Mori will think of her present. It's probably not the sort of thing he would consider buying himself. Still, that's all right. Presents should be things you don't even know you need.

At the next traffic lights, Angel kicks the slingback off her right foot, feeds a reggae cassette into the music-machine. The car becomes a disco, thumping beats from eight speakers. Strong happy sounds, the kind that make you forget. She wasn't planning to leave this city so soon, but there's no choice now. The plane ticket and the passport she carries with her all the time, just in case she has to move in a hurry.

Angel guns the engine, takes the lights on orange. She's leaving behind good friends, will never see them again. She's leaving behind the doctor – poor old guy will start his dying as soon as she's gone. She's leaving behind Mori, who looks at her in a different way from the others, who has a deep calmness that makes her feel calm inside too. But this Mori is too careless. Like all Japanese, he just lets things happen. Angel never lets things happen. She works hard to make sure things turn out like she wants.

Last thing she shouted at Mori: 'Maybe I give you a bigger present, detective-*san*!' Yes, after what she's just learned, Angel knows that Mori needs a bigger present. Bare foot pressing down on the accelerator, she starts thinking how to provide it.

Mori pulls the last of the wrapping paper off the saxophone. It's a Yamaha alto, top of the range. How did she know? He hasn't even touched one for years. Then he remembers a few lines of conversation on the long drive back to Tokyo. He'd just put on a tape. The girls hadn't liked it.

'Who made this crazy music?'

'A guy called Coltrane.'

'You like this stuff, detective-*san*?'

'Sure. I used to play it myself.'

'Used to? How come you stopped?'

'I got older.'

'You not so old, detective-*san*. I think you got stamina to handle all six of us girls, one after the other.'

'Hey, I go first!'

'No, me!'

'What about me?'

Shrieks of laughter, drowning out 'A Love Supreme'. But Angel remembered all right. You wouldn't think it, but behind that face there must be a mind like a computer.

At eleven o'clock, Mori calls the hospital, sweet-talks one of the nurses into giving him the latest news about Uno.

'Fully conscious now,' she says. 'Actually, he mentioned your name several times, Mori-*san*. He seems anxious to see you.'

'So he's going to be all right?'

'That's what the doctors say. Still, a total recovery will take months.'

Soft-faced Uno has a tough spirit, a strong will to live.

'He needs complete rest,' continues the nurse. 'The police don't seem to understand that. They say they want to start questioning him straight away. The doctors told them to wait another two days.'

'Do your best to keep them out,' says Mori. 'They won't catch the right guy anyway.'

That was the strong impression Mori got from his visit to the police station late last night. He went straight from the hospital, spent two hours explaining exactly what happened. From the hungry way they were looking at him, Mori was lucky to get out of there without being arrested himself. No wonder they're getting frustrated. The first shooting in Shinjuku for months, and they've got no witnesses, no leads, no motivation. Failure to grab someone for an incident like this could have serious consequences for next year's budget.

The nurse laughs uncertainly. 'Do you want to leave a message for the patient?' she says.

'No message,' says Mori firmly. 'Don't even say that I called.'

It'll be easier that way. Easier for Mori, easier for Uno and easier for Keiko.

Seconds later the phone starts ringing, this time a flat, official kind of sound. It's Shima, weary-voiced. He wants Mori to come over to the police station and make a formal statement, giving an hour-by-hour account of his movements for the past week and details of all the cases he's been working on.

'You know I can't do that,' says Mori.

'A comprehensive report must be prepared for the ministry,' says Shima. 'Haven't you understood what I mean, Mori?'

'Understood!' says Mori humbly. 'I will do my best to offer sincere co-operation.'

Shima meant exactly what he said. A comprehensive report must be prepared, and it must include many pages of plausible testimony from Mori. Shima also meant something that he omitted to say – the factuality of the testimony would be entirely at Mori's discretion.

Now it's time. The inevitable can't be delayed any longer. Mori goes over to the shrine on the wall, claps his hands, makes a few simple requests to the gods. Then he picks up the phone, calls Taniguchi.

'I need some more help,' he says cautiously. 'There are problems with this case I'm working on.'

Pause at the other end. He can hear Taniguchi's breathing, slow and deliberate.

'What case is that?' comes the reply.

Mori coughs drily in exasperation. Taniguchi's prodigious memory is one feature of his old personality that is still intact. Ask him about some thirty-year-old political scandal or the line-up of a pennant-winning Giants team, and he'll spit out every detail, no hesitation.

'You know – the health bureaucrat, dead in mysterious circumstances.'

'Ah!'

'I heard he was mixed up in some shady business, taking money from one of the drug companies. Is that possible?'

'Everything's possible,' Taniguchi mutters.

Sure enough, thinks Mori. That's what this business teaches you – anyone's capable of anything. It's not what the bad guys do that's so disturbing. You expect that. It's what the good guys can manage when they're pressed.

Mori asks if they can meet as soon as possible. Taniguchi agrees. They arrange to meet in a coffee-shop a block from Taniguchi's office. Neutral ground, thinks Mori. Better for objectivity.

Events are moving forward, the suspect within his grasp, the big bonus ripe for claiming. At this stage Mori usually feels exhilarated, eager to wrap the case up as fast as possible. This time, though, he feels only lethargy, banks of rainclouds piling up on his shoulders.

By the time Mori gets to the coffee-bar, Taniguchi already has two empty beer bottles on the table in front of him. He's scanning a tabloid paper, seemingly engrossed in an account of a Japanese pitcher's latest efforts in the US major leagues. He glances up at Mori coming through the door.

'Knocked out in the third innings,' he says, tapping the paper with his finger. 'Looks like the hitters are getting used to his forkball.'

'Shouldn't use it so often,' says Mori, pulling up a chair. 'Uncertainty is the best weapon for a pitcher.'

Taniguchi shakes his head, frowning. 'He needs more discipline. If he were playing for the Giants, the coaches would train him harder, improve his control.'

'If he were playing for the Giants, he wouldn't be able to think for himself at all.'

Mori's comment is deliberately harsh, but Taniguchi just chuckles, carries on talking baseball. Mori realizes that this is going to be more difficult than he expected. He needs to be cold and forceful. Instead, he's just sipping beer, smiling and nodding while Taniguchi explains how the Giants' system of 'controlled baseball' will always triumph over the uncoordinated individualism of the Hantetsu Porpoises.

'Discipline, control, teamwork – that's why the Giants won all those pennants! That's why we've beaten the Porpoises eight times already this season!'

When Taniguchi talks about the Giants' victories, he looks years younger. That's good to see. Mori lets the conversation roll on a little while longer.

'Maybe you're underestimating the Porpoises. They know what they're doing.'

'What do you mean? The players make stupid mistakes all the time, and that manager's tactics are nonsense.'

'The Porpoises know how to lose, Taniguchi-*san*. They lose a lot better than the Giants win.'

'Unacceptable!' roars Taniguchi, face flushed. 'Losing is a great disgrace!'

'Everyone loses in the end,' says Mori, looking his friend in the eye. 'The Porpoises have that wisdom. Maybe you should have it too.'

Taniguchi's glass smacks down on the table. There's a pause in which the two men gaze at each other. Mori sees confusion ghosting across his old friend's face.

'What exactly do you want to know?' says Taniguchi finally.

No point in delay – go straight to the nub. 'I want to know where you were on the evening of February the third.'

Taniguchi doesn't even bother to fake any surprise. 'You mean the night that Miura died? I was at work, working on a piece about secret cartels in the chemical industry.'

For a moment, Mori is lost for words. Taniguchi has obviously come well prepared.

'Is there any way to confirm that?'

The reply is instant. 'No problem. I spent most of the time on the phone to one of my contacts, a guy who was forced out of the ministry in a power struggle.'

'Can you give me his name?'

'Sure, I'll write it down for you.'

Taniguchi takes out one of his own business cards, scribbles a name and a phone number on the back. Mori picks it up, then puts it down again on the table.

'What's the matter? You don't believe me?'

Taniguchi is smiling, but Mori reads the tension in his face muscles.

'I know you killed Miura.'

'You do? What makes you think that?'

Mori shakes his head, buries his surprise in his beer glass. He'd been assuming that one straight question – enough to show his determination – would do the trick. Taniguchi would crumple, tearful, angry. Mori would be left with the ethical problem of what to do next. But Taniguchi is refusing to follow the script. Defiant, he's even gone to the trouble of preparing some ridiculous alibi. All right, if Taniguchi wants to go through the motions, Mori is ready to oblige. He drains the beer glass, wipes his mouth with a hand-towel.

'Tell me about your research assistant,' he says.

The smile disappears from Taniguchi's face. 'What research assistant?'

'The one with the interest in video games.'

Taniguchi's fingers twist into knots. 'I don't know what you're talking about,' he says.

Despite himself, Mori is starting to get irritated. This is all so pointless, mutually embarrassing.

'Then let me tell you my theory,' he says tightly. 'Afterwards you can point out the flaws.'

Mori's theory says this. You are an alcoholic, with manic depression bad enough to worry the few friends you've got left. Your political views are increasingly bitter, as revealed to me when I visited your apartment the other week. You uncover a major scandal, involving top bureaucrats and reformist politicians, but no one will publish the exposé you write. That fills you with anger. You decide to take revenge.

It so happens that the research assistant you're using is a video-game developer. He sees that you're an expert on the Edo period, consults you about a game concept. That gives you the idea of using the Black Blade identity, pretending to be a crazed stalker obsessed with video games. After killing Nakonishi you go for Miura. And after Miura, what next? If you're going to eliminate every scandal-tainted bureaucrat and businessman in Japan, you'll end up in the *Guinness Book of Records*, the biggest serial killer in history.

Those are Mori's thoughts. His words are simpler, sharper.

When he has finished, Taniguchi gives a little laugh of

pretended incredulity. 'And you think that's plausible? You've got no proof, nothing there at all.'

Mori sucks air through the side of his mouth. Taniguchi is forcing him to be much tougher than he wants. 'All right – I'll hand everything over to the police. There's enough for them to mount a serious investigation.'

'Is that necessary?' says Taniguchi, much twitchier now.

Mori gives a little shrug. 'Not necessary at all, if you agree to my terms. I want a full confession, all the details. Then I want you to check in for psychiatric treatment.'

Taniguchi blinks in bewilderment. 'Psychiatric treatment!'

'That's the deal,' says Mori coldly. 'Now, are you going to agree or not?'

Silence stretches as Taniguchi gazes blankly into the ashtray. Finally he heaves a sigh and nods, the answer they both knew he had to give. Mori reaches across the table, grabs him by the hand.

'They'll take good care of you,' he says. 'Don't worry – you'll do much better work afterwards.'

Taniguchi says nothing. He pours himself another beer, gulps it down as if it's his last.

After Taniguchi has gone, Mori sits in the coffee-bar watching raindrops dribble down the steamy window. This is a strange rainy season, seems to be going on for ever. His father used to say that rainy seasons were either masculine or feminine, 'the difference is just like the pissing'. Masculine: short bursts of heavy rain, interspersed with blazing sunshine. Feminine: light drizzle dragging on, day after day. Well, the old man would have been confused this year. The weather has turned as androgynous as the college kids who swarm through Shibuya. Water falls from the sky every day, sometimes quick, sometimes slow. What it never does is stop.

Mori swills beer round his mouth, oppressed by more than the weather. The Miura case is over. Kimiko Itoh is going to be pleased. But the confession was the result of a crude threat, the sort of thing the dumbest cop could have done. That's not the way that important cases should end, with only the vaguest understanding of how the whole thing fitted together.

What was it about Miura that especially enraged a hardened observer like Taniguchi? And why the change of attitude today, from stubbornness to submission in a matter of seconds? Mori's dissatisfaction mounts – at Taniguchi, at himself, at the impenetrable strangeness of human beings. He glances at the card that Taniguchi left on the table. A name, a phone number. By creating his bogus alibi, Taniguchi was challenging his competence as a detective. That's a challenge which – for no good reason – Mori suddenly feels it necessary to meet.

Mori goes over to the phone in the corner of the coffee-shop, calls the number. On the fifth ring there's an answer. The voice at the other end is stiff, a little nervous – just what you might expect from a deracinated bureaucrat. When Mori explains what he wants, the man sounds surprised, but agrees to help. Yes, he does remember calling Taniguchi several times one night. Exactly when he doesn't remember, will go and check in his diary. Mori spends a few minutes listening to papers being shuffled and drawers slid open. The answer when it comes is what he was expecting: February the third. Mori asks a few more questions, then puts down the phone.

Strong instinct: this man is telling the truth.

Which means that Taniguchi's alibi is good.

Which means that he didn't kill Miura.

Mori returns to his seat, orders a black coffee. His brain is fogging over like the window pane. He runs through the conversation with Taniguchi, step by step. What happened? At first Taniguchi was prepared to tough it out, confident in the alibi. Then suddenly Mori's crude threat – actually a bluff – caused him to crumble. Why confess to a murder which you can prove you didn't commit? One possible answer comes to mind. It's a strange one, but fits Taniguchi's character better than any other.

Mori glances at his watch. Taniguchi should be back in his little apartment by now. He goes back to the phone, dials the number.

'Who's there?' says Taniguchi, jumpy.

'It's me,' says Mori. 'Listen, I've just remembered an old girlfriend's coming to see me tomorrow. Why don't we have our next meeting tonight instead?'

'Impossible!' snaps Taniguchi. 'You said tomorrow morning, didn't you?'

Actually, it was Taniguchi who had suggested the meeting in Mori's office tomorrow, a formal setting for him to explain exactly what had happened. Mori had readily assented. He had assumed that Taniguchi needed the extra time to get himself ready. Now an alternative explanation comes to mind. Taniguchi needs the extra time to discuss the situation with someone else.

'All right, then,' says Mori calmly. 'See you at eleven o'clock tomorrow.'

He puts down the phone and rushes through the door to where the Honda is parked. Minutes later he is pulling into an alley fifty metres from the ivy-strewn façade of Taniguchi's building.

The vantage point Mori chooses is a bookshop on the ground floor of a 'pencil-building' so ridiculously thin and ungainly that the architect must have designed it for a bet. The shop itself is small, just a few magazine racks and tabled piled with stacks of bestsellers. The narrow aisles are packed with salarymen and students escaping from the dripping reality outside. Mori jostles his way between the silent hunched bodies, comfortable in their motionless commute. Limbs shift. A space appears next to the window, just the place for a view of Taniguchi's office. On one side is a middle-aged salaryman engrossed in a cookery magazine. On the other is a heavy-set guy in a leather jacket leafing through a manga, one page every four or five seconds. Mori pushes between them, picks a fishing magazine from the rack.

The air is damp, heavy with breath. Without looking, Mori feels crowded in by the images to either side: lush photos of brightly coloured vegetables; cartoons of big-eyed schoolgirls having candle wax dripped on their breasts. The magazine in front of his nose isn't much better. The kind of fishing it portrays is from another world, where tanned heroes reel glossy monsters on to the decks of yachts. The last time Mori went fishing was five years ago. His companion, a once great pachinko pro trying to recover his concentration. The place, a fishing trench in the industrial wastelands of Kawasaki City. For five hundred yen you can fish all day long. Anything you catch goes into a bucket of water, and at the end of the day the buckets get emptied back into the trench. Mori remembers the pachinko pro's chortling voice: 'Looks like the fish here are more experienced than the people catching them.' Dead six months later, cancer of the stomach. You know you're really getting old when your friends start dying of natural causes.

Mori's reverie snaps. Suddenly there's activity on the other side of the street – a taxi pulling up at the kerb, the blue sign showing it's on call. Minutes later a large black umbrella appears at the bottom of the staircase leading to Taniguchi's office. Mori cranes forward, squinting through the drizzle. The umbrella is just edging out on to the street when a bus comes rumbling across his line of sight.

'Hey, you're in the way,' mutters Mori under his breath. The guy in the leather jacket glances sideways, narrow-eyed.

The bus gives a hydraulic wheeze and – unbelievably – comes to a complete halt.

'Shift yourself,' says Mori.

Leather jacket turns towards him. 'What did you say?' he growls in Mori's ear.

There's no time for explanations. Mori shoves past, but leather jacket grabs his arm, won't let go. Mori twists round, fakes a stumble. His fist moves the minimum distance, thumping into the side of the guy's stomach. Leather jacket grunts in shock, sinks to his knees.

'Please excuse me,' murmurs Mori, bowing as he heads for the door. Not one of the other motionless commuters even looks up.

Outside, Mori marches around the back of the bus, then stops, hands on hips. Already the taxi is disappearing down the street, signalling a left turn at the junction. Mori can just make out the passenger bending forward to talk to the driver. His head is the shape of a dice, square with round corners. Taniguchi, no question! Mori turns, races back to the alley where he stowed the Honda.

It only takes a few minutes to catch up with the taxi on the main road to Ikebukuro. Mori stays in the middle lane, keeping at least a dozen cars between them. The taxi goes straight through Ikebukuro, joins the roaring traffic of the loop road. Then, after five kilometres, it suddenly turns into a rent-a-car lot. A hundred metres behind, Mori stops at a bank of vending machines. Even in the old days, Mori never saw Taniguchi driving a car, never heard him talk about driving. Yet here is now, emerging from the rent-a-car lot in a brand-new Daihatsu Move.

The Move is a beer-can on wheels – just six hundred cubic centimetres of engine – but Taniguchi takes up it to the speed limit straight away. Conclusion: the man is in a hurry. The traffic is thinning out now, giving Mori less cover. He drops back another few vehicles, hopes he doesn't lose the Daihatsu at a turning.

He doesn't. Next junction, the Daihatsu squeals left. Mori follows down a bustling shopping street, over a hump-backed flyover, through a succession of suburban streets that contain ever larger houses. Mori tries to keep his distance, but it's getting more difficult. Leaning the Honda into a sharp bend, he looks up to see the Daihatsu reversing into a parking spot. Just in time, Mori pulls into an empty driveway. By the time he has switched off the engine and pulled off his helmet, the Daihatsu is empty, Taniguchi nowhere in sight.

Mori glances around. Apartment blocks behind high stone walls, a children's playground, a red shrine gate. This is a high-class area. Mori knows that without even looking at the buildings. He can tell from the space between them, from the shape of the trees (big and sprawling) and the colour of their leaves (green, not grey). Ambient tranquillity, the most expensive item on the market.

Mori approaches the Daihatsu, tries the driver's door. It's unlocked. He slips inside, checks under the seats and in the glove compartment. All he finds are manuals and the rental agreement. Nothing in the car that belongs to Taniguchi, except an empty coffee-can and a book of matches lying on top of the dashboard. Interesting. Taniguchi doesn't smoke, so why a book of matches? Mori picks it up, opens the flap. On the inside, in smudgy blue ink, 'Toyo Inari Shrine'. Judging from the scrawl, Taniguchi must have written it down in a hurry. Mori gets out of the car, walks up to the shrine gate. Five metres above his head, emblazoned in

301

faded characters on the second tier of the arch, 'Toyo Inari Shrine'.

Mori steps inside. The shrine appears to be on top of a little hill. Mori follows a winding stairway, its stone worn smooth by centuries of shuffling feet. Halfway up he pauses. There's a noise, the dull boom of a big bell. It must be Taniguchi, making an appeal to the god of the hill. Mori moves faster, stooping forward when the stairway passes through a tunnel of miniature shrine gates.

The stairway ends, and Mori finds himself in a little clearing. The shrine itself is a plain wooden building, sheltered by trees girdled with sacred ropes. Nobody there, just the bell swaying gently from side to side. Mori hears the croak of magpies, the patter of rain, a small creature rustling through the undergrowth. Up here you could be lost in mountain country, a thousand years before the city was created.

The stone pathway passes around the side of the shrine. Mori follows, finds another smaller tunnel of shrine gates that twists between the trees and down the hillside. Inside is danker, darker, the staircase steep and coated with moss. Bent almost double, Mori treads carefully, one step at a time. Even so, halfway down he slips, has to reach out and grab the arch of a shrine gate. Just in time he stops it toppling forward and setting off a ripple of falling shrine gates that would reach the bottom of the hill well before he could.

At the end of the tunnel, Mori peers out into the damp light. Here the vegetation is thick, the path completely overgrown. It takes him a few moments to get his bearings. In front of him is a grove of tall bamboo, through which he can just make out a wooden fence and the white bulk of a building. That must be one of the luxury apartment blocks that face the street where he parked the Honda. Furthermore, something is moving on the other side of the bamboo, a splash of colour that Mori identifies as Taniguchi's dirty white windcheater.

Mori moves stealthily through the waist-high couchgrass. When he reaches the cover of the bamboo, he stops and watches in surprise. Taniguchi has grabbed hold of the top of the fence and is manfully levering himself upwards with knees and feet. Evidently, the man is in better shape than he looks. After a few failures, he finally manages to scrabble himself into a sitting position, from which he begins scrutinizing the apartment block through a pair of binoculars. A few seconds later, Taniguchi decides to come down again. This, though, proves a little more difficult, and he hits the ground too hard and falls flat on his back.

Mori squeezes through the bamboo, walks over to where his old friend lies puffing and groaning in the wet grass.

'That's not a good way to fall,' he says. 'You should bend your knees more.'

Taniguchi's eyes flash in panic. 'What are you doing here?'

'That's exactly what I want to ask you,' says Mori, reaching down a hand.

'Just some research. Nothing special.'

'Research into what exactly? Shrine architecture?'

Taniguchi shakes his head, grabs Mori's hand. Mori hauls him to his feet.

'What's going on?' he says tightly. 'Who lives in that place?'

Taniguchi glances over his shoulder at the apartment block, then suddenly stumbles forward, grabbing Mori by the shoulder.

'It's my foot,' he says, wincing. 'I think it may be broken.'

Mori bends down, eases off Taniguchi's left shoe. Indeed, the ankle is slightly swollen.

'Not too serious,' he says. 'Anyway, let's get you back to the car. I'll do the driving, and you can do the talking.'

Taniguchi puts an arm around Mori's neck and together they move awkwardly back towards the tunnel of shrine gates. Getting through the bamboo takes time as Taniguchi is unwilling to put both feet on the ground at once. Mori goes first then guides him through the criss-cross of leaves and long supple branches. On the other side, Taniguchi leans back against a huge green bamboo plant, as thick as a man's thigh. He looks pale, confused. Sad, thinks Mori. The sooner he gets psychiatric help the better.

'Think you can make it up the steps?'

'Maybe.'

Mori stares at him, senses the tension in his face. It's as if he's waiting for something to happen. Waiting for what? For the god of the bamboo grove to make an appearance? Mori holds out his hand.

'Come on,' he says gently. 'Let's get out of here.'

Then Mori hears a twig snap right behind him and suddenly long strong arms are reaching around his neck, pulling him off his feet.

'Yah!' he yells. 'What's going on?'

He twists, drives his elbow into ribcage, stamps heel on to toe. The only effect is that the pressure around his neck gets stronger.

'Don't hurt him,' says Taniguchi, who is no longer leaning against the big bamboo.

Wet cloth presses down on Mori's face. Chemical smell is fierce in his nostril, cold fog rushing into his brain. Now Taniguchi is moving away in the direction of the tunnel. Eyes swimming, Mori notices that the limp has gone.

Sensation dies in feet, knees, hands. Heart beats big and squashy. Face goes stiff, mouth fills with tongue.

Mori staggers free, twirls, crumples into long grass. Standing above him is a familiar figure – impossibly tall, black kimono.

'Black Blade,' shouts a voice in Mori's head. But Mori's lips are no longer taking instructions, and his eyelids are resolutely closed.

Seventeen

In a Shibuya back street lined with love hotels and strip clubs, there's a single game arcade always packed with students and young office workers. True enthusiasts, they come because they've heard that the most exciting new games arrive here well before anywhere else. What they haven't heard is the reason – that the place is managed by a leasing company controlled by SoftJoy Enterprises. Three other things that they don't know. That hidden cameras are capturing their every word and gesture. That the machines themselves transmit details of games played to SoftJoy's host computer. That they are being observed from behind the grease-spattered mirror on the wall by cognitive psychology specialists employed by the SoftJoy Research Institute.

Standing at the back of the crowd, watching the bleeping flashing screens with rapt attention, is a small man with a face as round and plump as a pastry. His clothes – jeans split at the knee, check shirt, baseball cap drawn down over the eyes – are much like everyone else's. He looks neither rich nor poor, neither young nor old. The only thing that is unusual about him is his head, which seems much too big for his slender shoulders.

'Not good,' yells one of the players, twisting round in his seat. 'He should be dead! Why isn't he dead?'

On the screen in front of him a headless monkey leaps

into the air, twirling a sword so fast that it becomes a blur of flashing metal. Meanwhile, the severed head sits on the table, screaming insults. This game is the latest version of Monkey Magic, one of SoftJoy's steadiest sellers.

'Cut off his arm,' shouts one of the crowd. 'That way you'll be safe.'

'All right!'

The player turns back to the controls. On the screen, the samurai dances forward, then thrusts with his sword, slicing off the monkey's hand at the wrist. The monkey grimaces inanely as the stump sprays a bright red fountain into the air. There are squeals of dismay from the women in the crowd. But the severed hand is still clutching the sword, which continues to whirl and flash as if it had a life of its own.

'Not good!' yells the player, desperate.

Not good indeed. Seconds later, the samurai is lying on the floor, life leaking away through a wound in his neck. The monkey recovers his limbs, morphs into a handsome youth played by the lead singer of a chart-topping rock group. Pounding music booms from concealed speakers; several people in the crowd start mouthing the lyrics of the song. The small man with big head does the same. He knows those lyrics well, as he was the one who wrote them.

The player gets out of the control seat, makes way for the next person. He says nothing as he pushes through the crowd. His eyes are empty, his mouth shut tight. The small man at the back glances down at his hands, notes the twitching fingers. Judging from the physical response, it'll take another hour for the game's imprint to wear off completely.

In the early days. SoftJoy experimented with crude subliminal techniques. Messages and ghost images were flashed into corners of the screen at crucial moments, when the brain was most receptive to new information. The results, though, were poor. In one experiment, game-players were unconsciously bombarded with the word 'thirsty' and pictures of sand dunes and glaring suns. Unfortunately, the effect on drink-purchasing patterns was statistically indistinguishable from raising the room temperature two degrees.

The human mind can't be manipulated like a machine, but it can be guided into certain emotional states by carefully assembled stimuli. That is the basis of movies, ads, all other visual fictions. It is also the basis of the CHI system. SoftJoy's researchers developed an abstract approach, using light pulses, colours and shapes to accompany the simple narrative of the games. Configurations were identified that could stimulate responses such as fear, anger and exhilaration. More work showed that intensity could be improved by the use of certain frequency variations in the sound effects. In the first arcade trials, the games with these features generated fifteen per cent more revenue than average. In subsequent versions, that ratio rose to twenty, then forty, and the repeat use ratio rose to the amazing level of forty per cent, too. In other words, if you played the game once, you couldn't stop going back for more.

Monkey Magic is an ordinary sort of game, nothing innovative or sophisticated. But the man with the large head knows that it can stimulate real fear, send real adrenalin coursing through the central nervous system. That's why the player pushing past on his way to the entrance was so grey-faced, so hunched in the shoulders. That's why many unfortunate people have experienced epileptic fits for the first time in video-game arcades.

A pager beeps in the small man's pocket. He takes it out, reads a message confirming the meeting due to start in his hotel room in two hours' time. Unobtrusively he moves to the door.

Mori . . .

Pushing through the thronging festival crowds . . .

Rushing to escape . . .

Fireworks over the river, flowers of light, exploding in the indigo sky . . .

The throwing-star spinning out of the ninja's gloved hand, floating above the heads of the crowd . . .

Mori dodges to one side. The throwing-star adjusts its course, comes curving and dipping towards him. The ninja's aim is uncanny. There is only one way to avoid those whirling blades. Mori must open his eyes. But his eyelids are made of cement. They refuse to obey. Mori raises his fingers to his eyes, forces them open.

The ninja disappears, as do the festival crowds, the fireworks, all the bright hard colours.

The world goes greenish-grey, greyish-green. Mori finds himself lying on his back, surrounded by couch-grass, bamboo. He rolls on to his haunches, sucks damp air into his lungs, tries to remember where he is, who he is.

There is no sign anywhere of either Taniguchi or his friend.

Something else – a thin column of smoke curling above the tops of the bamboo.

Mori's eye traces it down the sky to an open window in the apartment block behind the fence. From the same direction come noises, people yelling, the whine of sirens.

Last time he looked, that window was not open.

Last time he looked, there was no smoke.

Instant decision: this is not a good time to stand around theorizing. It's a good time to be gone.

Mori scuttles through the tunnel of shrine gates, races

past the shrine, then down the stone staircase to the main entrance.

Out on the street, the Daihatsu has gone, but a fire engine has stopped in front of one of the apartment blocks. Firemen in shiny silver suits are rushing around, lugging giant hoses. Mori appears casually curious as he strolls towards them. One of the firemen is standing back from the others, bellowing orders through a megaphone. He glares suspiciously at Mori, who therefore has no choice but to play the typical bystander. He stops, hands on hips, and gawks.

'What's happening here?'

'Fire,' says the fireman expertly.

'No one injured, I hope.'

The fireman shakes his head. 'No one there at the time. Luckily, because the place is completely burned out.'

'Really! Which apartment was it?'

'Number three oh three.' The fireman gazes at Mori as if he expects him to say something. Mori nods, keeps quiet. The fireman looks puzzled for a moment, then gives a little laugh.

'I see. Living in an area like this, you're used to having celebrities all around. I don't know – maybe you're a celebrity yourself!'

Mori smiles enigmatically. 'Maybe,' he says.

'Still, I've been a fan of Naomi Kusaka ever since I was at high school. Tell me – is she as cute in real life as on TV?'

Mori considers the question for a few seconds.

'Cuter,' he says finally.

The fireman wipes his face with a silver sleeve. For the moment he has forgotten about the fire completely.

'I thought so,' he says. 'By the way, I'm sure I've seen you on TV too. There's something pretty hard to forget about your face . . .'

Mori tunes into a sound in the distance – the unmistakable shriek of a police siren, probably just turning off the loop road.

'Wait a moment!' continues the fireman. 'You're a ballad-singer, one of those guys who used to be popular when I was a kid.'

Mori opens a mouth to make a speedy denial, but the fireman holds up a gloved hand.

'Don't tell me your name! Let me guess!'

For a moment, the two men gaze at each other in silence. Then a broad grin spreads across the fireman's face.

'You're Masao Kanda, aren't you?'

'No, I'm not.' Mori turns away, but the fireman grabs him by the elbow. The siren is closer now, no more than a couple of kilometres away.

'Jun Ishikawa?' he breathes in Mori's ear.

'No!'

'That tough guy – what was his name – Yamazaki?'

'Absolutely not!'

'I know – let's ask a few of the other guys. One of them is bound to know!'

The fireman puts the megaphone to his lips, is about to start bellowing when Mori yanks his sleeve free and marches down the road.

'Hey – wait!' blares the megaphone. 'Are you sure you're not Masao Kanda?'

Mori's only response is to break into a jog. He hurries into the empty driveway, straddles the Honda. As he noses out into the road, the police car comes squealing round the bend, lights flashing. The celebrity-crazed fireman is still bellowing names through the megaphone. Mori leans low over the handlebars, heads for home.

Richard Mitchell gazes grimly at the object on the table in

front of him. That rhomboid of grey plastic is responsible for one of the worst half-hours of his life. In appearance it is harmless enough, a multi-directional speaker-phone designed by someone with a fondness for Bauhaus architecture. In actuality, it is bringing him intense suffering. If only it would short-circuit, burst into flames, melt into a pool of sticky grey gunk.

The conference call was Sasha de Glazier's idea. It was time, she said, for the clients to have a chance to quiz Mitchell directly on his latest recommendations. Not yet, pleaded Mitchell, give me some time to prepare.

'What's the matter?' said Sasha, fixing him with the voodoo gaze. 'You scared they're going to chew on your *cojones*?'

Not far from the truth. For the first few minutes Mitchell leaned over the plastic rhomboid and gave his usual spiel about technological trends in the video-game market. Then, as soon as he mentioned SoftJoy and Mega Enterprises, the interruptions started. His attempts to answer the interruptions were themselves interrupted as fund managers and analysts from six different time zones queued up to denounce him.

'You're still recommending this stock?' comes an angry Australian voice. 'Un-bloody-believable, mate!'

'You've lost me much money,' accuses Jacqueline, perfect in Paris.

'These forecasts are way out of line . . .' grumbles Ahmed.

'Measures may have to be taken,' threatens the man from the Singapore government.

'This stock is dead,' says public school Sebastian. 'Why not have the decency to bury it?'

'Thirty per cent down in the first quarter. That's not funny, I think . . .'

'Mega is good stock, no? That stock goes up, no?'

'Get real, buddy. SoftJoy's down the tubes.'

'Take a grip, man, this is financial necrophilia . . .'

'My government says . . .'

'Don't you get it, you schmuck . . .'

'A complete load of crap . . .'

'Camel dung . . .'

'*Merde* . . .'

Mitchell emerges from the conference room with his back soaked in sweat. He walks back to the research department and slumps down at his desk. Nobody talks to him, not even the office ladies. Already they sense his defeat.

Mitchell switches on his computer, clicks up the chart of Mega's stock price. What he sees: a rising parabola now accelerating into an almost vertical trajectory. How would his old boss Yazawa describe that? Would he consider it as 'escalator ride to the moon', meaning an ascent so strong and meaningful that it can never be reversed? Or is it more like 'the ejaculation of the sleeping monk', a frenzied surge that is followed by collapse then years of lassitude? Yazawa never bothered to explain his terms, but one comment does stick in Mitchell's mind: 'Beware of escalators that lack steps.' Mega has risen continuously over the past year, not a single correction of more than five per cent. Thanks to the heavy buying whipped up by Scott Hamada and his cronies at Silvermans, this escalator has no steps at all.

Hardly daring to hope, Mitchell switches off the machine, gets ready to leave. Just as he's packing his briefcase, his human Geiger counter registers a tingling presence at his shoulder. It's Sasha de Glazier. Today she's dressed completely in black – black cotton dress, black stockings, black earrings, even black nail varnish.

'So what happened? Are your *cojones* still intact?'

At first Mitchell thinks she's going to reach down for confirmation. He takes an instinctive step backwards.

'No problem, Sasha.'

He attempts a nonchalant grin. Sasha doesn't respond, and the grin rapidly fades. She gazes at him, eyes narrowed. They're standing close enough for Mitchell to note a faint smudge on her upper lip, the shadow of a moustache.

'Excellent,' she says at last. 'In that case I want you to repeat the exercise every week.'

Mitchell nods dumbly. Sasha de Glazier marches off towards Hauptman's office, high heels stabbing the carpet.

Mori gets back to his office at six o'clock. He pours out a glass of Suntory, sits down heavily on the sofa. Just a couple of hours ago, the Miura case was drawing to a tidy resolution. Now everything is messy, stupidly complex.

The confession in the coffee shop was a trick, and Mori fell for it completely. Taniguchi has an accomplice, some crazed fantasist willing to follow his orders even to the point of murder. Taniguchi himself has a watertight alibi. And far from accepting the need for medical help, he is continuing with his campaign of murder and intimidation.

But why set fire to Naomi Kusaka's apartment. Why? Why pick on a celebrity who hasn't been in the news for more than a decade? Mori knows little about show business and cares less, but he does remember Naomi Kusaka – tall, short hair, sang terrible songs in a good strong voice. She started out with Takarazuka, the all-female theatre troupe, playing the male lead in swashbuckling romantic comedies. After that she had some success as a pop singer and actress in 'trendy dramas'. Then what? Mori has a vague recollection of a scandal, a tearful press conference, head bowed in contrition. He needs to know more. The person to ask is

314

Hayasaka, once a director for TV Kanto, now proprietor of a tiny vaudeville theatre deep in the heart of the old town.

As the years roll on, Tokyo shifts ever westwards. The old town on the east side of the river gets left further behind. The buildings get shabbier, the people get older, their tastes and customs more remote. These days women's magazines run specials on what kind of food to eat there, treating the place as if it were some quaint foreign land. Hayasaka is from the old town. One day he suddenly decided to go back.

From what he told Mori, it all happened after he got assigned to prime-time comedy, the one department in which TV Kanto regularly topped the ratings. The comedians he was working with – mainly guys who had come up through university talent contests arranged by TV companies – were incredibly popular. They endorsed hundreds of products, put out best-selling CD collections, had their pick of the high-school girls who hung around outside the studios all hours of the day and night. They were arrogant, of course, but Hayasaka didn't mind that. What began to trouble him was that they didn't make him laugh, not even crack a smile. At first he thought it was his own problem, getting out of touch or burned out or whatever. So he went to his friends, asked them to explain what the funniest gags were they had heard lately. Nobody could remember a single one. Conclusion: people were laughing not because of what these guys did or said, but because of who they were. These days laughing at the antics of a big-name comedian was no different from bowing to the boss at work.

Just at that time, Hayasaka happened to read a news item about an old theatre closing down. He recognized the name, flashed back to visiting the place with his uncle forty years ago. He remembered how his uncle used to laugh, face crumpled up, mouth so wide open you could see halfway down his throat. Because he knew what he was doing, he had quit his job, borrowed thirty million yen from his wife's father and talked the studio hands into renovating the place for free.

The theatre is located at the end of a winding alley that smells of yakitori and echoes with karaoke. It is a squat concrete building, festooned with red lanterns and wooden boards portraying the great vaudevillians of the past. A poster on the door advertises one of tonight's attractions – Pango the Snake-Charmer. The picture shows a man in a turban playing a flute. On the table in front of him is a large straw basket from which is emerging a woman dressed in a snakeskin sheath.

Mori clumps up the stairs to the manager's office. Inside Hayasaka is sitting at his desk, a long cigarette holder poised between his fingers.

'Ah, Mori-*san*,' he says, looking up from the ledger in front of him. 'You're just in time.'

'In time for what?'

'In time for the show, of course!' says Hayasaka, oozing enthusiasm. 'Tonight is Pango's comeback. He's been in retirement for fifteen years, but I managed to persuade him to return to the stage.'

'Really?' says Mori carefully. 'I had no idea.'

'You didn't know? In that case, you're extremely lucky. You'd better hurry up, Mori-*san*, the show's going to start any minute now!'

'Wait – I'm not in the mood for comedy.'

'It's when you're not in the mood for comedy that you need it most. You need it, Mori-*san*. That was obvious from your face when you walked through the door.'

'I'm here for a reason,' says Mori, finding it hard to hide his impatience. 'I came to ask for some information.'

Hayasaka flourishes the cigarette holder. 'Really? What sort of information?'

'Naomi Kusaka, used to be with Takarazuka. I need the full background on her – men, money, everything ...'

'Naomi Kusaka!' says Hayasaka, head on one side. 'That's a very interesting lady.'

'Interesting? In what way?'

There's a burst of noise in the hall below, applause and shouts of delight. Hayasaka points a finger downwards.

'I'll tell you after the show,' he says. 'For good friends like you, tickets are half-price.'

Mori shakes his head. 'This is urgent.'

'You can wait another hour, Mori-*san*. After all, Pango's been waiting fifteen years. Come on, I'll show you the way.'

Hayasaka was right. An hour doesn't make much difference. And, furthermore, Pango is excellent, impossible to watch with a straight face. The snake-women pop out of the baskets. Pango gazes at them with a mixture of bewilderment and goggle-eyed lasciviousness. He scratches his head, looks up at the audience, defies you not to laugh. Mori laughs, loud enough to surprise himself. And once he's started laughing he finds it difficult to stop.

A rapid series of gags – old friends that Pango makes you glad to meet again – then suddenly the hour is over. Walking up the stairs to Hayasaka's office, Mori feels lighter, younger.

Sprawling on the sofa, a glass of whisky cradled in his hands, Mori listens to the complex history of an ambitious young woman called Naomi Kusaka. The scandal that he remembered concerned the operator of a pyramid investment scheme. It turned out that the gifts he had lavished on his favourite actress – including diamonds, a sports car, and an apartment in Hawaii – had been financed by 'insurance premiums' collected from farmers' wives in Tohoku. From that time on, Naomi Kusaka was more careful in her choice of sponsors. First came a real-estate tycoon who suffered a fatal heart attack in a hot-spring bath. Next was the president of a movie company. A comeback movie was planned, a big budget French-Italian-Japanese co-production. It was cancelled when the company got into financial difficulties, had to sell its studio to a joint venture set up by Mega Enterprises and Rupert Murdoch.

'So what happened after that?'

Hayasaka places the cigarette holder between his lips, takes a long contemplative drag.

'From what I hear, Naomi is being unusually discreet. There are always rumours, of course, but nothing credible.'

'Nothing credible?' says Mori, frowning. 'These days everything's credible. If you were in my business, you'd know that.'

Hayakawa shrugs. 'Well, in my experience, seventy per cent of all rumours are false. The one I heard about Naomi Kusaka just doesn't sound like it belonged to the other thirty per cent.'

'Try it out. I'll give you my opinion.'

'All right, then. Would you believe that a well-known politician would get involved with a woman with that kind of history?'

Mori leans forward on the sofa. 'Yes, I certainly would.'

'Wait a moment,' says Hayasaka. 'I don't mean some medium-ranking dietman. I'm talking about a man who could be the next prime minister!'

'You mean, a man willing to dedicate his life to national regeneration?'

Hayasaka lifts the cigarette holder from his mouth, gazes at Mori in surprise. 'What – you heard the same rumour?'

'I heard nothing,' says Mori. 'It was just a strong hunch.

And in my experience, seventy per cent of strong hunches are correct.

He finishes the whisky, gets up to go. On the way out he buys a couple of advance tickets for Pango's next performance.

Outside the rain hangs in the air. The Honda weaves through the cramped and shabby streets, past shop awnings that haven't changed colour for decades, past shrine buildings that haven't changed shape for centuries. Mori crosses the river and leaves the old town behind. By the time he gets back to Shinjuku, the great city has already crept another few millimetres to the west.

Yoichi Sonoda leans back in his chair, eyes closed, hands cradling his neck. He is thinking pornography. Not the images themselves – all that human meat sweating and straining interests him not a jot – but the market they comprise, a market waiting to be seized and transformed.

The principle is simple: artificial stimulation of certain neuro-receptors through defined sets of sensory information. The usual methods, though, are highly inefficient.

Think of all the magazines, the videos, the cinemas, the telphone talk-lines, the websites, the strip shows, the lingerie bars, the lap-dance clubs, the 'fashion massage' parlours, the pink cabarets, the soaplands, the SM salons. Think of the huge sums of money spent all over the world, every day of the week.

Now imagine just a few per cent of that expenditure channelled to a new sort of video game, one that offers the richest, most intense eroticism ever experienced. A game that is polymorphic, customized to suit the private fantasies of every player. You choose the environment. You choose the characters – historical, whatever you like. You become the characters. You meet other characters chosen by other players.

The company with the right product would generate enough cash flow to control the entire industry.

Sonoda knows that his analysis is far from unique. For several years now, virtual pornography has been the great hope of the game industry. Researchers at Mega Enterprises have already produced a number of prototypes. The example that Sonoda saw was tacky, vulgar, no more than a 3-D video with a couple of interactive functions added. As usual, Mega is approaching the idea from the wrong angle. All they're doing is packaging pornographic images in a new format. When the first SoftJoy product is ready for the market – five years in the future, maybe eight – it will be something completely different. Not a new type of pornography, but a new type of sex.

A knock at the door.

'Enter.'

Okada appears, hands Sonoda the latest briefing from their mole in Mega's finance department. It contains the release schedule for the summer. Sonoda scans, nods approval. Predictably Mega have decided to rush out the game they stole from SoftJoy via the disloyal developer. According to the schedule, it should be in the shops by the end of the month.

'No wonder they are in a hurry,' he mutters abstractedly. 'This has the potential to be their best-selling game of the year.'

Okada looks puzzled, which is not surprising.

'What about our own version?' he says. 'Wouldn't it be advisable to bring forward the release date?'

'Inadvisable!' says Sonoda sharply. 'Better delay it for a couple of months.'

'Delay it!' says Okada, eyes wide with astonishment.

'You heard what I said.'

Better scrap it altogether, in fact. In a few days' time that game's job will have been done.

There are certain strategic necessities which someone like Okada could never appreciate. Which is why Sonoda decided to keep him in the dark. After the disloyal developer was identified, Sonoda took personal control of the little project. He interrogated the man alone, used extraordinary threats and bribes to win his co-operation. The next day, he sent the developer to meet the top people in Mega's production department. The developer handed over a revised version of the game, different from the previous version in one or two visual details. And also in a couple of lines of code, compressed and hidden where they would never be found by Mega's salaryman testers.

Richard Mitchell stands gazing nervously at his watch. Reiko was supposed to pick him up at the Akasaka crossing at nine o'clock. Now it's already a quarter past, and he's starting to get restless. Maybe he got the time or the place wrong. Maybe Sonoda got busy, decided to cancel the meeting. Maybe there never was a meeting, just Reiko enjoying a perverse joke at his expense. Whatever the reason, she hasn't appeared, and Mitchell is starting to have bad thoughts. No meeting means nothing to show Sasha de Glazier, which means no chance of keeping his job.

Taxis swish over the tarmac. Raindrops drip from his umbrella, a dark knobbly handled model that he bought especially for the occasion. 'British Simple Conservative' said the label at the Mitsuya Department Store. The price was about the same as a box seat at Wimbledon.

Suddenly a jacked-up Isuzu Bighorn with enormous wheels and a picture of a surfboard on the side comes cruising past, much too close to the kerb. Gutter water sprays over Mitchell's ankles.

'*Hoi!*' he bellows. 'You stupid octopus!'

The Bighorn squeals to a halt. The passenger door slides open and a young guy jumps out on to the pavement. He has a scrubby little beard and a mane of 'tea-coloured' hair flowing on to his shoulders. Passers-by stop and stare, no doubt hoping to see some trouble involving the big foreigner and the surfer.

'Look at this,' yells Mitchell, pointing at the dark patches on his trouser legs.

'You shouldn't stand so close to the kerb,' says the surfer, a supercilious smile on his face. 'That's a good way to get wet.'

His English is perfect, which somehow intensifies Mitchell's frustration.

'Wet? I'll show you wet!'

The smile disappears from the surfer's face as Mitchell drops the umbrella and advances towards him.

'Wait a moment! Stop!'

But Mitchell is in no mood to stop. He grabs the surfer by the shoulder and shoves him backwards against the side of the Bighorn. His opponent, though, is surprisingly lithe. Somehow he slips clear, and suddenly it is Mitchell who finds himself jammed up against the car door, wet metal cold on his body. Now each of them is gripping the other by the collar, pulling and twisting. This contest is hardly fair since the surfer is bare-chested beneath his cotton bomber jacket whereas Mitchell is wearing a monogrammed shirt and a silk Valentino tie recently purchased in Singapore airport.

'Yah!' breathes the surfer.

'Hah,' grunts Mitchell.

'Yah!'

'Let him go!'

It's a woman's voice. The grip around Mitchell's collar lessens. He turns to see Reiko Tanaka standing next to him, hands on hips.

'Come on,' she snaps. 'There's no time for fooling around!'

'Fooling around?' says Mitchell indignantly. 'Maybe you didn't see what happened. It was all the fault of this creep here!'

Reiko gives an impatient shake of the head. 'Don't you understand? This man is a key member of SoftJoy's marketing department.'

Mitchell gazes in astonishment as the surfer takes a wallet from the inside pocket of his jacket and slides out a name card.

'My name is Takeuchi,' he says, bowing as he proffers it to Mitchell. 'Humbly at your service.'

Mitchell accepts the name card and hastily produces one of his own.

'At your service,' he mutters.

The two men stand in the drizzle examining each other's name cards with exaggerated respect. Reiko walks around to the driver's side of the Bighorn and climbs inside.

The meeting with Sonoda is to be held in the Seikyu Hotel, an establishment in which the staff comfortaby outnumber the guests, though neither are often seen, and the hubbub of the city seems as distant as the peak of Mount Fuji. The peculiarity of the Seikyu – the feature which attracts most of its regular guests – is the rigour with which all elements of conventional hotel-ness are excluded. No atrium filled with birdsong, no grinning bell-hops, no 'complimentary' fruit or chocolate in your room, no signs indicating approved methods of payment, no check-out desk at all, in fact. If you want to leave, you just go. If you want anything, you just ask. The hotel knows who you are. If it didn't, you wouldn't be there.

Reiko leads them through the lobby – no chandeliers, no pianist in a cocktail dress, no newspaper kiosk – to a door half-hidden in an alcove. When she approaches, the door slides open. On the other side is an elevator containing no muzak, no gilt mirrors, no panel of numbered buttons. Instead, Reiko feeds a plastic card into a slot in the wall. The hotel's approval is instant. The door eases shut and the elevator purrs into motion, so discreetly that whether it is ascending or descending is impossible to tell.

Sonoda is waiting for them alone in his suite – bare feet, jeans, plain white T-shirt. With his Beatle fringe and his soft round cheeks, he could be a college student or a trainee chef.

Mitchell moves cautiously into the middle of the room. Should he shake hands or bow, speak in English or Japanese, address the man as 'Sonoda-*san*' or 'President' or perhaps even 'sensei'? Mitchell has been in Japan long enough to appreciate the heaviness of the situation. Not just what you say, but the way you stand, the way you breathe, the placement of the chair you choose, how quickly you reach for the tea cup on the table in front of you – all such acts are pregnant with meaning, raising complex issues of status and face.

'You are Richard Mitchell.' The words are spoken flatly, in unaccented English. Mitchell nods. All of a sudden his carefully prepared words of explanation have evaporated.

'Richard is one of SoftJoy's biggest supporters in the financial market,' says Reiko helpfully.

'The only supporter left, I think,' says Sonoda, a slight smile on his lips. 'And even your estimates of our future earnings are much too conservative. If you want to encourage investors to have confidence in SoftJoy's potential, you should have more confidence yourself.'

'I do have confidence,' protests Mitchell. 'Actually, I am just revising up my earnings forecast for this year.'

Sonoda pokes a finger into Mitchell's chest. 'You are revising up by fifteen per cent, which is a trivial amount. That should be fifty per cent, perhaps seventy.'

Mitchell gazes at him in amazement. 'How did you know about my estimates?'

'I have fast ears?' says Sonoda, his smile widening.

Fast isn't the word. The fifteen per cent figure was something Mitchell decided on just two days ago. He hadn't mentioned it to anyone. Only this morning did he enter it into the half-completed report on his computer.

'What's the problem?' continues Sonoda, obviously enjoying Mitchell's discomfiture. 'Don't you think another seventy per cent is attainable?'

Mitchell pauses before answering. 'Sounds pretty difficult. After all, given the current conditions in the video-game market . . .'

'Don't worry – the current conditions in the market are about to change dramatically.'

'Change how?'

'I'm sorry,' says Sonoda smugly. 'That information is extremely sensitive.'

Mitchell is starting to get impatient. Sonoda is toying with him, treating him like a junior member of staff.

'Well, I have some sensitive information too,' he says. 'Information that could do plenty of damage to your company.'

'Hah – so if I don't reveal corporate secrets, you'll use this information against us. What you're suggesting is a form of blackmail, isn't it?'

Try as he might, Mitchell can't keep the irritation out of

his voice. 'That's completely unfair. I've staked my whole career on the success of your company. If the stock price doesn't recover pretty damn quick, I'm going to be fired, no question about it.'

Sonoda seems only half-satisfied by the answer. 'So why is it that you persist in recommending SoftJoy? Why not recommend Mega, like all the other analysts do?'

'That's easy. Mega's games are boring, nothing creative at all.'

'And our games are not boring?'

Mitchell shakes his head. 'SoftJoy games are not boring. Sometimes they're too weird or too violent for my tastes, but they're never boring.'

He becomes aware that Sonoda's pudgy face is beaming with pleasure, like a schoolboy who has just been praised by his teacher.

'Tell me, Mr Mitchell,' he says. 'Which of our games is your personal favourite?'

The young foreigner's favourite, it turns out, is Meiji Restoration, a complex role-playing game based on the opening of Japan to the world in the mid-nineteenth century. Meiji Restoration happens to be one of Yoichi Sonoda's favourites as well. Sonoda likes the game so much because he originated the idea himself and led the team of developers who turned it into a minor bestseller.

'So what's your usual score?' he asks the young foreigner.

'Around five hundred points.'

Sonoda is impressed. The way the game was designed only the top decile of players should win more than four hundred points. Five hundred is a score that Sonoda himself has achieved only rarely. But is the young foreigner telling the truth? There's only one way to find out.

'Let's play,' he says.

Mitchell looks dubious. 'What, you mean now?'

'Certainly!' snaps Sonoda. 'There is a console set up in the next room. The game can be downloaded in a matter of minutes.'

Until this point, Reiko has been standing near the door, watching them in silence. Now she breaks into the conversation. 'Are you sure there's time for that, President?'

Sonoda's excitement is rising. It has been a long time since he played a game for fun.

'No problem,' he says, jumping to his feet. 'There's two hours until my next appointment, plenty of time to see which of us is stronger!'

'But Mr Mitchell has important business to discuss with you, a serious problem with one of our game developers.'

Sonoda flashes a glance at Reiko. An annoying woman, but with some sharp and useful instincts. As for the young foreigner, he still looks hesitant, no doubt worried by the prospect of losing his job. That gives Sonoda an idea, something that will make the contest between them even more entertaining.

Mitchell follows Sonoda into the next room, waits uneasily as Meiji Restoration is downloaded from SoftJoy's host computer. Sonoda is even more eccentric than the press reports suggest. First of all he breaks off a business meeting in order to challenge Mitchell to a video-game contest. Then he offers a bizarre 'prize'. If Mitchell wins the game, he gets the right to question Sonoda on any subject he wants. If Mitchell loses, he must reveal what he knows and leave immediately. He could have refused or tried to argue, but with a man like Sonoda there would have been no point. So Mitchell's fate is to be staked on the outcome of a bleeping flashing video game. Better that than the mercurial temperament of Sasha de Glazier or the wiles of Scott Hamada.

The download finishes. Sonoda pulls two helmets from a

box, hands one to Mitchell. His cherubic face is glowing with a strange energy.

'Ready?'

'Ready.'

Mitchell puts on the helmet and enters a world of political turmoil, frantic conspiracy and bloody assassination. Should he ally himself with the crumbling shogunate or the rebellious Satsuma clan? Should he trade with the ever-encroaching foreigners or expel them from Japanese waters? Whom should he trust, whom should he betray? History has delivered its own answer to these questions, but in SoftJoy's video games the outcomes are never fixed. A skilful player can, through the force of his choices, create a different Japan, one in which the old order triumphs, the modernizers are defeated, and the samurai continue to wear their top-knots and carry two swords.

Mitchell sides with the imperial forces.

Sonoda sides with the shogun.

Battle is joined.

Eighteen

Mitchell leaves Sonoda's suite at one o'clock in the morning, shirt soaked with sweat, brain aching with images. He has just finished the most intensely gruelling video-game session of his life.

The first contest built up slowly, evenly, clan against clan, stratagem against stratagem. Somehow, though, Sonoda forgot to win the allegiance of the Zen monks of Mount Hie, crucial allies in quelling any uprising. Mitchell moved in, made a secret pact in exchange for some rare Buddhist scrolls that he had looted from a temple in Nara. Sonoda's position was fatally weakened and Mitchell coasted home, four hundred points to three hundred and sixty.

Sonoda's frustration was something to behold. He barked at Takeuchi to cancel his next appointment and demanded an immediate rematch. This was over quickly, Mitchell losing by a sixty-point margin as his retainers scattered before the ferocious assaults of Sonoda's shock troops.

The third game was stalemated for over an hour, both men concentrating furiously as they strove for the upper hand. At last Mitchell identified the spy whom Sonoda had insinuated into his inner council. Judicious torture revealed the details of Sonoda's agreement with the French government. That gave Mitchell enough of an edge to force a victory, five hundred and thirty points to five hundred and twenty.

Thanks to the long hours Mitchell has been spending in his apartment with SoftJoy video games, the modernization of Japan was secure.

Hands trembling, he pulls off his helmet, shakes away the dizziness. Sonoda is staring at him, a strange nostrils-flared grimace on his face. There is a moment of silence as both men struggle to regain their breath, then suddenly Sonoda thrusts out a hand.

'Congratulations, Mr Mitchell,' he says tersely. 'You are a man who knows how to play seriously.'

That, Mitchell realizes, is Sonoda's ultimate compliment. He nods, clasps Sonoda's sweaty hand.

Tall glasses of guava juice are waiting in the next room. For the next fifteen minutes, Mitchell listens while Sonoda sketches out the future course of the video-game market. The long-term picture is fascinating, but it is the outlook for the next few months that fills Mitchell with a surge of excitement.

Apparently there are technical problems with one of Mega's next batch of game releases, serious enough to cause the cancellation of all their releases for months to come. What kind of problems and how Sonoda knows about them are questions which were answered with an enigmatic smile.

The president of SoftJoy is a weird character. When Mitchell tells him that one of his developers was involved in a murder based on the content of the Black Blade game, he grins as if he had just heard the greatest joke in the world.

'I would be humbly grateful to learn this man's name,' says Mitchell, turning up the courtesy level to maximum.

Sonoda gazes at him with detached amusement. After all, the identities of SoftJoy game developers are the company's most closely guarded secret.

'Why do you want to know?' he asks finally.

'A friend of mine is a detective,' says Mitchell. 'He's trying to find out the truth of what happened.'

'The truth?' says Sonoda, enunciating the word as if it were from a foreign language.

Takeuchi steps forward. 'This is serious, President. If this incident is widely known, much bad publicity will be created.'

Mitchell shakes his head. 'Not as bad as if the police have to mount a full-scale investigation. That would probably mean questioning every single one of your developers, their names in all the papers, Mega getting hold of every last detail of your operations.'

Takeuchi looks horror-struck.

Sonoda gazes at Mitchell, eyes narrowed. 'I'll see what I can do,' he grunts.

Then, without another word, he turns and walks out of the room. The meeting is over.

Reiko and Takeuchi stay behind in Sonoda's suite. Mitchell walks alone down the empty corridor – no room-service trolleys, no 'Do Not Disturb' signs, nothing and nobody likely to make any disturbance at all – into the unelevator-like elevator, across the unlobby-like lobby and out into the glittering Ginza night.

Exhilaration fuses with nervous exhaustion. As he crosses the street, his face is numb to the drizzle, his ears deaf to the roar of the traffic.

Standing at a window ten floors above, Sonoda watches Mitchell walk across the street and flag down a taxi. The young foreigner was not lying: he is truly a five-hundred-point man. Of course Sonoda made some concessions in that last game. He could have poisoned the sake or blackmailed one of the geisha into stealing the letter to the British government. Instead, he stuck to conventional tactics and lost by the thinnest of margins. Next time they

331

play – and there will be a next time, he will make sure of that – Sonoda will operate under no such restrictions.

Mitchell's taxi disappears into the river of tail-lights. Sonoda turns away from the window. Reiko and Takeuchi are standing at the door trying to avoid his gaze. They have never seen him lose a game before.

'Bad publicity,' he muses. 'I don't really think so.'

'Not if we act first,' says Takeuchi. 'I can remove all trace of the man from our records, make him out to be a mere sub-contractor.'

'That wouldn't work,' says Reiko. 'Everyone knows that all SoftJoy's game developers are under the personal control of President Sonoda.'

'So what do you think we should do?' says Takeuchi, irritated. 'Nothing?'

'Exactly,' says Sonoda.

The other two turn and stare at him. Sonoda turns away. Both of them are mediocre players, unable to understand that doing nothing is sometimes the strongest move of all. He picks up the helmet and fits it on again. It's time to practise some new tactics.

Nineteen

Mori wakes just after dawn, disturbed by a metallic scraping sound out on the balcony. Without bothering to look, he knows it's the same crow in exactly the same place. He crawls out of his futon, snatches the baseball bat, sweeps open the curtain. The crow twists its head towards him, glaring defiance. Mori shakes the bat menacingly. The bird opens its beak and gives a long caw of derision. The wings give one mighty flap, but the talons don't loosen their grip on the rail.

Empty gestures aren't going to work this time. In fact, every threat that's not carried through just emboldens the creature. This particular crow has probably lived for years in the city. It knows how weak-willed human beings are, how they jump up and down and shout and wave their fists and in the end do nothing at all. This crow is unimpressed. You can see that from the glint in its eye. It's planning to carry on the harassment campaign, until either Mori gets serious or the whole thing gets too boring.

Mori decides to get serious. He closes the curtain, goes to the cupboard in the kitchen where he keeps his tools for the Honda. Obviously disappointed by the briefness of the confrontation, the crow has started the scraping noise again, louder than before. Mori pulls out the materials he's looking for, spends a few minutes getting them ready.

The balcony runs along the east of the building. The

kitchen faces north. Mori eases the window open, climbs over the sink and gingerly steps out onto the ledge. Twenty metres below someone has parked a Subaru Domingo van. If Mori fell, he would smash through its shiny white roof like a fist through a paper screen.

Left hand clutching the drainpipe for support, he edges towards the corner of the building. The crow continues the scraping noise, occasionally punctuated by a flap of its giant wings. The next bit is tricky – one foot on the window sill, one foot stretching around the corner for the end of the balcony rail. Mori lets go of the drainpipe, and for a moment he is straddling the empty air. Then he grabs at the balcony rail and pulls himself around the corner.

The crow is three metres away, wings in mid-flap. The head jerks round, emits a caw of angry warning. Beady black eyes train on Mori as he scrabbles astride the rail. Now would be a good time to attack. A wing in the face would knock Mori off balance, send him plunging to the street. But the bird senses his purposefulness, moves a few inches down the rail.

Attack or flee: the judgement instinct that all creatures are born with. But this crow has got too used to the city, feasting on the richness of its garbage, leading an unchallenged life of safety and comfort. It's forgotten what's real. Instead of attacking or fleeing, it just sits there, glaring at Mori as he steps on to the balcony.

Mori leans against the rail, glares right back. He's close enough to jump the creature, snap its neck before it has time to flap those wings again. But he doesn't do that. He reaches under his jacket, pulls out the spray-gun. The crow cocks its head, gazes curiously at the object. Mori raises it, aims the nozzle at the centre of the bird's chest. The crow opens its wings again, gives another caw of derision, less convincing this time. It backs away, but not far enough.

Mori presses the trigger, sends a jet of liquid bleach shooting through the air.

Bleach splatters over the glossy black chest. The shock causes the crow to loosen its grip on the rail and drop to the ground. Mori takes a step forward and shoots again, this time drawing a large white blotch over the bird's back and wings. The crow screeches in dismay, lifts off into the air. As it wheels past, Mori has a split second to twist round and squirt the last of the bleach over its belly.

The crow heads for the sky, wings flapping urgently. Looking like a giant magpie, it passes high above the rooftops, sails into the distance.

We've got to stop these creatures now, thinks Mori. If we don't, what will the city be like in another quarter of a century?

After a long night's work, George the Wolf Nishio likes to take a sauna before going home to bed. The place he favours these days is in Gotanda, a few blocks from the station. Above the reception desk hangs a sign reading, 'No Admittance for Customers with Tattoos.' Nearly all the high-class saunas have that sign nowadays, a product of one of city hall's periodic anti-gang campaigns. George's chest and shoulders are covered in tattoos, the best that money can buy. The manager doesn't say anything about them, neither do the massage girls or the other customers. That's because, as everyone knows – the massage girls, the customers, the police – this establishment is owned by a finance company controlled by the old boss.

After steaming himself for fifteen minutes, George returns to his private room, gets a can of Budweiser from the fridge, picks up the phone. He requests the same two girls as last time, trained experts at making a man feel completely relaxed. When they arrive George is already lying flat on an airbed, naked except for his mirror-shades and the shark's-tooth pendant around his neck. The girls bow gracefully, chirrup the formal greeting. George watches as they strip off their kimonos and prepare themselves, rubbing aromatic oils into each other's breasts, bellies and thighs until the skin glistens with a moist golden light.

They set to work slowly and purposefully, slithering down the length of his body, strumming taut nipples across his thighs, sliding his toes into the clefts of their apple-shaped buttocks. George lies motionless, completely passive. No commands need be given, no words need be spoken. All is silent, apart from George's breathing, which is getting progressively rougher, and the gentle sucking noises made by the women's greased bodies.

An hour later, George takes breakfast at a fast-food joint near his apartment. He chomps a chilli-burger, watches the salarymen hurrying past the window clutching their umbrellas and briefcases. This is one of those moments when he really loves his profession. The lives of those men must be so pathetic, so dull. Imagine waking up the same time every day, taking the same train to the same office and sitting at the same desk, doing the same rot-brained tasks! Thinking about the absurdity of the idea, George almost laughs out loud. How can they look at themselves in the mirror every morning? Where is the pride, the honour?

The guy behind the counter has a radio blaring out pop music. Not exactly George's taste, but he's not in the mood to complain. Opposite him a group of middle-school girls are chattering away, bursting with life and energy. Are they going to turn into wives for the kind of men that scurry to work like ants? What a tragic prospect! One of them stands up, a tall girl with tinted brown hair and full breasts. How old? Fourteen, fifteen? George sees something in her face, the slightly cruel jut of her lips – an instinctive awareness of life's possibilities. Give George a couple of weeks and he could turn that awareness into real knowledge. He's done it before, got them to try things that teachers and parents don't like to talk about, that deep down they know are going to be fun.

The pop music is interrupted by a news bulletin. George is gazing out of the window when suddenly – with a leap of joyous pride – he realizes that the subject of the bulletin is himself. Just a couple of lines – 'the shooting in Shinjuku earlier this week ... recovering slowly from serious chest injuries ... police looking for a man in his mid-thirties' – but it's enough to put a big grin on his face.

'Serious chest injuries' – certainly no less than the guy deserved for obstructing the revenge of George the Wolf. He's lucky George didn't put a bullet in his belly.

The tall girl is moving towards the door now, waving goodbye to her friends. George feels like going after her, explaining coolly that he was the man responsible for that shooting. What would she say? She'd be shocked, of course, but somehow she'd be fascinated too. She's been told by her parents and teachers that hurting people is wrong. But already she sees that life isn't so simple, that respect goes not to the weak and obedient but to men with the ruthlessness to force their will on the world. That much is obvious from a middle-school textbook. Those big-spirited heroes – Julius Caesar, Napoleon, Hideyoshi and the rest – what kind of guys were they really? If alive today, would they choose to be salarymen or yakuza?

Back comes the pop music, as light and empty as before. The tall girl walks past the window, a cheap see-through umbrella over her head. From the way she walks – hips rolling, breasts flouncing – she could be nineteen or twenty. Still grinning to himself, George watches her disappear into the crowd. Before too long his deeds will again be featured in the news bulletins – top item this time, ahead of all the garbage about exchange rates and elections. That will be the moment to make her acquaintance fully.

The streets are already bustling by the time George gets back home. Suddenly exhausted, he kicks off his tight white trousers and collapses on to the bed in shirt, briefs and socks. Shafts of light are slanting between the permanently drawn curtains of his bedroom, but behind George's dark glasses night reigns supreme.

He is just fitting his earplugs when a bleeping noise comes from the mobile phone on the dresser. For a few seconds he glares in vexation, then picks the thing up. Just as well, for at the other end is a senior syndicate man with some important information. A big meeting is going to be held at four o'clock, and the old boss has particularly requested George's presence.

A glow of satisfaction spreads through George's being. Obviously he is back in full favour.

'So what's the purpose of the meeting?' he asks. 'I mean, do you want me to prepare anything in advance?'

'Cockroach!' bellows the senior man, so loud that George has to hold the phone away from his ear. 'Men who make big mistakes shouldn't ask insolent questions. They should learn to keep their mouths shut!'

'Sincere apologies, I just thought it would be better ...'

'It doesn't matter what you think! Nobody cares what you think. It's better if you don't think at all! Understood, cockroach!'

'Understood.'

The phone goes dead. George takes a deep breath, raises his face to the ceiling, gives a long howl of rage. Then he drops the phone to the ground and stomps – once, twice, three times. The thing is surprisingly tough. He has to go and get a hammer to finish it off.

*

Mori gets to his office just after nine. He makes coffee, munches a couple of pickled-plum riceballs, scans the newspapers for news about the arson attack on Naomi Kusaka's place. Surprisingly there's nothing, not even a couple of lines in the social affairs section of the *Kanto Shimbun*. He switches on the TV that stands on a pile of old books in the corner of the room. This machine was out of date when he bought it second-hand a dozen years ago. These days the treble-vision picture jumps and wobbles all over the place. When he's got a serious hangover, he daren't even look at the thing.

For the next twenty minutes Mori sips black coffee and grazes the showbiz and true crime shows that dominate the airwaves at this time of day. Nowhere is there a single mention of Naomi Kusaka. This is even more surprising. The smarmy creeps who host these programmes usually churn out even the most trivial gossip about minor celebrities whose fame won't outlive the cicadas in Shinjuku Park.

The ring of the telephone cuts into Mori's thoughts. Could it be Taniguchi, distraught over last night, ready to explain everything? No, the sound of the phone is coldly efficient, no contrition there at all. Mori picks up the receiver. It's Keiko, Uno's fiancée. She was at the hospital last night, says Uno's looking much stronger already.'

'That's great,' says Mori, with sincerity. But he has a strong suspicion that she isn't calling just to tell him that.

'The police have been bothering him, trying to find out what happened. Unfortunately he doesn't remember anything at all.'

'Not surprising, I'd say.'

'So I spoke to them directly, told them what I think. You see, they haven't got any clues yet. They seem to think it's connected to a feud between two factions of the Chinese mafia.'

'Really,' says Mori drily.

In police terms, that would make perfect sense. They could claim credit for solving a violent crime and at the same time lock up a Chinese hoodlum for a few years and then have him deported. No doubt an appropriate suspect has been identified already.

'Anyway, I told them that they'd be much better off talking to you, Mori-*san*. After all, it's obvious that you were the real target. The criminal is probably one of your known associates.'

'You said that?' says Mori, frowning.

'Certainly. I told them exactly what kind of man you are.'

'I think they know that already.'

Keiko's tone was frosty enough to start with. Now it plummets another couple of degrees.

'Maybe, but my fiancé doesn't. He still seems to think you're some kind of hero, even now.'

'Ah.'

'Do you remember, Mori-*san* – at the hospital I asked you for a favour? I wanted you to talk to him directly, try to force some common sense in his head.'

'Of course I remember. I'd be happy to do it whenever—'

Keiko cuts in ruthlessly. 'Wait – I've changed my mind. Requesting common sense from a man like you is like asking for fish at the greengrocer.'

A phrase that Mori last heard on the lips of one of his schoolteachers. This woman is going to make a strict wife, an even stricter mother.

'Meaning what exactly?'

'Meaning that I want you to stay away from him, permanently. You've done quite enough damage already.'

The phone goes dead. For a couple of seconds Mori sits in silence, gazing into the purring receiver.

Ten minutes of reverie: another cup of coffee; a Gerry Mulligan album on the turntable. Then back to work. Mori calls Kubota, the eldest son of one of his old karate teachers. Kubota is an assistant section chief at a fire station in Nerima Ward.

'I want you to do something for me,' says Mori. 'I need some information on a woman called Naomi Kusaka – used to be a big name a few years back.'

'Really?' says Kubota, impressed. 'Would I recognize her?'

'Doubtful,' says Mori. 'She was a singer, not a porno video star. Anyway, there was a fire at her place last night. I need to know the inside story.'

'Leave it to me. I'll call you back in five minutes.'

Which he does, but his punctuality turns out to be more impressive than the quality of his information.

'Small kitchen fire,' Kubota reports. 'Minimal damage. The cause was faulty wiring in the electric cooker.'

'What are you talking about?' snaps Mori. 'There was black smoke pouring out of the window. Whatever was inside that room must have roasted like a stick of yakitori!'

'Impossible,' says Kubota smartly. 'I have all the details on the screen in front of me. I just downloaded then from our central computer!'

Mori thanks him and rings off. For a man like Kubota, the more advanced the technology, the more worthy of respect the information. Arguing would be a waste of breath. Mori makes a few more enquiries, hardly expecting to turn up anything important. He expects correctly. Clearly someone has invested a lot of effort into concealing what happened last night.

For the next half hour, Mori sits at his desk, sipping

coffee, mulling over the case right from the beginning. He thinks of élite bureaucrats, their character and patterns of behaviour. He thinks of Taniguchi, the kind of man he was, the kind of man he is now. Once so urbane and cynical, now all twisted up by anger and bitterness. What could drive such a transformation? Why would a worldly middle-aged man suddenly turn to indiscriminate terrorism?

The question is baffling. It needs to be rethought, looked at from a different angle.

The death of Taniguchi's daughter, the event which shattered his life into fragments.

Or maybe not. Maybe the event which brought his life into focus, lending a purpose which it had previously lacked.

What kind of purpose?

Thoughts form in Mori's mind, instincts and suspicions. Some he casts away. Some he retains.

Richard Mitchell stands at the coffee-machine, watching Sasha de Glazier and Hauptman walking through the dealing room, locked in conversation. Today the market is surging. The phones are ringing non-stop, and the air is full of excited yells.

'Mitsukawa Heavy Industries – ninety thousand at market!'

'Seikyu Real Estate – fifty thousand done!'

'Raise the limit, raise the limit!'

Occasionally when a stock reaches a particularly important level, the room echoes with applause. Hauptman looks content. Because the market is strong and the dealing room sounds like a zoo, he assumes that his operation is making money. He leans down to pass a few words with Nakahama, the chief derivatives trader. Nakahama is a red-eyed, yellow-toothed, sour-breathed, Tagamet-popping, flabby-bellied old man of thirty-five. His daily risk positions are many times larger than the combined lifetime earnings of every individual in the room. Hautpman always treats Nakahama with the utmost respect, and will continue to do so until the day he has to fire him.

Nakahama takes his cigarette-holder from his mouth and blows a plume of smoke into the air. Already the ashtray in front of him contains a mini Mount Fuji of butts. He tells Hauptman what he wants to hear. Hauptman nods approval, gives him a slap on the shoulder and then steers Sasha over to his office. As they disappear inside, Mitchell notices the position of Hauptman's hand, which is resting on Sasha's back, three quarters of the way down. A few more inches and he would be touching her buttocks. The idea makes Mitchell feel slightly queasy. He has never viewed Sasha in those terms before. Of course she does have buttocks and breasts and the rest, rather well formed too, as far as the eye can judge. Technically speaking she is definitely female. But as for her sexual orientation, insofar as Mitchell thought about it at all, he assumed it was arachnoid, satisfied by the ritual consumption of healthy young males.

'Matsui Cement – sixty thousand to buy . . .'

'Mega Enterprises four hundred thousand to sell . . .'

Applause and whoops all round the trading desk. Four hundred thousand is a huge order for a high-priced stock like Mega. It will take several days to complete. And as Mitchell is the analyst responsible for the company, he will get a share of the sales credits – more credits, in fact, than he has managed to chalk up for the past three months. He wanders up to the salesman who yelled out the order.

'Where did that come from?' asks Mitchell casually.

The salesman takes off his headset, and pushes out his chest. He's preening himself like a fighter pilot just back from a mission. 'Some hedge fund in Hong Kong, first order we've ever got from them.'

'Are they getting our research reports?'

'Not yet. The account's only just been opened.'

Mitchell glances at the order ticket on the desk. The client name is 'Chi Associates'.

'This has got nothing to do with you at all,' says the salesman smugly. 'If I were you, I'd enjoy your luck while it lasts.'

Now the key panel is flashing, meaning that another call is waiting. The salesman slips the headset back on.

'Two hundred thousand? Yes, yes. Thank you very much.'

He gets up on his chair and bellows over to the trading desk. 'Two hundred thousand SoftJoy. Buy at market.'

More applause, whoops, zoo noises. Mitchell walks back to his desk, examines the action on his stock price monitor. Already Mega is weakening. When the market begins to sense the true extent of the selling pressure, the stock will plummet.

The call from Takeuchi comes through just before lunch.

'President Sonoda expresses gratitude for last night. He wants to know if you will be available for another meeting of the same nature.'

'Of course,' says Mitchell. 'Whenever you like.'

'Excellent. Now, about the information you requested last night . . .'

Takeuchi supplies a name and address, which Mitchell scribbles down on the back of a laundry receipt. On the screen in front of him, the SoftJoy stock price has suddenly surged five per cent. Mitchell clicks up the two-year chart of the stock's performance. The trend reversal he hardly dared to hope for is actually starting to happen. In Yazawa's language, today's move is the first step on the escalator. And where does this magic escalator take you, bucking and twisting and accelerating into the skies? That is something you never know till you get there. You just hold on tight and don't look down.

When Mori's Honda pulls up outside Taniguchi's building, the little yakitori restaurant is packed to bursting point and there's a line of salarymen and office ladies waiting outside in the drizzle. The reason is clear from the handwritten sign in the window: 'Idiotically Cheap – Ten-stick Lunchbox, three hundred yen each.'

Peering through a split in the awning, Mori glimpses the master's face, red and sweaty over the grill as he labours to satisfy the demand he has created. It's the busiest most profitable time of day for him, but when he sees Mori he hurries to the door.

'Problems?' he says, his brow creased with concern.

'Maybe,' says Mori. 'He didn't come back last night, I suppose.'

The master shakes his head. 'Usually we hear the music when he wakes up. But today there was nothing.'

Mori glances round. The line of people is getting longer. The master can't afford to stand around chatting.

'One last question,' says Mori. 'When we first talked, you mentioned Taniguchi-*san*'s research assistant. Do you remember what he looked like?'

'That's easy. He was one of the tallest guys I've ever seen, big heavy shoulders too. Looked like he'd make a good volleyball player.'

Mori thanks him. The master gives a quick yell of 'Welcome, welcome' to the people in the line, than hurries back to tend the grill. Mori trudges up the steep wooden staircase, past the hostess club, to Taniguchi's room. Nothing much has changed since he was there last. The same piles of magazines and books on the floor, the same crumpled heaps of sheets and blankets in the corner. Mori walks over to Taniguchi's desk, stares at the line of framed photos on the wall. The sparkling-eyed little girl at the shrine is clearly the same person as the pretty college student sitting in the park. But it is not Hiromi that interests Mori, but the young man whom she's nestling against on the bench. Compared to his bulky shoulders, Hiromi's head looks no bigger than that of the little girl that she was a dozen years before.

Mori lifts the picture off the wall, drops it into the inside pocket of his jacket. On the way back to Shinjuku, he ponders two key questions about Hiromi's death. This was an event which shattered a man's life to fragments, unbalancing his mind, provoking him to acts of crazed violence.

The first question: what kind of death?

The second question: what kind of man?

For it's gradually dawning on Mori that his first instincts may have been right. Circumstantially Taniguchi fits well. He is drunken, obsessive and teetering on the verge of a nervous breakdown. He may even have the right kind of motive. Still, as a crazed avenger he lacks credibility. In Mori's judgement, Miura's killer was driven by an uncontrollable sense of outrage. For all his bitterness and despair, Taniguchi lacks that depth of feeling. He's too old, knows too much about the way the world works.

Shinjuku is as dank and steamy as a sumo wrestler's armpit. The sun is invisible, as it has been for weeks, but ultraviolet rays are pouring through the cloud cover, sapping the energy of the human population, stimulating feverish procreation amongst the insects. The rainy season is finally drawing to a close.

346

A group of schoolkids is just coming out of the karaoke box place on the ground floor of his building. Mori can't help staring at one of them as he passes. The kid has got dyed blond hair, green contact lenses, shaved eyebrows and a nose stud.

'What's the matter, uncle?' grins the kid, pushing his face right into Mori's. 'Never seen a Japanese like this before?'

Mori grabs his ear, gives it a harder twist than he intended.

'Yoww,' yells the kid. His friends' voices rise in protest. 'Scary uncle!'

'Hey, maybe we'd better call the cops.'

'Bullying young people, that's big trouble for you!'

Mori carries on up the stairs, slightly surprised by the strength of his own irritation. These kids are truly pathetic, swaggering toughs one moment, squealing for help the next. And when they're on their own they've got no character at all, don't know what to say, don't know what to do. But the kid was just the target of his frustration, not the cause. The real problem is that Mori can feel the Miura case slipping away from him.

As ever, the lights are off in the little trading company on the third floor. Mori glances at the advertisements pasted to the window. There are three new ones.

'*Magnetic Mesh Briefs – Effective Against Impotence, Premature Ejaculation and Warts...*'

'*New Brain Food – Raise Memory to Genius Levels With Miracle Enzyme Discovered by Jewish Scientists...*'

'*Don't Waste 30% of Your Life! Study Foreign Languages While You Sleep – Forty-Stage Programme of Cassette Tapes...*'

Don't waste 30 per cent of your life – words that stick in Mori's mind as he continues up the stairs. How about 100 per cent of your life? Is it possible to miss the whole thing,

347

like drunken salarymen sometimes miss the last train home? Every night there's one of them, vaulting the ticket barriers, racing along the platform, thumping his palms against the closed doors of the carriage. The people inside gaze out blankly, secretly glad that someone has been left behind. Then the train jerks into motion and the salaryman slopes back the way he came. Mori knows that feeling. He's had it on and off for a quarter of a century.

Just as he's passing the floor occupied by the plant-leasing yakuza, Mori hears the phone ringing up in his office. It sounds urgent. For once he decides to hurry.

At the other end, a voice speaking painfully correct Japanese in a foreign accent.

'Mori-*san*, I managed to get the information about that game developer. Do you still need it?'

Mori needs it, fiercely.

Twenty

Akihabara, an electronic souk. Switches and capacitors lie heaped in trays like candy. Optical fibre cables dangle from the ceiling like strips of sausage. The dingy arcades are jampacked with stalls selling motherboards, modems, scramblers and descramblers, phreakers, bleepers, tracers, EPROMs and S-RAMs, high-frequency oscillators, infrared sensors, digital imagers, computer body parts and software of all varieties, bootleg and legitimate, antique and yet to be marketed. If you wanted to build an electronic warfare capability from scratch, this is where you would come.

It doesn't take Mori long to find the building, a grey concrete box with a dozen company names on the information board outside. The one that Mori is seeking is housed on the third floor. Coming out of the elevator, Mori is confronted by a metal door, battleship grey, firmly locked. He presses the buzzer. A woman's voice answers, cautious.

'Yes?'

'I'm looking for Nova Dream Company.'

'And who are you?'

Mori adopts a tone of fussy arrogance. 'Mori of the city government workers' health and welfare department. I'm conducting a survey of employment conditions in the small company sector.'

'Employment conditions?'

'That's right. Nova Dream has been chosen at random for participation in the twenty-fifth biennial survey. Of course your co-operation is totally voluntary, but . . .'

Mori leaves the sentence hanging in the air. No small company wants to antagonize the local welfare bureaucracy, thereby risking visits by all the different varieties of inspector, demands for submission of impossibly complex documentation, long investigations into breaches of regulations that no one even knew existed.

A moment later the door clicks open and Mori pushes inside. He finds himself in a shabby office, no bigger than his own. There are video-game posters on the wall, stacks of computer magazines on the floor. Also a smell of incense in the air, with the trace of a sweeter, heavier smell underneath. The girl sitting at the reception desk – short hair, glasses, dungarees – gazes at him blankly. There is no one else in the room.

'This is the head office of Nova Dream?' asks Mori, puzzled.

'Yes.'

'So where are all the employees?'

The woman smiles. 'The others don't actually work here. There's no need. They send in the material on-line, whenever it's finished.'

'And who are you exactly?'

'I'm the co-ordinator,' says the woman, using the English word. 'Now, what's all this about?'

Mori produces a name card and slides it across the desk. His politeness is cold, aggressive. 'I humbly request your help.'

'And you're from the city government?'

The co-ordinator looks dubious, as well she might. Mori is wearing a short-sleeved nylon shirt and baggy grey trousers, appropriate clothing for a low-ranking official. He has also gone to the trouble of acquiring a clipboard and notepad, the first few pages of which are covered with official-type verbiage. Nonetheless, Mori is only too aware that he'll never make a convincing bureaucrat. There's something wrong in the angle of his gaze, in the shape of his mouth when he talks, in the thrust of his shoulder when he walks.

'Yes, indeed. I'm a mid-career recruit, just five years on the job. What I lack in experience I make up with hard work and thoroughness. Nothing gets past me, absolutely nothing!'

The co-ordinator glances from Mori's face to the name card on the desk, then back to Mori's face again. The name card looks reasonably authentic. The phone number belongs to a call-box in Shinjuku, just a few hundred kilometres from the monstrous new City Hall building. If she decided to make the call, there's just a tiny chance that some passer-by might pick up the phone and answer. In which case Mori would be out of there like a rat with a red pepper suppository.

'I see,' she says hesitantly. 'Well, what exactly do you want to know?'

'First of all I want to see the personnel files. I need the number of employees, average ages, names, addresses – the usual stuff.'

'Impossible, I'm afraid. That information cannot be released.'

Mori takes that badly. 'Cannot be released! What are you talking about? This survey depends on proper answers to these questions.'

The woman shrugs, still trying to be pleasant. 'Perhaps you don't understand this industry, Mori-*san*. The only assets that companies like this own are the game developers

351

themselves. Information about them is a valuable commodity, so valuable that our competitors are always scheming to get their hands on it.'

Mori raises the pomposity level a few notches higher. 'Perhaps it is you who doesn't understand. This is a government survey, and the patriotic duty of every Japanese citizen is to offer sincere co-operation.'

She shakes her head. 'I'm sorry.'

Tough woman, this one. Mori approves. What he has to do next is unpleasant but necessary. He raises his face, takes a deep sniff.

'Now, what's that smell?' he says, phoney curious.

'You mean the incense?'

'I mean the other smell, under the smell of the incense. Is it cannabis? Are there drug addicts amongst your personnel?'

'Absolutely not!'

'Have you considered introducing compulsory blood tests?'

'Blood tests?' The woman looks shocked.

'Yes. There are many undesirable and unhealthy elements around these days. We must be vigilant. It is important to monitor the mind and bodies of our young workers, passing the results on to the police whenever necessary.'

At the mention of the word 'police', the woman's fingers knot together on the desk in front of her.

'This is a difficult problem,' Mori continues sternly. 'It would be normal to make such a recommendation in my report. Unless, of course, it is certain that your company philosophy is entirely lacking in antisocial tendencies . . .'

'It is certain,' says the woman, pale but still calm.

'But can you prove that?'

'Prove it how?'

352

'Through sincere co-operation with the twenty-fifth biennial survey of employment conditions.'

She manages to keep some sort of smile going. 'Of course. I will co-operate with pleasure.'

Mori nods gravely. He has surprised himself with his talent for bullying. Maybe he could have made it as a yakuza boss or a right-wing intellectual or a pitching coach for the Giants.

What he finds in the file: Nova Dream has only ten employees, six men and four women. Three of the men are in their early thirties, outside the age range. One of the others works from Kyushu, which rules him out on grounds of distance. That leaves two: Abe and Furumoto.

'You don't have any photos of these two guys?'

'Photos? Why?'

Mori explodes again. 'It doesn't matter why! Show me the photos!'

'I can't. There aren't any.'

'What! You mean you don't keep proper personnel records in this company?'

'There's nothing wrong with our personnel records,' she protests, hot with injured pride. 'Why are photos necessary? We know what we look like already.'

'Really?' sneers Mori. 'You know what you look like, do you? In that case, please tell me the exact height in fractions of a centimetre of each one of your employees.'

'The exact height? That's impossible.'

'According to our new regulations, it is compulsory to register that information with the Health and Welfare Bureau. Have you done that?'

The woman bites her lower lip. Good self-control again. 'Not yet,' she says.

Mori glares at her with withering contempt. 'All right, then,' he sighs, as if humouring a stubborn child. 'I shouldn't really do this, I know. Give me your estimates of the heights of the employees, and I'll see that the information is submitted in the right place. Do you understand?'

'Yes, I understand.'

The woman looks confused. Her instincts are telling her to obey the man from city hall, but her common sense is telling her that something is wrong. Luckily for Mori it is the instincts – *authority is dangerous, never question it* – that have the upper hand.

The woman gazes at the wall, tries to picture her colleagues lined up in a row. Mori coaxes the answers, softer attitude now. The woman comes up with some numbers. Mori notes them down on his clipboard. Only one thing matters – the relative heights of Abe and Furumoto. The way she tells it, Abe is a fairly big guy, a couple of centimetres taller than Mori. Furumoto, though, is a giant.

Mori nods in satisfaction, puts away his pen. 'Your sense of duty is impressive. It will be mentioned in my report.'

'Thank you,' she says.

'Not at all.'

She gazes at him, brow furrowed. Mori recognizes his mistake immediately. Too considerate. No official would utter those words in that tone of voice.

He grunts a few words of dismissal, makes for the door. Seconds later a phone starts ringing in a call-box a couple of hundred metres from City Hall in Shinjuku. Pulling on his helmet, Mori fancies that he can hear it faintly in the distance. He revs the engine, goes slicing through the dense commerce of the Akihabara afternoon.

The streets are clogged. It takes Mori an hour to get to Furumoto's address, as noted down from Nova Dream's personnel file. Why does the rain make everyone drive so slowly? It always makes Mori want to go faster.

Furumoto is the man, no question about it. The man who killed Miura and Nakanishi. The man who attacked Mori in the grounds of the shrine and set fire to Naomi Kusaka's apartment. The man who was sitting next to Taniguchi's daughter on the bench in the photo.

And why? Mori still has no idea, but the pattern is getting clearer. Everything starts with the suicide of Taniguchi's daughter. That was what pushed Taniguchi over the edge. That was what caused Furumoto to murder a high official at the Ministry of Health and the president of a major pharmaceutical company. Thinking about it, Mori realizes with a shock that he hardly knows anything about the circumstances. Taniguchi was tight-lipped about the whole thing, once muttering a few words about 'chronic depression'. Mori didn't like to ask for details. He didn't get any.

The Honda thunders through kilometre after kilometre of near-identical suburb, then out into a rawer landscape of wrecking yards, love hotels, cheap restaurants. One thing about this city – no matter how many decades, how many lifetimes you spend here, you keep finding yourself in places you've never been before. The area where Furumoto lives is new to Mori, not at all what he was expecting.

Mori was expecting the standard habitat for a young guy without much money – cheap apartment blocks, a couple of convenience stores, a dinky railway station with a level-crossing that goes 'bink, bink, bink' eighteen hours a day. But he was forgetting that just because Furumoto is twenty-five years old and works for a company with a head office not much bigger than a lunchbox, it doesn't mean the guy is suffering financially. Not these days, it doesn't.

It turns out that Furumoto doesn't live in an apartment block, or anywhere near an apartment block for that matter.

355

On the plot that matches the address stands a two-storey building, dark wood, gleaming wet tiles. With its long eaves and heavy shutters, it looks as if it dates from the Taisho era, which would make it about the same age as the oldest recorded jazz music or the current minister of education. Mori drives past, then pulls in behind a row of vending machines thirty metres further down the road. He buys himself a stamina drink – ginseng, beta carotene, snake-blood – pushes up his visor, swigs and scans.

Furumoto's place is actually a small factory, the kind with a workshop on the ground floor and accommodation for the owner and his workers – probably his wife, mother and daughters-in-law – up above. But the era in which Fujisawa Commercial Garment and small businesses like it could prosper has long gone. The characters on the wooden signboard have almost faded away, and the rice-paper screens behind the window glass are full of holes. What kind of twenty-five-year-old would choose to live in a place like this? A pretty strange one, that's for sure.

Mori takes the next turning on the left, then turns again. He parks the Honda outside a medium-sized pachinko parlour. Inside – flashing lights and blaring music and row after row of empty seats. It's a depressing sight. If the pachinko people can't get any customers, what hope is there for the detective industry? Mori walks through the empty store-yard at the back of the pachinko parlour, stops in front of a wall topped with broken beer bottles. Good enough to deter schoolkids, but not much more. Mori levers himself up by the fingers, uses the heel of his shoe to crunch away at the broken glass. Finally there is enough space for him to swing a leg up, then his whole body. Half-crouching, he edges along the top of the wall, one painstaking footstep after another. At the corner it meets the perimeter wall of the grounds of the old wooden house.

Mori raises his head, gazes at a window on the upper floor. Behind the milky opacity of the rice-paper screen a patch of darkness seems to recoil. A trick of light, thinks Mori, his own silhouette reflected in the window glass. He turns, springs lithely to the ground.

He is in a small garden, curtained off from the house by a clump of bamboo. Immediately in front of him – a pond, a mound of rocks, a strip of overgrown grass. There are no carp in the pond, only cigarette butts and aluminium ring-pulls. The rocks are cracked and caked with grime. No doubt old Fujisawa once tended this garden proudly, seeing a universe of meaning in its tiny space. Now it stinks of decay.

Mori peers through the bamboo leaves. The long room facing him is probably the work area. No light through the slats of the shuttered window, no sound except the dripping of the rain. He waits a couple of seconds – ears and eyes straining – then makes for the door, his movements as smooth and efficient as a cat's. Surprisingly, the door is unlocked. Mori slides it open a couple of centimetres, puts his face to the crack. Nothing, just dusty darkness and the smell of rotten tatami. He eases the door another few centimetres, ghosts inside.

How many years ago did Fujisawa Commercial Garment close for business for the last time? Not long, by the look of it. The machines are still there – gawky metal insects squatting at the shadows – and there are several sheets of paper pinned to a corkboard panel on the wall. Mori scans them. Pencil sketches of simple designs: padded jackets; serge overalls; baggy canvas trousers. Hard-wearing useful clothes, not the kind of stuff you'd see on a catwalk. Or if you did, it would be part of a mocking charade staged by some celebrity whose designs never get worn by anyone.

One sketch in particular attracts Mori's attention – a dark

357

kimono with wide sleeves. It's the kind of thing you might see on the proprietor of a rice-shop – tough enough for work, but respectable-looking too. Mori has seen an example of that design very recently. The kimono was worn by the man who lives in this building, who is probably somewhere upstairs right now. Furumoto is dangerous. Mori wants to talk to him, to persuade him to give himself up. But he knows that he may not get the chance. On a table in the corner of the room is a rusted carpet-knife. Mori picks it up, slides it into his pocket.

The door at the far end of the room turns out to be locked, but there is a wooden ladder leaning against the far wall, above it a panel in the ceiling. Mori puts a foot on the bottom rung. It creaks loudly, thinks about snapping then decides against it. Carefully testing each rung, Mori pulls himself up to the ceiling, lifts the panel open. Inside is some sort of storeroom, grey light filtering through a small square window. Dust dances. Mori sees cardboard crates, plastic dummies clothed in kimonos, row after row of jackets and coats hanging from wires. Soundlessly he hauls himself inside, replaces the panel.

Mori pads down the aisle between the rows of clothes, stops suddenly in front of one of the dummies. It is wearing a black kimono, clean, no coating of dust. Mori fingers the sleeve, lifts it to his face. There's a distinct smell of soap.

Next to the door are some heavy rolls of cloth and a pile of dismembered dummies, gleaming plastic buttocks, chests and forearms. Mori is gently twisting the door handle when he hears a little scraping noise a couple of metres to his left. One of the dummies' heads starts rocking from side to side, then slowly slips off the pile. Mori leaps backwards, heart thumping. The head topples to the ground and rolls over, face down. Something black shoots out of the bottom of the pile and disappears behind the rolls of cloth. A cat! Mori breathes a sigh of relief, swings the door open. Then there's a blur of movement, and something hits him in his chest as hard as he's ever been hit in his life. The force of the blow sends him reeling backwards, crashing into a row of coats. He grabs at one for balance, ends up on the floor covered in stiff black serge.

For a moment he lies there half-stunned, blinking in confusion. Then he drags himself upright, goes plunging through the next row of clothes, then the next, working his way diagonally across the room. When there's enough distance between himself and his assailant, he inserts himself into a row of kimonos, crouches down, listens. The footsteps start on the other side of the room, come slowly closer, up and down each aisle in turn. Once or twice they stop, and there's the swish of clothes being pulled off their hangers and thrown to the floor.

Finally he comes to the last row, the one where Mori crouches in hiding. The footsteps come to within a few metres, then stop. There's a moment of silence, then they turn and go back to the end of the row. Mori hears a puzzling sound – metallic scratching – then suddenly all the kimonos go jerking sideways and fall to the floor. The wire that they were hanging from has been cut.

Mori looks up to see Furumoto striding towards him. Mori has forgotten how big the man is, chest like a sake-barrel, fists like lumps of stone.

'Wait,' Mori calls out. 'I'm here to talk.'

'Too late for talking.'

'I'm trying to help you.'

'You're the one who needs help.'

Judging by what happened to Miura, that's a reasonable comment. Furumoto is big, fast, strong. Most important of all, he's young.

Mori backs away until he feels the cold wall behind him.

Furumoto's face is a mask of rage. He comes forward in a fighting stance, jabs a giant foot at Mori's groin. This time Mori sees it coming, turns to take it on his hip. Still the impact sends him staggering. Furumoto follows, his fist moving with enough power to crush a man's nose. Mori ducks away. Skipping sideways, he aims a punch at Furumoto's head. The punch is good, thudding into the cheekbone. Furumoto doesn't even blink, just keeps on coming, fists and feet moving like pistons. Mori keeps his distance, dodging and parrying until a whirling foot catches him full in the sternum, slams him back against the wall. He shakes his head, rolls aside just in time. Furumoto's lightning reverse kick smashes into the wall, throat-high.

Muscles too taut, brain too active. A voice from the past sounds in Mori's head, the old sensei from the high-school karate club. 'You can't beat strong men with strength, or fast men with speed. Move like water! Keep moving until they drown!'

Mori slows down his breathing, draws the air deep into the pit of his belly. Vision sharpens, a soft calmness rises through his veins. He glides forwards, glides backwards. He doesn't dodge Furumoto's kicks and punches. He flows past them, lets them explode into the empty air.

The sensei's voice again, urgent, practical: 'The weak spots for big men are the knees! Keep attacking the knees.'

Mori's mind floats away. He watches himself from somewhere else, slow motion, sinuous. He watches Furumoto fighting his own anger, breath rasping, power wasting in the violence of his blows. Mori waits for the moment, sees it coming well in advance. Furumoto feints a jab, then tries another full-power reverse kick. Mori dances forward, sweeps the foot away with his forearm. Before Furumoto has recovered his balance, Mori gets down low, drives his heel into Furumoto's left knee. Furumoto stumbles. Mori kicks again, aiming for the soft cartilage on the inside of the knee-cap. Furumoto grunts in pain, takes a step backwards. Mori repeats the action. This time he is perfectly positioned. All the kinetic energy that his body is capable of generating surges down a line ending in the heel of his right foot. Furumoto collapses to the ground, then rolls over on his back, big hands wrapped around his knee.

'My leg!' he yells. 'You've broken my leg!'

Mori moves fast. He pulls a belt off a kimono, loops it around Furumoto's wrists and pulls tight. Furumoto doesn't attempt to resist. Mori wipes sweat from his eyes, gazing down into the big man's grimacing face.

'Right, are you ready to talk?'

'Talk about what?' snarls Furumoto.

'About Miura.'

'Miura? I don't know any Miura!'

Mori shakes his head in sad exasperation. 'Listen, if you don't want to co-operate, that's fine. I can call the police, sit here and wait until they come. Or maybe you'd prefer the national security people.'

'National security people?'

'That's right. With those guys you won't have to worry about trials and lawyers and all that. Once they've got hold of you, nobody'll ever see you again.'

'That doesn't scare me.'

'What about Taniguchi-*san*? They'll be coming for him too.'

Furumoto's face darkens. He uses a clothes-rail to haul himself upright, then launches himself at Mori. One stride and his leg buckles under him. Mori sidesteps and plants his foot into Furumoto's stomach, just hard enough to show that there are penalties. Furumoto's breath leaves his body faster than scheduled. Mori squats down on his haunches and gazes into the gasping face.

'Listen, I told you I was here to help. If you give me what I want, I can make things a lot easier for you.'

'Give you what you want,' groans Furumoto. 'What is that supposed to mean?'

When the rage has gone, Furumoto looks completely different. Big-boned though he is, there is something soft, almost feminine in his face. With skin that smooth, he probably doesn't need to shave more than a couple of times a week.

Mori nods. 'It's like this. You're responsible for the deaths of two men. Don't try and deny it – there's no point.'

Furumoto doesn't try and deny it. He just stares up at Mori like a junior-school kid at a particularly hated teacher.

Mori continues. 'Now I need to know exactly what happened, why and how, right from the start. Help me with this, and I'll see you get good treatment from the police.'

'Good treatment?' says Furumoto.

'That's right. I've got a personal friend, a guy in a senior position, who would handle everything. All you've got to do is come down to Shinjuku with me and walk straight through the door. No fuss, no TV cameras, no need to involve Taniguchi-*san*.'

Furumoto is quiet for a while. 'Crimes like this usually get the death penalty,' he mutters finally.

'Not in your case,' says Mori. 'The death penalty's for hardened killers. If you surrender yourself willingly and show sincere remorse, you should be okay.'

'You think so?'

'I'm certain.'

There is another aspect to Mori's confidence that he doesn't mention. Anyone who behaves like Furumoto must have a pretty good chance of convincing the authorities that he's mentally unbalanced.

'So come on – let's hear your story. Start with the death of Hiromi. What's the connection with Miura and Nakanishi?'

Furumoto's eyes flash anger. For a moment he struggles for words. When they come out, it's in a staccato burst of outrage.

'The connection? It's obvious, isn't it? These are the men who killed her!'

Mori stares at him in bewilderment. 'What are you talking about? The girl killed herself, didn't she?'

'That's what everyone says! Actually—'

There's a slight rustling sound behind Mori's shoulder. Furumoto's eyes widen. Mori wheels round, too late. A man's figure comes hurtling through the row of kimonos, sending him sprawling to the floor. Mori keeps rolling, but a flying foot catches him on the side of the jaw. For a moment Mori lies stunned, face against the cold tile. Then Furumoto is on top of him, big knees grinding into his back, big hands looping around his neck. Mori's body arcs backwards like a bow. He gurgles for air, thrashes his feet, tries to squirm sideways. No good, he can't escape the grip on his throat, the tearing pain in his shoulders. Furumoto grunts as he raises the pressure another notch.

'Enough!'

Mori's forehead thumps against the floor. Through swimming eyes, he sees Taniguchi gazing down at him.

'I still don't understand you, Mori-*san*. You try to make things better and you always make them worse.'

'Worse for who?' gasps Mori.

'Worse for everyone,' says Taniguchi, slowly shaking his head. 'But mainly worse for you.'

Twenty-one

George the Wolf Nishio leans against the wall, toothpick in mouth, staring disconsolately at the carvings on the big wooden door: dragons; writhing snakes; gnashing lion-dogs. On the other side of that door are the old boss, the young prince, a dozen of their most trusted men, also representatives of the West Japan affiliates. Outside in the hallway, the junior members sit around gossiping, reading comic books, playing mah-jong.

Inside: power and respect.

Outside: anonymity, dispensability.

What is the subject under discussion? Amongst the juniors, opinions are divided. Some say a contract for a toxic waste dump on Kyushu. Others say there are problems with Korean groups, now arrogantly demanding a larger slice of the soccer World Cup. George's own theory is that there's going to be a declaration of all-out war with United Prosperity. And if it hadn't been for the fiasco with those foreign whores, he'd be in there listening, giving his advice whenever the old boss asked.

George crunches a Benzedrine tablet, flicks a steel comb through his quiff. In front of him, a couple of juniors squat on their haunches, slurping cup noodles and chatting.

'Seems there was a shooting in Shinjuku the other night. Some guy took two bullets.'

'What's that? A professional job?'

'Impossible. Whoever did it was a complete idiot, got the wrong guy then panicked and ran down a street full of people.'

Cackling laughter. 'Somebody ought to do something. The streets just aren't safe any more, right, Wolf?'

The junior turns up his snickering monkey face. George's lips ghost a smile. He doesn't need to talk to tofu-head juniors like these, men who haven't accomplished a tenth of what he has and never will. As for the hit on Mori, that was just bad luck, nothing to worry about. Next time he'll make sure. He will put the gun in Mori's mouth, watch him whimper and beg. And then he will stare straight into Mori's eyes and squeeze the trigger.

When he's finished, he will get a new tattoo. He'll go to the guy in Ueno, the finest artist in the whole Kanto region. George already knows what he wants. In the middle of his back, a slavering wolf's head, done in gold, crimson, black. A fitting emblem of the spiritual regeneration of George the Wolf Nishio.

The big wooden door swings open. The old boss appears, sombre-faced, austere in his dark kimono. Behind him is the young prince – crisp Italian suit, bouffant hair, smug little smile. The old boss barks an order. The juniors jump to their feet, form into two lines. They bow deeply as the guests pass between them to the entrance. The room echoes with the ritual shouts of farewell. George approves. This is traditional, everything as it should be.

After the visitors have been escorted to their limousines, George is summoned into the big room. The old boss sits at the head of the table. He stares into space, tapping a closed fan against the back of his hand. The young prince stands behind him, hands on hips.

'There is an urgent transportation job,' says the old

boss, sounding tired. 'You must travel to Yamanashi immediately.'

'The resort project is at risk,' snaps the young prince. 'If you hadn't lost those whores, all the contracts would have been signed by now.'

George gulps guiltily. So that is what the meeting was all about – negotiations on the resort project have been going badly. Now George understands why the old boss looks so gloom-ridden. This is a fifty-billion-yen project, with heavyweight political backing. According to the blueprints, there are going to be convention halls, a high-tech resort with artificial coral reefs and indoor ski runs, lifesize models of famous European buildings, permanent homes for twenty thousand rot-brained bed-pissing 'silver citizens'. If all goes well, it could provide the syndicate with years of lucrative work: chasing out local residents and buying up their real estate; paying off environmental groups; making sure the right politicians get elected; organizing construction worker unions, trucking cartels, prostitution franchises, protection services for shops and businesses.

'A special gift will be prepared,' says the old boss. 'You must handle it with great care, not let it out of your sight under any circumstances. Understood?'

'Understood!'

George backs out of the room, his face a grinning mask of humility. He waits outside for twenty minutes, then the young prince calls him into the room again. Standing on the table is a stone Buddha one metre tall. George doesn't know much about antiques – old stuff is depressing, just like old people – but the statue's blurred features signal great age, great monetary value. George lifts it gingerly into his arms, staggers a couple of steps backwards. It's much heavier than he expected.

'Watch out!' grunts the old boss. 'That's a delicate piece, has to be kept upright all the time.'

The young prince claps a hand round one side of George's face, forces George's ear towards his mouth. 'Take better care of this than you did of those whores,' he whispers. 'If you don't, you'll be going on a one-way helicopter ride.'

George thinks of half a dozen snarling answers, swallows them all unsaid.

The Buddha doesn't fit into the Mazda's boot, so George decides to keep it beside him, on the passenger seat. He drapes his jacket over it, makes the seat belt good and tight, then heads for Yamanashi.

He has been driving for just half an hour when his mobile phone starts ringing. The voice is female, hard.

'Nishio-*san*? Do you remember me? I'm Chen-li, the enemy of the whore called Angel.'

George remembers now – the short-haired girl in Wang's Chinese restaurant. It was her information that enabled him to find Mori.

'Are you interested in finding this Angel?' says Chen-li.

George's neck muscles lock rigid. 'Of course I am!' he growls.

Just the thought of the woman makes George feel savage. She's done just as much damage as Mori. Thanks to those two, a fifty-billion-yen project is hanging in the balance!

'I told you before she was staying with a doctor somewhere in Yokohama. Now I have discovered the name and address of this doctor.'

George's left foot stamps on the brake pedal. The Buddha jerks forward, restrained by the seat belt. George's jacket slides away, revealing its blotchy face.

'Give me that address!' barks George.

'But you must hurry. She is leaving the country tomorrow, never coming back.'

'Give me the address now!'

The Mazda squeals to a halt in the middle lane of the expressway. Cars swerve behind him, horns blaring. George ignores them, scrabbles in the glove compartment for a pen. Luckily he finds one, scribbles down the doctor's name and address on the back of a thousand-yen note.

'You sure she's going to be there?' he hisses.

Chen-li pauses for a moment. 'She'll be there all right, getting ready for the trip home. This is your last chance, Wolf-*san*!'

The phone goes dead. George's spirits soar. The woman Angel, he had assumed he would never see her again. Now she has suddenly fallen into his grasp, a dream come true. What about the old boss's request, the precious statue by his side? Loyalty dictates going to Yamanashi immediately, doing his best to save the bidding on the resort project. But honour and respect dictate something different – going straight to the doctor's place in Yokohama and slicing up that whore into human sashimi. Loyalty verses honour, the classic dilemma of traditional drama.

George ponders for about three seconds. Then he twists the steering wheel, sends the Mazda crashing through the chain of plastic bollards that separates the opposing flows of traffic. Horns blare at him, headlights flash. George turns in a squealing, rubber-blistering arc. The Buddha bounces around the passenger seat, its lips curved in a beatific smile, its sightless eyes gazing at the road to Yokohama.

Mori – blindfolded, wrists and ankles tied to the chair – sits and listens. There's something about not being able to move, not being able to see, that heightens all your other senses. So it was that time when he was buried up to the neck in radioactive sand, undergoing nasal therapy. So it is now. Furumoto and Taniguchi have gone to the next room to talk in secret, but their murmuring voices vibrate through the pipes, filter through the air-vents. Mori's hearing has never been sharper.

Furumoto is agitated. 'It's a simple choice – him or me. Look, I don't want the death sentence.'

Taniguchi sounds calmer. 'Don't worry. Nothing will be proven.'

Furumoto: 'But when the police start investigating . . .'

Taniguchi: 'This story will never be brought out into the open. There are some powerful people who will make sure of that.'

Outside a single-cylinder motorbike goes buzzing past like a demented bee. When the noise finally fades into the distance, the voices have moved further away, allowing Mori to catch only the odd phrase.

Furumoto: 'national security people . . .'

Taniguchi: 'probably bluffing . . .'

Furumoto: 'too dangerous . . .'

Taniguchi: 'do what is necessary . . .'

Another inaudible exchange, and the conversation winds down. A door closes, quiet footsteps approaching from behind, then the blindfold is eased, rolled up on to his forehead. Taniguchi stares at him thoughtfully.

'Not an easy decision,' says Mori, staring back.

Taniguchi flinches. 'What are you talking about?'

'What you're going to do with me. That's a difficult decision, right?'

Taniguchi shakes his head angrily. He looks pale, twitchy around the eyes. He needs a drink badly, thinks Mori.

'What are you doing here, Mori-*san*? Why did you have to get involved?'

'I got involved because somebody paid me money. For

most people, that's a good enough reason, though you probably think it's pretty contemptible.'

'Contemptible?'

There's uncertainty in those blood-shot eyes. Taniguchi really doesn't know what to do. Mori talks faster, louder, trying to dominate the situation.

'Don't you remember what you told me the other week? The whole country's gone crazy for money, everyone's selling themselves? Well, I'm one of those people selling themselves. I call it doing a job. In my opinion, that's a pretty harmless activity. If everyone stuck to making money, the world would be a better place.'

'You didn't think like that twenty years ago.'

'I grew up,' snaps Mori. 'You're going in the opposite direction, Taniguchi-*san*.'

'What's that mean?' says Taniguchi, grey-faced.

'Taking revenge on the establishment for Hiromi's death – that's fine for a crazy young guy like Furumoto. You should know better.'

There's a noise behind him, close, then a blow to the side of the head which sends the chair lurching sideways against the wall. It takes Mori several seconds to blink away the impact. Through swimming eyes, he sees Furumoto standing in front of him, almost dancing with rage.

'Those men deserved their punishment,' he shouts. 'What they did to Hiromi was murder. To make more profits they gave her poison, filled her with death.'

Mori glances at Taniguchi, who is standing hands on hips, sombre-faced. He nods. 'What he says is true, Mori-*san*. One year before she died Hiromi got sick. She was diagnosed as anaemic, nothing serious, just needed regular treatment. The drug she was prescribed was new on the market, but very popular with doctors. Can you guess why it was so popular with doctors?'

'I don't know. It must have been the most effective, I suppose.'

'Wrong! It was the most popular because it was by far the most expensive. That meant when the doctors prescribed it, they could get huge rebates from the manufacturer. And can you guess why this drug was the most expensive?'

This time Mori has a fair idea, but he says nothing. He knows that Taniguchi is going to tell him anyway.

'Because that was the price set by the ministry's panel of experts,' says Taniguchi savagely.

Mori nods. He doesn't need to be told that the manufacturer in question was Nakanishi Pharmaceutical, or that the panel of experts was under the 'guidance' of a certain senior bureaucrat.

'You mean the drug didn't work?' he says softly.

'It didn't work half as well as the existing drugs. But that's not the point. There were side effects, Mori-*san*, ones that should have come up in the first clinical tests.'

'Should have?'

'The results were manipulated, the risks minimized. Very simply done, Mori-*san*. I found that out when I investigated the company later. Anyway, within three months my daughter had serious liver damage, so painful she could hardly walk. The treatment for that would have blown up her body like a balloon, and the chances of success were next to zero.'

Taniguchi sits down heavily on the floor. From the misery in his crumpled face, it could have happened last week.

'And that's why she killed herself?'

This time Furumoto speaks, the anger gone from his voice. 'Yes, it was all in the letter she left. She wanted me to remember her at her best, like the cherry blossom in full bloom. And that's how she died, as pure and beautiful as ever.'

Taniguchi stares at the floor, as silent as a stone. Furumoto stalks out of the room. Mori hears his heavy footsteps entering the storeroom, then a furious yell, a crack, and a sound like a ball skidding across a floor. It takes Mori a few moments to work out what it was. One of the plastic dummies has just lost its head.

Taniguchi doesn't look up from the floor. Mori doesn't disturb him. Time drizzles by, five minutes, ten minutes, half an hour. Finally Taniguchi hauls himself upright, sighs like it's the last breath he'll ever take.

'There's nothing you can do,' says Mori. 'She's not coming back.'

Taniguchi frowns at Mori. 'I know that,' he growls.

He reaches into his trousers pocket and takes out a ten-centimetre length of black plastic. He points it at Mori, and a thin metal tongue shoots from the front. The switch-blade looks strangely out of place in Taniguchi's pale hand.

He steps towards Mori, face heavy with tension. The blade flashes under the bare neon light. Mori catches a trace of whisky in the air. Probably Taniguchi knocked back the drink before leaving the other room. Probably he felt he was going to need it.

Taniguchi moves behind the chair, outside Mori's line of vision.

'Looks like you've made your decision,' says Mori, vainly trying to twist around. The cords are too tight, biting into his arms and legs.

'It's not my decision any longer,' Taniguchi says quietly. Mori glances at the door. Furumoto's bulk is blocking the light. His eyes are trained on Mori, expressionless.

'You mean it's his?'

'I mean it's yours.'

The blade starts to saw at the cords. Mori waits until the last one has been cut. For a moment he just sits there, rubbing his wrists and ankles. Then suddenly he launches himself forward, grabs Taniguchi's arm and twists the knife free. Taniguchi puts up little resistance, but Furumoto comes forwards, hips rolling in that familiar karate stance. Taniguchi puts up a hand to stop him, then turns to Mori.

'Well?'

'Well what?'

'Well, what's the decision?'

Silence hangs in the air for a long moment. Mori turns his gaze from Taniguchi to Furumoto, then back to Taniguchi again. He wrinkles his brow as if his memory is giving him trouble.

'Aren't the Giants playing the Porpoises at home tonight? And didn't they lose the last three games in a row?'

Furumoto stares in suspicion. A complex of different emotions flits across Taniguchi's troubled face.

'Tonight they don't lose,' he mutters finally.

'I say they do,' says Mori smugly.

'Not possible!' says Taniguchi, indignant now. 'Tonight they're fielding their strongest line-up!'

Mori nods slowly. 'Well, here's an idea. Why don't we go along and see for ourselves?'

He makes for the door, then spins round and jabs a finger at Furumoto.

'You'd better come too, ninja. You need to forget things for a while.'

They all need to forget things for a while. Maybe longer, much longer. Mori leads them down the staircase. Outside nothing has changed. The sky is the colour of blank video. Rain is raining on rain.

The doctor lives in a high-class suburb of Yokohama.

George cruises the narrow streets, peering in fascination at hedges chopped into funny shapes, wrought-iron balconies, yards full of barbecue equipment. This place is like a foreign country, no noise, no neon, no surging crowds. Something about it makes him feel uneasy. There's too much space, too much geometry. Where's a man supposed to hide?

The Mazda jerks to a halt in front of a large white-tiled building, separated from the road by an ocean of lawn. George glances at his map, tries to get his bearings. The doctor's house is supposed to be somewhere near. There are words on the gate, written in Roman letters for some reason. George squints at them, takes a few seconds to decipher the 'sideways writing'. It's the doctor's name, sure enough. Which means this huge building must be his house, and that BMW in the driveway must be his car.

George parks the Mazda. Closing the door, his eyes rest on the Buddha. That smile he finds irritating – what's so funny, anyway? Life isn't funny, nor are the principles of loyalty and honour. Still, what to do with the thing? George remembers the old boss's warning: 'Don't let it out of your sight.' Reluctantly he pulls the Buddha out of the car and lurches towards the gate of the doctor's house. You can't be too careful these days, not even in a classy neighbourhood like this.

It's a dark evening, rain sputtering from a churning sky. The gate opens to George's push, not a squeak. George steps inside, leans the Buddha against the trunk of a sculpted pine-tree. He scans the house. There's only one room with a light, there on the third floor. The window has been left open a couple of inches. George catches the faint pulse of music, happy disco stuff. That sounds promising. He crouches down behind the BMW, keeps his eyes fixed on the window.

It doesn't take long to get confirmation. A woman's

figure flits past, tall, with long frizzy hair. Seconds later she's there again, gazing out of the window. For a moment she seems to be looking directly at him. But that's not possible: in the darkness he's too well hidden. Anyway, she soon turns away, reaching a hand behind her back. George catches his breath as she unloads the bra. His fingers twitch at the thoughts of what he's going to do to those heavy bells of flesh.

As soon as she's gone George scuttles across the lawn, mud squelching under the heels of his snakeskin boots. At the side of the house, he pauses, strains his ears to catch any motion inside. Nothing, just the whirr of machinery, the gurgle of pipes. Then suddenly behind him, a rattle and crash. He wheels round, sees a flowerpot broken on the stone path, the huge two-headed toad hopping through the undergrowth. That's a bad omen, causing George to clutch at the charm he keeps in his wallet. He looks closer, then smiles with relief. It's not a two-headed toad, but two toads mating. A good omen, hinting at the entertainment that lies ahead. He checks his pockets for gun, flick-knife, brass knuckles. Angel's last show on earth is going to be her best, the kind she never dreamed of in her worst nightmares.

George creeps round to the back of the house, finds what he's looking for straight away. There on the second floor – a small window left a few centimetres ajar. Probably a bathroom, thinks George. He climbs on to a ledge, uses a drainpipe to lever himself up to the right height. For several long minutes, he hangs there, three metres off the ground, gently sawing through the mosquito netting with his knife. Then a little jog of the blade and the catch jumps free, allowing him to pull the window open and squeeze inside. George steps lightly to the floor, gives his eyes a few seconds to get used to the darkness. It is a bathroom, with a large circular tub in the middle, the kind with bubble jets on all

...d waterproof video screens. George dips his hand
...he water. It's still warm, which is good. He has always
...ted to use such a bath. Tonight he will have his chance.

George takes out his gun, edges up the staircase to the third floor. The disco music is pounding loud. At the top of the stairs George sees a door half-open, light flooding through. Angel is in that room, maybe dancing naked to the beat. George hopes so. Then he can sit down, gun in lap, and make her dance some more. After that he'll make her crawl across the floor like the animal she is, complete submission in her eyes. Just the thought has his groin tingling.

George pushes open the door with his foot. But the room is empty, no Angel to be seen. Frowning, George walks inside, glances around. Lying on a glass table in the middle of the room: brassière and panties, sheer black lace. George picks up the panties, takes a good deep sniff. The jungle tang is hot and strong, enough to make his eyes water.

There's another door on the other side of the room. Softly George twists the handle, eases it open. Dim lampglow lights the interior. What he sees: a large bed, a woman's curves under a single sheet. George licks dry lips, steps into the room.

'Hey, Angel!' he hisses. 'It's time for the show!'

The woman makes no response. She's breathing deeply, sound asleep. George goes closer, yanks the sheet clean off the bed, revealing the woman's naked body. He stares down in dumb amazement.

'Chen-li! What you doing here?'

But Chen-li is in no position to answer. Her eyes are bandaged, her mouth taped shut. George's stomach ices over. Something's going horribly wrong, just like that time with the customs guy at Narita.

Suddenly the lamp goes off, the door slams shut.

George wheels around. 'Who's there?'

No answer, just pitch-black silence. George aims his gun in the direction of the lamp, shoots twice. Big noise fills his ears, afterwards nothing. George roars rage, stumbles to the door, sending a stool crashing to the ground. He feels for the door handle, twists savagely. It's locked.

'Open or I kill you!' he yells, flat hand thumping the door panel.

Then there's a tiny sound, right behind him. Even as he wheels round, George knows it's too late.

A crunching impact sends him staggering to the ground. The gun slips from his grasp.

George sprawls flat out, wondering if he's been hurt or not. No pain, he thinks, so maybe not. But then he puts a hand to the side of his head. The ear isn't there any more, just fragments of bone, wet warmth running through his fingers.

'Pig!' A woman's voice, seems a long way off. George peers around, still can't see anything. The situation is shocking. How can he work with no ear, with a piece of his skull missing? But then it occurs to him – strange fact – that he isn't going to work any more. He is going to die here in the dark.

Another sound. She's behind him somewhere, getting into position. He isn't even going to see her face.

George scrabbles to his knees. 'Wait,' he gurgles. 'I'm sorry, I'm sorry, I'm sorry . . .'

He wants to carry on saying the words for ever, but George the Wolf Nishio's last breath has already left his lips. Now the axe blade is slicing the air, heading straight for the line of his slickly combed parting.

As soon as it's over – two more blows to be completely sure – Angel goes to the bathroom and has a shower. After washing the blood and bits of brain out of her hair, she ties it up in a bun. Then she puts on jeans, apron, rubber gloves, turns up the volume on the disco music and sets to work.

The first time Angel saw a pig being killed was when she was five years old. The first time she helped was when she was nine. It's a messy business, lots of blood and smells and ugly noises. After a while, though, you learn not to notice all that. You learn to think of other things, people you haven't seen for a long time, interesting things you're planning to do. Your hands work – stabbing, carving, pulling – but your mind is somewhere else entirely.

Tonight Angel's mind is elsewhere for many hours. And when she's finished, it takes a long time to clean up: the bedroom; the bathroom; the garage; the tools. Conveniently, the black plastic bags just fit into the boot of the BMW. She drives down into the Miura peninsula, buries them up in the mountains, a few kilometres apart. The head she buries at the highest point, giving a good view of the flat ocean.

By the time she gets back to the doctor's house, grey dawn is seeping through the eastern sky. For the first time Angel notices the Buddha lying on its side next to the pine tree. She inspects it curiously. From the front the statue looks old, but the back is too clean, seems to be made of a different material. She goes into the garage, gets a hammer. One blow and the back shatters into a thousand fragments. Inside is a layer of orange packing foam. Angel pulls it out, revealing what's underneath – twelve compartments, each containing a block-like object wrapped in traditional handmade paper. Angel inspects them, one by one. She finds nine gold bars, three fat wodges of banknotes. The Buddha and the gold bars she puts in the boot of the BMW. The banknotes she takes back into the house and counts out on the kitchen table. Each wodge contains five million yen: enough money to build a fine house with a courtyard. She puts each block of money into a plastic bag, rolls them up in towels and stuffs them into the bottom of her suitcase.

Upstairs Angel changes into her favourite T-shirt. On the front, a print of Bob Marley, dreadlocks flying. Next door in the bedroom, Chen-li is making little snuffling noises. Another hour and the drug will have worn off. Angel hauls her downstairs, shoves her into the back seat of the BMW, drives into the heart of Chiba City. By the time she arrives, Chen-li's eyelids are starting to flutter. Angel leaves her slumped against a vending machine in a deserted back street lined with cut-price pink salons. Then she drives down to the waterfront and parks amongst the warehouses and scrap-metal yards. She breaks the Buddha up with the hammer, and throws the pieces into the greasy water of Tokyo Bay.

As for the gold, what can you do with that? Angel stares at the dull yellow blocks, senses the dangerous weight of their wealth. She already has ten million yen in banknotes, plenty for a good house, happiness for her family, all her dreams come true. This gold must be worth much more. The sort of dreams it will buy are someone else's dreams. Angel doesn't want the bad luck that comes from dreaming someone else's dreams.

For a moment she considers sending a couple of bars to Mori. She flashes him quitting his work as a detective, turning into a bored rich man with expensive clothes, an expensive mistress in the Ginza, expensive hobbies like golf or collecting Chinese porcelain. The thought is half-funny, half-sad – a Mori that is no longer Mori. No, decides Angel, the bad luck should not be passed on.

Beyond the wharves is a landscape out of a science-fiction manga: windowless rhomboids of bone-white concrete; pipes and pylons and overhead walkways; spherical tanks that look like giant ping-pong balls. From its midst a thin jetty reaches out into the bay. Angel drives slowly over a couple of hooped bridges, parks in front of the jetty. No one is around. All is clean, still, singing with the hum of invisible machinery. 'Water Treatment Complex' says the sign. Something different from the way waste is treated in the city where Angel was born. But if she had to choose one of them as a place to live, she would settle for the dead dogs and broken glass and rotting food.

Angel makes five trips along the jetty, a gold bar in each hand. She goes right to the edge, drops her load deep into the greasy black water.

Last journey to the doctor's house. Angel spends an hour tidying up, puts everything into order. The sheets are washed, the plates and bowls put away, every hair removed. Hardly a trace of her presence is left. She puts a simple note on the doctor's pillow – no explanation, just thanks for everything. The BMW goes back into the garage. The music tapes she takes with her to the Mazda.

Angel likes to leave things neat behind her. There is enough mess in the world anyway, enough ugliness. But things don't arrange themselves neatly on their own. Someone has to do the work. Angel worked to make the doctor's house neat, scrubbing away the stains on the carpet, wiping the mess off the walls. She worked to make Mori's life neat too, wiping away the ugly danger. That was her present, something he would have never done himself.

It took careful planning. First of all Angel and a friend called Crystal went to a recently bankrupted striptease club. The friend called up Chen-li, said she needed to make a purchase in a hurry. Being a good businesswoman, Chen-li wasn't going to refuse. When she walked into the musty darkness of the theatre, Crystal was squatting on the stage, looking desperate. Behind a curtain Angel was waiting, a sock full of hundred-yen coins dangling from her hand. Just a flick of the wrist: Chen-li went down like a sack of yams. They tied her up with bondage equipment they found in the costume chest, gave her a shot of the doctor's morphine, stuffed her into the boot of the BMW.

Back in the doctor's apartment, Angel pulled the leather mask off Chen-li's face, woke her with slaps and cold water. Then she explained exactly what she wanted done. No threats were necessary. Smart girl Chen-li saw the big axe gleaming on the table. She read the message in Angel's eyes and voice.

Everything went smoothly, neatly. Now the ending will be neat too: gold bars missing; the Wolf missing; his Mazda left in the long-term car park at Narita airport. Mori will continue being Mori, as he must. The doctor will face the death inside him alone, as he must. And Angel will fly away home, as she must.

Bare foot on the accelerator, she turns the music up to maximum. The Mazda eats up expressway.

Twenty-two

Mid-August, the Festival of the Dead. Six million salarymen have gone back to their home towns, packed in trains filled to one hundred and eighty per cent capacity. For the few days of their absence the streets are strangely slow and quiet. The bars and restaurants of Ginza are mostly shut, but Shinjuku stays in business for those who have no home town or no salary or just prefer not to move around too much in the sweltering heat.

Today Mori's office – no curtains, no air-conditioning – is a concrete oven. Feet up on the desk, he flaps at his face with a paper fan emblazoned with the character for 'cool'. The sight of that character helps a little. Crunching ice-cubes between his teeth helps some more. That's a habit he learned from his father. Something else Mori's father used to do when the heat got this intense – take off his trousers and stroll the neighbourhood in his cotton underpants. You can't do that nowadays. The neighbourhood wouldn't stand for it, nor would the clients. Especially not the particular client who'll be knocking on his door any minute now.

Mori turns to the window. The sky is a deep, oppressive blue; not a wisp of cloud, not a breath of wind. In the little shrine across the street the cicadas are screeching from the trees. Right below him a taxi comes gliding to a halt. The door flicks open and a candy-pink parasol emerges. That has to be her. Who else would carry something like that in a place like this? Confirmation comes when a pale brown shape lollops out onto the pavement. That's Kenji, the dog who's taught himself to bark silently.

By the time the buzzer sounds, Mori has put on his shoes and socks, buttoned his shirt and prepared two glasses of iced coffee. Kimiko Itoh walks into the room, imperiously elegant. Kenji trots behind her, his pink-and-black tongue flopping from the side of his mouth.

'Sit!' orders Kimiko Itoh. Kenji plumps his sagging belly onto the floor and folds in his legs. He looks worse than when Mori saw him last, fatter and paler. Silver streaks run from the corners of his eyes, make it look like he's been weeping. And what could cause a German shepherd to weep? The past, of course, and the lost future. All the deer he never killed, all the bitches he never mounted, all the dogginess that has been extracted from him by the ruthless kindness of Kimiko Itoh.

Her eyes interrogate the room. 'So this is your office?'

'That's right,' says Mori, apologetic.

'It's so hot in here. Don't you find it difficult to concentrate?'

'You get used to it.'

Kimiko Itoh nods. She's made out of porcelain, looks as if she's never emitted a molecule of sweat in her life.

'Iced coffee?' Mori gestures.

'Thank you so much.'

She smiles professionally, then gives the sofa a little brush with the side of her hand and sits down. The iced coffee she doesn't touch.

'In your message, you said that the investigation came to a successful conclusion. That's very good news, Mori-*san*. Your high reputation is certainly deserved.'

'Thank you.'

'And what are your findings?'

Mori takes a plain brown folder from the desk. 'All here in the report, together with a day-by-day log of my research activities, comprehensive summaries of all interviews, any detail you could possibly want.'

Her eyes bore into him. 'What I want is the name of the killer.'

'It's all here.'

Kimiko Itoh puts out her hand, palm upwards. Mori picks up the folder and gives it to her with exaggerated care. She takes a pair of bifocals from her bag and wedges them on the end of her unnaturally high nose. While she's reading, Mori walks over to the window and listens to the high-decibel panic of the cicadas over in the shrine. There's always one that starts it. Then the rest automatically join in, forming a wave of sound that gathers to a peak before suddenly crashing and ebbing away to nothing. Highly consensus-oriented, these insects. They think there's safety in numbers. But in a matter of weeks they'll be alone, each one writhing to death amongst the fallen leaves.

Kimiko Itoh browses in silence, turning the pages with a vicious flip of the wrist. When she's finished, she places the folder on the sofa beside her.

'This is a strange story, Mori-*san*. Are you sure you've got the right man?'

Mori sits down on the edge of the desk, nods with slow confidence. 'No question about it.'

'But there isn't any real proof here.'

'Real proof!' exclaims Mori. 'You've read his confession. That's good enough, isn't it?'

'Oh? Is that what the police say?'

'They don't say anything yet. I didn't want to bring them in without your approval.'

The elegant eyebrows take a short journey upward. 'You mean, this man is still at large?'

'Yes, kind of.'

'Kind of?'

Mori shrugs, fatalistic. 'His car was found in the long-stay car park at Narita airport. It looks like he's fled the country.'

Kimiko Itoh gives Mori a long hard stare. 'This isn't good enough, Mori-*san*. The task I gave you was to identify and secure the arrest of the man responsible. You've identified him – at least, that's what you claim – but he hasn't been caught.'

'So what are you saying? No bonus until he shows up?'

Kimiko Itoh smiles, saccharine-sweet. 'Sorry, Mori-*san*,' she coos. 'Not just no bonus. No payment at all.'

Mori jumps off the desk. He'd been expecting difficulties about the bonus, but the standard fee was agreed in advance!

'Wait a moment! What about all the expenses I've incurred? What about all the other work I had to turn down?'

Kimiko Itoh gets to her feet. 'I pay for results, Mori-*san*. That's my style of business. You give me results, you get rewarded. You give me nothing, and there's nothing in return. Find that man, and don't call me until you do!'

Mori watches in silence as she tugs the dozing Kenji to his feet and leads him to the door. Then she turns and makes a formal bow.

'Please pardon me for any disturbance caused.'

Politeness as aggressive as a kick in the groin. Mori listens to her high heels clattering down the staircase. It's unprecedented for a client to renege on the terms of agreement. But he can't really complain. What he did was unprecedented too.

He got the idea after Angel called from the airport.

'No need to worry, detective-*san*. No more Wolf.'

Exactly why there was 'no more Wolf' Angel didn't

explain, and Mori didn't ask. But gifts that are offered with generous intentions should always be accepted with grace, even when they're not exactly what you wanted.

With Taniguchi under treatment in a psychiatric clinic and Furumoto safely in California, Mori thought he would try his luck with Kimiko Itoh. It didn't work. She's gone, taking with her the sofa, the new cylinders for the Honda, the complete set of Thelonius Monk albums he saw on offer in a collectors' magazine. All that expenditure will have to be postponed indefinitely, like so much else in his life.

Mori unbuttons his shirt down to the navel, and pops another ice cube in his mouth. The heat is starting to get to him.

Over the past few weeks Mitchell's life has picked up speed. Suddenly everyone everywhere wants to talk to him – analysts, strategists, fund managers, even members of the main board in Frankfurt. Already he has made one round-the-world marketing trip – front of the plane, stretch limos from the airport – and Hauptman is pestering him to make another. But Mitchell no longer needs to travel to get his message across. Media sorcery has made him ubiquitous. His comments flash across Reuter's and Bloomberg screens across the world on a daily basis. He has been interviewed by CNN and the BBC, quoted in *Business Week*, *Forbes* and the *Economist*, made the subject of a short profile – complete with flattering pencil sketch – in the *Wall Street Journal*. He has even taken part in an all-night debate about technology, society and the future of mankind on Asahi TV.

Still better is the change in the attitude of his colleagues. When he walks through the trading-room, traders and salesmen gaze up at him with innocent greed, like sea lions waiting to be fed.

'Anything special today?'

'Any good information, Mitchell-*san*?'

Men who used to gaze at him with frozen contempt now greet him with smiles and bows and high fives. Women who ignored him completely now supply him with cookies and shoulder massages, compliment him on his dress sense, make coy hints about disco dates and trips to hot-spring resorts.

Why so popular? Because suddenly Richard Mitchell is the hottest analyst in the market, the man whose aggressive 'Sell' recommendation on Mega Enterprises appeared just days before the stock took 'the geisha's suicide leap'.

Richard Mitchell is the man who immediately grasped the implications of the company's virus problem, accurately forecasting the enforced recall of all games shipped this year.

Richard Mitchell is the man whose negotiating skills have brought in the biggest corporate deal of the year, SoftJoy's acquisition of a major American networking company.

In short, Richard Mitchell is the man whose ideas have been generating the trading profits, sales commissions and advisory fees that are fattening up the bonus packages of everyone in the office.

Today Mitchell sleeps late, recovering from a gruelling video-game contest with Sonoda that went on until three-thirty in the morning. By the time he gets to the office, afternoon trading has already started. And from the look of things the SoftJoy stock price has just taken another step on the magic escalator.

As soon as he sits down, a call comes through from Hauptman.

'Would you step into my office, Richard? Miss de Glazier is keen to have a few words with you.'

Mitchell's mood of well-being disappears in an instant. Sasha back in Tokyo? He has heard nothing about that. But

Sasha rarely announces her visits in advance. She just arrives, list of names in hand.

'Right now?'

'You heard what I said.'

Hauptman sounds uncharacteristically tense. Mitchell can guess why. Hauptman has probably been trying to persuade Sasha to back off, pointing out the value of Mitchell's recent work. But that would just strengthen her determination. Sasha is undeceivable, undeflectable. Like the Canadian Mounties, she always gets her man in the end.

Mitchell knocks on the door of Hauptman's office, pushes inside. Hauptman is alone in front of his huge desk, the phone still in his hand.

'That was quick,' he says.

'You said immediately.'

'Did I? Ah – well – what I meant was . . .'

The man is definitely flustered. He raises his hands, drops them, then twitches a smile.

'It's probably better if I leave you two to discuss this matter alone.'

With that he bolts out of the door, moving at the speed of an Olympic walker.

There's no sign of Sasha. Mitchell strolls over to the window, frowning. Suddenly his skin is itching all over. He had supposed he was home safe. After all, he had brought in new business, just as promised. But, as Yazawa used to say, there is nothing in the universe strong enough to escape its own karma. No stock or bond or currency, no human being, no insect. You can't defeat your karma because it is you, your innermost thoughts, your dreams, your spiritual DNA.

'Stop scratching yourself, Richard!'

Mitchell jerks round. Eerily Sasha's voice is booming at him among the bank of machines on Hauptman's gigantic desk. Edging closer, Mitchell notices something flickering in the middle of the control panel. He peers into the tiny liquid crystal screen. Sasha glares out at him. The picture quality is poor, but her hair appears to have changed shape, possibly colour too. There is a fringe, which makes her look like an earnest schoolgirl, and ringlets falling on her shoulders.

'I like your new hairstyle, Sasha. It really suits you.'

'Sit down and shut the fuck up!'

Her voice hasn't changed at all. Mitchell obeys, gingerly placing his slim buttocks into the large indentations in Hauptman's leather-cushioned chair.

'I have an important announcement to make, Richard. It may come as a shock. Are you ready?'

Mitchell takes a deep breath, closes his eyes. 'I'm ready.'

'Well, here it is. This is the parting of the ways. As of the end of this month, you're not going to be working for me any longer.'

Sasha pauses for dramatic emphasis. 'Oh,' says Mitchell dully. There doesn't seem to be anything else to say.

'You see, I've just handed in my resignation. They want me over at Silvermans'. I'm going to be Director of Global Information Resources.'

Now Mitchell's eyes are wide open. 'Oh,' he says again, this time with a completely different intonation.

'They need someone to carry out a drastic downsizing programme. It looks like things have got totally out of hand over there. That guy Hamada is a perfect example, don't you think?'

'Absolutely,' Mitchell stammers. It's taking time for Sasha's words to sink in.

'I mean, what a jerk. Does he really think he can get away with that corny act for ever?'

389

From her tone of voice, Scott Hamada won't be getting away with it for much longer.

'One other thing,' continues Sasha. 'I want everyone to understand that my decision to leave WBS was based on purely professional grounds. Got it?'

'Got it.' Mitchell gives a big grin. In fact, it's all he can do not to burst out laughing.

'I'm glad I had the foresight to keep you on, Richard. From what I hear, you've been making excellent progress. Of course, that was all horseshit that time in the restaurant, wasn't it?'

'Horseshit? What do you mean?'

'I mean you went there to spy on me. There was no client with you. I checked at the counter.'

Sasha's gaze is dark and lethal. Even on the muzzy little screen her eyes are like gun-barrels.

'Wait a moment...'

Sasha cuts him off. 'Forget it. I know you've got some weird shit going on out there, but that's not my business any more. Okay?'

'Sure, Sasha, sure. Anyway, congratulations on your new job. When are you planning to start?'

'October the tenth. That's exactly a week after my due date.'

'Your what?'

'Didn't I tell you? I've decided to give birth. And now is the ideal time to do it.'

Mitchell stares at the little screen in amazement. Sasha has 'decided to give birth'. What is that supposed to mean? Artificial insemination? Parthenogensis?

'Give birth,' he repeats, stunned by the idea.

'That's right. We're both delighted, especially Klaus. This'll be his first son.'

Klaus! Hauptman's first name is Klaus. Hauptman!

Surely that can't be right! Hauptman is so bulky, so German, so post-war. Then Mitchell recalls the embarrassed expression on Hauptman's face as he scurried out of the office. Maybe it is right. Hauptman did get divorced recently. And from Sasha's perspective he's good genetic material, a Prussian aristocrat, a fitness fanatic, at least six feet four inches tall . . .

'Well, congratulations,' says Mitchell feebly. 'I wish you both every happiness.'

'No time for that, amigo. We'll only be in the same time zone a couple of weeks a year, at max. Actually, we're thinking of doing the wedding on the Internet.'

Sasha flashes a smile. 'That's a joke by the way.'

Mitchell nods, bemused. He has never seen Sasha smiling before. He has never been able to imagine her smiling.

The liquid crystal screen flickers and dies. Sasha has to attend a meeting with the Indonesian minister of finance. Mitchell has to get back to his desk. There are telephone calls to make, people keen to hear his ideas.

'That sounds jolly interesting . . .'

'Way to go, Ritchie babe . . .'

'My government is quite satisfied . . .'

'Your spirit of sincerity is strong and impressive . . .'

'Next time you're in Paris, why don't we taste wine together . . .'

Mitchell leans back in his chair, watches the SoftJoy stock price take another lurch upwards. For the moment the wind of the gods is blowing in his direction, full force. Needless to say, it won't last. Never has, not once in the history of the financial markets. But while it does, you might as well enjoy it.

Standing at a window on the top floor of a select hotel is a small man with a large head. Seen from a distance, he looks like a child. Seen from close up, he looks like an uncommonly large dwarf. Standing, he moves not a muscle. Staring, his eyes are locked still, not even the blink of an eyelid. Some part of Sonoda's brain processes the image of the city, the buildings, the signs, the traffic, the human events. But none of that holds his attention. His mind is far away, roaming over fabulous dream landscapes that no one but himself can even describe.

Sonoda sees new art forms, new forms of reality. He sees a networked future of limitless computer capacity. He sees games that are always different, always developing, because the players generate the events themselves, make the rules as they go along. Games that have no beginning and no end. Games that tens of thousands, millions of people can play at the same time, safely, pleasurably, doing no harm to themselves or anyone else.

He sees heaven.

He sees hell.

Welcome to the world of Yoichi Sonoda.

Once you log in, you'll never log out.

As evening fades to night, the temperature in the city stays in the mid-thirties. Heat rises from the baking concrete, the spongy tarmac, the millions of air-conditioners chugging away full blast. Something in the air distorts the light, makes the moon seem much closer than usual. The silver disc hangs huge in the sky, the only cool thing in sight.

In his apartment Mori takes out the saxophone that Angel gave him, fits on the mouthpiece. He blows one note, quietly. The tone is good, so good that he has a sudden urge to play properly. But where? Not inside, not at this time of night. Not out on the street either. In this dense-packed suburb, someone would call the police straight away.

There's only one place that will do, the empty space under the expressway bridge.

Five minutes later he's there. First of all he tries a few scales, just to test his lungs. His fingers move with surprising agility. They seem to remember the patterns without being told. Next he plays a simple blues, then a freaky disjointed piece that he composed himself a quarter of a century ago. 'Samurai Boogie', that was the title. Not many people liked it – all those honks and squeals – but it was plenty of fun to play.

While Mori stands under that bridge, time freezes over. The moon hangs still in the sky, close enough to reach up and touch. Mori blows fast and furious, slow and dirty, his only audience the big trucks rumbling overhead.